WANDERERS FROM THE STARS

WANDERERS

FROM THE

STARS

C.M. Chadwick

Matador
Unit E2 Airfield Business Park,
Harrison Road, Market Harborough,
Leicestershire. LE16 7UL
Tel: 0116 2792299
Email: books@troubador.co.uk
Web: www.troubador.co.uk/matador
Twitter: @matadorbooks

ISBN 978 1803132 129

British Library Cataloguing in Publication Data.
A catalogue record for this book is available from the British Library.

Printed and bound by CPI Group (UK) Ltd, Croydon, CR0 4YY
Typeset in 11pt Adobe Jenson Pro by Troubador Publishing Ltd, Leicester, UK

Matador is an imprint of Troubador Publishing Ltd

*I would like to dedicate this book to Lyn Humphrey
in memory of the happy times we spent talking
about space flight and time travel,
when we were very young.*

The inspiration behind the 'Boskop 2' archaeological dig described here, and the peculiarities of the remains found there, is of course the skulls found at Boskop in 1913 which had an enlargement of the cranial cavity, a fact that I have gainfully elaborated on.

Several well-known people grace these pages in a manner in keeping with their lives, which are well-attested. For example, it is known that Dennis Wheatley entertained Freddy Gordon-Lennox, that both had an interest in UFOs, and that they discussed this matter together with the defence of the realm, a subject on which Wheatley's views are well-known. Similarly the character and disposition of Atlee, Macmillan and Truman are known; while Sandys, Dowding, Carrington and Heath are also important historical figures. As leaders of their respective countries they will have discussed the security issues surrounding this subject.

All other characters are wholly fictitious, and any resemblance to real people, whether living or dead, is coincidental.

The Silpho incident was real, as was the scepticism surrounding it.

Experiences concerning the soundless release of vast amounts of light are real, and were experienced by the author over the Marlborough downs during 2009, at a time when many similar reports appeared in the news.

ONE

A CRISIS FOR INTELLIGENCE

It was a Friday in August 1950, when the notable author Dennis Wheatley opened his front-door to his personal friends Freddy and Betty, who had come to stay for the weekend. Freddy was better addressed as Frederick Charles Gordon-Lennox, 9th Duke of Richmond, 9th Duke of Lennox, 9th Duke of Aubigny and 4th Duke of Gordon; his wife as the Duchess Elizabeth. They were of impeccable standing in society and it was not surprising that men of such high stature sought each other's company. That weekend the weather was warm and the author's home in Hampshire idyllic. They walked in sunshine and Wheatley showed his guests his beautiful garden. Later, they drove to the New Forest with a packed lunch and ambled about, watching the ponies and chatting like the old friends they were. At mid-day they brought deck chairs from their car and the four of them ate a light lunch from a hamper.

Soon, Joan Wheatley and Betty strolled farther, leaving Dennis and the Duke to chat. Conversation at first was light-hearted and friendly, dealing with friends and mutual acquaintances. Inevitably it became more serious as their discussion turned to aviation and the future defence of Britain. These were topics that were not spoken of in a casual manner and they held each other's opinions in the highest regard. At first, their conversation dealt with the navy and the development of modern military aircraft. But eventually there was a pause. The Duke paced about a bit. He seemed concerned, his brow furrowed. He returned to his seat and looked towards his companion as though unsure whether to continue. Eventually he said, 'The powers-that-be are a bit worried, Dennis.'

'So what's wrong, Freddy?'

'Well, down at Tangmere one of our planes reported an unidentified flying object at 20,000 ft. It was also seen on the radar nearby. The performance of the object vastly exceeded that of our own aircraft.'

'It was a jet, perhaps, or maybe a rocket plane?'

'No. And the feeling was that although research is proceeding at a great pace neither we, nor the Americans or Russians, could possess anything like it. It was a saucer-shaped craft, moving at a quite amazing speed. The thing is we know, as do the Americans, that many of our installations have been buzzed by such objects a lot recently.'

'Buzzed?'

'Yes. It goes back a bit, too. And the Americans let on that they were seen hovering around when the first two bombs went off in '45.'

'Does the Ministry of Defence regard it as a threat?'

'Perhaps not; there are no signs of an invasion. It's only a real threat if it turns out to be the Russians. But these are just the latest in a long line of sightings going back years, even centuries. There are old records, Dennis. It's just that with the advent of powered flight, now jet flight, and particularly with the atom bomb, these visits have increased. But of course we may be more sensitive to it.'

'So there have been more since the bomb arrived?'

'Yes, we're quite clear on that.'

The Duke spoke slowly: 'In public, we laugh it off. But that hasn't stopped the MOD from setting up a special working party to look at the subject. They are due to start in October under Sir Henry Tizard.'

'What do you think they will find out?'

'The truth: it will be quite clear that we are visited by flying craft from outer space.'

'And what will happen?'

'It won't get out, of course, although we have definitely reached the stage at which it needs to be publicly investigated. The real findings will be hushed up.'

Wheatley said, 'What's the point then?'

'Just this: I would expect the outcome to be carried to a meeting with our allies. We shall have to agree what to do. And the Americans will tell us enough of their own findings to enable a joint working party to reach a consensus for action.'

'But I just can't imagine all those tough military types *saying* such things! Are you seriously telling me, Freddy, that there really are flying craft from outer space? You make it sound as though the MOD actually believes in little green men!'

'That's just it, they do. But they can't come out in public and say so. Everyone would think they had suddenly gone barmy. Fleet Street would have a field day.'

'Yes, I see what you mean. At worst, it could reflect on the Government.'

'Exactly, and people might start to panic and begin to hoard food.'

Wheatley, the inveterate story-teller, said, 'I must say I fancy using some of these ideas in a novel. It would be fun to write about aliens abducting our people and whisking them away to Mars. I've never written a science fiction story before and I'm not sure it's my cup of tea, but at last it might be a good idea[1].'

'Dennis, pass me another sandwich please. Oh, and by the way, they don't come from Mars, it's a dead world—thanks, cucumber—but yes, the MOD and all the others, they know for sure that we have interplanetary visitors. However we don't know where they come from or why they are here.'

---

1   Dennis Wheatley published the excellent novel 'Star of Ill Omen' in May, 1952

'Is there anything we *do* know?'

'Yes. We know what the craft look like and a little about their performance. We also know, via the Americans, what kind of materials they use and what the people who fly them look like.'

'Since when?'

'Since a small vessel crashed over there in 1947.'

Both fell silent, and Betty and Joan returned from their stroll. They noted the distracted air of the men and Betty said, 'Missing us?'

'Surely! Come and have some of this excellent Champagne.'

—∞—

Later in that same month Prime Minister Clement Atlee sat in his private office in Downing Street. A studious and competent man, he sighed at the size of the file at his elbow, opened it and read from the papers it contained. He made corrections in black ink and reflected for a while. Then one of his telephones rang. It signified interest from a secretary outside. She said 'Sir, I have Sir Henry Tizard to see you.'

A door opened and Tizard entered. Atlee knew that Tizard's advice on questions of technology was of the highest calibre. The two men had shared memoranda on the subject of unidentified flying craft over Great Britain and following Tizard's request for a working party to investigate the subject, it had been Atlee who had suggested the present meeting. Atlee said, 'We are concerned obviously. Flying craft from space are very much in the newspapers these days. You've seen the news campaign?' Tizard nodded. 'Mountbatten supported it. The RAF has said they are worried by it. They say that visitors have been flying near to air bases and around our nuclear storage facilities.'

Tizard said, 'I know about at least some of that. The RAF has tried to photograph them on several occasions but they can't get near. As soon as one of our fastest jets approaches, they accelerate away at an unimaginable speed.'

'Then it can't be the Americans or Russians who make them. We are all in the same boat as far as our abilities are concerned.'

Tizard looked more closely at Atlee. They both had a natural hesitancy in discussing a subject which had been ridiculed by the press many times. He thought that Atlee might even prefer to discuss religion. After a brief pause, he followed: 'I've spoken to Dowding and he's taking this very seriously. He is quite convinced that we're being watched by visitors from space. Coming from a man like Dowding we have to listen.'

Atlee replied, 'I agree. We've got to look at it. I've agreed your suggestion of a working party with representatives from the various ministries. There will be all the resources you need.'

'Thank you. I'm glad, because this has been going on for quite a while. Sir Winston was worried about it as far back as 1941. We were preoccupied at the time, but now that's all over we need some kind of agreement on what to do next.'

'How quickly can you report?'

'I would think by early next summer.'

Atlee said, 'Make it sooner if you can. There's no panic, but some of the files on the subject have been getting rather thick.' He waved towards his desk. 'And we need to let it be known that it's in hand.'

'I'll get on it. But tell me, is there anything big that I should know about?'

'There's new stuff all the time. The big news was obviously Roswell three years ago. It's common knowledge that the Americans used a site in New Mexico to develop their nuclear program. They used an airbase near Alamogordo in support. Given our own experience, one might have expected alien visitors to turn up there. And inevitably, they did.'

Tizzard said, 'I heard about the crash there. Perhaps they are as error-prone as we are.'

'Perhaps they are, Henry. But although the Americans closed it down quickly, they were not quick enough. News got out and members of the public saw the site, the remains of the craft and its occupants. I hear we have done something on it ourselves?'

'Yes, we actually had a chap of our own nearby. He did nothing to upset the locals and was pleasant, open and conciliatory. That's always the best cover. He had enough influence to collect some basic information on his own account. A friendly policeman, you might say. He spoke to original witnesses and found they were under intense pressure to keep their mouths shut. But he did obtain enough information to draw his own conclusion only a little time after the event.'

'He was fully independent?'

'Yes, and the interesting thing is that witnesses spoke of having seen the bodies of humanoids. But the scene was cleaned up pretty quickly and everything was taken away to the airbase for forensic examination.'

'There's more?'

'There is. The Americans were very clever. Once they knew it was out, they turned the whole incident into a Hollywood-style epic and the so-called Roswell Incident ended up as a joke, complete with little green men and themed restaurants.'

'So do you believe any of it?' Atlee, a pipe smoker, waved some of the tobacco smoke away.

Tizard shrugged his shoulders and as always, his instinct was to present matters in the most careful light. 'Privately, I do. But I cannot pre-empt the findings of my own committee. We had better wait for the case studies.'

'Well alright. But returning to *that*, there must be enough of an outcome to satisfy anyone who tries to lift the carpet. It must be properly forensic, but leading inexorably to a negative outcome,' Atlee paused: 'at least, for public consumption.'

'I understand. So the truth is only for us.' Tizard smiled sadly and stood up. They shook hands, Tizard left and Atlee turned back to his files. In the fresh air and hazy sunshine outside, Tizard walked along Downing Street.

On the following day Atlee authorised the release of files for use by the working party, and by October it was time for a first meeting. Soon Tizard met the other representatives and their brief was concerned with procedures that were to be adopted when they next met. He summed up at the end of a short interval, 'In the first instance, we have agreed to collect as much information as we can. We have several recent sightings by RAF personnel and have taken witness statements from them. We agree that this should be extended to naval personnel. A request from one of us will be adequate for any case, thought to have merit, to be carried forward to the next reporting stage. Any example deemed to be insubstantial will not be carried forward. Our conclusions will be passed to the Prime Minister and a permanent record will be kept by the Ministry of Defence. Our findings will be top secret and it is essential that they should remain so.'

There was a general murmur of agreement, and further discussion followed about the criteria for case studies to be passed forward. First, they began sifting out the many reports without supporting witness statements. Only where a statement was obtained from professional people, from police or those of similar standing, was it carried forward. None was accepted if it contained any reference to apparently psychic experiences. Tizard himself considered an observation by a pilot flying out of RAF Tangmere, who had observed a disc flying at 20,000 feet while revolving and emitting light. His fountain pen paused while he read further. Eventually he added his initials to the bottom and wrote: 'Observation confirmed by RAF Radar; their plan position indicator was able to confirm both the height above ground and the distance of the object as it flew east over Portsmouth; case to be carried forward to committee stage.' A little later, he added another note to the report: 'There is a similarity between case numbers 46 and 14 in that light was seen to be emitted from the UFO by both witnesses.'

Painstakingly the committee advanced, and from the very many cases examined there was a clear consensus for those they chose to carry forward. Finally, a report was ready, which Tizard sent to Atlee in June, 1951. In the following month he was called by Atlee to discuss its findings. Atlee said, 'There were hundreds of sightings. Are you happy with just the three that made it to the end?'

'We had to exercise the most rigorous standards otherwise the report would have been meaningless. You will recall that its aim was to investigate whether UFOs exist, and only those with reliable witness statements could be included.'

'Of course.' Atlee glanced at a note in the margin. 'I see that you retained the case supported by the radar station. You considered it to be a national security issue. Can you say why?'

Tizard said, 'Certainly, the MOD was particularly worried by it. The very nature of the contact, and the fact that several witnesses were of an impeccable standard, meant that we had no choice but to include it. The pilot saw it and his observation was corroborated by no fewer than four officers, all a pretty experienced lot. We couldn't doubt their testimony.'

'Yes, I see. So even with the fullest rigour, UFOs must be real. What about the others?'

'We passed the case of the test pilot flying at Farnborough. He saw a disc-shaped craft, grey in colour, performing very high-speed manoeuvres over the Royal Aircraft Establishment there. He estimated its speed at 1000 mph and its control and agility as exceeding anything our technology could offer. The point is that even if we dismissed that observation, a similar craft was seen by no fewer than five respected RAF personnel two weeks later. It carried out manoeuvres that would not be possible for our own aircraft. They described one as the 'falling motion of an autumn leaf'. It would have required a gyroscopic control and the fine directional application of power that we can only dream of.'

'And what about the many cases which didn't make it through?'

'I think that by weight of numbers alone, they must have had something in them. They described features which many seemed to have in common: the shape of the craft, its abilities, and the issue of light from its perimeter.'

Atlee grimaced, 'And now for the whitewash.'

Tizard, noting his distaste, said, 'What else can we do? So here'—he opened his attaché case—'take a look at page two.'

Atlee swallowed his reluctance and glanced where directed. 'Test pilot's observations were an optical illusion eh? Alright. But how do we argue away all those witnesses in the radar episode? Ah, I see…became influenced by the contents of the earlier observation into expecting a UFO…rational thinking must conclude…a conventional craft… so near to the airbase. It will have to do; please write it up.'

They contemplated the report for a while and with a consensus reached, a more relaxed air came over them. They were able to speak informally, and it was clear that one or two things remained to be said. Tizard said, 'It's a shame there wasn't an easier way. And it took nine months just for a whitewash! It seems an awful lot of effort just to cover something up.'

Atlee replied, 'Some kind of accommodation with the general public has been coming for a long time. And there are wider considerations: the Americans need to be satisfied.'

'Why?'

'They have come to exactly the same conclusions and they want to hush it up for exactly the same reasons. We can't afford to be shown up because all kinds of defence cooperation depends on us being taken seriously. Our aim is to get UFOs out of the news and it has to be done on both sides of the Atlantic. It can only be done if we show we have investigated the matter.' He followed, 'Have there been any more rumours from Alamogordo?'

'No, but I spoke to a few scientists about it. I told them about the fact that there were humanoids, alive and moving, many hours after the crash. They were small, and must have breathed oxygen. Their bodies were of a plan similar to our own. They were not only vertebrates, but also primates with bipedal locomotion and an opposable thumb—'

Atlee looked directly at Tizard and said, 'Go on.'

'—and the fact that they were pretty brainy. Their cranial capacity was enlarged in proportion to their body, as were their eyes, but their body was degenerate compared to our own. They were androgyne.' Atlee waited.

'So I put some of this to them. They told me they couldn't see how evolution on different planets, so far apart, could have given such a similar body plan. They were clear that the similarities I described would tell us as much about our own origin as that of life from elsewhere.'

'I don't quite understand you.'

'They felt that if we are so similar, we probably had a common origin.'

'And this is not science fiction?' Atlee raised an eyebrow.

'No, they were informed and were willing to make suppositions from what little I could tell them.' Atlee listened, fascinated.

'They found it incredible that evolution on different planets could give any such similarity. They said that every environmental aspect and influence would have had to be exactly replicated: the sun, the atmosphere, the presence of water.'

'Go on.'

'Why did they have a backbone and walk upright? Why were they not quadrupedal? Why not three eyes, which would have been better than two? Why not the thicker legs needed for a planet with higher gravity? Why humanoid at all?'

Atlee said, 'Meaning?'

'First, I go to church and regard myself as a Christian. I don't believe in all that evolution stuff. But the scientists did. They were clever types at Oxbridge, quite open-minded and not talkative for its own sake. The facts spoke for themselves—their words not mine. They said we must have come from some common beginning. One said the evidence could still be in the fossil record. If we found it, then it would suggest that an advanced civilisation left here aeons ago and developed elsewhere, leaving the rest of us to evolve as we might.'

Atlee said, 'No wonder the Americans want to hush it up. Heaven help us if any hard evidence gets out. Are you sure your contacts can be trusted?'

Tizard leaned forward and exclaimed, 'Trusted, certainly; they are a bright lot. But anyway, the evidence *is* out! It could be uncovered by any competent investigation. That, presumably, is why we are speaking! Our only defence is propaganda and disinformation. We make sure that our conclusions are restricted to unusual weather patterns, misidentified aircraft, meteorological balloons and hoaxes. But we are only safe until somebody comes along with enough intelligence to it investigate properly.'

Atlee said, 'Well newspaper men are bright. I suppose we should anticipate further action in the news. What happens if there's another campaign like the one led by Mountbatten?'

'Then we would need to set up our own campaign. We could suggest a continuous observation of the skies by interested parties, cameras, radar stations, and record sound waves we receive. We could mention those big concrete sound collectors on the beach at Folkestone. It would peter out in the news and the general public would find nothing.'

'And meanwhile we can release the conclusion of our report.' The meeting ended. Neither man had enjoyed the degree of cynicism that had been necessary in its making.

—◠◠◠—

The following year was a hot one throughout the northern hemisphere, and in Washington DC, the sky was the blue of hot steel and the sun shone with a white ferocity. All this was noted by Harold Schaeffer when as a clerical officer for a bank, he left his workplace on a minor errand. Shortly, the slightest exertion made him perspire, and so he was relieved when obliged to slow to a halt where, among a throng of pedestrians, he followed their gaze upwards. They were spellbound, their eyes high above in the clear sky. Schaeffer began to squint as his eyes followed theirs, his hand held to his brow to shade them from the glare.

Above the skyscrapers were two saucer-shaped craft, hovering, and quite still. They were made of metal and reflected sunlight, yet their edges also emanated light in the form of discernible rays. Schaeffer could see that far away on the horizon, three fast jet aircraft were approaching, their white vapour trails clear against the brilliant background. They made straight for the hovering craft which in an instant, accelerated away at an enormous speed, estimated by some to be 8000 mph. They easily outpaced the aircraft following them which, left far behind, returned the way they had come.

There was an astonished murmur from the crowd. Schaeffer walked on in silence, bought a small lunch and returned to his office. There, preoccupied with his own thoughts, he completed his day's work without further incident. However he worked slowly, from time to time switching his attention to sheets of paper on which he drew the strange craft in all detail. When he left for home, he waved towards to the foyer with the barest attempt at pleasantry. That evening, he listened to a short report in the local radio news, which contained a description of the event seen clearly by so many. The newscaster said, 'Today, spectators in the capital reported aircraft of various kinds, all seen above the city in high speed manoeuvres. The Army Air Force would like to reassure all concerned that matters were routine and that joint training exercises took place between jet trainers and helicopters.' Bemused by the newscaster's description, Schaeffer looked at his drawings once again and shook his head.

A week later, further flying discs were seen by the general public over Washington. Matters had reached the stage at which the Government had to take notice. Eventually, President Truman sat down to a meeting with representatives of the Airforce and National Security Council at his office in in Washington. Their aim that day was to assess the risk and make recommendations to the President.

Truman sat in a high-backed wing chair and faced the meeting around a table. The atmosphere was cordial and respectful and his manner formal, as was his nature in such meetings, 'There have been hundreds of reported sightings of spacecraft. They aren't our planes, are they?'

'No, Sir,' said an officer, 'they aren't ours, and they don't belong to the British or the Soviets. They are too quick, too manoeuvrable, too big and too alien.'

'They *are* spacecraft, are they not?'

'Some call them flying saucers, but I prefer to call them unidentified flying objects because that is what they are. But not to mince words, they do not come from our own technology.'

Truman replied with his firm, but amiable manner, 'Nor from our allies or ideological opponents?'

'No. The British are about where we are with airframe and jet engine development, the Soviets a little behind. No conventional jet or rocket craft could do what was seen.'

'Can there be any reasonable doubt about them?'

'We doubt some, of course. But the more recent sightings have been wholly corroborated.'

'So what do they actually look like?'

'If they reflect radar they are probably metallic. All witnesses have said that they reflect light and are silver in colour. Some say they leave a trail of light. They are too fast for us to catch.'

Truman turned his head towards a National Security Council representative. He said, 'Your assessment of the risk to national security please.'

The representative replied: 'We don't think there is any military risk. They have never behaved aggressively. Nor has there been any destruction of military property apart from a couple of our aircraft that were lost. They got too close and were burned up. There has never been any aggression towards the general public, or to our cities and government buildings.'

'And is there any wider risk?'

'Yes. The reports unsettle the general public. That in turn unsettles the normal governance of our great country.'

Truman said, 'What are they doing here in Washington?'

'If they were of this earth I would say monitoring air traffic.'

'But so close to the White House?'

'Nothing we can do about that.'

'And your recommendation?'

'We should set up a panel to monitor witness statements and influence public opinion. We need to take the heat out of the newspapers. And get them to look again at the remains we obtained from Roswell; I hear that there are things still kept in storage.'

'OK. I want it to settle down again.' Truman remained totally and calmly didactic.

'It will.'

Truman said, 'Let us forget the science for a minute and speak informally.' He nodded to the secretary taking minutes, and she stopped as he had requested. 'What are we dealing with?'

'They are craft from outer space, Sir. We are visited regularly and probably observed, although we don't know why. They are very advanced, certainly an older civilisation than our own. We think their interest is benign, but we cannot be sure of that.'

Truman nodded to his secretary again. 'OK, let's keep this out of the papers. Oh, and talk to the British again as well. We know this has been a busy time for UFOs over there too.'

It became common for official spokesmen to reassure the general public. Such reassurances were successful and there was no military crisis, no run on a currency or any international incident. Often, radio commentators returned to the supposed panic caused by the broadcast by Columbia, in 1938, of a narration of the H.G. Wells novel War of the Worlds. 'We are wiser now,' people were reassured, and appropriately cynical about UFOs they remained interested, but unworried by the topic.

Back in Britain, times slowly changed. Eventually in 1957 a necessary strategic decision caused the subject to be reopened by Macmillan's new government. Following the resignation of Anthony Eden he had been Prime Minister for only a month before saying, 'Let me see the cumulative file on contacts with unidentified flying objects. And please would you ensure that Duncan has a copy in advance of our meeting on the 3rd?'

In fact Macmillan had quite a bit of policymaking to do. He had become Prime Minister after the Suez crisis and in the midst of regret at the loss of British influence in the Middle East. There was interest in how the country might develop a more contemporary role. As a part of this, Macmillan had authorised the preparation of a white paper on defence. In setting the future of the British Military Services, it had a particular effect on the indigenous aircraft industry. Much would be trimmed. In a preliminary discussion Macmillan met with Duncan Sandys, the secretary for defence. At 11 o'clock, Sandys was ushered into Macmillan's office. As they sat down, Sandys opened his briefcase to remove two folders and got straight to the point. 'The outlines of the white paper are clear. We need to decide on what to cut and what to keep. Here are my recommendations. I want to run them past you before we get to the stage of a first draft. There may be political ramifications from some quarters.'

'Certainly, we must try to keep everybody on side.'

Sandys made some marks on his notes. Then he said, 'The main changes are to the Royal Air Force. The world has changed and new technology has made many of our former proposals obsolete. It would be pointless going forward with some of our older ideas. Nevertheless there is one particular project that I think we should keep.'

'Which in particular?' Macmillan listened carefully.

'The P1 interceptor.' Sandys had his arguments rehearsed: 'It's already developed and ready for production. We are just too far ahead to throw it away and arguably we still need it. We have to chase bombers away from our airspace and rockets can't do that. We either fire them or we don't, and if we do its war.'

'I see. So if we keep that, what can we reasonably cut?'

'We can talk about the combined jet and rocket interceptor, the SR53.' In fact he looked regretful.

'If we accept a need for the P1, is the SR53 strictly necessary?'

'I suppose not. We do need to be able to shoot down any bomber armed with nuclear warheads. But the P1 can do at least some of that, and we are developing surface to air missiles that can do the rest.'

'But there is one further factor. Have you seen the news—about this Silpho object?'

'Silpho?' repeated Sandys. He had not expected such a connection with defence matters.

Yes. What do you make of it?

Sandys said, 'It may be a hoax.'

'Perhaps, but Dowding has seen the object and he said, straight out, that it's extra-terrestrial. We have to give him some kind of credence. Could it affect our decision on SR53?'

'It's hard to say. Has anything else been done about it? I mean other than having seen it in the news.'

Macmillan replied: 'It's very difficult to decide what we *can* do about a metal ball which suddenly falls to earth in a meteor storm. We saw inside, of course. It contained copper sheets of an unusually high purity. They had hieroglyphics on them like those on the Roswell crash. There was nothing else inside. Nothing could possibly have lived in there, and it contained no machine. It had no motive force of its own, so it was a projectile of some kind.'

'So you want to keep SR53 to shoot down another Silpho?'

'Not necessarily Silpho, but something like it.'

'I see. You mean we ought to be worried about our defence against fast projectiles launched in a similar manner.' Sandys had made a statement rather than a question.

'Well, I don't think we can requisition the development of armaments against an imaginary foe. But there are the flying saucers too—one of the legacies of my predecessors is this file.'

'Yes,' said Sandys, 'I've seen the reports of their capabilities. But if they are real, then we can't stop them anyway, and certainly not with SR53.'

Macmillan replied: 'So SR53 should go?'

'Yes, I think it must.'

'Very well, but regarding the file I mentioned, we must carry on with our former policy, which is to hush it all up. Have you taken any steps with that object?'

'Yes. Silpho has been put away in a box. A few people looked at it but we intend to make it disappear very quickly. I asked the Science Museum to archive it with especial care. It won't be found again for many years to come.'

Some thirteen years later, with SR53 gone, the P1 interceptor, by then called Lightning, was in the middle of its operational lifetime. It had become an icon for British defence capability since its performance was outstanding. That point was recalled by Edward Heath early in 1970, when as Prime Minister it came up in discussion with Peter Carrington, the secretary of state for defence.

'We've lost a jet from RAF Binbrook,' said Carrington, 'and the pilot is missing.' He had a cultured and precise articulation and did not waste words unnecessarily.

'Yes,' said Heath, 'I had a call from the airbase. It was an American pilot, just three days before his 29th birthday. Is there any news of him?' His was a more provincial voice which some said was the product of elocution lessons.

'No news. Captain Shaffner was a very experienced pilot. He went out with two other aircraft, but he was the first to get there.'

'Responding to the Soviets?'

'Perhaps. We got a radar blip from Staxton Wold and whoever it was ignored our orders to withdraw. When he got close enough Shaffner said there were bright lights in the sky, but no aircraft. So it wasn't the Soviets. Then we got another radio message to the effect that his Lightning had become uncontrollable. It went down in the sea.'

'Let me know when they find the aircraft.'

Three weeks later Heath received the expected call from Carrington. 'They've found the Lightning.'

'Had it broken up?'

'No. It was in one piece and must have come down pretty gently. It was ditched by the pilot, but he was no longer with the craft.'

'Perhaps he was lost from his dinghy?'

'No, he cannot have got out because the canopy was still in place. But he was gone. It's unthinkable for a pilot to get out without having jettisoned the canopy beforehand. There was every means of doing so. But he was absent altogether.'

'So what do you think happened?'

'I don't know. The other aircrews said the unidentified object was an extra-terrestrial craft. They were rather blasé about it as though they often see them. They usually describe them as shiny spheres or huge metallic cigars. They can easily outpace a Mach 2 interceptor with the fastest rate of climb.'

'We're really sure there was something there?'

'We are. And it was tracked by the Americans too.'

'Well let them know. Put out a suitable press release and keep the rest quiet.'

TWO

THE HACKER

By the year 2022 the conversation between Heath and Carrington was long in the past and 50 years had come and gone. Many of the intervening summers had been hot and sultry, but few more so than the August day when, in east Sussex, it was still warm and humid despite the sun having gone down two hours before. To Janice Ericson and Charlie Fellows, youngsters in leather bike gear, it was an ideal time to be out on Charlie's motorbike.

The big old bike was Charlie's pride and joy and had chrome which shone in the evening sun. It was right for the small lanes and chalk paths leading to the Firehills, a high point on the downs, where among the yellow gorse they held picnics and talked of the future. On that occasion they dismounted and strolled around to stretch their legs. The hot engine cooled and clicked in the quiet air while they sprawled on the short turf nearby. They removed their crash helmets, looked upwards into the darkening sky and chatted as lovers do. Minutes passed quickly, the warmth of the grass faded, and they watched as the sky changed from blue to violet, then to black.

They lay on the springy turf, their eyes facing upwards. The night sky was like a huge canvas in which the stars came alight one-by-one. There was no cloud and it was clear enough to see great distances into space, to the Milky Way and beyond. Eventually the whole was filled with tiny lamps and their light was unblinking, so that Janice remarked that they did not seem to twinkle. There on the Downs the stars seemed closer and brighter than from the dusty conurbation of Hastings to the west or Eastbourne a little farther.

Janice, a pretty girl with short dark hair, pointed to the moving lights of a meteor shower in the south. Charlie followed her eyes and he could see starlight reflected in them. Neither was drawn to speak since that idyllic aspect required no explanation. Then the meteors were alight in her eyes too, but unlike the stars they fell in a swarm and vanished in a final blaze on the crest of the hill. Meanwhile another, larger glow seemed to be travelling straight towards them in a distinct and unusual trajectory. Unlike the other incandescent lights it seemed to persist rather than disappear, and they ducked instinctively as it went overhead, too shocked to say much. Despite the dark, they could see a long gouge in the grass where it had fallen in the next field, leaving a mark just visible in the light of the stars. They were within easy walking distance. Charlie, a tall, willowy lad with a vestige of the old Sussex country accent, said, 'Come on, let's go and find it.'

After ten minutes, and with the aid of a torch, Janice came first to a gash in the turf about three feet deep, but becoming shallower, until at its very end an object could be seen in its own faint glow in the chalky debris. Shining a torch they could see that it was hot, and in the shape of a sphere, with slight projections above and below which made it look like a spinning top.

Charlie peered forward, then placed his arm on her shoulder and drew her back a little. He said, 'It isn't a meteorite.'

Janice shook her head. 'No,' she said, 'that's obvious. But it may be dangerous. Better not get too close.' They waited while the object hissed against the soil and like their bike, clicked as it cooled. Its colour slowly changed from blue-white to black, and in the dark Janice said, 'I think we should leave it until tomorrow. It's getting late and I want to get my head down. I can't see anyone else coming up here before breakfast time. Can we come back?'

'Sure. I'll come round early.'

They retraced their footsteps and Charlie dropped Janice home. She was ready at seven thirty the next morning and the object, now cool, was still there among the sheep that were cropping the short turf. In the daylight they could see the lightest of etchings on its surface: each one a careful shape with a particular texture that made it visible from some angles only.

The object looked so benign that Charlie was drawn to touch it, and this time, Janice did not think to warn him. It was smooth, but when he withdrew his hand it was black, as from soot; while where his hand had been were revealed concentric circles of silver, copper and grey. They tried to lift it and found they were easily able to do so. Janice said, 'Well, if this is made of metal it isn't solid. It bet it's hollow inside.'

'Yes, I doubt whether it's even half an inch thick. It's so light! Look at the marks though.' He pointed to them, standing proud of the surface as though they were meant to be touched as much as seen by eye. Brushing them to remove more of the black dirt, they felt rough to his fingertips, which noted the striations from which they were made.

Janice said, 'What shall we do with it?'

'Let's speak to Guy. He's interested in this stuff. I'll get him back here with his van. Can I use your phone? We can have breakfast here in the meantime. Here's some bread and cheese and a flask of coffee.'

'Guy Meredith?'

'Yes. It will interest him.'

Later, Meredith's telephone rang and Charlie Fellows was on the line. 'Hello Guy. Thanks for your tip about the bike, by the way. It's running pretty well. Hey, did you see that meteor storm last night?' Charlie's country burr was pleasant and reassuring. He was accomplished at making it so, and was pleased that most of the unease which Guy exuded in company was now absent.

'I certainly did. The sky was very clear. I think some of it may have hit the town. I'll go and see later. What about you?'

'I was out testing the bike with Janice. We saw something pretty interesting and we wondered whether we could get you to look at it!'

'Something to do with the bike?'

'No, something to do with the meteor shower. We thought you might want to see it. We're on the Firehills overlooking the sea. You know that narrow path near the top, where we go for a picnic? We don't want to leave it, so can you bring your van along?'

'Sure, I can go into town later. Give me a few minutes. I can make a space in the back first.'

An hour later, a van pulled cautiously up the narrow track. On the side was the slogan Meredith Security. Janice and Charlie had made a point of never asking about his work and seemed happy to restrict themselves to knowing that he worked in computer security. He had never enlarged on this, and they had rightly assumed he would be coy about his work and who his clients were. That aside, he was generally amenable and quite open about his hobbies, which he shared readily. Meredith was interested in astronomy and had a very large telescope which he used to observe the planets—they had seen Jupiter with it. Such an instrument was a magnet to like-minded people, and Janice and Charlie were drawn to his company just as enthusiasts of classic bikes were drawn to theirs. They had known each other for a while. Meredith was pleasant but rather solitary and they sometimes thought him nerdish or even autistic. He had the obsession to detail characteristic of autism, and usually needed to 'work up to' social meetings rather than have them happen suddenly. Other than that, they got along well.

They found it easy to place the object in Meredith's van. He offered to drive it anywhere they liked, but Janice and Charlie suggested Meredith's place, where he had a large garage for his telescope, computers and various other machines which made it a place half for work and the rest for hobbies. In fact Meredith probably spent most of his day there, visits to clients aside. They spent ten minutes looking over the meteor, then wrapped it in a white sheet in the back of his van. It seemed an innocuous object in daylight, now that it was cold and black. They agreed to follow Meredith home. Charlie kicked the starter and there was a burble as his bike chugged downhill.

Charlie carried the sphere while Meredith unlocked his garage. He said, 'I'll get some coffee first: three cups?' They agreed, despite the fact that there was still some of their own in the thermos flask. They knew that he ate little but drank a lot of instant coffee, which they did not particularly like. It did not suit the couple's own calm and relaxed disposition.

Meredith returned and said, 'You say it just fell from the skies?'

'It just did,' replied Janice, conscious of the irony. 'But it also happened to be in that meteor shower over the downs.'

'It's got marks on it. It reminds me of something else I read about a while back. There was something like it many years ago. It fell to earth and caused a lot of publicity, but then it disappeared and the whole thing fizzled out. I think it ended up in a museum. But that was maybe 50 years ago.'

Charlie said, 'Can you find out more about that?'

'I expect so. But before I do, I can tell you that this isn't a meteorite.'

'Janice and I are heading off into town for a couple of beers this lunchtime,' said Charlie. 'There will be a few bikes there—do you fancy dropping along?'

'Ok, I'd like to. Can I meet you in that car park? You'll see my van.'

—m—

Ten days later, Meredith entered the office of a Mr Robert Hawkins at the Science Museum in London. Hawkins was charged with liaison with the general public, which meant answering a barrage of scientific questions, often from schoolchildren, on everything from perpetual motion to the colours of the rainbow. He dealt with many enquiries by correspondence, some by interactive lectures, and fewer by interview with any member of the public with a more serious question of a scientific nature. Clients of these meetings were usually schoolteachers, journalists from Sunday colour supplements, or the occasional representative of a television show. Meredith, however, was one of the few: an apparently serious private astronomer and authentic scholar, hoping for a sight of the Silpho artefact. Meredith had said nothing about Janice and Charlie's fortune on the downs and had come without the intention of doing so. Hawkins had agreed to show him the Silpho object and had had it raised from the museum archives. He was hospitable and offered coffee. The other accepted with thanks and Hawkins recognised the habitual coffee user: Meredith could be seen immediately to relax. He sipped gratefully and said, 'It appeared half a century ago?'

'More than. It appeared in 1957 and disappeared soon after. They put it away in a tin box and archived in a way that makes me think people wanted it to disappear.'

'So it wasn't a hoax?'

'The official line was that it *was* a hoax. But that didn't stop it from being put away in case of trouble. Today, of course, we would probably say it's a bit low-tech for a flying saucer.'

'And it just fell to earth?'

'Maybe. A local businessman said he saw a glowing object fall from the skies. But he was too late to retrieve it. It fell onto Silpho Moor, and when he got there, it was gone. He placed an advert in the local paper—there was a reward, too—and another chap brought this metal flying saucer to him. It may even not have been the same one that he saw; we shall never know.'

'Was there any evidence,' said Meredith, 'that it might have been a real UFO?'

'It was a time of intense media coverage of the subject.' Hawkins mused, 'but the object was handled by no less a person than Air Chief Marshal Lord Dowding.'

'And he was satisfied?'

'Apparently so, but you can see it and judge for yourself.' Hawkins lifted a steel box onto a table and opened the lid. He said, 'We like to keep it with the box it was stored in. There is the historical aspect to be considered.' Out of the box it sat awkwardly on the table, leaning to one side.

Meredith said, 'It's pretty dusty,' but he pulled out a tape measure and used it to measure the size of the sphere. It was a little over 16 inches across. Then Hawkins offered to place it on a balance. It read 9.97kg, and Meredith wrote down both measurements in a small notebook. To Meredith it seemed rather homespun, like a model from a metalwork class, without the precision of manufacture that he would have expected from anything connected with a UFO. He looked doubtful until Hawkins proffered: 'Remember, it was supposed to have fallen to earth. It probably got very hot.' Meredith nodded and asked whether he could photograph it. Hawkins agreed.

Meredith lifted the object once more and turned it over in his hands. It was copper-coloured and carried a number of small engravings. It opened to reveal what Hawkins described as 'the works,' but which in fact were a few thin copper sheets that had marks on them like those on the outside. All were indecipherable, but he had a vague feeling that they were familiar, and almost said so. Hawkins, however, remarked: 'I don't think anyone has managed to make any sense of them. Someone did come up with a story that they were a message from an alien called Ullo. But I can't see why anyone would bother to tell us that we must improve or disappear because let's face it, we probably realise that anyway.'

Meredith nodded. 'But they could actually mean something; and I think that the shapes are beautiful. It would have taken a lot of care to make them and they are the one thing I could believe in.'

'But not Ullo then?'

'No, Ullo is out as far as I'm concerned.'

Meredith made a few notes which, together with his camera, he packed away in a bag. Then lifting the sphere he gesticulated towards its box, which Hawkins turned to find. A considerable amount of black dust fell from the sphere, which he collected in an envelope. Then, he brushed his fingers together as one would with the dust of years of storage. Meredith offered his thanks, they shook hands, and Hawkins put the lid back on the box.

When he got home, he phoned Janice and Charlie and suggested they might like to come over that evening. Later, he described the Silpho object to them and projected his photographs on a screen. The hieroglyphs were small, and they walked closer to see. He voiced the words he had almost uttered to Hawkins: 'They look like yours, but apart from that I can't remember where else I've seen them.'

'I know what you mean,' replied Janice. She thought for a while, and then shook her head so that her dark hair flapped about, 'They almost look Egyptian, but they're not quite there. And it looks a bit like ours, but it's smaller. It's more like something home-made. Was it light?'

'Yes, it was hollow, so it was about what you would expect. But it was very dirty, and I don't think that was from being stored. We can try a bit of chemistry on it.'

'Chemistry?' Charlie raised an eyebrow.

'Yes, I pick up quite a lot of it in my line of work. I need to know what metals I'm dealing with.' He opened the envelope. 'I collected a bit of dirt from the object. The chap didn't seem to mind too much. Perhaps he didn't see.'

Janice and Charlie watched as Meredith emptied the contents into a test tube. He held it to the light and said, 'Ok, there are two kinds of tiny particles: orange and black.' Then he carried out a number of careful manipulations, first with water and then with acids. As they sat to watch, he told them not to get too close. Janice and Charlie, as easy-going as ever, were unfazed by Meredith's authoritative manner. Charlie said, 'I wouldn't like to get that stuff on my bike!' But their attention stayed as the mixture changed colour. Finally, Meredith gave a modest, but satisfied smile in their direction. He said, 'The orange particles are copper and the black powder is copper oxide. I sometimes see it near electrical circuits when they overheat. It tells me that this thing got very hot.'

'I suppose it suggests,' said Janice, 'that the object is real?'

'It supports the idea that it fell to earth, anyway.'

Charlie said, 'As did our own object.'

'Yes, but I don't think that either could have come from a very great height, otherwise they would have melted. And if it was from a low-altitude, then it wasn't a proper meteorite.'

'That ties in with what Silpho witnesses were supposed to have seen, doesn't it?' replied Janice.

'Well it does tie in with what you and Charlie saw on the Firehills.' There was a short pause as they digested these conclusions. Janice said, 'I feel like I'm taking part in a detective story,' and smiled in her engaging way.

Meredith went out to get more coffee, and as he drank gratefully, he seemed to lose some of the agitation he felt in company. He then said, 'The next thing is to find out what we can about your Firehills object. He cleared a space on his bench and set up his chemicals again. Janice sat at a distance and said, 'I was never much good with experiments!' Charlie grinned and held the object while Meredith scraped it to obtain material for his tests.

None were surprised when the outcome was similar. Meredith said, 'It's copper as well, and it got as hot as the Silpho thing. But they don't look as though they were made by the same hand. Yours is bigger and better.'

Janice joined them at the bench and said, 'Perhaps that's because it's less bashed about. The other one looks as though it lived a harder life.'

Charlie said, 'They probably opened it with a hammer!'

Meredith followed, 'In that case, what's inside this one?'

—⁓—

Guy Meredith lived in a provincial seaside town at the foot of the South Downs, where he was adequately comfortable in a rambling house inherited from his parents. It was larger than he needed, but he was used to it and felt secure there. Nevertheless the expression 'adequately comfortable' would have been misleading from his point of view. Since he had little interest in comfort, he would actually have preferred an uncomfortable home had it given him more solitude and security.

His activities had naturally spread into a large garage, complete with wooden ceiling and a room above, where he usually worked. Although he used a van for business, it lived outside in all weathers and so both floors were available for work and leisure. Prominent within it was his telescope underneath a skylight on the top floor, and the machines on which he worked for a living. Inside, it was often hot, and there was a continuous whirring of cooling fans. But the lifestyle, the few armchairs and the litter of bachelor living: the cups, kettle and television, suited him. There were other things too: his work and hobbies were blurred into one so that under a workbench was a trunk, hidden under a few old curtains. It contained the odds and ends relevant to his hobby, and it was there that he agreed to keep Janice and Charlie's object among the similar things that were of interest to him.

The autistic Meredith, security consultant and a clever individual, was aware of his awkwardness and rather cautious in all company. Yet he also understood he was improving and that his intelligence could create paradigms for social interaction. He was not intentionally solitary, but his solitary work suited him and his interests were complimentary. At times he had learned to like at least some companionship, and then he made an effort to introduce inflection in his voice and vary the stock of conversation pieces he had carefully acquired. However under duress he sometimes forgot and his voice would then become curious so that his conversation, usually diverse and articulate, became flat and monotonous as though he had forgotten the carefully-learned phrases.

Nevertheless he was a decent and prosperous individual and very good at his job. And this had enabled him to indulge in a more private obsession. It was known that he was interested in astronomy, but in private he pursued it to a more unusual extreme. He had an ardent interest in space travel and the unexplained, and he knew that official—mostly defence—records would demonstrate the truth of their existence. It was a singular attitude towards official records, so dependent on his computer skills, which made his activities necessarily covert and clandestine. Yet it would have been unwise to consider Meredith as just a computer hacker. He had no interest in the act of breaking and entering in its own right, and justified his actions quite simply: there was no material gain. Nor had he caused any material damage. He considered that the fundamental injustice was the withholding of knowledge by the authorities. Nevertheless, he had been warned by the police, and he had even appeared in the local news where a mildly nefarious reputation had increased his standing among his clients.

Thus it was a few short days after his meeting with Janice and Charlie that he sat alone at his computer. On a Friday afternoon and in an unnecessarily furtive manner, for he was alone, he opened a file held on a computer at the British Ministry of Defence. It was dated 1952 and had sub-folders with secretive-sounding names such as Joint Intelligence Bureau. He opened one, a folder about 70 years old and past any possible relevance to the security of the realm. He had wished to find more about Silpho but had not been successful. Yet he had found something else that was just as interesting. He thought it strange that it was still marked with a code for restricted access.

Restricted certainly, and access had not been easy, yet with a diligent application of his abilities, the foremost of which was patience, he had eventually found a way in. He thought about the physical length of the connection, about 50 miles. It was strange that a combination of copper wire and fibre optic cables worked as it did. He visualised the copper wire as an extension of his own fingers and felt as though he were a spider at the middle of a web. Or perhaps he was the fly? If so, he would need to ensure that his opponent the spider, while feeling for any movement in the connection, should know nothing of him. He concentrated his attention on the screen to the exclusion of all else, and avoided moving the cursor over the document.

He thought their level of security unprofessional and muttered to that extent in the privacy of his room: 'They don't seem to learn.' By exercising care, Meredith had managed to minimise the risk. It was wrong that they should be so secretive, but that, in any case, was the game: they were the target of his endeavours just as he was the target of their security. He had felt a familiar rush of adrenalin as he created that 50-mile link. It was a compulsion, like gaming or gambling, both at which he excelled. It was a disorder that he found stimulating.

He read titles only, conscious of the constraint of time. It was clear in the subject matter and from the manner of its construction, that his intended document was not a hoax. Some 70 years after the 1950s UFO scare, Meredith saved to disc a file entitled 'Airfield Incursions, Witness Statements'. He did not attempt to read it online because he had learned not to spend too much time connected. Suddenly the cursor began to move independently of his own hand. He knew the signs and closed his connection. He doubted they could trace him, yet he was not sure. The adrenalin had been worth perhaps 10 cups of coffee.

—∞—

Eighteen hours later Meredith walked into town, went straight to an internet café and ordered still more coffee. Then he opened the file on his memory stick and read quickly. It was concerned with witness statements to Scientific Intelligence officials and had a moderate security status. The interviewee was a Flight Lieutenant, a witness to a putative unidentified flying object. He made a short inspection of the photograph for signs of the grainy background characteristic of an airbrushed image, but found that it had not been altered. The photograph remained clear, a passport back into a post-war world of black-and-white. It contained a silver-white disk above the control tower of an airbase. An adjoining script was difficult to read but was legible with the help of a magnifying glass. He read:

INTERVIEW ONE

Interviewer: 'State your views on the general notion of extra-terrestrial life.'

Client: 'I have an open mind. I accept as true only those things for which the evidence is clear.'

Interviewer: 'Describe the circumstances in which you saw the unidentified object.'

Client: 'I was at the airbase on a warm day, and the air was quite still. There was no aircraft in the air and none on the ground with an engine started, so all was quiet. I turned to see a flying object approach from behind me. It wouldn't be correct to say it intentionally approached *me*; it was just traversing in my general direction from some distance away.'

Interviewer: 'What did it look like?'

Client: 'It was a saucer-shaped object, a flying saucer. It had a grey colour and it moved with a subsidiary rocking motion. But it was pearlescent. It shimmered in the manner of mother of pearl.'

Interviewer: 'Any idea why it rocked?'

Client: 'No, but such a rocking motion might have facilitated the collection of data, rather like an old-fashioned biplane rocking its wings to increase the area of ground-coverage in a series of photographs.'

Interviewer: 'Any other visual characteristics you recall?'

Client: 'It was grey, but it reflected light as metals do. It went overhead very quickly and I saw that its edges looked a bit different. They gave out light, but it was not a reflection. It was a light source, with little sparks and crackles like static electricity at its edge. It resembled a massive electric generator. I smelled ozone and the smell was exceedingly strong. As it traversed, it made the air feel charged in the manner of an electrical storm or as though within a power station. It was about 100 feet in diameter and moved at about 500 mph. Other than that it was smooth and featureless.'

Interviewer: 'Where do you think it came from? Perhaps the Russians made it?'

Client: 'No idea. It wasn't one of ours, nor of the Americans. The Russians are still farther behind. I would describe it as not of this world.'

Interviewer: 'You sound as though you're joking!'

Client: 'I don't joke in interviews of this kind.'

INTERVIEW 2

Interviewer: 'You saw the 'craft' a second time?'

Client: 'That sounds like a question rather than a statement. You know it; that's why we are here.'

Interviewer: 'Quite. Well tell me how it was.'

Client: 'I was watching the maiden flight of a new aircraft about a month after my first sighting of the unknown craft. That would make it during September 1950. The maiden flight was of a joint British and Australian fighter plane with a swept wing. It was an attractive, good-looking design that was easy on the eye, but its engine wasn't really suitable and we only made one which was destroyed in an accident the following year. Shame really.'

'So I was watching the flight, and apart from the new prototype there was nothing else around. I was above the flying control building and it was a cloudy afternoon; there was good visibility but only below about 5000 feet. Above that height there was 100% cloud. I saw the plane do its flight and return after about 20 minutes. There were quite a few of us there. Then I saw the unidentified flying object at a distance.'

Interviewer: 'Did you consider that the unidentified object might be an aeroplane?'

Client: 'We all saw it at the same time. Its effect on us was similar; we were all quite shocked. And there was no question of it being any kind of aeroplane with an aerofoil wing. It had some other means of flight and propulsion. It resembled a gyroscope with the ability to remain just stable. That might account for the rocking motion I mentioned in our last meeting. Then it would fly off at incredible speed and at an angle which suggested some hugely powerful method of propulsion and fine control. It was farther away than when I saw it the first time, but in all respects the object was identical to the first.'

Interviewer: 'What would the effect be on any humans inside?'

Client: 'With acceleration and g-forces like that? I would imagine unconsciousness or even instant death. It would have had to be automated or controlled from elsewhere, or alternatively it would have needed some way of mitigating the g-forces.'

Interviewer: 'Was it spinning?'

Client: 'It seemed to have the same pattern of gyroscopic stability you get from a spinning object.'

Interviewer: 'You all saw the same thing?'

Client: 'Yes, some of my comrades hadn't believed me the first time and they were obliged to apologise! We were dumbfounded.'

Interviewer: 'What do you think it was?'

Client: 'It was not of this earth; its abilities were just too far in advance of those of today.'

Interviewer: 'Let me be clear: you must speak of this to nobody. This may be an issue of national security. I must make it clear to you that this matter must not be spoken of either within the airbase or with people outside. I intend to speak to each of the group concerned and will make the same point. Can I confirm that this is quite clear?'

Client: 'I am very clear on this point, thank you.'

Meredith closed the file, pocketed his magnifying glass and sat in silence. He brooded for a few minutes and slowly drank his coffee, which was now lukewarm. Now that he *knew*, he felt sated. But it was one thing to 'know' and another to 'do'. What could he, what should he 'do'? He mused on his findings, what indeed? This and other matters were worthy of consideration by the Network.

He was by no means the only person of such a disposition. There were many others around the world, particularly in the United States, who shared his interest. They were members of what by then had become a network of like-minded people, tantamount to a formal organisation. It was an enterprise that had grown in many countries and the number of participants had become considerable. It was now a group certainly of three figures, perhaps even four.

The Network existed to share information of a technical nature. It had started as an email club, but like many such groups it had grown to provide newsletters and conventions. It had become large enough to have policies and influence, and its members accepted a number of fundamental truths. It was held as certain that UFOs existed, since there was quite enough evidence of that from photographs taken by all kinds of aircraft. And it was accepted that humankind was under surveillance for the same reason. More recently, the Network had also become speculative and technical: a discussion forum for questions of advanced technology. Yet it was careful to omit articles that were a product of the imagination or which contained pseudo-science; all could recognise them. Thus it promoted exchanges of real scientific interest in which material evidence was circulated, and evaluated as though a scientific paper.

Meredith's article on the airbase incident might add to evidence from that period, and it would certainly attract interest, yet it was old-hat, a concern of 70 years before. Anything on Silpho was similarly yesterday's news. Continuing to reflect, Meredith was handed a menu, which he declined. Razor-thin, he ate little and preferred the impact of caffeine on an empty stomach. With a clear mind, he decided immediately to circulate, under a pseudonym, a file on the interviews.

What, though, to do about the Firehills projectile? Should he, Janice and Charlie wait on that? Could it be that news on the subject was too speculative? Quickly, he made up his mind. He would avoid the Network but speak to one or two of his more private contacts. This was not unusual with more important findings because it was generally understood that the Network was monitored by the American and British security services. Members had occasionally been chased down and questioned about their sources of information and some said—it was rumoured—that they were occasionally made to disappear. Accordingly, the Network had developed a surreptitious side, with exchanges that were not for more general consumption. Individual contacts?—he would speak to Bud Lynch first—were always a source of wisdom.

Meredith continued to think: he had been busy recently and had not noticed the obvious. The Network was more than usually alive at the moment. Several small, but individual strands of evidence had surfaced together. It was as though something much larger were afoot. Any further action demanded extra care. And extra care was needed because he knew that he had become newsworthy again. The recent meteor shower had dented several cars in town and he had been with Janice and Charlie when a local reporter photographed the results. They had been close, quite by chance, and it had not helped when Charlie, standing nearby, had said, 'Another unidentified flying object.' That alone would not have been enough for him to appear in the local news, but his previous form on the subject had made him newsworthy. Had the reporter known more about the events of the night before, then his own exposure would have been considerably greater. The reporter had not known, of course, but Meredith was careful to prime his friends on what not to say in case of continuing interest from that quarter.

A little later, Meredith spoke again to Janice and Charlie. They were in his garage looking at the Firehills projectile. The young couple were pleasant and lively and he was pleased to see them. The projectile stood on a workbench and they had decided to take a longer look at it.

Meredith said, 'So you saw it land?'

'We were looking up at the sky and we saw it land. It was hot and it glowed, so we saw it hit the earth. We don't think it landed in any controlled way. It just hit the ground at an angle and it made that big scrape in the soil.'

'Thanks. Was it in the meteor shower?'

Janice said, 'It arrived at the same time. But the funny thing is that we saw it come down at a different angle. It was a much shallower—what's that word?'

'Trajectory?'

'That's the one. When it landed, it made that long scrape in the soil. If it had come straight down I think it would have made a big crater and would probably have been flattened. But it wasn't even dented! Thanks for helping us to get it back, by the way. We could never have done it with just the bike.'

'That's OK.'

It was bright in Meredith's garage, and quite hot. There were extra lights overhead and the place contained many powerful computers, cases removed and their components open to the eye. They were working hard: there was a whir of cooling fans and lights flashed as they used electricity. Meredith saw them looking and said 'Bitcoin. It helps pay the bills.'

Propped up in the middle of all this the projectile stood on the bench, undamaged. Meredith said, 'We agreed it's probably hollow, so there might be something inside.' He added, 'But I don't want to break it open.'

'Maybe we should hand it in?' said Charlie, his Sussex burr quizzical, ironic.

'Not just yet. No, please don't. The thing would disappear. It would get carted off by some official agency and it would vanish, and nobody would be the wiser, least of all us.'

'OK,' said Charlie, 'I suppose it's only fair that we should get a first crack at it. Anyway, it may be nothing important.'

Janice was used to tempering her boyfriend's enthusiasm and she was a bit more cautious about it: 'But what if it's dangerous? It might give off a cloud of gas or contain deadly spores. It might cause a new pandemic!'

'And it might not. Anyway, it got hot, so the deadly spores are probably dead anyway!'

'Well alright, I suppose we can't sit here staring at it. Let's turn it over to see whether there's any way of getting inside.'

They turned it over. There were the few hieroglyphs on the surface that could be seen easily, but overall the object remained black, its surface a mass of sooty copper oxide and hand-prints. They decided to clean it first, and Meredith fetched a damp cloth.

His ministrations restored a shiny surface, not copper-coloured, but of a lighter metallic hue with a red tinge to it. He thought it perhaps an alloy of some kind. The hieroglyphs, now clean, were a suitable subject for his camera. He moved some lights around, took photographs and then turned it over in the hope of finding a crevice or seam. While he held it, Charlie pressed its surface in diverse ways; then they each grasped it and turned hemispheres in opposite directions. There was no result.

Charlie said, 'We need to decide whether to get a can opener!' Meredith had also wanted to say this but thus far had been reluctant.

Janice replied, 'I don't think we want to break it. I just think we need to understand the marks. They may be instructions for a way in.'

'Ok, marks first then. In which case, we've gone as far as we can today. But the marks, they aren't really my kind of problem,' he went on, 'but I do know a guy.'

'Is he discreet?' said Janice.

'He's a client, so he's as discreet with me as I am with him. He's in the computer algorithms business, which isn't strictly relevant, but he's also good with shapes, forms and mathematical representations. He runs a magazine on it. I saw it once and it was full of that kind of stuff. Also he has his own business contacts—I'm sure he could put a problem about. He's a guy called Peter, and we chat quite often. I do general computer repairs and security for him. It's either that or we have to get rough with the object.'

Charlie nodded. 'Good idea.' They were all relieved to agree. 'We don't really want to cut it open, it seems a shame. By the way, can we please keep it here? You've got that trunk there'—he pointed—'and it'll be inconspicuous; better than my place for sure.'

Janice looked at the open trunk with its mass of wires, Meccano frames and bits of twisted metal. She said, 'There's no chance of putting it on the bike, anyway. By the way, what *is* all that stuff?'

'Oh, it's just a load of junk I've collected over the years; some of it's supposed to be interesting. Most of it, just bits of rocks or metal, came from exchanges with other people. But thank you for reminding me, I need to get some of it checked out soon. I know another guy: we talk from time to time.'

'You seem to get around, Guy,' said Janice.

He said, 'Yes, I probably do.' To the others, the combination of his self-effacing, retiring manner and his sharp brain seemed incongruous, but not unpleasant.

Later Guy Meredith encrypted a two-page missive on the Firehills projectile and sent it to Bud Lynch, a correspondent in the United States. Lynch was a fellow member of the Network whom he knew through video conferences. Several exchanges had built a measure of confidence and familiarity, and they had become assured enough to share material which could cause trouble if released more widely. In due course, material objects had been exchanged, among them some of the hardware now hidden in his trunk. Lynch was a materials scientist and his opinion added credence to observations concerning hardware that had been salvaged from aircraft or supposed spacecraft. Thus it was reasonable that he should be the first to benefit from findings regarding the Firehills projectile. As he pressed 'send,' he was grateful for the means of encryption he had arranged with Lynch beforehand. The file of interviews he had already dealt with.

—⚏—

A week later, Meredith was with his client Peter Pargeter, who was working in his office. Pargeter's was one of the comfortable village homes, some way to the west, which many professional people had taken rather than commute to a larger town or city. Village homes were small, but many had substantial facilities at the rear. A group of bespoke wooden sheds offered a larger floor area than the house itself. And they were pleasant; a breeze brought the scent of roses in to where Pargeter sat at a large desk, alternately deep in thought or scribbling on rough paper the incomprehensible mathematics particular to his business.

Pargeter jumped to his feet as Meredith approached along a path outside, and welcomed him with a smile. A professional man of middle age, he had run to fat and waddled about on worn heels, toes outwards, rather like a duck. He had receding hair which he tried to compensate for by combing it forward over a bald patch, and he often held his head in an unnatural poise to avoid disturbing it. In most other respects the two men were quite different, one middle-aged, the other young. Meredith was aware that Pargeter's figure was a product of 30 years of indulgence and that he would never have accommodated Meredith's diligent avoidance of lunch. Other than that, Pargeter had a friendly and open disposition, considerable charm, and enough natural authority to get noticed among those in high places. In turn, he had often wondered why Meredith seemed to need a period of notice in order to accept a proposed meeting. Perhaps he needed to get used to the idea first?

Despite their differences they got on well on a professional basis. They had known each other for a couple of years and Pargeter admired Meredith's 'flair' in problem-solving. For Meredith, who hoped to enlist Pargeter's help, on that occasion the boot would be on the other foot. In fact, it would be the first time that he would ask Pargeter's help on any matter. In so doing he suspected that Pargeter would take like a leech to any kind of mathematical problem and would probably welcome it as a diversion. He had decided to keep the Firehills projectile out of their discussion and intended to broach the subject of the hieroglyphs, so called, only on a general basis.

Pargeter knew that Meredith drank coffee whenever he could, and he was happy to oblige while the latter rebuilt his machine and tested it. Later, with their business over, Meredith passed the photographs of the Firehills hieroglyphs to Pargeter, who had guessed from his unusually preoccupied look that something else was on his mind.

Meredith said, 'What do you make of these unusual symbols, Peter. Any ideas?'

Pargeter said, 'Gosh, they look interesting. Were they on a metal surface? It looks shiny.'

'Yes, they were on a metal.'

Pargeter counted the hieroglyphs. 'I think I can see twenty five different symbols, is that all you've got?'

'I think that's it.'

'Can I ask where they came from? Abroad, surely; South America or China, perhaps even Egypt?'

'Not sure where.'

'Well they may be hieroglyphic.' Pargeter looked at them closely. 'That's funny, one or two look familiar, but when I think about it I can't place them at all.'

'You say they are hieroglyphic? Like letters of an alphabet?'

'Not quite. There are various kinds, of course. The simplest are no more than pictures of the object they represent. But they can represent many different things, sounds, a syllable or even a whole word. With use, they often get reduced to simple brush strokes and straight lines. I thought these were Egyptian—they are often recognisable—but on reflection perhaps not.'

'So there's nothing at all familiar?'

'I'm not sure. But I do find it strange that among them there should be no representation of an agricultural artefact. I would expect the horns of a goat, a domestic cat, a kitchen implement or a plough at least: homely things, important to the average bloke in the street. I would also expect many more than twenty-five.'

Meredith said, 'So what's the point of them? Do they have any particular advantage?'

'They may do. Where speakers of distinct dialects can't understand each other, a common system of hieroglyphs can be understood by both. But more importantly they remain the cultural property of a nation, rather like its language. In some cases they are revered for their mystical quality and are seen on religious monuments.'

'How did you find out all this stuff?'

Pargeter smiled, 'Oh, when I was a lad, I spent hours in the reading room at the local library. That's where I started on geometry, for what it's worth!'

'I see! But from the point of view of finding out what these few mean, could they be an alphabet like our own?'

'I suppose they could. Twenty five symbols would certainly be enough to represent all the sounds in modern English, anyway.'

'But what if they are numbers?'

'Then I doubt whether there would be more than ten. Nobody with any sense would count in anything other than tens.'

'So can you make an informed guess about their meaning?'

'Not without some kind of key. I don't suppose you have a Rosetta stone?'

'No. Any idea what to do?'

'Leave the photographs with me. I will try to look at them over the weekend.'

THREE

David Elliott, a journalist, hesitated at the entrance to Jonathan Burgess' open office door, but he tapped on the glass and walked straight in for the meeting with his editor which, on a Monday, had been arranged last thing on the Friday afternoon. Burgess greeted him and waved his hand towards the chair opposite. His was not a particularly formal manner, and he usually dispensed with greetings. Characteristically he launched straight into the reason for their encounter: 'Here, David, I've an assignment for you.' He passed over a brown envelope from which Elliott withdrew a sheaf of papers.

Elliott was pleased, because an unusual assignment was usually a bit of relief from everyday routine. He did not dislike a visit to the law courts, and he actively enjoyed a lunch meeting with a junior minister if he could get one. Yet he had a raffish streak about him, and a 'more creative' investigation would be a welcome diversion. Could this be one? As the recipient of a proverbial brown envelope, Elliott liked to think that Burgess had high hopes of him. The envelope was undoubtedly a favour, and he hoped to do well with it. If so, it would be better than the last one, a case which unfortunately had fizzled out.

Burgess pointed to the envelope. 'This could be just as interesting. It's classified, and the military and security services don't like it. It

43

may be a fairy tale, but it's worth a punt to try and get inside.' He added, 'I like hackers, they lead to bigger things.'

Burgess turned away to look at his desk. His conversation was always marked by frugality, and he didn't say anything further. Elliott thanked him, picked up the file and made for the door. Burgess did nod at him as he left, which Elliott took as a sign of a small measure of approval. But it was not as though Burgess had shown him any other courtesy, and he was known to want results. Later, Elliott sat at his desk. He opened the folder, which contained a selection of press cuttings together with the photograph of a man of about 30 years. The face was of an individual driven by nervous energy, and it looked emaciated. The hair was cropped short, and the complexion was pale as though of an office worker who spent long hours away from the sunshine. The eyes were unfocussed and although he looked clever, he seemed scruffy, as though indifferent to any audience.

Elliott read the contents of the file, a job which took about half an hour, and he made a few notes as he went on. The case hadn't made the national news—Elliott thought 'not yet, anyway'—and much of the material was from provincial newspapers. But there were old press cuttings too, which suggested a long-standing history of interest from officialdom. It seemed to Elliott that they were anxious to make the subject look a public fool, and to make an example of a man who knew too much of their business. His instinct confirmed that of Burgess, who with his unerring eye had sensed mileage in the case still.

The file dealt with the case of Guy Meredith, a computer consultant, who several years before had managed to hack into the computers of defence installations in the United States and Britain. His interests were harmless and rather cranky, and he was considered as no more than a highly competent pest. However he had resurfaced recently with the suggestion that there was 'something big afoot in the world of UFOs' and he had got into local news, if only in a small town by the seaside. Elliott supposed that it was more correct that the suggestion had accompanied him, rather than being made by him, but that was beside the point. As far as his audience was concerned, there were observations about a meteor storm, and reports of lights in the sky at a place called the Firehills.

Elliott looked for the young man on social media and found his page with ease. It was in fact substantial and wholly public, as though he enjoyed notoriety. Nevertheless he also had few social media contacts as though he was shy or made few relationships. It was an open invitation to contact its owner, which Elliott did as soon as he had found a number. He was simple and direct: 'Hello, I'm David Elliott, a journalist for a London paper with a large circulation. We hear you're in the local news. Can I make an appointment to see you? We are interested in what you do.'

Meredith was pleasant in return, 'I'm not sure I can do justice to a fully-fledged city paper, but if you aren't worried about my wasting your time, then it's OK. But there isn't really very much that's new.'

'Don't worry about that, perhaps we can be of help to each other.' Elliott thought that Meredith might like more publicity than a social media page could offer.

'Yes, it's surprising how beneficial journalism can be. How long do you need?'

'Let's say about an hour or so.'

'OK, but I would much prefer to meet in town. What about a coffee shop?'

'Not at your home?'

'No.'

Elliott said, 'Sure, name your place.'

'The Aroma Cafeteria in Victoria Street, it's an internet café which I use quite often. I like to get out and about in the mornings. How about 11.00 am tomorrow?'

'Yes, that would be fine.' Meredith hung up and sat down to ponder. Fifty miles away Elliott had a quiet evening at home and then turned in at 11 pm.

The next day, Elliott arrived at the railway station of a quiet seaside town on the south coast. It nestled under the South Downs with the Firehills to the east, but was served poorly by main roads and slow diesel trains. The air was fresh and salty, however, and the cries of seabirds recalled half-remembered childhood holidays by the seaside. It was early, so he walked a circuitous route over the mile or so to their proposed meeting place. The town did not seem especially prosperous, but the centre was busy, with a constant flow of buses to and from the sea front. Walking east on the promenade, he saw a shingle beach with much flotsam and jetsam and to his left, a few antique shops and half-timbered pubs. Most of the townspeople seemed to dress very cheaply and the shops were priced accordingly, but the fish and chip shops were full, as were the amusement arcades. It was one of the many English seaside towns caricatured cruelly in French films, but it was better than Boulogne or Calais anyway, and unlike those places, it had an unselfconscious gaiety about it with holidaymakers arm in arm, sporting funny hats and candy floss.

Elliott eventually found the cafe and sat at a small table. A waitress brought coffee and he looked out of the window at passers-by. He was still a little early, had finished his coffee and was thinking about another, when Meredith entered. Elliott knew him from his photograph, waved, and Meredith joined him at the table. The latter said, 'You made it then.' He spoke informally but didn't seem particularly at ease at first, and with his gaze darting around the room, he seemed unsettled. However after coffee he seemed to relax more and was at last willing to meet Elliott's gaze.

'Yes, I got on an early train and I was here with at least an hour to spare. I saw a little of the sea front. An up-and-coming town, but it could do with a lick of paint?'

'Yes, Brighton along the coast is in a much better state of repair.'

'But I had a good walk anyway. You preferred to meet in town?'

'I like to get out. That's the one difficulty in working from home. I keep busy, of course, but when I'm not with clients I look forward to the simplest of excursions. Could I see some identification, please, before we talk about anything?'

'Certainly, there you are.' Elliott showed him his press cards and Meredith compared the photograph with the face. They matched, and Elliott was smart and good-looking. There was no sense that he was ingratiating, and he was polite and straight to the point. Meredith took to him straight away.

Elliott said, 'I read about your case and hoped that we could benefit each other. You will be familiar with the story in the local paper. While it wasn't an extensive piece, I thought that a better-written story, maybe with a few original strands, might be worth a larger audience.'

'That's just what I want. I don't regard myself as a criminal, but that hasn't stopped the various security services who occasionally threatened me with incarceration.'

'Surely a bit of hacking isn't really worth a long stretch?'

'Not over here. They say I cost them millions and damage their systems, but it isn't really true. All they need to do is change a few passwords. I have never deleted or broken anything.'

'Do you expect to get caught?'

'You don't think about that. And anyway, it adds to the excitement. The challenge is to be invisible while you are doing it.'

'What kind of stuff do you actually want to see? Surely you aren't after defence simulations or codes for pressing the nuclear button?'

'Lord, no. I'm interested in things from outer space. Astronomy or space travel. And if there's anything I can purloin about unidentified flying objects'—he seemed to relish the term—'then I would go straight to that.'

'So UFOs come under defence?'

'I didn't think so, but now I know they do. The giveaway is that the chap who denies everything is always from the military. They always sound as though they have something to cover up.'

'So you got into their systems. Did it take long?'

'That makes it sound like breaking and entering. Well, you don't just break in overnight. It took six months, but it was part-time. I had to wait. You need to make the software and then wait for it to harvest things like passwords.'

Elliott was pleased with the way Meredith had warmed to their conversation. It was approaching mid-day. He said, 'More coffee, or can I buy you lunch?'

'Well I suppose lunch if we're going to keep the table.'

'Sure. What can I get you?'

Meredith settled on quiche and salad and a foaming concoction called a Toffee Crisp milkshake. He ate quickly, and was unconcerned by continuing the conversation with his mouth full, 'It actually took me a full month to make the gear myself.'

'The computer?'

'No,' said Meredith. 'I meant the bits of software to do the job.'

'You already knew how to make it?'

'It's my job to know these things anyway.'

'You are employed at present?'

'Consultant.'

'Do you get work very easily?'

'I do now. The funny thing is that it loosed a few contracts from official sources. I won't say who because there are confidentiality agreements.'

'So how did you get into these UK or was it US defence systems? Surely they were all behind walls and protected by passwords so that only authorised people can get inside?'

'Well yes. It was both countries actually. And there were various levels of security, so that the higher the degree of national security involved, the fewer were authorised to have access.'

'And yet you managed to get inside.'

'It wasn't exactly a case of switch on and get inside, but I did, yes. Look, can we keep the technical side simple, please?'

'But you were never a danger to their systems.'

'No, I'm completely harmless. I'm only really interested in UFOs and interstellar travel.'

'But I bet you could tell me what the United States would do in the event of a nuclear war?'

'I looked at some files, yes. The Americans have simulated every possible war that you might imagine, including one in which they need to 'take out' a Marxist British prime minister.'

'And you don't intend to talk about it?'

'No. It just isn't worth my own safety. I'm not saying our lot are as bad as the Russians, but look at what *they* did. They poisoned a chap with radioactive polonium. They slipped it into his cup of tea. These things do go on. Who knows what might happen!'

Elliott felt he needed to change the subject. He finished a mouthful of salad and began to talk about the town itself. 'I strolled around a bit on the way here. It was interesting. There are postcards of tall wooden buildings on the beach, and there's a fishing fleet as well.'

'Oh yes. I've lived here much of my life. This place gets under your skin after a while. It's the sound of the place, the salt smell and the shrieking gulls. It has history too. There were guns on the promenade in the war.'

'I'm a Londoner.'

'Did your grandparents ever visit the hop farms?'

'I think they did. But that was a long time ago.'

Meredith had finished his lunch. Elliott sensed that he'd had enough and said 'Look, Guy, I think we can do each other a lot of good. Can we arrange a longer session, so that we can actually discuss the UFO side of things in proper detail? I agree that there's not much mileage in the security aspect. And I don't want to hog a table here. What do you say?'

'It will have to be a week-end. Now I know you, perhaps we can do it at my home. I can show you things. Phone me, no, my mobile please.'

Later, Elliott spoke to Burgess again. 'I met Meredith and had an introductory session over lunch. He seemed rather nervous and I kept on wanting to soothe him. But he's very bright.'

'Do you think you will get a story?'

'Yes, but it will take some careful landing. I have a sixth sense about it: it could be huge.'

Following a respectable interval, Elliott telephoned Meredith and was soon with him at his home. He asked whether he could record their conversation, 'It's better than taking notes.'

'I expected it. And besides, I would rather you had an accurate record. But I would like a copy of the recording, please.' Elliott agreed and switched on.

Meredith seemed quite eager to pick up where they had left off, and he seemed more relaxed on his home territory, or perhaps because he knew what to expect. 'I do worry about letting the wrong things out, so no defence issues today. It's not that I know much about that aspect anyway; I was never really interested in it.'

'That's fine; we can leave it out and stick to UFOs.'

'Good. Both the British and the Americans have a lot of files on the subject. Some files carried notes to show they were examined by no less a person than the President. I found one which referred to forms of propulsion that might have a potential for space travel.'

'What, rockets?'

'No, no! Hardly more advanced than the bow and arrow. It dealt with zero point energy and the generation of gravity waves. And there was a bit on photon mass propulsion.'

Elliott didn't pretend to understand and in any case, he wanted Meredith to run under his own steam. He made a more general question, 'Was it concerned with extra-terrestrials visiting the Earth, or was it more about our own space travel in the future?'

'More about them visiting. We cannot be anywhere near the technology of the people who come here. Compared with them, our science is primitive. All the evidence: the photographs, fragments of material from alleged crashes, anecdotal evidence from people who have seen them, everything was concerned with them visiting us.'

'You use the word 'people.''

'Sure I do. I can go into that later. But as far as official records are concerned, I made it clear to the security people that I failed to record what I saw.' He made a gesture for Elliott to turn off the recording. 'I suppose I can rely on your confidence in this?' Elliott nodded but said nothing. He wanted to let the other speak without the kind of technical interruptions that spoil a football match.

Meredith opened up. 'Well I did manage to get copies. I can show you pictures, details, statements. I can point you towards people in the United States who can tell you more.' He seemed animated, as though finally able to unburden himself. 'I said I hadn't, but they didn't believe me and they seized my computer. In fact I'd saved everything elsewhere. It served them right! If that makes me a crook, I don't care.'

He nodded for Elliott to turn the recording back on.

Elliott said, 'Tell me about interstellar travel.'

'There are unimaginable distances. Our Milky Way is 100,000 light years across. With its 300 billion stars—that is a 3 with eleven noughts afterwards—there are at least enough stars in our own galaxy to interest human-kind for all eternity. And the latest estimates tell us of 2 trillion galaxies. We cannot grasp the number of stars in our universe or the almost infinite number of planets. Some of them must be like our own. Life has flourished on our own little world and it's absurd to propose that we are alone. If not, it would mean that basic chemical evolution has worked in only one in 300 billion solar systems, which is ridiculous. Why, we have even shown aspects of it ourselves in the laboratory.'

'Of chemical evolution?'

'Yes. We know that electrical discharges—lightning—can cause the assembly of some organic molecules. And we've shown chemical catalysis on the surface of clay particles.'

'So you don't believe that bacteria come from the space dust distributed by comets from outer space?'

'No, that panspermia idea is a bit far-fetched. I think genesis and evolution happened here.' Elliott nodded, although he was not in a position either to agree or disagree. And he had no doubt that Meredith had meant what he said. He continued to listen in anticipation.

'The trouble is that we have a rather pathetic status in the greater scheme of things. We can't get very far with rocket propulsion. Not even to the limits of our own solar system. But I know it's possible.' He went to a folder of papers and extracted some enlarged and rather grainy photographs. 'Look at these.'

The first was in monochrome and showed a view from within the cockpit of an aircraft. However, visible through a window was a very large object which took up three-quarters of the picture. Elliott said, 'A giant airship?'

'No, it's not. And it's straight-on in the field of vision so it can't have been caused by a refraction. In fact it's a UFO. It was photographed inside a passenger airplane over the Atlantic. The crew and passengers all told the same story that it flew alongside for thirty minutes and then disappeared at high speed. Now look at this one.' He showed a similar picture, differing only in that the craft was replaced by a weather balloon. 'This is the airbrushed version. It was considered not in the best public interest for the truth to be known.' He shook his head.

Elliott compared the two pictures: 'What exactly is it in the original?'

'A cigar-shaped craft about the size of the Hindenburg airship. You would never believe it from its appearance, but it can hover effortlessly or accelerate to very high speeds. All witnesses said it was smooth and had no port for jet or rocket propulsion. It was probably made from metal and the owners had no concern for staying hidden.'

'Not a saucer-shaped craft, then.'

'No, but there were saucers in some other photographs I found. They are smaller and more numerous.'

'Why two designs?' said Elliott. 'Or could it be different visitors?'

'I would say two designs for different jobs. I think the saucers are local devices for use on arrival. The cigars, which are much larger, are probably used for deep space.'

Elliott said, 'You spoke of work on a method of propulsion.'

'Yes. There was talk about photon capture, but there's no indication that it's in use yet.'

'You mean propulsion by light?'

'Yes. Any such craft would need very large sails, and they would gather sunlight as a sailing ship gathers wind. They could use giant lasers, of course. But there were no sails in any photograph, and not one of those flying cigars had them.'

'Sails sound rather far-fetched anyway.'

'It may be for *them*, but not for us. I hear that NASA is actually working on this right now and they estimate a flight-time of only 5 months to reach Mars.'

'Then what about interstellar travel?' said Elliott. 'Surely a laser couldn't beam out that far?'

'It would, but since light from our sun is barely visible that far away, there wouldn't be much of a push from even the largest laser. Then it would need rockets to stop, and the return journey would be impossible unless we deposited another laser on Pluto with a suitable energy source. So I think we need to look elsewhere for a means of propulsion.'

'OK, so how do we get to the next star system?'

'Hang on a minute.' Meredith went out to the kitchen and returned five minutes later with coffee. It tasted good and it helped Elliott to think. He had to admit that he was intrigued, and also that Meredith was knowledgeable and interested in facts. The conversation continued.

Meredith said. 'So no, there's no photon capture by UFOs.' Then, 'We can speculate, but the physics is beyond both of us. What I do know is that our civilisation is only five thousand years old. In two hundred years we have moved from sailing ships to supersonic flight. So imagine what a civilisation might be like after 300,000 years!'

'I see what you mean. But do you really think that a ship could travel the width of our galaxy to visit? Could even a culture of 300,000 years master a distance of 100,000 light years?'

'In time, I think it probably could. First of all, I doubt whether any such civilisation would be centred on a single solar system. I think it would spread in jumps. They might already know of us from a base, say, ten light years away. At one quarter of light speed they could visit us in forty years. Farther afield their culture could have spread to a settlement, ten light years distant, in the other direction. And perhaps they think our short lifetime is insignificant.'

'Let's get back to basics. Can you let me have the whole of this file to look at?'

'These are actually my own copies, but I did collect some things I would like you to have at this stage. It contains the original and retouched photographs of what I think are spacecraft, together with smart materials taken from Roswell. It also contains a copy of autopsy reports on part-decomposed bodies made soon after. And by the way, the Americans released reports which were so patently ridiculous that everyone made fun of them. But these are the real ones, untouched and uncorrupted.'

'I didn't realise that.'

'Well there's more: I have a bit of a file on reverse-engineered ceramics which the Americans use to make their stealth fighters.'

'Are you serious? If I do a piece on that, all hell will let loose.'

'You think so? You are more likely to be treated as a crank. There would be open derision and you would be publicly ridiculed. Nobody would believe you any more than they believe the infamous tabloid story about a WW2 bomber found on the moon. But if you got hold of a sample and showed it in public, or if you had a preserved specimen...'

'Then what?'

'You would have incontrovertible proof. So despite the fact that I'm in this for a bit of publicity myself, it's why you should wait for an altogether bigger scoop.'

'And if I don't wait?'

'It will die the death. And after the ridicule, you can expect a visit from the security services. They would also visit your editor. Take it from me, you need hard evidence.'

Then Meredith followed, 'And here is a bit of hard evidence to get you started.' He held out his hand, clutching a small grey artefact. Elliott tried to hold it. It was a flat plate, small enough to cover the palm of his hand and about as thin as a coin. It was slippery and he had trouble holding it. He cupped it in both hands.

'What is it?'

Meredith said: 'I'll show you.' He took the object back and carried it to a workbench, where he picked up a further disc, identical to the first. He was excited, his voice raised, 'See these?

They are similar in size, but this other one is made from steel. I know that, because I had it made. 'You can just about bend it in a vice by using this mole wrench. See? Now try the grey plate.' Elliott exerted his full strength, but without success.

Meredith said, 'It's stronger than steel. I have never seen the like.'

Elliott said, 'And it weighs almost nothing!' Again, he had difficulty in holding it, 'And it's so slippery!' The object remained innocent-looking, a featureless grey plate. He said, 'A while back, I asked about your use of the word 'people'. Did *they* make it?'

'Yes, they did. It's stronger, lighter and more slippery than anything I have ever seen.'

'So it's not a plastic?'

'It looks like a plastic, but it doesn't behave like one. It conducts electricity and has incredible strength and lightness. I tried putting it in water to see whether it would rust. It didn't. It's also frictionless— you saw for yourself—so it can't be held easily.'

'And there are other examples which can be induced to become very powerful magnets, while some seem to scatter light and have a strange optical image, quite unlike that given by a mirror.' Meredith paused for breath. 'And where do you think the Americans obtained their material which absorbs radar signals? They found *that* very useful, believe me: it ended up in stealth bombers. They have almost no radar signature!'

'Can I take it away with the file?'

'Yes, I'd like you to. In fact it's better that it doesn't just stay here forever. I've sat and wondered about if myself, for quite long enough!'

'But where did you get these things?'

'I'm in touch with people on the Network. This example came from the Roswell crash. I've no proof of that, of course, but I do have proof that someone had it as far back as '47. And *that* was way before our own modern plastics and smart materials. We did have nylon and Bakelite, and I think Teflon since 1938, but not much more. So take it from me, the provenance of the piece is beyond question. It isn't man-made.'

'I suppose the proof is that we still couldn't make it now?'

'No.'

'Look, Guy, can I speak to any of your leads in the States?'

'I can check.'

'That would be great.'

Elliott had been there for an hour and he didn't like to overstay his welcome. He could also sense that Meredith, if he gave too much away, or if he felt his contacts were compromised, might regret it and close up like a clamshell. So he said, 'You have been more than helpful. Let me look this over, and perhaps we can get together again. In your own time of course; here's another card with my number on it.'

Their talk had been a start, but Elliott knew that Meredith was correct about the evidence. It wasn't comprehensive enough for the kind of story he wanted. He was unsure why Meredith had been so helpful. It was strange that a man so concerned with security should be so forthcoming with a journalist. Shortly, as Elliott packed up, that question was answered:

'I do have my own interests to consider, and most of this is old-hat anyway. These photos were news 50 years ago, but not now. So is the grey plate. I think they should be out in the open where people can see them at long last. And there's new stuff out there, which is where I'm headed. I may be able to let you onto that in due course, but I need to know more myself.' He had decided not to mention the Firehills projectile that day nor the incessant messaging that was a feature of the Network at the present time. They parted amicably, with handshakes, and with expressions of future cooperation.

A few days later, Meredith received a telephone call from Peter Pargeter, who had spent a while looking at the page of hieroglyphs that Meredith had brought him. He made the usual pleasantries, complemented Meredith on his recent work—'outstanding, thank you'—and said: 'I'm afraid I've drawn a blank with that. I think I saw some similarity between a few of them and the ancient Egyptian scheme of writing, but I couldn't be sure. I would need to see more examples, or see them in use in order to make more progress. I'm sorry I can't be more helpful.'

Meredith thanked him for his comments and they agreed to think about it.

—∭—

Deep among the rolling chalk downs John Buchanan, a genial blond-haired man with a bushy beard, finished a breakfast that had come straight from his farm. It was of large proportions, but he knew that it was very important. He believed in the well-being of the hens that scratched their happy way in his barn, where they laid their golden eggs; and in the bounty of the pigs in the meadow where, among the Yarlingtons and bitter Foxwhelp apples that fed them, they gave the bacon he so enjoyed. And he believed in the cider, dark, sharp and strong, a recipe that had been passed down by his great grandfather, a man of iron will and with iron in his blood. So when the time came for that precious bittersweet juice to ferment John, his earnest successor, always bowed to tradition and threw into the mix an old horseshoe. In that way iron was restored to the blood and his lineage had prospered.

Later that day, Buchanan worked hard on the farm among his many children, who laughed and cavorted and offered their earnest assistance with the apple harvest. Lord knows, how many had they scrumped to fill their bellies! It was a good job their digestions worked so quickly, otherwise that old yeast would ferment inside them! And what would happen then?

He stopped at lunchtime for the West Countryman's traditional bread, sharp cheddar and raw onions. Replete, he washed it down with cider, then lay on the grass for an hour and watched the bees make their merry way among the lavender and clover. Life couldn't be better than this. Some said that his hamlet was cut-off, an oasis of country ways and generations behind the times. Yet it was not the opinion of those who lived there; they knew it as a happy place.

Buchanan chuckled again. He was inspired by a cider called 'Croppie,' the home-made brew sold at the 'Hoar Apple Tree,' and prepared to venture out later to make just such a mark on the countryside. It had become a tradition: country folk knew they should dance around a crop circle when the harvest was good. It was only natural to celebrate.

He had promised to meet friends Tara and Tony, with whom, armed with the rope, flails and motor mower already in the back of his Land Rover, he would ascend a notable hillside to the east. They would probably be joined by Jason, a man who still practised at the butts every day with the longbow. His right arm was of considerable proportions and, practising in case he was ever needed to face the French, he used the most powerful bow possible. Sympathising with him, they actively encouraged on patriotic grounds the amount of food he ate to maintain his colossal strength.

That evening they met as arranged and John lit his pipe, which contained a tobacco so fierce that at times, he almost blacked out. He was joined by the lovely Tara, a dark-haired beauty, who accepted some of his tobacco with a smile and promptly rolled it into a cigarette, 'The better to smoke it,' she said. Meanwhile Jason eventually joined them; his aim with the clothyard bodkin that afternoon had been deadly.

They parked at a suitable layby and collected their appliances from the back. It was dark, but a faint luminescence arose from stars in a clear sky. Calmly, the four friends climbed towards a site known to be perfect for their endeavours. Tara led the way, providing an occasional admonishment when the men deviated from their path. All were in good spirits as they prepared to make a crop circle at the summit.

At the top of the hill, and exactly where they had intended to make their own circle, they saw a silver-grey saucer, standing upright on the grass. It issued forth a great amount of light and the image of saucer and landscape was burned into their retinas, there to fade very slowly over the next ten minutes. There was also a metallic smell which John had known once before, when the battery of his tractor had arced to an electric fence. Meanwhile, in the all-pervading static electricity, Jason's right arm contracted with an involuntary flexion of the muscle so that Tara, thinking he had made an improper suggestion, gave him a slap on the hand.

Darkness returned very slowly and the four friends inched forward. The hillside was now completely bare, the silver craft gone. At last Tony said, 'Someone else has done our work for us!' He pointed at the blackened surface of the soil, still smouldering with strange shapes and patterns. In awe they turned tail, returned to the Land Rover, and were just in time for a last pint before the Hoar Apple Tree closed for the night. Doubly appreciative of the brew, they savoured its hypnotic powers and swore that they would plant the Yarlington themselves, so that future generations would benefit as they had done.

—m—

That evening, an attractive blond-haired woman called Freya Sampson drove over the same chalk downs. She ran a programme on local affairs for a radio station in the Thames Valley area, where she had worked for three years. In it, local news and events were discussed live, and people occasionally telephoned in with comments and further contributions. On that day she had chosen to follow a story that had arisen during an earlier live session in which an unusually large number of people had called in to talk about the same thing. They had all spoken of very bright lights in the sky. Such sightings were not unheard of in that neighbourhood, but the number had increased to the extent that a sighting could almost be guaranteed if out after dark. She had decided to speak to witnesses with a view to inviting a few them into the studio. There, they would have an opportunity to enlarge on their earlier observations and speculate further.

It was dark and her lights were on. She stopped at a junction on the downs where a minor road gave way at the approach to a village. The road ahead was clear and she made ready to pull out but as she did so, her car stalled and she found herself in complete darkness. She fumbled with the starter but found that all electrical systems were completely dead. Fearing an incursion in the dark, she locked her car from the inside. All the roadside lights were extinguished so that the downs were as dark as they had been in the time of her grandparents. Everywhere was an inky blackness in which the night sky with its stars was suddenly the lightest object.

In an instant all changed. For three or four seconds her surroundings were as light as day and she was able to see not only the road ahead, but also the surrounding streets. She could make out the broad vista of the countryside farther afield, with its trees and farms, steeples and telegraph poles. It was as though a giant lightbulb had been switched on to illuminate the countryside for miles around. Then, the light failed without a flicker so that an inky blackness returned. It became a dark in which her eyes took time to acclimatise, the brilliant image slowly fading as she looked around.

Shortly, she unlocked her door and stood outside. The air was silent and still. There was no perturbation of the atmosphere with wind, nor was there any noise of an explosion or other detonation. There was no febrile weather system, no rain or thunder and no lightning. She smelled a strong metallic smell like that of a working photocopier. It was ozone, but far stronger and more persistent than she had ever known. Quickly, she held a paper tissue to her nose, entered her car and closed the window.

After two or three minutes the streetlights flickered and came on and her headlights started to glow faintly. She turned them off, hoping to restart her car. The engine fired, but it took about a minute for her headlights to reach their former brightness. She hesitated for a minute or so, her engine running, until confident of driving away safely. By the side of the road a couple of cats howled, their fur crackling with strange flashes of static electricity. All around, the weather remained quiet and sultry.

She drove on her way and said to herself, 'Not of this earth.' Later, her radio program was one in which scientists were invited to speculate on the kinds of natural phenomena that could bring about an all-pervading electrical drain and a massive emission of light energy. They suggested sunspots and adverse weather, but spoke as though the subject had been rehearsed beforehand. Her programme lacked its usual spontaneity and it was not an edition of which she was proud.

―〰―

Three thousand, five hundred miles to the west, a Pennsylvania day was as hot and humid as is common in that latitude. The sycamore trees, scorched by the heat of the outgoing summer so that their bark peeled, had begun to drop their leaves, where in the street they were stirred by the same stifling breeze that helped to clear away the diesel fumes given by passing buses. Cicadas creaked and rasped in the undergrowth and their noise became frantic as the advancing day brought still greater temperatures. Young people walked arm-in-arm in the lightest of clothing, and went to baseball games or played tenpin bowling. They ate their ice cream hurriedly and there was a general gaiety among the student population of the many colleges and universities for which that particular town is noted.

At a large University there, Joseph Dorkin, professor of anthropological molecular biology, entered the mailroom and claimed a large box, together with assorted other mail. The box was heavy, and he carried it to his office with difficulty. Pushing the door open with his foot, he dumped everything on his desk and made a pot of the strong black coffee favoured in those parts. He dealt with an assortment of envelopes first, then walked around his laboratory and spoke to the half a dozen research students there. It was a Monday morning and they were disinclined to speak.

Dorkin was a well-respected individual whose interests were many. His research was on the topic of human origins, yet unlike that of other anthropologists, it was diverse. Besides the study of cultural and archaeological artefacts he was interested in the molecular aspect of evolution. In all this, he was known for his interesting observations on palaeontological records and his research group was prosperous, well-financed and publicised.

Dumping the rest of his correspondence in a waste bin, he turned his attention to the box on his desk. Its contents had been loaned to him by a museum following his interest in a catalogue of artefacts acquired by them from a source in Central America. It contained layers of soft cotton packing which he carefully removed before placing a pair of metal objects on the desk. They were statuettes, tarnished, dull and very old. He was pleased to find that there had been no attempt to clean or polish them even though they had passed through the hands of the original native finder, a broker of antiquities, and the person from the museum who had catalogued them. Each was a likeness of the human form and despite a small size they had an imposing presence. Their dull, metallic eyes stared back at him, while their pouting lips and hook nose gave them an obstreperous and surly attitude.

He turned them around, one after the other. The first was nine inches tall, a standing figure wearing a skirt or kilt. The second was smaller, a man sitting on a chair or throne, while in his right hand was a circular object, perhaps the calendar typical of that region. Their hair was long, but barbered and tidy under a head-dress. Each had a barrel chest, very broad shoulders and was overtly masculine.

Dorkin took photographs and wrote a general description. Lifting them he was reminded of their weight and wrote 'check composition'. In fact, such a check was of particular interest to him because he intended to date them by analysis of the metal from which they were made. He wrote: 'in the style of the Mayan god Itzamna, origin the Chiapas state of Mexico, near to the Guatemalan border', then, 'found in deep jungle by a native labourer'.

Very carefully, he weighed each statuette and measured its volume by placing it in a tank of water. Following a simple calculation he wrote, 'density $11.3 \text{g}/\text{cm}^3$, composition confirmed as lead'. Finally, he used a file to remove a few grains of metal from the base of each and after repacking them in their box, sent the filings to be analysed by the department of metallurgy.

A month later, Dorkin opened a report from that department.
It read:

'Samples a and b are over 99% lead, but unusually they contain
60% of the lead isotope ^{207}Pb. In general, that isotope is never
more than 22% in naturally-occurring lead samples. It is noted
that where the proportion is higher it can only be a result of the
decay of fissile material, namely uranium-235. Our studies show
that samples a and b emit small amounts of radiation consistent
with the presence of traces of that isotope of uranium. It is our
view that the metal was refined to purify the lead before being
worked, although not to the degree necessary for them to be made
harmless. We are concerned that those people who were in contact
with samples a and b may have been exposed to radioactivity.'

Dorkin considered the letter with disbelief. Then he wrote to the
museum, asking them to check the provenance of the two statuettes.
His letter said:

'I have doubts about their provenance since both examples
reveal a level of ability with metal refinement consistent only
with modern scientific methods. I feel they cannot have been
made by the primitive metallurgical skills of Mesoamerican
craftsmen many thousands of years ago, among whose remains
the statuettes were supposedly found.'

A little later, the curator of the museum replied:

'We were concerned enough by your letter to check the
provenance of the Mayan statuettes. In particular, we have
again spoken to the broker of antiquities for that area. We
vouch wholly for our broker, whose record for us is impeccable.
He has stated that the objects were retrieved from a chamber
under the remains of a dwelling of the Mayan early preclassic
period. It was found among other objects consistent with that

*period, including fragments of pottery and fired clay, examples
of which we obtained at the same time. Further, the statuettes
were cast in crude moulds and are perfect stylistic exemplars of
the time. The chamber had not been disturbed since the contents
were interred. Under the circumstances, I have no doubt about
the authenticity of the statuettes under discussion.'*

Dorkin returned a brief letter of thanks and pondered.

—⁓—

When Elliott was next in his London office, he asked to see Burgess.
The latter had some tea and drank without looking up. Elliott knew
better than to interrupt him while he finished reading a letter and
appended his signature. Only then did he speak.

'Well, Elliott, what did you find out?'

'Dynamite. He's a lot brighter than I thought. Not just an
autistic young man. He may be a bit of a nerd but at least he's the
real thing, not just a guy putting on an act. There's a whole lot
which the public doesn't know about. He could be about to stir up
a hornets nest.'

'So what exactly is your angle?'

'I don't think we can help him by endorsing a view of him
as a simple figure. I said as much, and we need to play down the
personal side and concentrate on the science, which speaks for itself.
He's happy with that because it will keep him out of trouble while
delivering the facts, which are considerable.'

'And?'

'Already I have a load of real evidence. There are photographs,
files, and names too. One lead, perhaps a big one, is abroad. As soon
as I hear that Meredith's contacts are willing, I want to go there.
There's new stuff about the crash as well.'

'What crash? You can't mean the Roswell incident. That's dead
meat as far as news is concerned. Don't even go there or we'll just
get laughed at.'

'OK Jonathan, point taken. But this will probably grow. Roswell may be dead, but there's someone over there who can tell me a bit about the materials UFOs are made from. Yes, really!' He held out his hand with a grey object sitting on his palm. Burgess, with his curiosity aroused, peered at it.

Elliott said, 'It's some kind of material with properties we've not yet come across. Meredith gave it to me. I think it was a bit of a sacrifice, to be honest. And I was astounded to hear him say, outright, that it's not from this earth. He got it from a contact, a like-minded enthusiast.' His voice was carefully-moderated to contain no trace of cynicism. 'And it's a suitable calling card for the guy I want to see next.'

'So who are these enthusiasts?'

'They share things via a so-called Network. They run a secretive internet blog which deals in any evidence they can find. I'm told that quite a lot of hardware is actually in circulation. They want a convincing public case before they bring it all out in the open. That's where they need a guy like me.'

'And they think they are in some kind of danger?'

'Apparently. Some of these materials may have been reverse-engineered by defence people. They don't like their secrets getting out and they tend to get heavy if crossed. But that's beside the point. He can tell me why this object is more advanced than our own stuff. I want to see it in action and take a video clip if I can.'

'Are you sure his contact will actually want to speak to you?'

'I hope to find out soon. Meredith's in contact with him. What's slowing things down is the fact that although they want publicity, they are also pretty furtive. Meredith was forthcoming with me, yet when he spoke about his contacts he was clear there was a risk. I got the impression he was worried about people having disappeared, and about heavy-handed US and British agencies.'

Burgess said, 'I'm sure you wouldn't want to cry off having gone this far, but you can always come back if you feel you are getting into hot water. And you know the score; we can pick up any reasonable expense for this one.'

'Don't worry, I mean to see it through if I can.'

Elliott telephoned Meredith some time later. They were now on first-name terms: 'Guy, you mentioned your contact in the States. Will he see me?'

'You're lucky. He said yes, and I can give you a letter of introduction beforehand.'

'Is that really necessary?'

'It's an elementary level of security. I did say the Network is probably monitored. It wouldn't be impossible for someone to pose as you to obtain an introduction.'

'Alright, you know best. Can you give me his details? I can make arrangements to go over.'

'But why don't you just Skype him and save the ticket?'

'That's easy. I hope to be referred to other people. I think this matter can grow, but not from this end, or at least not in the same way. Anyway, what's the guy's name?'

'He's called Bud Lynch, a man-mountain. He likes his food.' For a second, Meredith compared a mental image of himself: a gaunt, fleshless individual subsisting mostly on coffee, with that of Lynch, whose cheeks were puffed out and who had a gross belly, a result of constant indulgence. Still, he supposed that he had his own vices.

FOUR

NEPAL AND BOSKOP

Far away, on the other side of the world, a Nepalese mountain guide called Vivek Adhikari looked up towards the magnificent snow-capped peaks in the far distance. He was of long experience, but the sight of the mountains and valleys never ceased to delight. Prosperous visitors from western countries found him a competent guide who helped to fulfil their ambition of a once-in-a-lifetime pilgrimage to the highest places on earth. Yet often, they departed wondering whether their rich lives were poorer than his own.

Yet his work was very dangerous. The mountains were fickle and treacherous and some said they were the preserve of spirits who valued their solitude and privacy. A climber might make a mistake in a place in which a blizzard could erupt from nothing. Then, the landscape would seem to scowl and grimace as a trespasser faced the grim reality of ice and wind; while the demonic screams of a biting tempest would howl like a demented being. It was then that they called for Adhikari, a man who had saved many lives. In so doing he felt that the spirits smiled on him, so sincere a man and with such good intentions. Perhaps they knew he desired no fame and was content with small things.

On that day Adhikari was uneasy, for the weather was poor and the forecast was for worse. He was worried, not for himself, but for a climber whose partner had returned with the news that the other was stuck at altitude with a broken ankle. A bivouac was seen high on a snowfield, but the owner was unable to descend. Any rescue would of necessity be by helicopter, yet the winds were too high and heavier snow was starting. It had fallen to Adhikari's team to provide consolation and medical care for a man who was unable to move and perhaps stricken by altitude sickness.

Yet he had known worse, and walking out into the ice-cold air with his team of three compatriots, he began his climb towards the great grey-brown mountain with its jagged edges. At first, he walked in a low valley of pine trees, the snow falling from branches with a slight hiss. Later, he traversed sparse vegetation, hard rock and compacted snow. The great peaks were hidden as snow fell, while wind brought forth flurries of dense whiteness. Overhead grey-yellow snow clouds began to displace white, and the two swirled for ascendancy in a frantic circular motion, white opposing yellow. It was ten o'clock in the morning, yet the night would present temperatures of -30°C so that those without shelter would succumb to frostbite in the rarefied air.

Crossing short tough grass, the small party passed onto an older snowfield where Adhikari was able to follow the footprints of climbers before him. For an hour the air cleared so that no more snow fell and all was strangely silent. When he could, he paused to examine the mountainside using binoculars, but saw no trace of the bivouac. In his own case he would have sought shelter in one of the crevices or myriad other places where the wind was less. He was pleased; the absence of the bivouac suggested that its owner was at least *compos mentis*.

By mid-afternoon they were at their intended altitude but could see nothing. The team had traversed all the relevant snow faces to the height at which the bivouac was expected, yet without result. As light began to fade, they made for a ridge 500 yards away, where behind a pair of jagged stones in the shape of eye teeth, they made ready to spend the night.

The dawn was overcast and the sky heavy and yellow with unshed snow. Miraculously the great mass of snow was held in reserve as though the mountain intended to punish its interlopers at its own convenience. They climbed higher over cracked rocks and snowfields, higher than they had intended. Eventually, they were above the height at which the missing climber might reasonably be found.

At last the snow fell, and he made the decision to send the rest of his party down the mountain, leaving the greater mass of supplies with him at altitude. Later it became very overcast as clouds covered the sun and blizzard conditions prevailed. He decided to make one further traverse to the north. Before long, he began to descend as the wind became worse. It was then that he heard a faint cry for help and although the sound was blown away, it was towards his right and fairly close. He called back and was answered. It was no mistake.

After ten minutes he came upon a forlorn figure propped under a rock overhang. Reaching him he said 'Namaste[2],' and asked the name of the individual in slow English. The prostrate man said 'Dhanyabaad[3], and bowed his head. Then he said, 'I'm Callum Dood, sorry to be such a bother. My ankle…' It was clearly broken, and they faced a night in a bivouac under poor conditions.

Dood had some whisky, which Adhikari declined. He knew better than to dilate his blood vessels by that means. Dood had clearly drunk some, he began to sing; it was the onset of altitude sickness, a delirium he had seen many times. In Dood's case the whisky helped to fortify him against the cold, the pain and the rarefied atmosphere, but Adhikari knew its effects would pass within the hour.

It was clear that no rescue would be forthcoming until night had passed, and even then the opportunity for a helicopter depended on the weather. It began to get colder and snow fell heavily, an evil discoloured sheet given a yellow tinge by the sand blown from far away. It began to pile around them and they huddled together within the tent that Adhikari had been able to erect, thankfully out

---

2   I salute the God within you.
3   I am profoundly grateful.

of the direct blast of ice-cold air. By morning more snow fell, and conditions were still too poor for an aerial rescue. They spent the day sheltering, although they were able to eat a little food. Throughout Adhikari made an effort to prevent the snow from covering them and flew a flag on a pole to mark their position.

By the second night Dood was failing and Adhikari knew that help must arrive soon or all could be lost. Yet the cold increased and the snowfall became prolonged and heavy. It settled on their meagre tent and their flag became a limp rag. He remained calm and collected, and was surprised by a resurgence of strength in his companion, who had just smoked some concoction made from leaves. It seemed that it enabled him to avoid pain and remain in a state of quiet tranquillity. Later all became quiet as snowfall became the merest rustle: a downy blanket that calmed the chaotic currents above them. He knew they were buried, although insulated from the air outside. They both slept for a while.

At 1am Adhikari woke. He heard voices outside and sat up in anticipation. They were the sounds of a language he had not yet heard: staccato and guttural, and it seemed to him a language of consonants only. There followed the scuffling sound of digging, and eventually the flaps of the tent were opened. Dark figures gestured for them to leave. Adhikari pulled his companion out and they grabbed their belongings. Dood was unable to stand, his limbs cold and stiff and his broken ankle lying at an unnatural angle. Waiting were four strangers, presumably a rescue team, who gestured that Dood should lie on a stretcher. They began to carry him down the mountainside, one man at each corner under conditions in which Adhikari could barely see them. They were not members of his own rescue party, and they seemed to avoid his gaze. Perhaps they were from another part of his country of many different peoples? He thought them strangely small for members of a mountain rescue team.

However they were stubborn. By dawn they had descended to the lower slopes of the mountain where, just 500 feet below them, they could see a larger rescue party climbing up. The four waited and gesticulated towards the new group, but strangely declined to meet them. With ten minutes to spare, they waved to indicate their own withdrawal. By then all could see more clearly in the morning light.

They were odd. Adhikari was drawn to their expressions, which were strange—watchful, and almost cat-like. Their eyes seemed to hold the particular wisdom which Adhikari had seen in the few hermits and religious aesthetes who lived in caves or small hovels at remote places in the mountains. Adhikari bowed low and knew he had finally met the Meh-Teh, the 'Old Men of the Mountains'. He had seen their footprints in high passes in the snow, where they sometimes walked with bare feet despite the cold. There were many legends surrounding them in Nepal and in ranges of mountains far to the north. He said, 'Meh-Teh' to Dood, who promptly replied, 'Yeti?'

Quickly, for it was still cold, Adhikari collected a compacted footprint and placed it inside a plastic bag. The larger party successfully returned home, and all were thankful. Later, the icy footprint had turned to water, but the bag still contained a few hairs shed by their former owner. It had been an unusual rescue and one which, although successful, made Adhikari decline further work on the mountain for a while. His was a reflective holiday, a time during which he sent his specimen to a museum in Kathmandu, where it was received with interest.

Six months later it reached Professor Dorkin in the United States, whose reputation was well-established. At first he viewed it only with passing interest. Then, when he obtained the result of a DNA test on it he was heard to remark: 'That's very strange. It's an Asian sample and I suppose I expected to see something like the orangutan. But it doesn't have 48 chromosomes like the orangutan, nor even 46 like humans. It has 44, for heaven's sake, and I really don't know what that means.'

The result remained at the back of his mind and he returned what remained of the sample to its owner, together with the result. Then he turned his attention elsewhere. Far away, Adhikari left baskets of fruit at places in the high passes, while the museum in Khatmandu made an exhibit from the material returned to them. In time, Callum Dood returned to Europe with his ankle in plaster, but having discussed his escape with Adhikari was more thoughtful than he might have anticipated.

—m—

Joseph Dorkin was soon preoccupied by his lead statuettes and unwilling to dismiss them as fakes. It remained for him to trace them back to their former owner and the place in which they were found. Yet in the first instance his attention was drawn to yet another find, not archaeological, but palaeontological. He marked it as even more interesting than his other concerns to the extent that it took immediate priority over all else. It could have been designed deliberately in order to tantalise. Accordingly he postponed his attentions with regard to Central America and prepared to take two companions to South Africa on a dig.

Like many such digs, it was not intended to be an exhaustive study of the site; at least, not in the first instance. Instead, he expected to carry out a preliminary examination to establish whether it was worth devoting more time to it. Two companions would suffice, but he had not been able to ignore the strange sixth-sense that, rather than being a waste of time, it would prove to be significant. He had felt that sense before and it had proven to be unerringly accurate. He chose his companions carefully: a postdoctoral research associate named Carmen van Brouin, a woman of 30 years; together with a younger graduate student, a dark-haired man called Simon Wiener. They made preparations for a trip of two weeks but could stay longer if necessary.

Professor Dorkin was an academic at the peak of his powers and widely renowned in his field. He was a still-sprightly man of 50 years, trim and fit, and although single, or perhaps because he was single, he remained completely dedicated to his work. Some acquaintances questioned his monastic lifestyle, and it was true that he did seem indifferent to at least some social pleasures. Yet none could find fault with his professional attitude and manner, and most simply shrugged their shoulders and ignored his indifference to women, and men for that matter. Perhaps he had been different when he was younger.

His considerable energy had enabled him to make outstanding progress with his work on comparing DNA samples from ancient human settlements. In applying to continue this research he had been very pleased with a recent application for funds from the US Government. He guessed that they were more interested in the technology itself and less in the palaeontology, and had noted that his success was inexplicably linked to his present choice of personnel. Carmen had almost seemed to bring funding with her. Perhaps she knew someone? It was not, however, a subject that one could constructively dwell on.

He was fully versed in the story of Boskop Man, by now over a century old. A few finds, namely fragments of skeletons, had prompted a dig in the early 20th century, so another investigation could not properly be described as new. Yet Boskop had 'resurfaced' recently with a further find at some distance from the original. While other parties had tried to play down its significance, Dorkin had seen great potential. He had decided to reinvestigate without delay. 'Our target,' he said, as he drove a truck out of their hotel car park, 'is Boskop.'

As Dorkin, Wiener and van Brouin drove southwest from Johannesburg, they surveyed their surroundings with some interest. Their way led towards Potchefstroom, a journey of about an hour and a half on reasonable roads. It was dry, and a white cloud of dust marked their passage. The wayside was of calf-high grass, brown in the hot sun, and the landscape prairie-like, without much cover. By the side of dry fields was a network of ditches with a little water in a few of them. It was not a tropical climate and the humidity was moderate. It reminded them of Spain or Italy: hot but not unbearable, and with relief to be found in the shade.

After a while they stopped by the roadside for refreshment. The road was quiet and they stayed for fifteen minutes, walking around a little. For a minute Dorkin stood with his eyes to the north where a few low hills, green-grey on the horizon, could be seen about ten miles away. A deeper green lay around them, the colour of twisted and stumpy trees growing there. Carmen, an athletic, intelligent and personable woman of Dutch extraction, joined him and followed his gaze. She said, 'What exactly are we looking for?'

'We need to find a new cave. As you know, the original skulls were found by some Afrikaaner farmers about a hundred years ago. They were handed to a guy called FitzSimmons to look at.'

Carmen, with her characteristically assertive manner replied, 'Who the hell was he?'

'He was interested in snakes, a herpetologist. And there are plenty of those here. You had better watch yourself.'

'Interested in snakes?' She pulled a face, and her brown eyes showed her dislike of the idea.

'Yes, I guess it was his hobby. But he was also a doctor, and a recognised anthropologist. He reconstructed some human skulls from fragments and wrote a few papers about them.'

Simon Wiener, younger and more diffident but equally thoughtful, said, 'And did they—the skulls—actually prove anything?'

'I wouldn't say prove. At least, not what the people at the time wanted. They were of great age and of considerable interest. They were described as fine examples.'

'Fine?'

'They were well-made, supposedly superior. The skulls were enlarged at the front, which was thought to provide the potential for advanced intelligence. Perhaps they were brighter than we are. That was back in the 1930s, at a time when such matters attracted attention. The Nazis became interested in them because they were obsessed with comparative anthropology.'

Carmen said, 'So why the interest today, if eugenics is out?'

'Well, from our point of view the original finds are of no particular significance. But there was a new find this year. A further cave was discovered by a young boy. If it was seen a hundred years ago, which I doubt, then its significance was missed at the time.'

'So we are the first to have the opportunity?'

'Yes. There are no older records of it. The local government has kept quiet to avoid people crawling all over the place. If we can tie the palaeontology into our work on DNA variation, it could be interesting. It would certainly be a PhD for Simon and fame for us all. See those hills ahead? No, a little to the right. That's where we're going. When we get there, please make sure you wear the long boots. We shall have to walk some distance.'

'Any people around?' said Simon.

'Sure there are, but not many. Mostly they speak Setswana, the language of Botswana, but there are Afrikaaners too. Carmen, you might understand what they say. There's not much American around here.'

'I doubt it,' said Carmen, 'my father spoke Dutch, but apart from a couple of words I can't understand it myself.'

'Is there a hotel?' said Simon.

'Ha, sure there is!' replied Dorkin, 'for a local population of 200 and no tourists at all? No, it's back to base before nightfall or stay with the truck. Anyway, this is just to look around.'

After another half hour of driving they reached the low hills they had seen earlier. Although it was hot, they changed into long boots and protective jeans. Collecting some equipment, they locked the truck out of sight and followed a narrow path around the base of a hill. There was a perpetual rustle of insects all around, and flies, beetles and spiders were everywhere. Several snakes basked in the heat, their tongues darting out and with cold eyes watching. It was a hostile countryside, dry and rugged, and with its occupants committed to predation.

'Snakes,' said Simon, 'look at that sonofabitch over there!'

Dorkin replied, 'Be careful, it's a puff adder,' and backed away as the culprit raised its head and opened its mouth to reveal exceptionally long fangs. They increased their speed and eventually the animal slithered away. He added: 'This damn place invented snakes; they are everywhere.' He pointed to a group of three evil-looking animals, small and brown, that watched him and stuck their tongues out as though tasting a kill in advance.

With packs on and heavy clothing, at least from the waist down, they became very hot and bothered and they seemed to toil forward with increasing difficulty. After a further mile the path ended at a rock face where an elevation of flint reflected light as well as heat. There, they were relieved to turn right and avoid the sun even though a visible path was lacking. From then on their way was rough, over stones and flattened yellow grass and around many potholes. Shrivelled and forlorn shrubs hung disconsolately, while large horseflies hovered menacingly and refused to back away. Meanwhile, a few haggard birds sent raucous calls into the gulley around them. They were not surprised that few people came that way.

Eventually Dorkin said, 'Almost there!' and after a further 100 yards stopped and removed his pack. He pointed at a small opening to his left, a dark recess that could be reached only by climbing over a large boulder. Nearby, and scratched into the rock, was the mark of a simple circle with a cross above it. Carmen remarked that it looked like the cartoon version of an upside-down flower, but they were more interested by the boulder, which looked like a defence for the opening behind it. Before deciding what to do, however, Dorkin said, 'This is what we want, but first we need to rest.'

They sat and wiped away the sweat. The sun had reached its zenith, but since they had rounded the hill to the east they were out of direct sunlight. They drank water and cooled slowly. Soon Carmen seemed ready to start, and her enquiring expression brought a positive nod from the others. She said, 'Well, we've come this far and we don't want to go back empty-handed, do we? So if you guys are happy, let's take out the flashlights and try our luck.'

Wiener offered to go first. His feet found marks in the boulder, toe-deep, to facilitate entry. The others passed their packs to him and followed. Inside, the strong sunlight faded, but by torchlight they could see that the place had walls of rock and was evidently stable. Before them a short passageway and a low ceiling made them stoop. It continued for ten feet and then narrowed to allow only one to pass at a time. At its end they were obliged to squeeze around an upright slab fixed to the floor, which presumably served as some kind of defensive measure in placing any intruder at a disadvantage. On the other side they passed into a large cave with walls of rock and brown shingle underfoot. There, a little light entered through a fissure in the ceiling so that the place was in twilight rather than darkness. There was fresh air and the place was dry, which augured well for the survival of any relics they might find.

'The first thing,' said Wiener, 'is that anyone who ever lived in here must have been able to use fire. We can just about find our way around without a lamp, but that's all. I wouldn't want to live in here otherwise.' He added, 'And I wouldn't want to get stuck inside.' He looked carefully at the roof overhead, but apart from the channel through which a little light entered, there was no other way out. They were barely able to see the extremities and shone their flashlights around.

The walls of the cave were seen to surround a roughly circular cavity which, near the back, had several recesses that were not quite rooms or tunnels. In places the shingle underfoot gave out to sand or compacted earth. They agreed that the shingle might have been brought in from outside. Dorkin's voice echoed in the stillness: 'I wonder how this cave was made. I don't think it was dug out, but I would suspect that it was enlarged by its inhabitants.' He looked around the floor: 'But they don't seem to have left anything behind and there's no suggestion that anyone has lived here for a very long time.' He followed: 'But I do think this place is very old. Maybe a stream hollowed it out.' His companions nodded in agreement.

'Okay,' he said, 'this is the right place. I suggest we take some measurements, photograph the place properly and then leave for the day.' He pulled out a camera and a laser distance metre. 'We can piece it all together back at the hotel. Then, we can decide where to dig.'

They spent an hour doing as Dorkin had suggested, and in due course Carmen examined the back of the cave. In a recess brown earth lay instead of shingle, but it also had a small area of crude paving around a hole that emitted a musty smell, although hardly worse than any other hole in the ground. She was immediately thrown off-balance while standing there, and paving and earth subsided under her weight. Then followed the sound of earth and stones falling, and when all had finished she shone her torch down to observe the debris below. She said, 'OK, no harm done,' and added, 'I bet this was a latrine. See how water could wash it out?' A conduit left towards the outside. Then she said, 'I expect some of the trash went down there too.'

After a time, they decided to leave for the day and were careful to leave no indication of their visit. Since the sun was lower in the sky the return journey was much easier, and they were barely troubled by the samples they had collected. On the following day they met in a private room in which, on a table, they spread a chart of white paper marked with an outline of the cave floor. Their few specimens and many photographs were then assigned to the parts of the cave from which they were taken. Accordingly, Carmen took a small bag of earth and emptied it into a plastic tray. She manipulated the contents and managed to separate from the mass of brown sand a few grains of a black and shiny substance. She passed these to Dorkin, who had just made a positive remark about renting their workroom: 'It means that we can leave all this stuff out.' He followed, 'So what's this?'

'They look like small black beads of something hard. They were in with the sand which I collected from that place at the back.'

'I see. Well they are round and smooth so 'black beads' is a pretty good description. They look as though they've been fused by heat. In fact, I would call them a simple form of glass.'

She replied, 'So you're saying they're man-made?'

'Yes, but not necessarily on purpose. You often get particles of a kind of black glass where sand has been used to surround a fire. Don't expect it to be transparent, by the way. We can take it as evidence that humans were there, but we knew that anyway.'

'You get black glass when sand is heated?'

'Not quite. It—the silicon dioxide in sand—can react with the alkaline constituents of wood ash or even burned animal bones. You get that in the high temperatures of a camp fire. Which sample was that again?'

'It came from that recess at the back. The one where we said they probably threw their trash.'

'Then I suppose that recess was a general rubbish tip—bones and stuff. They could have covered it with ash from the fire if they didn't like to leave evidence outside.'

'That sounds more than likely.'

She said, 'So Joseph, what do we do next?'

'We go back and lay in proper lighting. Then we take off the top layer of soil at strategic places, sift it carefully and remove any important artefacts. We photograph them and classify the hell out of everything. We stay for about two weeks and camp out.'

'OK,' said Carmen van Brouin, 'it's no shower for two weeks, but don't expect me to starve.'

'That's alright. We can come back here and clean up if we get desperate.'

During their next visit they renewed their particular interest in the far recess, and in the cavity beneath it. They dug more brown sand and sifted through it, revealing underneath a particularly dark soil not unlike potting compost. This contained diverse oddments which they took as evidence of former human occupation, such as fragments of bone and horn, together with an assortment of pieces of flint. One particular piece they identified with ease as a bone from an antelope. This, apparently very old, encouraged them to dig farther down and it became clear that their general view of the cavity as a refuse tip was right. For a time, they continued to work in the recess, scraping with trowels and sorting the various sizes of particles by using sieves.

In all this, they had not expected comfort, but with the need to crouch in a confined space they felt obliged to stand at regular intervals, or to walk around. On one of these occasions, and as Dorkin stood and backed out of the recess, Wiener moved a lamp that had formerly been directed downwards. Immediately, Dorkin's attention became focussed on a wall opposite, newly illuminated, and now facing him.

On it a few patches of colour, thus far, had been no more noticeable than any other indiscriminate marks. However they now took form before his eyes so that patches of ochre and the faintest of black lines took on the shape of a human figure. In the same manner, various small undulations and blotches resolved into the shape of a hill. Dorkin said, 'Look at this!' and was surprised by his own understatement. The others, normally puritanical when it came to swearing, let their principles fall with a resounding expletive which made the place echo.

All three were used to poring over primitive drawings and they immediately recognised the simple aesthetic which enabled them to describe it as art. It was not unexpected, because their experience had taught them that primitive humans and cave paintings went together. Yet they were surprised by the transformative effect that it had on their perception of the place. The faded colour elevated the cave and made it seem homely. Yet Dorkin was thoughtful. He muttered quietly, unaware that the others could hear: 'I'm sure I've seen something like it recently.' They saw no particular significance in his comment, but they did notice that he collected a tiny chip of surface material from an edge. Following these attentions, they continued their work in silence.

Their two-week stay continued but the significant finds they had hoped for were conspicuous by their absence. On the thirteenth day they decided to extend their investigation. Then, following a superficial dig in the main part of the dwelling that revealed little, they decided to look again at the recess. As Simon Wiener said, 'It isn't as though we have a better place to look for fossils.'

Their work continued to reveal only the characteristic dark soil, which they removed carefully. Continuing to dig they eventually reached sand, which suggested that they would find nothing further of any significance. Yet their work seemed to have affected the stability of an adjoining wall so that after a few fragments fell from it, Wiener began to divert his attention from floor to wall. He found that it was soft and unstable, a construction of dry mud and sand that was quite different from the supporting walls of the cave. It began to crumble under his attentions so that a significant assortment of detritus fell out. Dorkin said, 'Don't worry, I think it's only a partition of some kind.' Accordingly, there was no collapse of the ceiling; the cave remained intact, and the generator still chugged away. Around Wiener's feet, a pile of sand and gravel itself indicated why it had come down. It contained no natural cement and was little more than a simple cairn built to entomb the remains that were now exposed in it.

Here at last was their element of good luck. The fall had exposed numerous fossilised human remains. They had worked on enough examples to recognise them instantly. On their fourteenth day, enough palaeontological material had been revealed to keep them busy for a year or more. As they stared Dorkin said simply, 'I'm surprised that we didn't spot it as soon as we came in. It just shows how much we were concerned with digging down.' It was an anticlimactic statement which failed to hide his pleasure at their good fortune.

With such a find they knew that the ill-disciplined would dig with a shovel. Dorkin, however, cautioned against any such action. They continued to investigate the area properly, first excavating with trowels all parts that had fallen, and then around the foot of the cairn itself. They were pleased that time began to pass more pleasurably, with none of the perplexing frustration of other sites which failed to yield any evidence. They finished as quickly as had been anticipated, cleaned and made good the site, and then returned to Johannesburg. That evening, they celebrated with a few drinks in the bar of their hotel.

On the following days they pored over their finds and managed to assemble from the assortment a complete human skeleton; while other oddments were identified as the fossilised remains of several small children. Carmen displayed some sensitivity towards them, but was comforted by Simon, who suggested that they should walk in the sunshine. There, she became more composed and said, 'I guess it was long ago.'

Later, she sifted through more soil and found what she thought were pieces of flint. She passed them to Dorkin who held them to the light. He said, 'Scrapers they may be, but I don't think they are flint, which is crystalline and shows angular fracture lines. Again, this looks more like glass. Can you see how the breakage marks are concentric?' He passed them back again. 'So it can't be any crystal. I would say it's more like obsidian, but the thing is, there's none of that around here. You need molten lava to get it, which means a volcano.'

Carmen said, 'So what's wrong with that?'

'There haven't been any active volcanos in southern Africa for millions of years. It would have had to come from somewhere else. That means long-distance trade, and probably from overseas. But of course we need get these fragments analysed before we can be sure.'

Later, they began to examine some larger artefacts which had iron or the orange stain of rust within them. One particularly large example was heavy enough for Simon to compare it with a small cannonball. He said, 'I'm damned if I want this in my hand luggage.' It was an object, however, which made them wonder enough to earmark it for immediate analysis on their return.

With all kinds of interesting artefacts packed and numbered, they made ready to return home. They were delighted with their finds and could hardly wait for the flight. Dorkin said, 'It's been an easy dig. We came out just to look around. Usually I have to struggle to find things, but this time it was different. We unearthed all this without even going over the whole site.'

Carmen said, 'So do we have time for more? I mean, do we have enough stuff?'

'Sure we do.' Dorkin smiled. 'We could make a case for staying longer, but we already have a full adult skeleton and a few bits of several juveniles, including skulls complete with jawbones and teeth. We also have some artwork, together with enough evidence to date it. And there are the remains of what we think is ironwork; possibly even some kind of mallet-head. All this is much more than anyone got from the old Boskop dig a hundred years ago. And it's much more than from any other site I have ever visited. So I think it's enough for this trip, don't you?'

In fact, Dorkin was as excited as the others, but he was always careful to present the most moderate perspective. He said, 'It's almost too good to be true, so we have to be careful. There are people who will want to pick it apart. If we play it right, we can really hit the journals hard. And there's the DNA stuff to do as well. I think we've got enough to last us for a long time, but it absolutely has to be watertight.'

During the night Dorkin slept badly. He lay awake in bed and listened to the sound of insects as they buzzed about. Something nagged at him and it was to do with their investigation. He turned this over in his mind: was it the fossil remains? Perhaps something was amiss with them. He allowed his mind to wander. No, it was the wall painting. Following the excitement of the other finds it had barely been discussed. They had taken photographs but had worked quickly and with a view to continuing their survey.

It was strange that revelations came in the night, but the painting seemed familiar to him. Restless, he put on a dressing gown, unlocked their work-room and examined a photograph on his laptop computer. The picture was faint and old, yet the art was alive. It was simple, but not primitive. It showed a man sitting, perhaps on a throne. His outstretched hand bore small gifts which he meant to dispense to those around him. His cranium was large and his eyes exaggerated in size. Nearby, a path led to a hill on which a craft stood, a port open in its side. Dorkin smiled, and was satisfied. He went to sleep easily and dreamed of similar cave pictures he had seen at Mesoamerican sites, now 9,000 miles distant. It was an impossible distance for ancient humans to have travelled, so how had the similarity come about?

The day following was hot, and a haze lay over the Johannesburg streets when his team finished packing. He said nothing about his nocturnal reflections and began to set aside a small collection which they could take in their hand luggage. A few stones and a tiny fossil would pass scrutiny and would give them something to look at until the crate arrived by air.

Two weeks later, they met again in Dorkin's office. They were fully restored: Carmen was smart and wore her hair loose as she liked it; Simon was bronzed under his sallow skin and pleased to be back on his home territory. Dorkin had often wondered whether there was any attraction between them, but no, he had seen nothing. Their relationship was perfectly pleasant, but it was vocational, formal even, which he thought unusual in people of their age. Were they really only interested in palaeontology? Perhaps they were only ambitious, which was easier to understand. These, however, were special times, and Dorkin dismissed such thoughts and began to focus on the results of their trip.

Their most important prize lay on a workbench before them. Dorkin said, 'This is the skull of a human male, but look at the size of it. The forebrain is enlarged. I would say its capacity is 40% larger than the average modern human[4]. And the two children: I can't say how they died, but what *is* clear is that their forebrains are enlarged too, especially in the frontal lobes.' His use of the present tense made it sound as though they were still alive.

'And that's where the IQ resides,' said Simon Wiener.

Carmen stayed silent; perhaps she had not quite got over her previous tribulation with them.

Dorkin approached a chart on his whiteboard. It was divided into sections, each with ink of a different colour. He pointed to the blue: 'We need to get going on the next steps. First, we need to assemble the skeletons, which are all in pieces. And it needs to be done properly, so they must be wired together. That will take time.' He ticked his blue list.

He moved to red: 'We can do all the DNA stuff here in the department, but I'd like you to organise samples for dating by carbon-14. Go for the long bones, we should strike lucky with something to analyse.' He made a tick on his red list.

There was already a mark next to green: 'I sent those rusty iron

---

4   Skulls taken from the Boskop in 1913 showed a similar enlargement of
     the forebrain.

implements away to be X-rayed, and there's the chemistry to be done, as well. But I can tell you one thing already, they were iron tools, and not just iron lumps.'

A month later, they met in his office once again. Before them were three skeletons, fully assembled, and complete apart from a few chips and cracks. There were copious summaries in three colours on Dorkin's whiteboard. They were in a state of excitement.

Dorkin had written in bright red ink, 'skeletons 65,000 years old'. He tapped the board with a pointer.

Carmen said, 'Can we be sure about the age?'

He replied firmly, 'They are about 65,000 thousand years old.'

'But carbon-14 dating is supposed to be useless for samples older than 50,000 years!'

'That might be true under normal circumstances, but we *have* got large samples to test, so by using more material I've been able to stretch the method to its absolute limit of 75,000 years.'

'But we were expecting the settlement to be 3000 years old, not 65,000!'

'I do know that!'

Carmen persisted, 'But that would date the settlement as far back as the time when primitive man first spread out of Africa. There were supposedly no distinct races then!'

Dorkin seemed pleased, but having already seen the results he was not as surprised as the others. He said, 'If you think that's strange, just wait until you hear the DNA results. Over to you, Simon!'

Wiener said: 'Ok, here goes.' He attempted to suppress the excitement in his voice. 'The carbon-14 dating says these people lived 65,000 years ago. We checked it, and all three skeletons were the same. But we also looked at their mitochondrial DNA as well. We were successful because—the samples were so good I can hardly believe it!' He paused and looked at the other two, 'So we had enough DNA—we easily amplified enough to get good results. The limit for the method is supposed to be 1.4 million years old, but that would be for the very best preserved samples. Our samples were not quite that good, but their age was still no difficulty.' There was another pause, while he looked from one to the other. Carmen was on the edge of her seat. Wiener drew a deep breath, 'Now just to remind you, we know how quickly that DNA mutates, so by looking at its divergence from modern samples we can tell when they separated from the main human population. So, here's the interesting thing. Our samples show they diverged from modern man 450,000 years ago. These guys went their own way as a distinct population nearly half a million years ago. Dammit, do I make myself clear? They cannot have interacted with, or interbred with Homo sapiens at all during that time.'

Carmen shook her head and her face showed disbelief. She said, 'The divergence is one thing, but the rest is just crazy! We know they used iron tools, which must place them in the Iron Age. We agreed that those black lumps were tools, not just meteorites... the mallet, it had a metal core! And we know that the earliest iron tools appeared only after the Bronze Age ended, about 3,000 years ago. That's why we thought our fossils would be 3,000 years old! There must be something wrong if our results tell us that the Iron Age started 62,000 years before the date which everybody else has agreed!'

Dorkin attempted to instil a bit of authority into the proceedings: 'Okay, let's talk about possible contamination of the site. If modern man lived there later, it would account for the tools—*that's* the main criticism that will be levied at us—but there was no contamination. The animal bones in the waste pit were around 65,000 years old as well. There was no evidence of any later habitation. We went over the place carefully.' The others nodded. 'And,' he continued, 'there's that calcite chip which I took from the surface of the wall-painting. I sent it off to have it dated from the uranium-series isotopes found in it. There's a guy who makes a living out of it.'

Carmen said, 'So what did he find?'

'You tell me!'

'Alright, once again it was sixty-five thousand. But if that's really so, it's older than any other cave finds yet!

'They will only say it's a fake,' said Carmen. 'Remember Piltdown Man? It turned out to be an orangutan. And there are some,' she said, 'who may find a connection between Dawson[5] and Dorkin!' She laughed, pleased with herself.

Dorkin was slightly stung by this, not because he was angry with Carmen, but because the notion of their find being rejected by the scientific community was too upsetting to contemplate. He said, 'I know. We shall be asking everyone to accept almost unheard-of evidence about the occupants of our site. We find it questionable ourselves, and we were actually there. So the only way around this is to make our case watertight. *That* is what we must do now.'

He underlined all the coloured sections on his whiteboard and said, 'They lived there long ago, were brighter than we are and they were familiar with iron thousands of years before they should have been. Then suddenly they disappeared as though taken away.'

There was complete silence. The other two had a strange vision of a subspecies of Homo sapiens, living quietly by themselves in caves and avoiding all contact with the rest of humanity. In the silence Simon mumbled something about '—need more evidence,' and Carmen replied, 'We surely have enough with all this!'

'We had better wait,' said Simon, 'until we get the rest of the results back.' But Dorkin barely heard. He had an even stranger vision. He remembered the cave art that resembled the Mesoamerican examples he had seen. And shortly he would propose his strange solution.

Carmen studied Simon with her brown eyes. Dorkin still thought she remained indifferent to Weiner; he might have been an old man instead of a 25-year old. And her expression was guarded, Dorkin did not know why.

---

5   Charles Dawson has been proposed as the perpetrator of the Piltdown hoax.

FIVE

SUPERNATURAL OR PARANORMAL?

While Dorkin considered his whiteboard, the Reverend Callum Dood, several thousand miles to the east and recovering after his trip to Nepal, was in a reflective mood. His ankle was healed, but a slight stiffness remained while walking, which brought back his narrow escape from the mountainside. He had thanked Adhikari profusely, but had not been able to reward the benevolence of the strange people whom his rescuer, a man not known to mince words, had called the *metoh kangmi*. It seemed that they were known by many names and there were legends also, yet Adhikari had declined to say more when pressed. Dood understood his position: Adhikari was obliged to humour the many westerners who made trips especially to look for them. Some feared them; others said they were wise; all said they were reclusive.

Dood paced to and fro in the drawing room of his rectory. He was vicar of the small village of Peckling, deep in the Wessex countryside. It was a comfortable place and sociable, yet it was not parochial. Times were slowly changing and a recent influx of professional people had improved the place. They spent money in the village, attended church more often than the locals, placed their kids in the village school and ran clubs and societies. Very often they were sincere. The village was now more prosperous and Dood had more to do.

In many respects he was the ideal person for his position. In former years the village had been a farming community and his predecessor, a quiet man, was content to take his sermons from a book. Yet since the place was now a haven for professionals, so their requirements for vicar were different. Dood, among the less recent additions to the population, had been regarded as an enigma: solitary yet sociable; getting on a bit yet sprightly; clerical yet dishevelled; a man of God yet a purveyor of country wisdom; an aesthete yet reliant on herbal remedies. But if his activities were not wholly conventional, they were in keeping with the more recent influx, many of whom were unconventional in habit. They were highly educated and not quite 'country'. Paradoxically, he found it increasingly easy to fit in. Besides vicar, he might also have described himself as psychologist. Among the many aesthetic, esoteric and doctrinal matters there were stranger things to experience than evensong. And in that, he had on several occasions proved to be a more than robust member of the community. The diocese had noticed and although they would have denied it, they had taken a deliberate interest in his abilities. Some said he was the local exorcist, to which he might have replied 'hardly!'

He continued to pace his drawing room on a day in which his quiet solitude was beset with conventional routines. He was not forlorn however; the countryside gave pleasure with its long walks and fungal forays among the falling russet and gold. He was comforted by his garden and by his researches, botanical, mycological and mystical. And there was no lack of stimulation in a room in which, in great comfort, he was usually content to read, smoke, sketch butterflies, make sandwiches, and write his own sermons. Yet that day he paced on. Reaching the opposite wall, he turned away from his reflection in a mirror, spun on his heel and returned. A small scuff mark appeared on his rich Isfahani rug and noticing it, he changed the direction of his walk so that it lay over his 350 years old floorboards instead. Finally, he slumped into an armchair, thought about his latest botanical experiment and ignited it with a match.

He inhaled from his cigarillo, which contained a substantial quantity of the African Dream Root, yet it was no frivolous vice. The subject of psychology had taken him to the phenomenon of 'the lucid dream,' a condition quite distinct from the effect of any stimulant or depressant on the nervous system. In such a state one could observe an enhanced consciousness, together with vivid colours despite nominally being asleep. One could feel no boredom and would be neither vague nor temperamental. Adherents could enter into a deeply reflective state and be detached, yet retaining all mental facilities. They would be wholly lucid yet infinitely expanded. How else could the metoh kangmi have lived at such a height and in such cold? They had revealed a degree of mental preparation, perhaps an interest in the inner mystery. Dood nodded his head at the thought. He inhaled again and the rectory became timeless so that he was able to think about events as though he were above and beyond them. The mind was strange; it continually harvested tiny stimuli and considered the smallest pieces of information. When called upon by the will of its owner, it would muster a formal report. In his timeless and reflective state his mind floated over notable events in the neighbourhood: lights in the sky, strange sounds and marks in the fields, over crop circles and power failures. It decided that there was an issue.

The telephone rang from his hall. He awoke quickly, stubbed out his cigarillo, and all former thoughts were manifest as an underlying feeling of disquiet as he ceased his reflections and moved to answer it. Adam Shilto was at the other end.

'Hello Callum, this is Adam, can I come over please?' Adam Shilto was the local archdeacon, Dood's main point of contact with the upper echelons of the church and a close personal friend. Their relationship was concerned with work, yet it was also informal. Shilto lived locally, yet not close enough to walk into the village. In their meetings they often shared coffee and enjoyed a simple chat, but if Shilto called there was always the likelihood that he was concerned with business. And if Shilto had urgent business it was likely to be bad. As soon as he heard him on the telephone, Dood was aware of the nagging manner in his voice.

He replied, 'By all means Adam and while you are here, I would like you to try my distillate of the wormwood plant. Some call it the essence of Essence; I would be interested in your opinion.'

'Are you on that stuff right now?'

'No, I'm only having a smoke.'

'Well I'm not promising anything. But let me come over today.'

'Have you got anything edible?'

'Yes, some cake.'

'Consider me bribed.'

Later, Adam Shilto, a tall, broad grey-haired man of about 60 with a sub-fusc and moderate black woollen jacket and grey trousers, cycled over. He had a small plastic bag with him and withdrew a cake which he passed to Callum Dood. The latter dispensed it with surgical care and as they relaxed in chairs in his study, he offered Shilto a glass jug of wine, in the yellow depths of which lay a bunch of slender leaves, grey and white. He said, 'Try a glass!'

Shilto sipped curiously. He said, 'This is wormwood?' He had an open and friendly countenance and smiled willingly.

Dood said, 'Yes, an infusion in chardonnay…my latest project. Now tell me what's going on.'

Adam Shilto said, 'I'm not the only one who has started to wonder. I won't say that there's any disquiet yet, just curiosity. You remember those pagan activities on the downs five years ago[6]?'

'Don't remind me!'

'Well you needn't worry about any more of that.' Shilto read the curiosity on the other man's face. If it wasn't some spiritual problem, then Dood wondered what the present conundrum could be. He was about to give voice to the view that the church ought not to be interested in the preserve of politicians or social services, when Shilto followed: 'What's the difference between the supernatural and the paranormal?'

'It might be the difference between a ghost and a moving light. It might also be the difference between the church becoming involved

---

6   The Magdeburg Relic.

and calling the police. Perhaps you had better tell me what's going on.'

'Look, Callum, there are some peculiar sights and sounds around here these days. The police say they have enough to do. We don't know whether it's supernatural or paranormal. In fact, the more I try to distinguish between them myself, the more I become confused.'

'Well, what *is* going on?'

'There are lights over the downs. And I don't mean *on* the downs. There are marks in the fields. There is combustion and great heat, but no apparent means of having caused it. There are funny smells too, and people can't explain them. And there are journalists about. They are probably from London, as if we don't have enough of our own. They are digging around, asking things.'

'Is this really church stuff Adam?'

'We don't think it's a ghost if that's what you mean. Even the local Druids are conspicuous by their absence and all that pagan malarkey seems to be quiet. Here, have another slice of fruitcake.'

'Thanks. So where do *I* come in?'

'You know the score. There is nobody, not even the journalists—and let's face it, those guys are like terriers—who can uncover what you can, if there is anything there to uncover. Why don't you start in your usual manner with your own contacts? They are people these journalists wouldn't get to see. By the way, this stuff makes me feel a bit odd and mystical. It's almost as though my head has grown too large for my body. I seem to be living inside a giant skull.'

Dood nodded and poured more. Then he referred to the few notes he had scribbled down just before Shilto arrived. They concerned his researches that morning: *'The Dream Root will assist the brain to harvest subliminal messages from just below the conscious…am aware of lights and crop circles; there is local disquiet.'* He said, 'Funnily enough, my researches had drawn me to the same conclusion. If I must, then so be it. I'll look into it.'

'Thanks, Callum,' said Shilto.

Dood replied, 'By the way, I'm glad you liked the wine, but that wormwood infusion is only halfway there. Try some Absinthe instead. It's the real stuff, not just gin with an aniseed ball in it. Careful, it makes you go a bit crazy. By the way, your fruitcake was pretty good. If you like, I've got some biscuits with wormwood in them, just to see what happens. And you can crumble a little into a cigar if you wish...'

Later, when Shilto had left, Dood went out to his garden shed and read a learned article:

> '...the chemical essence of wormwood had been found to have a molecular shape similar to that of the psychoactive substance tetrahydrocannabinol and it could therefore be expected to behave in the same psycho-stimulant manner. Some authorities feel its action is due to the stimulation of neurotransmitters as has been found with extracts of other plant materials.'

Picking up his notebook he wrote: 'Wednesday 27th. A distillation of Cypress leaves using a method previously tested on the common sage. Today, 50 grams of Cypress leaves were ground with a pestle and mortar and infused with alcohol. They were left for an hour and filtered. The liquid extract was evaporated until dry and dissolved in a small volume of fresh alcohol. Pipe tobacco was infused with the resulting thujone extract for 24 hours, dried, repacked and test-smoked.'

He wrote the title 'Results' and with a pen at the ready, relaxed in his garden shed and smoked the first of several pipes. He thought about Shilto and his strange request. He had known there was a problem, of course, but the question was what he should do. He would start with the Dog and Duck. A public house of the best kind, it was the village moot hall, welcoming to all and sundry, the beer lover, the gourmet, the happy or sad.

—◊—

That evening, and wearing full clerical regalia, Dood walked the necessary 500 yards and ordered a pitcher of real ale. There, traditions were very much alive and it was still possible to buy beer in multiples of pints, of which the pitcher was one. Such a volume or beer, he considered, might conceivably attract any person with a tendency to be sociable.

The inevitable darts team was there, but they played a conventional 501 down and supped their lager. They were reasonably lively and from his position in a comfortable armchair, he watched them play. On occasions Libby Long, the ever-popular barmaid, came over to chat or top up his glass. She bustled about with her usual charm and energy, a free spirit and certainly without any interest in the concerns expressed by Adam Shilto. She smiled in a benevolent manner and served a few other people. Her other customers were similarly content.

His pitcher had no takers. Perhaps the locals knew they would be pumped for information? Libby Long smiled in his direction; she knew him of old. Nevertheless that did not stop her from pausing for a few minutes to talk, and she accepted a small wineglass of beer from him. 'If only to seem sociable,' she said with her usual charming manner, 'Anything going bump…?'

'Not really. The occult side of things is quite dead.'

She smiled at this. 'So this visit is just a social foray?' She sounded doubtful.

'Certainly it is. But if you *do* know anything about scorch marks on the downs, crop circles in the cornfields or bright lights overhead, you will let me know?' He smiled.

'Sure, Honey. But there's nothing along those lines here. Or if there is the local people aren't taking much notice.'

'Any angles for me?'

'I don't suppose the shepherds and poachers take much notice of stuff like that, not with all the cider they drink, so why don't you talk to professional people instead? You need to speak to clever people like the microlighters or the ones who race off-roaders on the Ridgeway. They all seem to write software for a living.'

'Any introductions?'

'Maybe. Start with the chess club. There's John Ellerington over there.' She pointed towards a man in his thirties with a labrador and muddy boots. In these days, a vicar did not normally invite himself to tea with people new to the village, so waving was considered adequate. He had certainly waved at Ellerington, who was not exactly a new face although they had not yet spoken. He had thought Ellerington a professional type although in what regard he was unsure. He was known to have two small children and a wife who walked them to primary school. Neither was immersed in the full round of village activities and they came to church only at Christmas time.

Dood collected chessmen and a board from the bar and laid it down next to his beer. He set the board up and in a slow and deliberate manner moved first the white and then the black. As he did so he referred to pages of a book which accompanied the board. His manner was bumbling, but he was an accomplished actor and did not meet the eye of those around him. Eventually he felt the eyes of Ellerington upon him. Raising his glass to sip, he nodded, smiled his least cynical smile and returned to the board, brow furrowed. Soon, Ellerington went to the bar and on taking charge of a drink, strolled over. He said, 'An amateur?'

'Certainly, just picking it up. I must say I can't make head or tail of it.'

'Well you surprise me, because what you have done is to use one of the more unusual openings. It's called the Orangutan, an opening developed in 1924.'

'Well I just opened this little book and thought I'd put it together. I must admit I'd been thinking about learning for a while.'

'Can I join you for a minute? You're the local vicar, are you not?'

'I try to be! Callum Dood, sermons and curry.' They shook hands.

'I'm John and I'm fairly new to the village.'

'Yes, I think we've passed in the street. Tell me, what's so special about the game?'

'Well, it is a strategic game, one which develops a highly-focussed thinking and mental stamina. Strangely, they are not the same qualities as those required by successful players of bridge. The inexperienced player of chess often plays with great bravura and naivety. They show a considerable artistry that may be absent from the long slugging matches of heavyweight, experienced players. That is why I welcome new chess players to our chess club.'

'That sounds like an invitation.'

'Sure it is. But it's only fair to say I've not reciprocated by attending church services.'

'Agnostic or atheist?'

'Lapsed. I suppose you hear that quite often! But I lapsed quite a long time ago.'

Dood said, 'Don't worry. A lot of people lapse and return later. They dip in and out or come along on big occasions. Folk have allegiances they half-remember, but they rely on them when the time comes. That's why hymns are important at primary school.'

'I'm sure you're right. But I know you will like our club, so please come over and play with us. We meet at one of about four or five homes on rotation. Some members live a bit farther away, maybe 20 miles but they are happy to come over. We are still a local group.'

'Well there is always the church hall if you get short.'

'Ah, we like to have a few glasses as well.'

'The offer is still open. We don't worry about the temperance pledge these days!'

A few days later, Dood strolled up the main street and stopped at a cottage. It had a beautiful rose garden at the front, and a large tabby cat in the window which held a most contemptuous expression. There was some pargeting on the front of the house that had been added very recently. He knocked on the door and was ushered in by the resident, a plump, balding man in middle age, with spectacles and a tweed suit, who introduced himself as Peter Pargeter and led him towards a sizeable annexe at the back of the house. Once there, he said, 'That's where I work,' and pointed to a closed door; followed by 'This is where I play,' and pointed to an open one. It proved to be a supplementary room with carpets, electrical radiators and many convenient and comfortable chairs that had small tables between them to accommodate a board. It was a comfortable and very convenient club room. Shortly, the cat joined them and sat watching as Dood set up chessmen and in a deliberate manner referred to a manual.

Pargeter sat down and said, 'Welcome Reverend. You are my very first guest to arrive. John will be along in ten minutes and we expect another half dozen tonight. So what do you know about chess?'

'It's a bit like the Gobi Desert. I've always known what it is but I've never managed to go there.'

'So why now?'

'I've come to save all these people from the Devil.'

'Are you serious?'

'No. Actually, I need the mental exercise and I like meeting new people.'

Pargeter looked relieved. 'Well you've come to the right place.' He set up chessmen on a neighbouring table. 'Can I start you off or are you content to think about your early moves? We like to show a few slides at the start and one of our members is due to chat about some kind of pet defence. Then after 15 minutes we settle down for an hour, break for a cup of something, then carry on for another… well…until people get fed up. Then we save our games until next time or call it a draw.'

Dood did not wish to start a game until he had met some more guests. 'I'm a real novice so…'

'Surely. There's the doorbell again.'

Ellerington walked in, followed by six other people. Three were women, all young. The men were in their thirties and looked prosperous enough to be the new kind of professional. They waved, and made ready for games around the room. Ellerington joined Dood and glanced at the manual he was reading. He said, 'Good to see you again. Come over here and make yourself comfortable.' There was a general movement towards a projector and then a laptop appeared. One of the new men said to another: 'So what kind of transport did you use to get here?' He pronounced it trahnsport. Ellerington said quietly to Dood, 'I think he works for the BBC.'

When all were seated the BBC man spoke about the King's Indian defence and made reference to some notable games in which it had appeared. After fifteen minutes the group, now comfortable and talkative, split into pairs and gravitated towards smaller tables. Ellerington faced Pargeter and they kept a friendly eye on Dood, an odd man out, and drew him into conversation from time to time. They told him they were evenly matched, that they played together regularly and would keep the proceedings informal that night.

Dood said to Ellerington, 'Are either of you competitive with chess? I mean, speaking as a complete novice, are you perhaps to 'county' standard in the manner of players of tennis?'

Ellerington replied, 'Lord no! We are only Peckling standard. We do it for the social life and for the fact that it helps our powers of concentration.'

Pargeter nodded and said, 'Certainly. I find it helps with my work.'

'Ah, that's interesting. Do you mind if I ask about your work? Professional or academic perhaps?'

'That's fine, but I don't think I belong to a recognised profession. I write algorithms. I work for myself.'

'Mathematical stuff?'

'Yes, but I'm as much employed with practical tasks as with pure mathematics. I write programs for computers so they can harvest data and make calculations. People hire me. I can't say who, but defence people find me useful and so do the financial services.'

'Funnily enough,' said Ellerington, 'people write programs so that very powerful computers can play chess. We can't get a game off them.'

'Do you mean to say that a computer can play chess better than the person who designed its program? How can that be?'

'Oh, the machine is more reliable and can do things more quickly, if not more intelligently. It needs only to understand some basic moves but it can analyse many more situations more quickly.'

'I had better not pit myself against either of you!' said Dood.

'I disagree. You may be brilliant from first principles. You may have insight, flair and artistry. You may surprise yourself but cannot understand why.'

'But surely, a move that has flair can also be predicted by a computer? Even though artistic, surely it remains no more than an ordinary move?'

'Certainly, but that does not explain why the great grandmasters can often beat very advanced computers. I have always wondered whether even the best program would have beaten Bobby Fischer. For me he was the most mercurial, temperamental and advanced player of them all. It might take a true 'artificial organic brain' to be unbeatable.'

Dood acknowledged with a nod, and asked what it might take to reach that level of ability.

'Total dedication,' said Ellerington, and then to Pargeter: 'Now you have the white, so let's start.'

They played some part games. Ellerington demonstrated some beginnings and endings and they worked through strategies, defences and set-pieces. Then he offered coffee and they brought the proceedings to a close at about 10.30 pm. Pargeter's cat had attached itself to Dood and watched contemptuously with its great golden eyes as he moved his chessmen about. Later it strolled around outside and accompanied him for 50 yards as he went home. Not yet a friend, he thought, but possibly not an enemy either.

Dood continued to play chess at the pub in a conspicuous manner, and he set up chessmen on a table by a window at the vicarage. He made progress with the game and found it brought forth waves and positive comments from other guests in the public bar. However, he was quite aware that he had not yet made enough progress to ask about odd lights or unexplained crop circles on the downs. Such a premature question would characterise him as an oddball, a situation he was anxious to avoid. Yet the new professionals might still be useful to talk to, so he carried on and met more of them when he could.

He began to read some back copies of the local newspaper. It proclaimed that three weeks before, a large circle had appeared in a field near a well-known iron-age hill fort. There had been lights in the sky and a general failure of supplies of electrical power at the time. Several farm workers had reported a crop circle the next morning and a local reporter had seen it. Later, a helicopter photographed the circle from above and the picture brought considerable speculation in the paper and on local radio. He looked at the letters page. One letter said, 'Hoaxers need to think about the damage to crops when trampling large areas in this manner.' Another showed the photograph of a jovial farmer with a bushy beard, who said, 'The marks are clear evidence that space visitors regard the downs as a point of reference in their interplanetary travels.'

He knew the radio presenter from an earlier period in which she had worked elsewhere. They had spoken a few times since then and their relationship was still on a friendly basis. Dood telephoned her: 'Hi Freya, I hope you remember me? This is Callum and I heard about your program on the radio.'

'Hello Callum. Which one? Do you mean the survey of local restaurants?' Freya Sampson's voice was cheerful and friendly.

'Actually I was thinking about your piece on the crop circle. What's it all about?'

'Well, people usually take a few crop circles in their stride. They laugh at anyone who talks about aliens and they think it's something to do with beer or Morris dancing. The trouble is that everyone's suddenly talking about it. You know how things are with Twitter when things go viral, well crop circles have gone viral without any social media connection at all.'

'Is there honestly anything more going on?'

'I think there *is* more than usual, and the more you dig into it, the more you find. I'm working on a story now, and I want to beat all my competitors down from London. They keep on turning up around here as though they feel some kind of scoop coming on. Journalists are funny like that, they have a sixth sense. Thing is, I think they're right. It's growing into a huge exclusive. It might even get my program onto national radio!'

'Let me come and see you.'

'OK. I can do it tomorrow lunchtime. You can buy me some pizza.'

'I thought you'd say that. But it would be a pleasure.'

At midday Dood entered a restaurant and observed Freya drinking coffee at a table by the window. She was dressed very casually in blue jeans and had grown her yellow hair longer than it had been at their last meeting two years before. It suited her and she looked prosperous, self-possessed and stylish. A petite and attractive individual, she was also tough and professional. She had entered the world of media comparatively recently and done well.

She waved him over and he sat down facing the sunshine. Freya thought he looked only a little older and still possessed of a kind of elemental energy that belied his age. She smiled at his hair, still on the verge of chaos, but could see that his inner vision was unimpaired. More than that, he was perceptive from his experience and by his unusual interests. He looked relaxed, and when the waitress approached he said, 'My treat. What would you like?'

'I don't eat much at lunchtime but I shall be out until late, so pizza would be great, thank you.'

'Do you want to share a large one?'

'Sure.'

'So what keeps you out working late?'

She preferred to start the questions. 'First of all, why did you call me yesterday? I wouldn't have thought that this kind of stuff would be of any concern to your bosses.'

'They have a general interest in anything out of the ordinary. There's no way of saying that strange lights are not supernatural. In fact, Adam and I were discussing how one might actually distinguish the paranormal and supernatural. They sent me out to look around, just like last time.'

'And what have you found out?'

'Very little more than you first told me. There are lights on the downs, funny smells, crop circles and failures of electrical systems. They seem to happen at once and they may be connected.'

'Is that all?'

'There's very little more. I tried to meet some new people: professionals, of the kind who might have an insight into scientific and technical matters. I met some clever people who write algorithms and things like that. But I'm no closer to finding out what's going on. That's why I telephoned you. I saw an article in the local paper. It mentioned your program.'

'Well, I'm glad they sent you to look into this, but I don't think you will find any ghosts. I think this is different.'

'Is there anything in it at all?'

'Yes, I think there is. When I started looking, I suspected the military, but now I'm not so sure. There are no army types about, so…something else…I don't know.'

'Perhaps we could share resources?'

'As always, Callum. I think we both need an edge on this.'

The pizza arrived and they ate while it was hot. After a few minutes Dood said, 'So where should I look first?'

'You could take a look at some of the marks on the downs. I think I actually saw some of them being made! I was driving over the downs when it was dark. Quite suddenly it became as light as day, but only for a few seconds. My engine stopped and my headlights went dead. The local street lights, they all went off. I can't think where such a vast amount of light could come from. There was no flame or explosion, no aircraft overhead, no storm, no lightning. It wasn't sheet lightning; I've seen that once before. And there was a smell—it was metallic. Shortly after that, the locals reported marks in the fields. It was a jolly chap called Buchanan who found them.'

'Crop circles?'

'Perhaps, but they were more like scorch marks. There was a distinct pattern in the scorched grass. I suppose the first thing to do would be to go up and look at them.'

'You could show me where?'

'I was going to offer. What do you say if we take my car?'

—◊—

On the hills ten miles east of Peckling it was a bright and blustery day, with a hint of rain in the air. The red kites soared effortlessly overhead, a twitch of the tail or wingtip sending them into aerial acrobatics as they cruised like nature's own drones, their eyes on tiny movements below. The two conspirators approached from the south west, from which a clump of beech, oak and conifer was a prominent feature on the summit of a low hill. Away to the south the homes and industrial developments were somehow invisible, while the flat farmland receded into the distance with small groups of cows fading to specks in green and windy fields. It was an exposed place, with excellent views for perhaps fifteen miles around.

Freya parked her car by the side of a muddy track and they walked north east into farmland, leaving the trees half a mile behind. In a field to the right a large circle could be seen. It lay in long grass that had a slight slope, but it was nevertheless symmetrical, as though whatever had made it had found no difficulty in working at an angle.

Dood said, 'This is an odd place for locals to have devised a hoax. They would have inconvenienced the farmer, and it would have been a difficult place to reach on foot with the stuff needed to make it. I don't think they trampled the grass down anyway.'

'Trampled? No, these are scorch marks!' Freya kicked away at the scorched turf as they walked around. A few clods of earth went flying to reveal soil blackened to a depth of at least nine inches. She said, 'And whatever made this was *very* hot. I can't see even a blowtorch reaching this depth.' She moved her hands to emphasise the temperature and they were as far apart as she could make them.

They continued to prowl around the perimeter until eventually, Dood said, 'This thing is so big that even a very large rocket couldn't have made it. And nobody could have brought a rocket all the way up from the road anyway.'

'No. And I can't see any rocket making such a fine pattern. The strange thing is that these scorch marks go deep but the surface is barely disturbed. I thought of one of those jump jets, but any kind of jet engine or rocket would have blown large chunks of earth away. This was something else altogether.'

'And what if a load of farm workers, out for a laugh, had just decided to blowtorch it?'

'It's too big, too symmetrical and just too deep. I can't see anyone having the patience to mark it out properly. It would take days, and they would leave traces of chalk or that white liquid they use to mark out tennis courts. We would be bound to see it and the footprints too. See how soft it is.'

Dood carried on pondering: 'I can only think of marking it out with a giant yardstick or a set of huge compasses, but what then? It would take ages to do. And I can't understand how even a very hot object could make a pattern with such well-defined edges. See how it seems to ignore the slope of the land and all irregularities on the surface.'

Freya replied, 'I may not be popular with the farmer, but do you think I could take away a bit of turf to be analysed?'

'I don't see why not. I expect he can afford to lose a bit. And any independent forensics lab could do the job. I'm sure they would take a commission from a local radio station.'

Dood smiled and turned his back in jest, while Freya collected some scorched turf and a little soil. As she sealed it in small plastic bags, he said, 'Is there an aerial photograph of this?'

'Yes, it was published in the paper, and I have an original that reached me at the radio station.'

'Do you think I could have a copy myself?'

'That's certainly possible. I'll get one printed out.'

Back in the car, she said, 'I'll try to get these samples tested. Perhaps you could do something about analysing the aerial view to see whether it means anything. And if you can tell me how I came to see that massive release of light, I would be grateful!'

'I'll do my best with those clever types from the chess club.'

She said, 'By the way, thank you for the pizza. It was rather a good lunch!'

At home, Dood walked in his garden and from a flowerpot picked a few leaves from a shrub called the Seer's sage. Walking farther to his garden shed, he boiled a kettle and infused the leaves in a battered old teapot. While the herbal tea brewed, he rolled a few cigarillos and crumbled further leaves into them. Sprawling in an old armchair, he sipped his tea and smoked his first cigarillo. The comfort, the heat of the tea and the sweet aromatic vapour enabled him to relax and turn his mind to a free and unburdened consideration of events. He examined a glossy photograph of an aerial view of the marks on the hillside. It was an exact circle, but it had a trailing line from the middle to the perimeter which made him think that in making it, a hot object would have needed to revolve like a Catherine wheel firework. Had he wished to follow this line, he would have walked to the perimeter on a trailing path of increasing radius, while taking an occasional sideways step. Yet even so, it was unclear what had made it. Had it been a revolving rocket craft, with individual rockets firing continuously, then the whole area would have been a uniform black. Any rockets must therefore have fired only intermittently. Yet since intermittent firing would have been pointless for propulsion, its only purpose must have been to make the marks.

With the onset of the effect of Seer's sage he felt a sense of revisiting the ring and of marks being applied while he watched. He sipped his herbal tea and felt a supplementary vision of motion far above. Then his mind became part of an alternative reality: a part of a fractal pattern and his mind within it. His sight advanced through a fractal of an infinite number of triangles and he understood its symmetry. Soon the crop circle became a part of that fractal and its trailing arm a message. He laughed and tears fell from his eyes.

He became infinitely calm. Settling further into his armchair, he looked again at his photograph and it became clear. Its meaning projected forth large, so that it displayed only the logic which the ring contained. Then his vision changed and his mind became a strange synthesis of fractal triangles and trailing radii. The circle became upright and flat, upon a flat, two-dimensional hill. He became ice-cold and slept for a while. Then in a cold trance he counted the step-like sideways radii, of which there were 4. He observed that the curved, trailing lines differed only in their length and that again, there were 4 such lengths. He sipped further herbal tea, now quite cold. The numbers and lengths were ratios. He relit his cigarillo, but his mind became confused as smoke supplemented his infusion of tea. Then he lay on the grass under a psychedelic rain of red, blue and green.

Dood awoke and felt the urge to play chess. He went to the Dog and Duck and ordered a bottle of wine. He set up a chessboard in his favourite corner and began to play by taking opposite sides of the table for each move, and required no manual to help with white or black pieces. He became engrossed, and beat himself easily. Soon, he became warm in the convivial atmosphere and began to listen to conversation from other tables and from the bar. He waved to Ellerington who was also present.

Ellerington watched him, fascinated, and said, 'That was remarkable. You successfully worked through Bobby Fischer's 'Bust to the King's Gambit' from his 1961 game with Boris Spassky. Did you read it up?'

Dood replied, 'No, my mind seems remarkably clear tonight.'

Ellerington said, 'You had better come to the chess club later this week. That was one of the greatest games of all time.'

At the chess club, Dood played as a novice and was content with an opponent of similar ability. It was a short game and he lost to his opponent. Sympathy and informality now beckoning, he had decided to show Pargeter his photograph. Later, there was coffee and they sat around in idle chatter for half an hour before going home. It was during this period that he spoke to Pargeter, who wore the same tweed suit as before. Pargeter was relaxed and seemed pleased with his game, so Dood showed him his photo of the crop circle. He said, 'Peter, I saw this pattern when I was looking at a maths problem in a book. I thought the mental exercise might do me good, but I have no idea what it means. I need someone with the right kind of mind to look it over. I wonder...'

'Well, if I can! My, it does have a deceptively simple form. It's funny, you know, but you're the second person to ask me something like this recently.' He studied it for a few minutes and said, 'Can I borrow it? I know a chap who can probably make some sense of it.'

'Why, what does he do?'

'He works in shape analysis. You know, in digital geometry. He analyses geometric shapes by using a computer. He gets the thing into a digital form and then his computer references the shape against a database of known models. Even if it's unlike anything seen before, it can still find points of similarity.'

Pargeter paused for breath and continued: 'And he can look for mathematical meanings. Your shape may be suitable for boundary representation. If anyone can find out what it means, then he can.'

'Boundary representation?'

'Yes. They look at topology and geometry. Umm...he's a busy man, so I shall probably need to slip him something drinkable.'

'That's fine, what's his poison?'

—⁓—

In a small laboratory in the midlands, a policeman called Briggs was talking to a young forensic scientist by the name of Jarvis. Briggs said, 'Tell me about the radioactive substances found in the soil sample.'

'In fact the level of radioactivity was low.'

'Then why are you worried?'

'Interested would be a better expression.'

Briggs had taken a dislike to Jarvis, who had a rather pompous manner. He said, 'Alright, tell me why you are interested.'

'My problem was actually the nature of the contents, rather than the level of radioactivity. The main thing was the presence of compounds of Beryllium 7, together with a range of unusual isotopes of elements with atomic weights up to 56. Not only that, there were substantial amounts of helium throughout the sample. These things are usually found where there have been nuclear fusion reactions.'

'Nuclear fission?'

'No, I said fusion. The end product of fusion is small stuff, like we found. The soil was moderately dangerous from a chemical viewpoint, and a little radioactive.'

'You say it was dangerous?'

'Well I wouldn't want to eat it, if that's what you mean.'

'Anything else I should know?'

'Yes, there was something really rather strange. We actually detected Boron 8. The amounts present were very low, but still detectable. The half-life of this isotope is 770 milliseconds, a long time by the standard of isotopes of that element, but still very short. There was just enough for us to detect.'

'Meaning?'

'The temperature of the sample, during whatever fusion reactions were taking place, was above 10,000,000 degrees.'

'That sounds hot.'

'It is, or was twice as hot as the surface of the sun. You had better get the Home Office down, Special Branch, MI6, the lot.'

—⚬—

Freya Sampson lived in a pleasant apartment block. Her neighbourhood was prosperous and populated by similarly professional people. It was 3 pm and she had intended to go the gymnasium for a swim and sauna. Having just changed into her tracksuit, she heard a knock on the front door and went to investigate. She had a chain on her front door, but removed it when she saw the two men outside, one of them a policeman in uniform. She asked for formal identification, was shown it by each of them and asked whether they could speak to her in private. She agreed and the small party was invited into her comfortable sitting room. Freya offered tea, which her guests declined, and she enquired of their purpose.

The plain-clothed officer, Briggs, said: 'We are sorry to disturb you, but we are here on a serious matter. You sent a sample of soil to be analysed by a forensics laboratory. Do we take it that your commission was on behalf of your employer?'

'Yes, it was. What exactly is your concern?'

'I expect you know that most of their case-work is related to toxicology, forensic biology, firearms and basic forensic chemistry?'

'Yes, of course. That's why I sent my sample to them.'

'Well, they also do work for the nuclear industry and they routinely check samples over for radio-emissions. Usually, their checks amount to nothing but in this case, there were traces of unusual chemicals present. They described the sample as being "worthy of more investigation". There are two difficulties here. We don't think you are guilty of any criminal activity, but we need to find out where your sample came from. We also want to get you checked over by the radiology department at the General Hospital. I am sorry to ask you this, but assuming you showered a while ago, can we arrange to check over your bathroom and other facilities while you are away?'

'Of course, but I'm surprised. Is there any risk?'

'We don't think so, but we were advised to make sure.'

'How long do they want me?'

'They said an afternoon. They want to carry out a whole body scan and will ask for samples of…I expect they meant the rest of the day, anyway.'

'Alright, but I'd like to pack a bag and make a couple of telephone calls first.'

'Certainly; you are not under arrest.'

Freya went to a bedroom where she made telephone calls to Callum Dood and her employer. Dood was surprised that their trip had ended on such a note and said, 'Perhaps I need to check my trainers?' There was a serious edge to his manner which she noted.

She replied, 'Perhaps I'll telephone when I get out.'

Back in her sitting room, she said, 'I'm ready now. Are you driving?'

Briggs replied, 'Actually, there's an ambulance waiting outside. We came in a car ourselves, but there was no siren or anything.'

Later, Freya was escorted through a labyrinth of tunnels at the local hospital. Briggs waited outside but the other officer had departed. She was given a chair and some tea, after which the radiology department completed its business. Later it got dark and she waited while staff muttered in a separate room. Finally, a doctor spoke to Briggs who then returned to see her.

Briggs said, 'You are clean, I'm pleased to say. Although you were exposed to dangerous chemical samples, most of the danger was contained in the small sample you sent away. There's nothing inside your body, anyway. Your shoes did have a few contaminants on them although the rest of your clothes and your home are clean. That is to say, they are now. And your friend the Reverend Dood, he volunteered to come in of his own free will. We looked him over too.'

'Can you take me home?'

'Certainly, but we want to ask you both not to return to the marks on the hillside until we have had a chance to cordon it off and clean it up. Someone mentioned something called Boron 8. I've no idea what that means, but our forensics chap said it was significant.'

'I don't think you need to worry about either of us going back there. And where is the Reverend anyway?'

'He's waiting outside.'

A police car drove them home. On the way back Dood said, 'I invited Adam around tomorrow. We quite often have a spot of lunch together. Can you come over too?'

She replied, 'Callum, you know I love your lunches; you can consider it a date!'

'Say about mid-day?'

'Yes, thank you.'

—m—

Freya Sampson arrived at midday and Adam Shilto a little after. She had come by taxi in the foreknowledge of his style of entertainment, whereas Shilto had less distance to come and had done so by bicycle. She had assumed their lunch would be a small party of three but Dood had invited Peter Pargeter also. A good host, Dood offered them a choice of sherry, beer or gin and tonic. He said to the others, 'I know Peter from my local chess club. I'm new there and Peter has offered to help me with that interesting mathematical picture I showed you.'

Pargeter had changed from his tweed suit to a tweed jacket of a different design, together with baggy green corduroy trousers. Despite his sedentary habit and a tendency to wheeze slightly, he looked the picture of comfort. He nodded and said, 'And I managed to enlist my friend at work. He does fancy things with mathematical symbolism. He was quite interested in your design and ran it through a computer.'

Dood said, 'Did he have any luck?'

'Yes, but I need something to drink before I can describe his findings.'

Dood sympathised and handed out drinks while they chatted in the comfort of his lounge. Pargeter had not yet met Shilto, but they took to each other well. They were both about the same age and had similar interests—albeit those outside work—travel, wine, music and in the case of Pargeter, chess. Shilto received an open invitation to the chess club and Pargeter to the amateur dramatic society.

Freya Sampson chatted to Dood about how clean and tidy the forensics people had left her apartment. She hoped he was not too perturbed by his own experience of them. They did not enlarge on the subject, however, due to a need for him to act as host. He said, 'I expect you are all starving and I've done something…well, I hope you like it. We shall find out!'

The others looked enthusiastic and their host led them into a large dining room. Pargeter said, 'You certainly have a lot of space to work in.'

'I know this place is too big for a single man but it does come with the job. I'm only a custodian, of course, and I do open it up for village functions.'

'Adam Shilto said, 'It has a lovely garden.'

'Certainly! In the autumn the lawns are full of penny buns and I collect a few to eat.'

'Penny buns?' said Freya.

'Yes, townies call them ceps, but anyone interested in the shires would use the old names. The French word is too…it lacks… whatever, they taste pretty good and I wouldn't want to spoil them with olive oil or garlic.'

'Callum is interested in conservation,' said Shilto. 'And if you like herbal lore, then this is the place to come.'

'And,' said Dood, pointing to some preserved butterflies in display cabinets on the wall, 'the more diverse the herbs, the happier the bees and butterflies.'

He returned from the kitchen and served up sausages and mash with fried onions. He said, 'Modest, but tasty!' The others tucked in and their host sent round a couple of bottles of a local red. He said, 'We're just getting there with the reds, don't you think?'

Pargeter swallowed a mouthful of sausage and mash and said, 'My colleague took a good look at your shape. Straight away, he wondered why I'd needed to ask him. He felt it was designed to test human intuition and didn't involve any calculation. Anyway, he looked at it with his intuitive eye and deciphered it in no time.'

Dood replied, 'Ah, human intuition. We cannot say why we understand things, but we do. Perhaps the part of the brain which solves mathematical problems is distinct and separate from the seat of consciousness!' The others nodded and avoided talking, their mouths full.

The wine circulated and Pargeter carried on chatting, while clearly enjoying lunch. He pulled a couple of pages of notes from his pocket, put his fork down for a minute and said, 'He said the radii are used to separate longer parts of the trailing line. Once he had established that, he said the rest was easy. The length of each section of trailing line was the significant factor and their measurements, together with other things such as the area of parts of the circle, gave two sets of numbers.' He looked at his notes again. 'I'm not sure why, but the first number was 17.1150.91.1793.'

'So what does it mean?'

'Hang on a minute, the circle also gave another number'—he

picked up the paper again—'and he seemed very pleased with it. He said it was a set of ratios thus: 0:7:4:0:4:8:0:4:8:9. I think he enjoyed the challenge to be honest.' He put the papers back in his pocket, took a sip of wine and suppressed the kind of splutter which comes from talking while eating. Then he said, 'It was this second lot of numbers which interested him. He popped them into his computer and the blasted machine said it was a representation of the Kepler conjecture.'

'The what?' said Shilto.

'He said it's how mathematicians describe the best way of packing spheres in three-dimensional space.'

'Eh?' said Shilto. He frowned, more attuned to the architecture of local churches than to spheres.

'If you pack tennis balls by dropping them in a box, or if they are shaken, they will take a position in which no more than 65% of the space is used up. Yet a closer packing can be attained by hand. This 'best' arrangement will utilise 74% of the volume, which is the Kepler's number I mentioned earlier.'

'But what's the point of it?'

'It tells you how best to stack cannonballs.'

'That's useful!'

'Even better, if atoms are stacked in different ways, the energies they contain are different. It could describe the energy given out when particles in crystals become randomised. Imagine the energy stored in a super-dense crystalline material. An alien spacecraft could use it as a way of storing energy until needed.'

There was silence until Freya said, 'None of us yet has spoken about spacecraft, so why suddenly that? And if it's as you say, could it be a message?' She looked around the table, noting each person's expression.

Pargeter smiled, 'Like a lot of people, I listen to local radio, and I do like your program, Freya. Everyone has heard about the lights and crop circles and that's why I mentioned spacecraft. But as far as the message goes, we already know about Kepler stacking, so I can't see the point.'

'Then maybe,' said Dood,'the Kepler conjecture, if so easily worked out, was just to show us that the circle contained mathematical logic. Having accepted *that*, then we would be more inclined to take the other number seriously. On that basis, the important thing would be the first number, not the Kepler conjecture.'

'I see your point,' replied Pargeter, 'but I would also point out that there are reports of some other crop circles containing the constant Pi and nothing else.'

'Then perhaps they also contained other information that was never spotted.'

'That's an interesting point.'

Adam Shilto said, 'Well that's given the game away! We all seem to be investigating alien spacecraft. To be honest, I'm pleased it's not ghosts!'

They had all known it, yet had not dared to say. But now that it was out at long last, they were all easy and unconstrained. They smiled, turned happily to their plates and topped up their wineglasses. Callum Dood asked them not to say anything interesting while he was out of the room. He jumped up, went out to the kitchen and brought back a massive steamed suet pudding with a sauce of hot golden syrup. It was full of fruit, sticky, and fortifying. They tucked in and the room was silent for about fifteen minutes.

Shilto said, 'What an amazing pudding!' He positively beamed. With effort, Dood left the room once more and returned with a large ripe Stilton cheese.

Freya said, 'Who needs a spacecraft when you've got one of these!'

Pargeter said, 'There's a lot of mathematics in a cheese like that!'

Freya added, 'It's magnificent! I doubt whether I shall be able to eat for another 48 hours!'

Dood said, 'Thank heaven it isn't a spaceship. We'd never get off the ground!' The conversation continued, accompanied by a clattering of plates.

Peter Pargeter finished first, and said, 'So, we are all engaged in the same quest. First, is all this stuff a hoax?'

Freya said, 'I certainly don't think my experience in the car was a hoax.'

Dood said, 'I don't think the crop circle was a hoax either.' They all agreed that it wasn't, and began to evaluate the evidence.

'With the circle,' said Dood, 'someone would have seen it. The farmer is out there every day. He would have seen people marking out the site or burning the ground. But it just appeared.'

Freya cleaned some syrup off her hair, ate a little Stilton and said: 'We dug up some soil and I had it analysed. The lab was worried about it, told the police and I was taken to the local hospital and checked over. They said I was OK but the policeman mentioned that the soil contained some strange chemicals. No casual mischief-maker could have obtained them. So it's either the government, or someone from over the rainbow.'

Shilto followed, 'So we agree that none of these things is a hoax. If they aren't, they must be real. And if so, they must have some purpose.'

Pargeter nodded and replied, 'But I think we need to deal with simple ideas. I don't think our visitors were trying to tell us much. We don't accept advice from people we don't know, or at least *I* don't. I think they just meant to give us evidence of their presence. That's why they sent us something simple. They sent us a message we could understand for what it is.'

The others ate cheese and finished their wine, happy to let Pargeter speak in his reasonable and logical way: 'So we need to look beyond the Kepler number. It's of no more use to us than the Pi we already know about. I think it's more likely that we need to understand that other piece of information which the circle contained.'

Conversation came to a stop in the face of the fact that none had more to offer about the crop circle. Dood stood up and said, 'Pop your plates on a pile and I'll deal with them later. Let's have a stroll around the garden.'

The others did as he suggested, and they strolled across a damp lawn towards a couple of pine trees. They reached a raised bed full of resinous sawdust, pine needles and crushed bark. A collection of large and noble-looking mushrooms was growing there. Dood said, 'This is the King Boletus, or penny bun. It is a lovely thing fried in butter and served on spaghetti, or baked in short crust pastry.' He pulled a cigarillo from his pocket and lit it, whereupon the air was fragrant with the smell of nutmeg.

Freya pointed and said, 'What's this other one?'

'Oh, *that* is Psilocybe cubensis, the Cuban magic mushroom. It started to grow here quite by accident. I had a bit of Cuban mahogany which I put outside and it must have had some spores on it. It's interesting to study. The butterflies seem to like it.'

Pargeter said, 'What exactly is that tobacco, Callum? I used to smoke Park Drive, but that seems a little more exotic?'

'Oh, it's just a little stimulant after a meal. It contains a substance called myristicin, which is an aid to reflection. Pretty mellow stuff anyway.'

Pargeter said, 'It seemed to turbocharge your chess game a while back!'

'Ah, that was something else!'

Talk returned to the markings on the down. 'So the Kepler number was only a calling card?' said Dood.

Pargeter replied, 'It seems reasonable to think so. They were probably trying to introduce themselves as intelligent and benign. Intelligent enough to message us with something we can understand; benign enough to cause no damage.'

'Yes, but I would never have guessed that you'd take an interest in a mystery like this!'

'I'd certainly take an interest if a mystery fell into my lap. And I wouldn't be surprised if they leave messages at intervals in case someone, someday, becomes knowledgeable enough to do something about it.'

The garden became colder as the sun disappeared behind cloud in the afternoon sky. It began to rain so they finished their stroll and returned with their host as he left to make tea. Then, with cups at the ready, they settled into armchairs in front of a log fire. After a while, Pargeter's cat appeared at the window and demanded to be let in. Immediately, he curled up in front of the fire in front of them.

Freya Sampson said, 'Briggs said they found something called Boron 8 on the hillside.'

Pargeter, who had been listening to Shilto, turned round and said, 'What did you say?'

'I said Boron 8.'

'Oh my Lord!'

'Well, tell us,' said Adam Shilto, who didn't seem to mind the loss of his audience.

Pargeter was silent for a while, and he looked around slowly, apparently lost for words. He took a sip of tea and spluttered a bit. Finally he said, 'It confirms all we thought, and it means your wish for a national radio slot'—he nodded to Freya—'has definitely borne fruit. If they found *that* on the hill, then for sure we are dealing with something not of this earth.'

Dood returned with a fresh teapot just in time to hear. He said, 'What?'

Pargeter said, 'A while back, I modelled something quite important for somebody equally important, and this came up in my study. Boron 8 has a half-life of milliseconds, so very large amounts must have been made for any measureable amount to have been found later.'

Adam Shilto said, 'Yes, but what is it?'

'It's a radioactive element made only in places that are astoundingly hot, and only by nuclear fusion reactions. Dammit, it means that nuclear fusion was taking place on the downs above our own little village. The temperature there must have been too hot for us to comprehend.'

Thus far, the four conspirators had been as polite as possible, with courteous gaps afforded in their conversation for those who wished to intervene, for tea to be passed around, and for various other civil interruptions. Yet with his statement Pargeter had changed matters so that his audience was on the edge of their seats, all civilities forgotten. They would certainly have ignored even the most polite intervention, as though the effect of the wine had suddenly passed.

Adam Shilto said, 'If this is all top-secret, then you needn't go on.'

'That's OK. I do work for physicists in defence industries, but the basic science is already in the public domain. I can tell you, straight out, that somebody was using fusion reactions to obtain huge amounts of energy, up there on the hillside. I expect that the release of energy was their prime purpose and that all the other evidence we found, the marks and all, were left behind to notify us of ...whatever their subsidiary intention was.'

'Huge amounts of energy?'

'Yes. And that might account for the massive amount of light released at the time. Then they were gone, leaving all this evidence behind.'

None of them minded Pargeter's monologue, and they continued to be spellbound as he continued thus: 'And all was quiet. If *we* had tried to do this, we should have needed a small atomic bomb just to set it off! We must be dealing with aliens, don't you see?'

'Not the Russians or Chinese?' said Dood.

'No. Like us, they would need nuclear fission to start a fusion reaction. They can do little bombs, but they *are* bombs, and it would still have flattened that hillside. So there were no Russians on these downs, no chance.'

'So what do we do?' Freya wondered whether she had at last been confronted by enough material for her scoop.

'Well I don't think we are in any danger. If they wanted us dead, then we would be gone by now.'

Shilto said, 'If they left us a message it's because they want to hear from us.'

'Yes,' said Dood. 'I think that's clear. But how can we do it and what should we say?'

Pargeter avoided answering Dood's question and said instead, 'We need to be careful. If this gets into the papers right now, or if we annoy MI6, then we might be in trouble. I'm sorry, Freya, I know you are investigating on behalf of your news program, but can you take it slowly for a while?'

'I am sure I can find something else to do,' said Freya, who had been thinking hard. 'In any case I don't think I'm anywhere near ready. I can't just say Boron 8 and hope for the best. I'd be laughed out, just like all the other cranks.'

Their host said, 'We had better meet again in a few days.'

'OK, call me when we've got some ideas,' said Freya.'

'Please can I come in on this?' said Pargeter, rather plaintively, 'It's right up my street!'

—∞—

They met a week later at Freya's place. Anxious to return Callum Dood's hospitality, she had invited them to an old fashioned Edwardian 'high tea,' complete with an Edwardian cake stand. Pargeter had said 'Good,' and 'UFO hunters always think better on a full stomach.' The others shared his opinion, and Freya liked to cook, the more so when she knew she would have appreciative company.

When they arrived, she gave her visitors a pot of a delightfully smoky tea while she joined in general discourse from the kitchen. There, she put finishing touches to cakes, scones, vol-au-vent and a genuine hot Welsh rarebit. Soon she said: 'Come to the table while it's at its best.'

Unfortunately Pargeter had managed to get gravy on his lapel at their last meeting, but he now wore yet another tweed jacket, and his enthusiasm for the pleasures of the table was undimmed. He beamed and said, 'Absolutely wonderful!' There was general agreement that if Freya were ever to give up her news program, she could make a fortune running a tea shop. They all agreed that her table was the 'equal of anything at the Ritz.'

Freya confirmed that although she had 'managed to fill her time with run-of-the-mill cases that week, it had not taken her mind off their meeting.' The others then agreed that they 'should now be able to decide what to do.' Meanwhile, Adam Shilto ate a piece of Welsh rarebit and smiled as the horseradish did its work.

From the kitchen Freya asked, 'What do you think of publicising the whole episode as it stands?' Then, without waiting for a repeat of Pargeter's previous comment on the matter she followed, 'Think about it. If our visitors came with a view to making contact, then surely they didn't intend to meet the four of *us*. But if everything got into the news they might be induced to meet our leaders instead.'

Shilto said, 'I can see it might be pointless speaking to a vicar or an archdeacon.'

Dood followed, 'I can't see that anything would happen. That field on the downs has been cordoned off now and I think they had a bulldozer on it. MI6 already knows about the radioactivity and no news article would make any difference. They wouldn't actually do any more than we can, in fact probably less.'

'In that case,' said Shilto, 'we should do something ourselves. It's as much our business as anyone else's. But we need a few ideas on how to go about it.'

'I know another guy,' said Pargeter. 'He does my computers and he's interested in this stuff although he has no idea that I know. He was in the papers a while back. He hacked into some defence computers looking for UFOs. That's why I use him. I need security and he's the best.'

Freya said, 'I could go and see him with my journalist's hat on.'

'Good idea. I had better telephone him first though.'

—w—

Two days day later, David Elliott was getting ready for his trip to the United States when, quite unexpectedly, he received a text message from Meredith. It said, 'Are you free?' He replied in the affirmative and there was a delay of about a minute before his telephone rang. Meredith seemed to want to confide in Elliott although that did not alter his tendency to formality. 'Mr Elliott, it's Meredith here. How are you getting on?'

'Fine, thank you. I'm off to the United States soon. I hope to chase up that name you gave me.'

'Well, be careful.'

'As always, but why say that now?'

'I get the feeling I'm being investigated again.'

'Have you seen anyone?'

'No, but when you've been there before, you become familiar with the feeling. And I know I had someone in the house.'

'How?'

'I've been bugged. They are hard to spot because they are voice-activated and only switch on when someone speaks nearby. Then they transmit. But I happen to own a GSM bug detector that can detect a signal.'

'Don't tell me, it beeped.'

'It did. The point is that it only appeared after your visit. It was probably a result of my seeing you. So they must know about you as well.'

'Who exactly are *they*?'

'It might be some government agency, MI6 perhaps, but which one I have no idea.'

'Could it be a US agency? And if it is, are they just eavesdropping, or do they intend something worse?'

'I can't say for certain, but they both probably know that something is happening. Just mind how you go.' Elliott replaced the phone and considered cancelling his trip, but he dismissed the thought immediately. He was a cautious individual but had been fortified by the good luck message from Burgess. And besides, he had bought his ticket. It was too late to back out, whatever he felt. That evening he went out with a friend and they had an early dinner followed by a visit to the theatre. He tried to keep conversation away from his work but it was clear he was somewhat distracted. Eventually, his companion asked about his forthcoming flight.

'I get a flight from Heathrow to Toronto Pearson. There's a short stopover and then a connecting flight to Pittsburgh. At least I've got aisle seats so I can pace up and down.'

'And then?'

'I can hire a car at the airport, just for a few days. Then I shall have some more contacts to see in Pennsylvania and possibly in other states on the east coast.'

'OK, so where do we reach you?'

'On my mobile; it works over there. But if not, then try the Fairmont. It's supposed to be nice and I expect to be there for three or four days before moving on. Or I might stay longer.'

'Not going west, then?'

'No plans just yet.'

Elliott had brought a couple of paperbacks to read on the plane. The flight went well and he hired a car at the airport, drove to the city and booked into his hotel. Then he went straight to bed and slept for twelve hours. The following morning he had a light breakfast and made a telephone call from his room. 'Hi, this is David Elliott. We exchanged emails.'

'Sure, the English guy.'

'I'm in town and would like to see you.'

'That's OK. Come to my shop; I work in Shadyside.'

'Is it easy to find?'

'Yeah. You got the address? I'm just off South Highlands Avenue.'

It took Elliott about an hour to get there, find a place to park and walk to Bud Lynch's Computer store. It was a double-fronted shop, unusually dark inside for an American store, and with a large workshop at the back. Lynch emerged: a big man, wearing oversize clothes. His tee-shirt proclaimed "I beat anorexia" and he perspired freely in the heat and humidity. There was a pervading smell of heat and diesel from the buses outside.

Lynch waved Elliott through to his workshop, which contained many reviews and recommendations pasted to the wall. He was working on a machine and it lay open on the bench. Next to it was a full-sized pizza in its box, which he eyed hungrily.

He said 'Coffee? And by the way everyone calls me Lynch.'

'Great, that's OK and fine, thank you. And don't let me stop your breakfast.'

'Thanks.' Lynch poured two coffees, offered Elliott a slice of pizza which he declined, and then chewed thoughtfully on a piece himself. He said, 'You've come a long way.'

'Yes, I have.' He showed him his press cards. 'I've spoken to Meredith and I think we can get a sizeable story into circulation. That seems to be what like-minded people want.'

'Yes, but why didn't you just Skype an interview with me?'

'Meredith asked me that, too. It's because I've got something to show you and because journalists can't work like that. And he seemed to think you might get quite a few who want to chat, and that you may have to look out for security people.'

'And the object he mentioned, I suppose it's a kind of calling card?'

'I suppose you could say so.'

'Well, I guess you had better show me what he wanted me to see.'

Elliott retrieved his disc-like object, which looked an opalescent grey in the subdued light.

'You got this through customs?'

'There was no difficulty. I just said it was an engineering part, which is probably true anyway. The guy tapped it and weighed it. It was clearly not going to explode.'

'Just a minute.'

He took the object and placed it on a small balance, which promptly registered 5 grams. Then with difficulty he immersed the object in water, a step which caused a small amount to be displaced into a nearby container. He said, 'My goodness, 10 cm^3. That makes a density of half a gram per cm^3. The nearest we can get to that today is just under 1. Let's see what else it can do.'

Lynch, a very powerful man, tried to bend it, and as had been the case at Meredith's place, there was no result. He was barely able to grip it with his fingers, and when it inevitably fell to the floor, it failed to bounce or make any kind of noise as though it had absorbed all the energy of impact. Carefully, he turned it over in both hands and said, 'What a beauty.'

He started to moderate his voice so that he became more difficult to hear. He also angled his head, smiled and rolled his eyes around the four walls in a gesture which Elliott took to mean that he too should take care with what he said.

Lynch seemed genuinely enthusiastic about the object: 'Our strongest and lightest metals are the closed cell or syntactic metal foams. They are very rigid but none have this very low density. And I doubt whether even they are as strong as this. Also it has almost no friction at all. Where did it come from?'

'Meredith got it from someone else on the Network. He said it came from the Roswell site in '47. Is it the real thing? He suggested you could tell me a lot more about more general matters.'

'I can, but not right now. I think you need to go away and hide it. Let's do dinner tonight instead.'

Elliott was puzzled but said only, 'Yes, I expect you are busy right now. Where do you want to meet?'

'Here.' Lynch wrote down a name and address on a piece of paper. Elliott took it and read 'The Medina, South Highland Avenue'. He was just about to repeat it when Lynch placed a finger over his lips and said, 'Trust me. I'll book a table for 7 pm. I don't want to talk here for any longer than necessary. Leave your car at the hotel and get a taxi.'

He nodded in agreement and walked out into the street. As he left, Lynch tinkered with a computer with one hand and ate more pizza with the other.

Elliott had the better part of the day to fill. He returned to his hotel and made a makeshift hiding place for the disc in the lining of his suitcase. It was amateurish but better than nothing. Then he decided to spend a few hours looking around the downtown area. He ended up at Point State Park, where he walked around, enjoying the exercise. A wind whipped up a spray from the fountain and flung it towards him as he admired the handiwork of the gardeners nearby. The air was cooler there and clean, and with his mind refreshed he found it easier to consider his conversation with Lynch. The crowds seemed to drift by without noticing him and walking on, he soon reached a main thoroughfare where he bought a few small presents and had lunch in a salad bar. Then he bought copies of the New York Times and Washington Post and read them back at his hotel. Resting and thinking, he drank tea and pondered. Lynch hadn't wanted to speak openly at his own premises. Yet he wasn't particularly busy, was his own man and able to close his business whenever he chose. Elliott thought he had the same secretive manner as Meredith, and made a mental note to ask about surveillance in the US.

Later, Elliott dressed casually and took a taxi rather than his car. His attire, still, was more formal than is usual in an American late summer. He was positively encouraged to accept a business card from the driver, who indicated that he would be 'around Shadyside' at whatever time he might be needed, later on.

Avoiding Lynch's premises Elliott made for the Medina Restaurant, a smart place that advertised as a Mediterranean kitchen and wine bar. Keen to investigate this thesis, he entered exactly on the dot of 7 pm and found Lynch at the bar. Lynch waved him over. He had been drinking sparkling water for a while and was keen to try something a little stronger. He said, 'I fancy a cocktail. What would you like?'

'Thanks for inviting me. As far as ordering is concerned, I hope you don't mind if I place myself in your hands.'

Lynch called the waiter and gave an order; and to Elliott he said, 'You will like this, it's pretty easy to soak up!' The cocktail arrived and Elliott had to agree. It was a delicious blend and just what a traveller needed. He began to relax a little and asked why Lynch had suggested meeting there. Lynch said without hesitation, 'I believe I am being watched and bugged. This has gone on for quite a while.'

'How do you know?'

'I get a particular kind of radio interference. I bet they don't know that I can tell, but I easily recognise the symptoms. I've never managed to find anything that might cause it, but I expect it's only a pea-sized bug under a floorboard.' He paused, 'And there are people too. There's a small truck with antennae.'

'So how do you know they can't hear us here?'

'I don't, but they would need to bug every restaurant in Shadyside to do that.'

'And maybe they sent me?'

'I did think of that, but I know Meredith. He's straight and if I had to trust anyone, it would be somebody sent by him. Similar business, same interests.'

'But why would they want to bug you? And who are 'they' anyway? All this bugging, that's exactly what *he* talked about.'

Lynch paused to take a further sip at his cocktail. Elliott thought that he carried his drink well. Lynch followed in a considered manner: 'Some of your questions are easy to answer. First, my former employer was NASA and they are a suspicious lot. When I was with them, I was in materials science. I have no doubt they keep an eye on former employees and their activities are probably not limited to me. I always understood that their interest was precautionary and benign, but then I started to notice a bit more intrusiveness. Maybe they are interested in you too, and Meredith also; and maybe the CIA are in on it. There's no doubt that they monitor the Network.'

'What could they want from me?'

Lynch said, 'That metal disc, for one. Make sure you hide it away.' He finished his cocktail. 'But I feel a bit easier about speaking more openly here. You saw that I couldn't break it. It was incredibly light, almost frictionless and it absorbed all the energy produced by falling. There was no bounce, no noise.'

Elliott nodded and let him continue. 'But there were other materials too. I have seen a similar object start to spin in a strong magnetic field. One time I crushed an engineered structure in the palm of my hand and saw it spring back into its exact former shape. It was better than the best shape memory alloys we make today. And these things were taken from the Roswell site in '47. You really did get it from Meredith?'

'I did.'

'Okay. The CIA was too slow and a whole load of bits and pieces disappeared from the Roswell site before they got there. It was before my time, but their efforts to clean up suggested a massive institutional panic. They went over the place with a fine tooth-comb, and they also removed all the topsoil from the site over a wide area and intimidated everyone in sight. If Roswell was really only a crashed weather balloon, then why would they do that? And that brings me to their bugging activities. They may know you have a piece of the action. If so, they will want it in case it's something new.'

In an intentionally deadpan manner Elliott said, 'So I take it that you actually believe in UFOs?'

Lynch looked shocked. 'Hell yes! Why do you think there's bugging going on?'

He relaxed again when the waiter brought some menus over. The waiter was informal and said, 'Bud, do you fancy the cheese tasting today?'

Lynch waved the question over to Elliott, who said, 'No, I'd like to go straight into an appetiser, please.'

Lynch nodded, but ordered some olives and baba ghanoush 'to give me the energy to choose.' It seemed to work well because he opted for tuna tartare, which came with shallots, celery leaves, lemon emulsion, crème fraîche, caviar and grilled focaccia. Elliott chose charred octopus with fennel, citrus, parsley, prosciutto and a sherry gastrique. The waiter nodded in approval and wrote things down while they considered what was to follow.

An amiable host, Lynch recommended and Elliott accepted his suggestion of a red pepper casereccia with seared sea scallops, crab, roasted garlic and parsley butter. Each dish was notable for the diligence with which it was described by the waiter, and as Lynch said, by the skill with which it was prepared by the chef. It was some time since Elliott had met anybody as enthusiastic as Lynch at the dinner table and he felt that Lynch might have dined there regardless of the need for any private meeting.

The waiter indulged Lynch with more time, but eventually departed with his order for filet mignon with creamed corn and a confit of carrots, and with forest mushrooms, serrano chillies, oregano, 'moody blue' and quince jus. However the waiter needed to replace his pencil midway through writing down the requisition, which demanded a complete repeat of the order. There were gestures of appreciation from Lynch as he did so, and he was as lyrical as any musician while describing moody blue, not as a form of music, but in fact a blue cheese.

Having been shown to their table, they ate quietly and with concentration. Soon, Lynch seemed to relax as though gradually ascending after a dive in the sea. A metaphorical arm broke through a languid surface as he pushed his chair back a few inches and began to view his companion again. Elliott whistled and said, 'That was magnificent.'

Lynch nodded with pleasure and it was clear that he had found a new respect for his companion, who had at least kept pace with him. 'So,' he said, 'I was saying that yes, I really do believe in UFOs. But there are people around we have to watch out for. And there is also top-end research into the subject going on as we speak.'

'Research?'

'You bet. But I'm a materials man. They watch me because I left to do my own thing. The computers are just to earn a living.'

'They watch you always?'

'They know when there's any activity. The guys are CIA, but from a special section with a nasty man in charge. I've not met him of course, but I've heard about the disappearances and the unlucky ones who have tangled with him. And the previous nasty guy was replaced by an equally nasty guy when the first one retired. Rumour has it that the first one knew too much and didn't last long after he left. So you can see how I feel myself.'

'So what's the aim of this particular section?'

'They aim to cover up all discussion on the subject. They want to keep it out of the papers unless it can be made an object of derision. They want any technical advance to be used only in the US defence industry: in bioweapons, flight, power sources, medicines; anything that will give the US an advantage in military power, wealth or technical prowess.'

Elliott replied, 'Meredith said the Network is alive right now. He said there's something really big. But he didn't know quite what. Perhaps you know?'

Lynch's tone of voice was its own encouragement. 'I've also heard that. I can take you to people doing work on unusual forms of powered flight. It's interesting, and I know a guy in Cleveland. It takes a few hours to get there by Greyhound. But the big buzz is about something very big in the DNA line. I'm the wrong guy to speak to about that, but once again, I *can* introduce you to the people who know about it.'

'What, a local man?'

'Sure. We're not as parochial here as you might suppose. There is a lot of state-of-the art research into that subject going on in this city.'

'Can I see your man in Cleveland and then the other guy?'

'Sure. I'll set it up. Give me a day or two.'

—⁂—

Within the secret world of the CIA, Walter Stein held a modest post but in fact he commanded a considerable budget and an entire office of at least a hundred field agents. His responsibilities were therefore considerable. A few hours before Bud Lynch ordered butterscotch pot de crème with Chantilly cream and candied cashews, Stein sat in a late meeting with a few of his staff, in which he gave a brief summary of recent developments. He was always polite and courteous, but they were aware that he had a dark and petulant side and were careful to be attentive.

Stein said, 'I hear that Lynch has met a journalist called David Elliott. Our surveillance has suggested that he had with him an unidentified material.' (All knew well that particular euphemism for a material of extra-terrestrial origin.)

'Sir, should we apprehend him?' said an experienced surveillance agent.

Stein said, 'Not now. I have a feeling we are about to open a very considerable can of worms. We shall want the UM in due course, but I don't want to disturb Lynch or Elliott right now. They are just about to link into their contacts in a big way and I think that Lynch may be about to introduce Elliott to the molecular biologists. There is one called Dorkin who is too much the scientist to give a damn about our concerns. But one of our agents, a woman called Carmen van Brouin works for him. She gave us a whole load of information about Dorkin's recent trip to South Africa. In fact, almost everyone in that department is either doubling up for us or has had their grant agreed because of us.'

The agent said, 'In that case why don't we arrest Dorkin?'

Stein replied, 'Because he's the real expert we need. He may not be totally tame, but we still need to retrieve the data from our case and are certain to need him again in future. Our material was sent to his laboratory to analyse and I want to get the data back without difficulty. We would be foolish to have to enlist yet another scientist and be presented with the same security concerns. For that matter I don't want the original remains to escape either.'

'You mean the Roswell remains?'

'I do. They've been under liquid nitrogen for the last seventy-five years. We want them back when he's analysed them.'

Discussion continued for a while and it was then Stein's practice to release his staff, who trooped out gratefully. That evening, he perspired over a report for the head of the CIA and the President, intended for use in a meeting that had been arranged to take place two days hence. The meeting was to be held in Washington, where Stein knew he would be faced with a barrage of questions concerning Dorkin and Lynch. In due course, he sat at a table with a secretary and the head of the CIA while they waited for the President, who was exactly on time. The meeting started, and despite his misgivings, Stein appeared calm and collected. He gave an appraisal of the priorities of his work and the significance of current research in various clandestine technologies. The President then said, 'What exactly is different today from 'research' that has already been carried out over many years?'

'We always keep an eye on reports of UFOs, the appearance of extra-terrestrials, and any suggestion that advanced technology may have surfaced. There has been some over the years, but we have usually managed to keep a lid on it.'

'And what else?'

'Our own technology—molecular biology—has advanced a lot in recent years. We can now evaluate specimens from crashes like Roswell. We're watching a scientist called Dorkin, who is clever and useful, and we are also funding him, although he may not realise it. He's the kind of guy who can make hybrids and chimeras which may be of use to us. But there are other things I have to keep my eyes on. In particular, although a little UFO technology has surfaced over the years, recently it seems to have increased from a trickle to a flood. It's getting difficult to cover up.'

The President nodded and replied, 'Where does this new advanced technology come from?'

Stein said, 'It seems to start from Central America and drift northwards, a bit like the narcotics trail. Perhaps we need a wall of some kind.'

'No, we want that stuff to come in: the technology that is.'

'Sure, but chiefly we want to know about the source. It must be coming from somewhere. And there are reports of strange electrical storms over Mexico, together with brilliant lights in the sky. I mean huge emissions over an area of twenty miles. They only last for a few seconds or so. Everyone says lightning, but we think otherwise.'

'I don't like that in our own backyard. If something is going on I want to know what it is. How's the budget?'

'Well of course I could always use more agents.'

'And what would you do with them?'

'Apart from the usual domestic surveillance, I want to send some agents down to Mexico to look around. Van Brouin has to do whatever Dorkin wants. I expect that he will eventually look for artefacts down there; perhaps investigate the DNA too. And if he's successful it could be a revelation.'

'What's he going to do if he finds what he's looking for?'

'He will probably try to make a hybrid with the Roswell sample. And I bet he thinks that *I* have no morals.'

'OK watch him and make sure it all runs smoothly.'

—⁓—

Elliott and Lynch took a bus northwest towards the great lakes. It was still very hot and humid outside, but it was air-conditioned and so Elliott was discomforted, not from the climate, but from sitting next to the considerable girth of his companion. Lynch looked at the scenery for a while and then opened a box of Twinkies, which he continued to eat until they were all gone, whereupon he fell asleep for at least an hour.

The bus took three hours to reach Cleveland, where they stopped at a grey box-like building. Moving outside, they were accosted by one or two street vendors but Lynch soon hailed a taxi and supplied the driver with an address written on paper. They passed through a city centre that had many tall buildings; a dozen of them genuine skyscrapers, but it was not a very large city like Chicago.

Eventually the taxi entered a suburb which Lynch described as Little Italy, an area of attractive-looking shops and restaurants. A little farther on was an area of large Victorian-style villas, many of them divided into separate apartments. Another half-mile brought them to an estate of prefabricated industrial units behind an aluminium security fence, together with space for several parked cars. One unit bore the nameplate: *'Mann Flight, Commercial Robotics,'* together with some telephone numbers. Lynch pressed a button, was invited to identify himself via an intercom, and they were ushered in by a very personable personal assistant and offered coffee in an anteroom. Shortly an intercom rang and a voice asked that they be brought to the office of the principal.

Bailey T. Mann rose from his chair and shook hands with them both. He was an individual of informal disposition, without a tie, and with a jacket hanging from the back of his chair. His short-sleeved, part-buttoned shirt revealed an excellent suntan and he displayed the quick movements of the practised sportsman. Lithe and sharp, his contrast with Lynch was profound, yet they were familiar in each other's company.

Lynch said, 'This is David Elliott from England, a journalist looking at advanced technology.' His eyes met those of Mann as he spoke, and an understanding passed between them.

'Okay,' said Mann. He made polite enquiries about Elliott's journey. Then he said, 'Bud has told me how much you know. He trusts you implicitly, which is saying something these days. Let me show you my laboratory.' He picked up a white coat and put it on. The other two followed him through a door behind his desk and they entered a large laboratory that was air-conditioned to the point of distress: cold, deionised, filtered, clean and aseptic.

The laboratory contained ten people working at the bench using CNC controlled lathes and various machine tools. There was a hum, and nobody looked at them. Mann said, 'We design and make control systems and engineering parts for aircraft, helicopters and robots. But I expect you want to see the good stuff.'

They followed Mann to the far end of the room and through a door. Beyond was another laboratory of large size, but with only two people and most of the area given to space. It contained several machines which looked as though they were built to test various principles of flight. Those present welcomed them; Mann made comments about their work and asked whether they could see a demonstration. Elliott could see that the manner of all those present was egalitarian; they replied firmly and without deference.

Mann said to Elliott, 'Let's see the rest for a minute while they set things up.' They strolled around further, looking at part-assembled machinery standing on the floor or on the workbench. All was technical and thoroughly proficient.

'Look at this here,' said Mann, approaching a small aircraft on a bench. It was light: made of balsa wood and had a series of aerofoil wings. He said, 'You've heard of biplanes, well this is a decaplane. At the front of the machine you can see a naked wire: it has a charge of +25,000 volts. At the back, the wing itself is negatively-charged. The wire at the front will ionise nitrogen in the air, and the ions naturally migrate in the electrical field between the two electrodes. The flow of ions over the aerofoil creates lift. It's a good model system for motive force in a craft driven ionically.'

One of the white-coated researchers lifted the craft and flicked a switch on it. Giving the machine a gentle push, it flew in a circle for about 60 seconds before alighting gently. He said, 'That's a first. I adjusted the tail to give it a circular path.'

Mann nodded and looked approving. Lynch said, 'So how relevant is that to spacecraft?'

'We can never be sure when things will be useful. The use of ionic currents to create flight was first described a couple of years ago, but we have developed it further because we want to see whether it can power larger flying machines.'

Lynch said, 'Well, is there any evidence at all that the same principle could apply to a UFO?'

'There may be. We know that some reports described saucers as making a crackling sound, while having an electrical disturbance at the edge. The air around them also smelled of ozone, which is made by an electrical discharge. Ergo, flying saucers could utilise the same principle. The rim could have an enormously high voltage to make ozone from oxygen. We smell ozone as a result.'

Lynch replied, 'So flying saucers produce lots of static electricity?'

'Exactly, that's why we are looking at it. If *those* guys use a system like this, then rest assured it's a system with potential.'

'So this back room is really a large hobby room?'

'It is, and maybe I'm a powered flight fanatic. But I'm not stupid; the business can afford to do research on things like this and believe me, if we make something work, it will make millions.'

Elliott was quiet. He just about understood some of the principles, and was captivated by the enthusiasm of Mann, who spoke without inhibition. He asked what he hoped was a serious question and was pleased by how it was received: 'If an ionic wind has to pass over an aerofoil, could the shape of the edge of the saucer: curved above and flat below, create lift?'

'We did think of that,' said Mann, 'but we doubt it. Another principle might be a pressure effect at a trailing edge. On one side, oxygen is changed to ozone. This requires an enormous electrical discharge. The chemistry tells us that the number of particles must fall: there is less ozone than oxygen, which creates a pressure drop at that position so the craft is pushed forwards.'

Elliott said, 'But do you believe it?'

Mann said, 'Not quite, but ideas can be tested. Eventually one will work.'

Lynch said, 'Not that one, it's just too low-tech. How could it work in space? Don't forget, there would be no gas to ionise. And how do they hover?'

Mann sighed, 'I thought you'd say that, but there may be spin-offs!'

'And if it's neither of these, then is there anything else better?'

'Sure there is. Look at this. We call it our elementary force module. It's there, at the back.'

They were ushered towards the back of the laboratory, a slow process because on the way, Mann asked to see demonstrations of various miniaturised machines, some like helicopters, that had the capability of flight. He said, 'These designs are used to develop miniaturised robotics.' Eventually, they reached their destination, a far workbench, beside which was a large centrifuge on wheels. It was of very strong construction and designed to spin a container at its edge. It was painted with the initials EFM, and Mann regarded it with considerable appreciation. He said, 'No spins right now, but this definitely has considerable potential.'

'Okay,' said Lynch, 'tell us!'

'Well, I would draw your attention to what flying saucers are supposed to be like. That in itself could be the main clue to how they work. Some reports suggest that they behave like gyroscopes, just on the edge of stability, and are able to fly off at high speeds. They are obvious candidates for some kind of gyroscopic drive.'

'A what?'

'Consider this. What if they contain a centrifuge inside, rotating at a very high speed? It would need a large radius and would have to rotate a very great mass. What would happen if it suddenly stopped rotating, or if it were able to make the mass spend more time in one part of the circumference?'

''That's easy.' Lynch smiled. 'It would fly off in one particular direction.'

'Sure it would,' said Mann. 'But whereas our centrifuge has metal arms, I imagine the saucer having some kind of internal force to control the spinning mass. And I imagine the mass spinning through a sphere, not a circle.'

'You would have a gyroscopic drive, with the craft driven by inertia.'

'Thank you. And now, imagine a very large mass indeed. We are currently experimenting with osmium metal, which has a density twice that of lead. But I mean really dense: what's the densest thing you can think of?'

'The contents of a black hole?'

'Well yes. Or a piece of neutron star! Imagine if our aliens had *that*. Perhaps they have found a way to contain an object of immense mass. A teaspoonful of dead neutron star would weigh about a billion tons. And it they can accelerate such a thing, then perhaps they use it to bend time and space.' He sighed: 'We can only imagine the forces involved. It may be a long shot, but it's worth a punt anyway.'

They eventually returned to Mann's office, where he called for iced tea. Then he said, 'So you see, David, we have the resources to do something interesting. This may only be a personal hobby and I can't predict the outcome as far as my business is concerned, but Bud knows how I feel. I've been keen on UFOs for as long as he has.'

Lynch said, 'Well, your work is the nearest to that *big thing* we know we are missing. David had already heard about photon capture, but it isn't the answer. These alien guys, they travel vast distances at high speeds. Eventually, one of your ideas will be the right one.'

'Thanks,' said Mann. He mused sadly: 'But all these ideas require vast amounts of energy...'

The conversation came to a natural halt. Then, with his personal comfort in mind, Lynch said, 'Time is getting on, its 4 o'clock already. I know a hotel, but can you suggest a place we can eat?'

'I was just about to invite you to be my guests. You must stay at my house tonight. We can go out to Little Italy if you like traditional Italian food.'

Later, Mann was amiable and indulgent, his pocket easily encompassing the demands of his hospitality. At a restaurant Elliott found it easy to relax, and the pace of the occasion was dictated more by the moderate Mann than by the immoderate Lynch. Their talk returned to the Network, to space travel and to propulsion in space. Elliott said, 'Your business is for the most part a micro-engineering company?'

'Sure it is. I employ ten scientists in research here in Cleveland, and I also have a manufacturing facility the other side of town. It's a proper business, not just a hobby. And we have some big clients.'

Lynch said, 'Bailey and I go back a long time to when we were both at NASA. We have this common interest so we stayed in touch. And we are both members of the Network.'

'Yeah,' said Mann. 'But I always try to stay below the threshold of public interest. Bud vouched for you, but some of the work I do here is, let us say, better kept out of the public eye.'

'I'm told,' said Elliott, 'that NASA is building a photon-capture device. Why that if it's a bit low-tech?'

'It is low-tech. It may take us to Mars one day, but I don't think there's anything more in it. The same can be said for our decafoil: it will work in our atmosphere, but I'm realistic about its likely application elsewhere. That's why we are also looking at other things.'

Mann continued: 'I guess that now's the time to air it all. We can come up with ideas about making a spaceship move in space, but the problem is the energy required. As we accelerate towards light speed, which is necessary for these colossal distances, the energy necessary would increase towards the infinite. So these craft need great amounts of energy.'

'Fission reactions?' said Lynch, chewing thoughtfully.

'No. The conversion of mass to energy is too small. All the fissile material you could load onto a giant spaceship wouldn't be near enough.'

'Then what about the fusion of matter and antimatter? Every bit of mass is converted into energy.'

'Antimatter is difficult to make,' said Mann. 'I know they made it at CERN, so it's feasible. They kept a small amount in a kind of magnetic capsule, contained by electrical and magnetic fields. They managed to make antihydrogen and they kept it for a few minutes. But I still can't see *aliens* using that'—Elliott looked up at the word—'when they could do something a lot easier.'

'So,' said Lynch, 'Tell me, what's a lot easier?'

'Black holes: I mentioned them earlier.' Then he said to a waiter, 'Please can I have some more French dressing?'

An abstemious individual, Mann took a mouthful of crab salad and washed the food down with tonic water. He was sober and completely in earnest. He said, 'They are the only suitable source for all the energy needed. A 600,000 tonne black hole would give out enough energy to accelerate that mass to 10% of the speed of light in three weeks.'

'So how does it work?'

'Black holes emit Hawking radiation, which like rays of light, will give a push. You could place a black hole next to a parabolic reflector; the radiation would push it along. Or the front of a craft could be designed to absorb short-wave radiation while other wavelengths pass out at the back. That, too, would give a push.'

He finished a few more pieces of crab salad, but seemed more animated by his conversation than by the prospect of continuing to eat: 'It's a great idea and has many advantages over matter-antimatter fusion as an energy source. Sure, making and containing one would be difficult'—'he pushed his plate aside—'a black hole here on earth would end up at the centre of the earth straight away. But for an advanced civilisation those are developmental problems'—he smiled—'and the thing is, we understand at least some of the theory behind it. Once contained, it wouldn't blow up, and any mass which fell into it would be released later as still more energy.'

Elliott and Lynch exchanged glances. They were impressed by his sheer enthusiasm. He could almost be said to be fanatical, tolerating no distractions, but he was not in any way hermit-like. Elliott wondered how he might write Mann's story and what its effect would be on Burgess and their readers. What exactly would he be free to include? He hoped that Mann's enthusiasm would not be lost when the article was written. And now he was quite sure that the case would develop further. What, however, would be the outcome of his impending introduction to Lynch's 'DNA contact?'

They drew towards the conclusion of their meal and conversation turned to other matters. Mann asked about Elliott's job and his work in London. Later, after a stroll and a visit to a bar where Mann once again drank only tonic water, they took a taxi to his house and watched a couple of films.

The following morning Lynch briefly mentioned the 'DNA line back home,' and Mann asked to be kept informed. Then Lynch and Elliott made their farewells and embarked on their return journey. For most of the way they were deep in thought; Lynch was absorbed to the point that he did not to want to picnic, while Elliott was even more determined to create a blockbuster of a story and began to make a few notes on paper. When they parted Elliott renewed his request for the next interview and Lynch again asked him to telephone a day or two later.

—⁓—

Nearly four thousand miles to the east, Guy Meredith received a telephone call at his home. He was busy and let the instrument ring for a while. When eventually he picked it up he half-expected to hear Elliott phoning from the United States, but in fact it was a woman's voice at the other end: 'Mr Meredith?'

'Speaking.'

'I wonder whether you still talk to reporters these days? I'm a reporter with a local radio station. We cover south-west Oxfordshire and Wiltshire. I'm interested in your experiences and wonder whether I could set up a meeting?'

'No connection with the government or defence?'

'None. Why do you say that?'

He thought: 'I'm getting too much trouble for them. They're probably after a sting.' Instead he said, 'Just curiosity. You're the second journalist to say that in a month.'

'Let me come and see you, please. We have a mutual acquaintance, a Mr Peter Pargeter, who thinks highly of you, and I of him.'

'Yes, I know him. Alright, when?' He dismissed any uncharitable thoughts immediately.

A week later, Freya Sampson sat down in the Meredith's front room and said, 'Peter said I should telephone you. We got to know each other very recently. As I suggested, I'm a reporter with a magazine-style news program on the local radio.'

'Ok, so what can I do for you?'

'It's a very interesting time at the moment. A lot of local people have been talking about unidentified flying objects and more particularly, unexplained lights, crop circles and power failures. I have been following things up and that's how I came across Peter.'

'I'm surprised! I thought I'd covered my tracks as far as he was concerned.'

'He thinks you may have a bit of experience there. Do you believe in UFOs?'

Meredith replied, 'I seem to have been asked that question many times. The answer is certainly, yes I do.'

'I hope you don't mind, but I looked you up. You seem to be well-known for such ideas these days. How long have you believed in them?'

'I guess it started when I was a kid. Over the years I did a bit of research on the subject—it can be done—and I got the feeling that the whole thing was being covered up. That alone made it very likely it was real. I can't see anyone covering up a myth.'

'So you did some work on it?'

Meredith appeared uncomfortable and shifted in his chair. 'You could certainly put it like that. I tried to find out about it and I upset a few people. You had better be careful or you may make the same mistake.'

Freya was aware that Meredith would soon ask about her own experience, so she felt it better to show willing and raise the subject first. She said, 'I've seen some of the evidence myself, so I don't have the usual scepticism. We got Peter to look at some of it, and he's been a great help from a general scientific viewpoint. We think we may be onto a message of some kind and we would like to send one back. We don't know how to do it, and that's why Peter gave me your name. We were also concerned that our visitors might not be friendly.'

Meredith smiled, 'Yes, Peter's a clever guy. I'm flattered that he remembered me.'

'Yes. And by the way, *are* they friendly?'

'Up to a point. They are benign in their general attitude towards us and our lovely blue planet. They have no intention of destroying us or we would be long gone. But they wouldn't take kindly to a fighter plane armed with rockets, too near one of their own craft. They would probably view it as a danger and act first.'

Freya said, 'They left marks in a field. Peter found that it contained some kind of mathematical constant. And there were other strange things: there was radioactivity and some marks made by very great temperatures. He said they were caused by some kind of localised nuclear fusion. Call it a crop circle if you wish, but it wasn't made by the usual croppies with cider and a Land Rover. And there were strange lights and power failures. What do you think?'

She was speaking from experience. Meredith felt comfortable with the truth and his reply was as frank as he could muster: 'I think they leave little tests around in order to gauge our response to various kinds of stimulus. They probably know our stage of technical development because they can easily see it. So I think they may be more interested in our behaviour. It would be exactly as we assess the quality of behaviour in adolescents as they mature. They may feel we are a threat to them. Perhaps they consider us a threat to the whole cosmos. I can understand why.'

'Any proof?'

'I think so. There are files on US defence computers which suggest that nuclear devices were inactivated around the world at critical times. Not destroyed, but made inactive. And on both sides.'

'So they want to prevent the destruction of our world and minimise any danger we present to other worlds?'

'That's about it.'

'But how long have they been visiting?'

'Who can say? I think longer ago than the dawn of our modern civilisation. There are records in this country of large craft appearing in the sky as far back as the twelfth and thirteenth centuries. They were recorded by the scribes of the day, who were perfectly reasonable people. It's only the modern sceptics who doubt. They seem to strike an attitude of disbelief just for the sake of it. Personally, I have little doubt that one could look back a lot further. Our civilisation is young, as little as five thousand years old. Perhaps theirs is a million years old.'

'What do you imagine they're like?'

'In themselves they are probably little different from us. They must have physical bodies otherwise they wouldn't need to enclose them in spacecraft. Yet in terms of development they are very much more advanced. I use the term loosely, however. They certainly have abundant knowledge, but they may also have a society as regimented as that of ants. And their minds: they may have implants to control behaviour or to improve communication or reasoning. There are many who would say that such a society is more primitive than our own. We cannot necessarily describe them by using terms we apply to ourselves.'

'But in terms of their appearance, are they very different?'

'Like ours, their body chemistry must be based on reactions

which take place in water. The only alternative solvent that would behave anything like water in diverse chemical reactions would be liquid ammonia. And they would then be the product of an intensely cold, hostile world. That is extremely unlikely.' He paused, but Freya felt he hadn't finished and she decided not to ask a further question.

'So,' he continued, 'like us, they must be made of carbon compounds and as they developed, they were probably the subject of similar pressures of evolution. We know that intelligence can lead to survival. Eventually an intelligent life form with a culture would have developed. And after a million years of continuous technological and social development...'

'Mr Meredith, you are avoiding my question!'

'Well I don't mean to. From what I have heard, the suggestion is that they are humanoid.'

'Which means that...'

'It does. But let us stop for a while; I need some coffee. Perhaps you do too?'

'Yes please! I've a lot to think about.'

Meredith made a pot of coffee, a ritual he enjoyed, and they made general conversation for a while. Freya spoke about her work, and her experience with the bright light and electrical failures when out in her car. She also mentioned the many responses of local people, together with the fact that the subject was frequent in conversation wherever she went. Meredith asked about her companions and how they had sent her to see him. They finished their coffee and returned to the interview:

She said, 'Returning to the idea of sending a message back into space, if we want to get in touch with them, what should we do?'

Meredith shook his head. 'You are naïve if you think it would achieve anything. First, there is the obvious difficulty of how to send it. I suppose you discussed a radio message or laser light, or even making your own crop circle?'

'We did!'

'Well I doubt they would even notice it. And what about a suitable message? I expect you want to say that you are peaceful, would like to send them good wishes and that you've deciphered their crop circle?'

'I suppose so!'

'Well they may not even understand the notion of good wishes. And what can you give them that they don't have already? Why should they take note of any message from you? They know that you cannot speak for the whole of humanity!'

'Then a return message isn't practicable?'

Meredith was cautious: 'They probably monitor the state of the entire cosmos and if so, they will already know that we can fuse nuclei ourselves. If they already know things like that, they don't need messages concerned with small matters.'

Freya thought his response a little negative. 'Well we thought that the fact they sent us a message would mean they are interested in a response. We're not going to be deterred!'

'Well alright, so long as you don't expect too much!'

'And if, in the unlikely event that we are successful with our message, what about a possible meeting with them?'

'They would still know nothing much about you and your friends. Your only chance of a meeting is in the event that their visits are concerned with a larger matter: perhaps a long-standing quest which brings them here repeatedly. You would need to have something they particularly need.'

Freya felt at ease and asked to use his Christian name. He said, 'Oh sure.'

She said, 'Some kind of quest? That *must* be it. Of all the trips they could make, they come here repeatedly, so it must be something to do with *us*.'

Meredith considered. In his attempt to present a reasoned view, perhaps he should have given more weight to the recent increase in activity in the Network. And Freya's notion of a particular quest: she had emphasised a perfectly reasonable idea. He said, 'Perhaps you may be right. And if there are lots of visits right now...'

'Then, Guy, there must be something happening here right now.'

Meredith rose from his chair and looked out into an overcast garden with a little drizzle falling. He paced about, returning to the window repeatedly. He said, 'I'm very glad you came over. Sometimes it takes someone else's view of things to make sense of them.'

Freya was pleased that Meredith felt free to speak.

He continued: 'So all these small events may not be as small as I had thought. Perhaps they are connected somehow. And if something unusual is going on, then perhaps we may be in pole position to find out what it is.'

'Then do you have any ideas?'

'I've just sent a guy from your own profession over to the States. I'm in contact with a few people he's been speaking to. I heard he's about to strike gold with his investigation.'

'Gold?'

'Perhaps. Look, Freya, can you come back, or can we speak on the phone when I've found out? At last I'm beginning to see a bigger picture. I need to get in touch with my contacts in the States. Elliott—that's our journalist—is just seeing some important people right now. I need to find out what's come up before we talk again.'

'Yes, certainly.'

—m—

Meredith spoke to Budd Lynch the next day. Lynch had returned from seeing Bailey Mann in Cleveland and had just arranged for Elliott to meet his contact at the University. Meredith recounted his observations to Lynch and listened with interest to his reply.

Lynch said, 'We went to Cleveland. There was some interesting work on powered flight, but I doubt whether any of it is applicable to spacecraft.'

Meredith recounted his feeling that there must be something big going on. 'I'd like to know what it's all about,' he said. 'If it isn't powered flight, then it must be something else. Have you any idea what?'

'I may have. I sent Elliott to my other contact. He works at the

University. He's a clever guy, interested in anthropology—you know, the origin of human beings and such. He works on anything to do with ancient human remains, their genetics, evolution, cultural relics and so on. The word is out that he has made a big find. Not only that, he seems to have an interest in the Roswell smash. That's about it right now.'

'Can I mention this to my new contacts? There's a girl from the local radio.'

'As long as it doesn't implicate my sources.'

'It won't. But where exactly does this news come from...these rumours?'

'I wouldn't be surprised if someone has talked. It happens even in the CIA. Or perhaps it was at the University itself. Academics are vain, you know, and they like to talk...it's the prestige.'

Later, Meredith recounted his conversation in a telephone call to Freya at her home. He had been thinking, and had come up with an idea. A small spark of intuition at first, it had grown in his mind into a fully-fledged explanation for what was going on. He said to Freya, 'I wouldn't be surprised if this molecular anthropologist is making comparisons between ancient humans and material from the Roswell accident. Now *that* would be something which might bring our alien friends down to see us!'

'Then why to the Thames valley?'

'Now *that* I don't understand.'

—␣␣—

Freya Sampson, Callum Dood, Peter Pargeter and Adam Shilto were in conference at Pargeter's home. Pargeter said, 'Let's shut the chess room, shall we? Come through here, it's got proper armchairs. Have a glass of this.'

Shilto had cycled over, still a sprightly figure despite his years and relieved to have some diversion from everyday work. He said to Freya, 'Please tell us what happened.'

She replied, 'Meredith told me quite a lot. He agreed there are aliens out there, but he's not convinced that we can hope to message them. He came around to the idea that something big is happening, but he thought the trail had gone elsewhere for the time being. To the USA, that is.'

Like Shilto, Callum Dood was relieved to be in conference with his friends rather than having to write his weekly sermon, 'So what do we do next?' he said.

Freya replied, 'It might be a good idea to follow that London newspaper type to the States. I hear he has met some interesting people. I would like to speak to him. He's called Elliott.'

'What makes you think he'll share his story with you?'

'He may do if I share my own side of things. I may be able to convince him to join a joint enterprise. But I don't want to go alone.'

Dood said, 'Well, I'll go too. Adam, can you square that with the bosses?' Shilto nodded.

She replied, 'You had better watch what herbal remedies you take with you.'

Dood said, 'I shall limit myself to special teas.'

—∞—

Freya Sampson and Callum Dood prepared to follow Elliott to the United States. With a trip in mind they obtained visas and packed clothes for a hot autumn—Freya had asked about the climate—to which Dood replied, 'I think it will be very hot and humid.'

Having obtained his number from Meredith, Freya telephoned Elliott and introduced herself and Dood. She explained the reason for their trip and Elliott agreed to a meeting. Elliott, waiting to visit his contact at the University, agreed to book rooms at his own hotel and volunteered to meet them at the airport. When they eventually met about a week later, Elliott was quite taken with Freya and found her an attractive and pleasant diversion. In Callum Dood he immediately recognised a skilled diplomat and man of the world, yet he could not quite reconcile the mix of unspoken cynicism and gentle benefaction which he had not experienced before and could not properly name. However he dismissed such thoughts to the back of his mind, made the two welcome, and drove them back to the city. They booked in and he said, 'I'm sure you will want to rest and freshen up. Knock on my door when you've recovered. Here is my room number. I have plenty to do in the meantime. Say 24 hours?'

S I X

A STRANGE NEW SPECIES?

Elliott paused before a nameplate which read Professor Joseph E. Dorkin, and knocked gently. Immediately a voice said, 'Come in, Mr Elliott and have a seat. He pushed a chair over and sat down behind his desk. So you're a journalist?'

'I am. I work for this newspaper'—he pulled out his press cards—'and I was referred to you by Mr Bud Lynch, whom we both know.'

'Yes, Mr Lynch and I are old friends. Our work is quite different of course, but we do have a common interest. So welcome to the University. How do you like our city?'

'I like it. It has a good feel. So what kind of work do you do here?'

'We are interested in the origins of the human race. We look at historical and cultural artefacts, but our main work is in analysing palaeontological samples when we are lucky enough to find them. We pioneered a form of analysis using extremely tiny samples of DNA. We clone and compare them and we have also do a little embryo research.'

'So you get private funding?'

'Some, but mostly we are maintained by the University itself and through public funds.'

'Returning to your research, you work with DNA samples from ancient finds? I suppose that must place you right at the limit of the available technology.'

'It certainly does, which is why we get support from forensics agencies. They want to see the technology develop. Our main work is on sequencing the DNA remains from archaeological sites. We can start from very tiny amounts, much smaller than before.'

Elliott nodded in an encouraging manner.

Dorkin carried on, 'So we amplify these small samples for further analysis. We explore the genetic variation in human populations.' He smiled, encouraging further questions. His manners showed very little reticence and a clear propensity for self-advertisement. Elliott guessed that this was necessary in his business. He said 'Lynch tells me you may have new insights on samples of an historical nature.' He added, 'But he was as careful as ever.'

'Sure we do. It's not quite in the public domain, but it is in limited circulation within this building and among a select few'—he smiled again—'of my friends.'

Elliott nodded, 'You can tell me just a little?' He was confident of a positive response, suspecting that otherwise there would have been no interview.

'Yes. This project came to us with valuable funding. We took some DNA samples from very old paleontological sites.'

Elliott was anxious not to push Dorkin too hard and he visibly relaxed into his chair.

Dorkin carefully considered his words, 'We managed to obtain some DNA from interesting places. We tested samples from Homo heidelbergensis and managed to replicate them, even though they were pretty degraded. Those guys were exactly like modern humans.' He paused and seemed to reflect. 'Also, we looked at Boskop man. We went to South Africa and revisited the site of the original discoveries. There were new finds some distance away—we were very pleased because they were quite extensive and completely unspoiled.' He seemed to warm to their discussion. 'So there were new Boskop remains. They were of a great age, at least

65,000 years, maybe 70,000 years old—and although an original skull from the 1913 find was completely fossilised, our own finds were in a much better state of preservation. Now, this is the nub: the skulls were about 40% larger than the average for a modern human.'

'So what did the people look like?'

'A bit like Herman Munster. They had huge brains and small faces, and they were probably very clever. Their cranial cavity may have been up to 2000cc in volume, and one estimate is that they had IQ readings of 180. Not sure I agree, because it is the organisation of the brain rather than...' he paused. 'But if they were humanoid then humanoid criteria must apply, so that estimate of a very high IQ must remain.'

'And their DNA samples?'

Dorkin looked hesitant. He got up, walked about, and stopped at a window. Looking out, he rubbed his chin and seemed reluctant to go further. Then abruptly, he spun on his heel, sat down behind his desk and looked directly at Elliott as though taking his measure. Finally, he seemed to come to a positive decision and his momentary reticence fell away. He said, 'As you would expect, the Boskop samples were very similar to modern human DNA. But there were differences too. Quite a few sections were unique to Boskop Man.'

Elliott said, 'Would you call them human?'

Dorkin reflected. 'Well yes...' the sibilant hissed into silence. 'But let us get this into some kind of perspective. We share 96% of our DNA with gorillas and chimps and 90% with cats. But the new Boskop finds shared only 98.5% with us, so they may just have crossed the threshold of being a separate species. We cannot be sure, but I do think that they diverged from us a long time ago.'

'So what were their lives like?'

'They were more advanced than we were at the time; we know that because there were other finds. They used fire, because we found a simple kind of fused glass.' Elliott nodded.

'And there were advanced tools, not just the usual flint scrapers. They were made of iron. Some were little more than rust, of course, but that didn't stop us looking at them.'

'So what was so special about them?'

'They would seem pretty ordinary to us today. But let me repeat, they were made of iron.' He leaned forward. 'Don't you see, their iron age started at least 65,000 years before our own! There's no academic who would believe me. But that's not all: there were other things there.'

'Such as?'

'We found a composite tool: a hammer made of an iron coat over a mass of lead. You just don't get iron and lead composites from 65,000 years ago.'

Elliott said, 'That must mean contamination of the site by modern man.'

He expected a quick affirmation. Instead, Dorkin said, 'That's just it. They—all the artefacts—were under strata which showed no disturbance of any kind. It is inconceivable that they were mislaid or planted there.'

'So how do you explain your findings?'

'Hang on, there's more. We had the lead analysed.' He passed a paper to Elliott. 'See here, the ratios of three isotopes'—he pointed to the script—'suggest the lead was obtained from Central America. It must mean that Boskop men were somehow in contact with Mesoamerica. But how could there have been a trans-Atlantic passage 65,000 years ago? And that's not the only thing. We found cutting tools made from obsidian.'

'So?'

'Obsidian is a volcanic rock which is made by the action of great heat. There is no native obsidian at the Cape. The kind we found, well, it possibly resembles that of the Mexican peninsula of Yucatan, but we need to check it first-hand. And if so...'

Elliott said, 'It might all be a hoax, like the Piltdown find.'

Dorkin said, 'Believe me, we checked it out. And who's going to fake the skeleton and the DNA? And how could that have been achieved? Dammit, they are the real thing!'

They sat in silence for a minute. Elliott's mind worked overtime, but eventually settled on the main reason for his visit. He could see that Dorkin was watching him, probably aware of the nature of his impending question: 'Professor Dorkin, you have a common interest with Bud Lynch. I take it that this interest can somehow be applied to your present discoveries?'

'Yes. I had hoped eventually to get onto that. We also found ancient artwork. The main item was the depiction of a man surrounded by agricultural tools such as ploughs, scythes, fields of maize and the like. In the background were saucer-shaped craft and a path leading to it.'

Elliott knew that as far as his story was concerned, the floodgates were open.

'We are absolutely certain the drawings were as old as the human specimens. They were behind a calcite surface and the age of the calcite was the same. I collected some to test.'

'I can guess what you are trying to tell me. Clearly, you believe it.'

'I'd never get it accepted at a conference, but yes I do. It's not possible to envision a boat capable of crossing 8,500 miles of open sea. It can only makes sense, all things considered, if there were some more sophisticated craft capable of bridging the gap between the Cape and Mexico, 65,000 years ago.'

Elliott had not mentioned a connection with any classified aspect, but was aware that the time was right to do so. He said, 'You and Bud Lynch know each other well. He mentioned Roswell.' Elliott left it there.

Dorkin made a halting attempt at a reply, but followed: 'The advanced tools were one thing, but the DNA, that was even more... odd.'

'You said they shared 98.5% of their DNA with us.'

'I did. I have not spoken of this widely, but my laboratory knows. So it isn't in the public domain, but neither can I call it absolutely secret. The strange thing is that our samples from Boskop were similar to others that were sent to us by our government. They must have had their suspicions otherwise they would never have commissioned the work.' His expression was one big exclamation.

'Does that bring us back to your connection with Lynch?'

'Yes. Mr Elliott, you seem to have tied me down. These classified samples were taken from the crash site at Roswell in 1947. They were a bit degraded, but it was an easy task to amplify them so that we could compare the two. They were similar to those taken from Boskop this year.' He paused, 'But there was one difference; there was less of what we call junk DNA, less non-coding stuff. Large parts of it don't seem to do much; they just sit there with an unknown function. It was as though some of that, some of the Roswell DNA had been cut out, cleaned up. Those guys were like the product of some giant experiment that had gone a bit wrong.'

Elliott made do with, 'I think I understand!'

'Good. We looked at mitochondrial DNA too. We use it to study divergence, you know. It tells us when populations were separated. The Boskop guys became separated from modern man 450,000 years ago, long before modern man left Africa. And here's another thing. Although the basic genome of Boskop and Roswell man was very similar, the mitochondrial DNA showed that they, in turn, became distinct populations 600,000 years ago.'

'And neither was the direct ancestor of modern humans?'

'No, I don't think so. There are better candidates for *that*.'

'So do I understand this properly? You are saying that the basic DNA genome from Boskop man was similar to that from the Roswell crash?'

'Yes. But the two populations became separated 600,000 years ago. The tests are very reliable these days, and they gave us an indisputable test result.'

Elliott sat up in his chair and said, 'Look, do I get this right? Your results suggest the Roswell aliens left our earth 600,000 years ago?'

'That seems about it, but it may also be that small populations remained elsewhere, at various places and in secret, around the world.'

'And am I to understand that, much later, these aliens revisit us from time to time?'

'It looks that way,' replied Dorkin. 'They appear to have established links with parts of the world such as Boskop and

Central America, with a view to…well, offering some kind of help. Lord knows why. Later, our own ancestors became the dominant kind of human.'

'Have you any idea how controversial this is?'

'Certainly, it's impossibly controversial.'

'So what are you going to do?'

'Well, if I put all that into a scientific paper I'd never get any funding again. I would probably be ostracised by the scientific community for talking nonsense. But the thing is, the US Government is aware of all this and must have viewed the results exactly as I have done. They could do little else.'

Elliott said, 'Then, Professor, can I publish any of this in my newspaper?'

Dorkin said, 'I would be pleased for you to do something on our methods; it attracts grant money. And it would be great for the public to hear about our work on palaeontology and anthropology and our methods for the amplification of old samples. But if you include anything about Roswell, we are finished. And believe me, I think it might be very dangerous for you as well.'

—⚬—

'Professor Dorkin,' said Walter Stein, 'We studied your analyses of the material from South Africa. We want to find subsets of modern populations in which these ancient genes are preserved.'

'You mean you want to find more Boskop men?'

'If you put it like that, then the answer must be yes.'

'But they are extinct!'

'They may be, but some of their characteristics might remain in modern populations. They might be useful to us. Where's the best place to look?'

'There are only two places I can think of. The first is the Cape itself, but I don't think there's much likelihood of success there. There's been too much displacement of peoples, and there's too little archaeological evidence.'

'And the other?'

'I suggest you think about the Yucatan peninsula in Mexico. It contains isolated but still flourishing older populations. They show evidence of old languages and a continuity of cultural forms: the gods, the agriculture, the writing and other relics.'

'OK, we want you to attempt a survey of local DNA samples. Get into schools in native areas. No problem with funding.'

'It will take time.'

'Then you had better get started.'

'You guys have got me by the balls.'

'Yeah, and we're gonna squeeze.'

—※—

Callum Dood and Freya Sampson knocked on Elliott's door. Elliott suggested that they should make for the lounge bar because of the armchairs and the service available there. None of them was particularly hungry, but since it was 'coffee time' they asked for coffee and reclined for a few minutes. They were at ease and felt no need for elaborate courtesies when each described their background, their dealings with Meredith and in Elliott's case, with Dorkin. It was quite clear that they had a common interest and would make more progress by working together.

Dood said, 'So Dorkin thinks that Boskop Man and 'Roswell Man' are one and the same.'

Elliott said, 'Yes, and I would never have believed it. Yet all that stuff about DNA is supported by contemporary accounts of the Roswell crash. The survivors were small humanoids with enlarged crania and small faces. The skulls from Dorkin's dig were similar.'

Freya said, 'I don't understand all that stuff about isotopes of lead.'

'I did ask Dorkin a bit more. He said that samples of lead from around the world differ, so that it's possible to say where they came from. He felt that a lead tool found at Boskop must have come from Central America.'

Freya replied, 'So the Boskop people were in contact with the source of the metal?'

'Yes. Dorkin said that no simple boat, nor even a balsa raft like the Kon Tiki, could have travelled 8,500 miles across the Atlantic. There are mountainous seas there and it isn't a tranquil place like the Pacific!'

Dood said, 'Well then, a flying craft it must have been. Perhaps they ferried people about, too.'

Elliott said, 'Dorkin felt the scientific community would never accept it. My readers will say we are nuts.'

'They all thought the sun revolved around the earth,' said Freya. 'We can only try to prove it, but how?' She rang for the waiter and asked for more coffee. They sipped the strong, dark brew and stretched their legs, wandering up and down. Eventually, she said, 'Dorkin compared DNA from various sources. Do you think he has the record of a whole genome?'

'I wouldn't know, but I *suppose* he must have,' said Elliott.

'Would he supply it to us?'

Dood said, 'For what purpose?'

'I don't know really, but if there were some means of letting our extra-terrestrial visitors know that we know about them…'

Dood interrupted: 'I get it. You want to leave the details out for them to find?'

'Something along those lines.'

Elliott said, 'So you want to leave a 'genome' message in a crop circle? That's a lot of data! Would they visit again? And how long would it last before the weather blows it away?'

Freya replied, 'I know it sounds ridiculous if you put it like that. I hadn't begun to think of it in those terms.'

Dood said, 'We could telephone Dorkin and ask what he thinks.'

'Good idea,' said Elliott. 'Let me do it later. Give the poor guy a chance to get out of bed.'

Later, Elliott managed to get through to Dorkin, who seemed willing to expand on their earlier conversation. 'This genome project,' said Elliott, 'what kind of data does it deliver?'

'We end up with a series of letters. There are only four letters, but these are repeated over and over again in various orders.'

'And how could one record it?'

'The problem is not the complexity, but the amount of data. You cannot simply write it down. There are 3.5 billion pieces of information. You need a computer database.'

'Would a laptop be any good?'

'Yes. A large hard-drive could easily record that. One byte is a single character of text on a computer. A gigabyte is one billion. You need 3.5 billion to record a whole sequence.'

'Thank you, Professor, but I do have one further question. Suppose I wanted to beam it to somebody in, say, a radio wave. How could I do it?'

Dorkin chuckled, 'Ha, I can guess what you're thinking. You simply digitise the genome so that G is maybe a zero, C is one, with spaces between. You would need two more combinations for A and T. Any half-decent extraterrestrial could read *that*.'

'And can you give me the Boskop and Roswell data?'

'I knew that was coming. My own recent data from Boskop yes, but I can't do the Roswell stuff unless I check with my client. And it's a bit big to email. I could let you have it on a detachable drive, but I would need to copy it. That shouldn't take too long.'

Later, Elliott ascended the granite steps towards Dorkin's laboratory. He made his presence known, passed a secure door and a young woman introduced herself: 'Hi, I'm Carmen van Brouin, Professor Dorkin's research associate. I'm afraid he's overdue. He went out, but left a small package for you when you came.'

'Thank you; when was he supposed to be back?'

'An hour ago. You had better rearrange if you want to see him in person.'

'Well please thank him for his help.' He left, clutching his package. Back at the hotel, Elliott called the others and they met again in the lounge. The waiter came over and collected orders for lunch. By then they were quite hungry, and so they ate for about twenty minutes. Elliott told them that although Dorkin was absent, their quest had been fruitful. Eventually, they pushed their plates away.

'Well let's see inside!' said Freya.

'I doubt whether there's very much *to* see,' replied Elliott, but he unwrapped the package anyway. Inside was a note which he read to the others:

'*Hi Mr Elliott,*

I copied the details from Boskop Man as you asked. You will also find that I included data from the analysis of the Roswell crash material.

You may wonder why I did this after saying I couldn't. Well as you know, I am sponsored by the Agency and a lot of people tell me that agency work can be a bit dangerous. In case that turns out to be true, this will make sure that my work is preserved in the public domain. Please do some good with it.

There's one further thing. The drive also contains the sequence of a hybrid embryo that we made. We took some DNA from the Roswell samples and injected it into a human egg cell where it was expressed. It didn't live long but we have the technology to do a repeat. So, genetic experiments on aliens are possible, and perhaps that is what the agency wants to find out about.

I guess I believe more in my work than just being a stooge for the agency.

Joseph Dorkin.'

Dood said, 'I bet he thought his phone was tapped.'

'Yes,' said Elliott, 'but if there's going to be a problem with the ownership of that database, then we need to be careful ourselves.'

Freya said, 'The package hasn't been opened or it would never have reached us. But if they do find out, I think we can expect to lose it.'

Dood turned to Elliott: 'David, can you get someone to make a second copy? I want to send it off to a contact of mine. No doubt there are people here in the hotel who could copy it, but I would want to be a bit more discreet about things.'

Elliott nodded. Later, he went to see Bud Lynch in Shadyside. After brief greetings he said, 'I saw Dorkin and he gave me some information which I have on this detachable drive. I need a copy of all the data on it.'

Lynch picked up the drive, looked at it knowingly and smiled. He said, 'I thought he would be interesting to talk to. Sure I can copy that.' He disappeared into a stock room and reappeared after a couple of minutes, clutching a computer. It made a whirring sound for five minutes, after which he seemed satisfied. He said, 'All in a good cause.'

Elliott thanked him, they shook hands, and Lynch turned his attention to a large box of Twinkies, each of which he microwaved for three seconds before eating. Back in town, Elliott went to a post office and assembled a small parcel with a covering note to Peter Pargeter. Written earlier by Dood it said, *'Peter, I enclose a computer drive with three files of data. They will need to be sent in a radio message when we get back so please copy it, ask Adam to keep a copy and keep one yourself. Please keep quiet about it in case it excites an unusual level of interest.'*

—␣—

Joseph Dorkin held a meeting in his office with Carmen van Brouin and Simon Wiener. As was his habit at such meetings, he used a whiteboard covered with notes and referred to it from time to time, or ticked a statement or underlined a word in coloured ink.

Wiener said, 'So exactly what do you want us to do next?'

Dorkin replied, 'All seems to rest on our idea that there was a connection between the Boskop site and Mexico. We need to find the other end of the link. Of course, if we get any further evidence for our other findings, then that would be great.' He paused; it was his habit to draw as much from his colleagues as he could. Then he said: 'I thought I'd put this to you in case I've missed something.' He doubted it, having thought about little else for weeks.

Simon Wiener said, 'Well it seems clear to me. We need evidence that the lead sample we found at Boskop has an equivalent over here. And with what we know about historical trade routes and the fact that they passed out of Mexico, it's quite plain where we should look.'

Dorkin nodded, turned to Carmen and made a movement which elicited a comment from her, 'Sure,' she said, 'and while we are there we can do some genetics as well. We can look for Boskop-like genes in the local population. That would be the best proof I can think of.'

'Is that it?' said Dorkin.

'Well no,' she replied. 'We can also put our geologists' hats on and collect some obsidian as well. We need to find some samples like the ones we already have.'

'Very good,' said Dorkin. 'That will take us up a mountainside, but I'm pleased to have you volunteer.' He smiled at her, but she knew he was serious. 'And we can ask the chemistry department to do the comparisons for us.'

'Should we do the DNA ourselves?' said Carmen.

'We can certainly do the swabs. But the best thing is to send them away afterwards. I don't want to spend time on that if we can just pay someone.'

It seemed settled. The small party would travel into Mexico to begin what would surely be a period of painstaking evidence-gathering. They could not expect any immediate revelation: it meant a lot of uncomfortable fieldwork in an unfamiliar country. To that end, they began to prepare for a lengthy stay. 'But don't worry about food,' said Dorkin, 'we can buy it when we get there. You like Tex-Mex?'

'Practically live on it,' they said.

'OK,' said Wiener. 'But we *are* taking the truck, so make sure we take some Scotch.'

Ten days later, they crossed the border into Sonora. They were among the many Americans travelling south to do cross-border shopping. Yet unlike most of the other travellers their destination, the state of Veracruz in the Gulf, was far distant, over 2000 miles away. Their route, passing south through the states of Chihuahua, Durango and Zacatecas was a considerable journey in which they took turns behind the wheel, stopping every five or six hours for spicy meals in the local style or for the night at a roadside motel. They were unhurried and comfortable despite the semi-equatorial weather, and in the many hours of driving there was ample time to discuss their work.

Dorkin said, 'I think we need to investigate the easy angles first. They have a habit of growing while we do them. We should look for our geological samples and then separate and share out the remaining tasks.'

Carmen replied, 'So we collect obsidian first? I mean, will it just be lying around?'

'No it won't. And we need to be the ones to find it. We can't just turn up at a museum and ask for a piece. There must be a record of when and where.'

'So where?' said Carmen.

'Let's go straight to the Vulcan de St Martin and then we can do the El Chichon volcano. If they are no good we can try others. There are over forty so I hope we strike lucky early on. We shall have to wait for the analyses of course.'

'So you haven't forgotten the other matters?' said Weiner.

'No. When we separate, Simon, I'd you to do the genetics. Your Spanish is good, mine isn't, so I would like you to visit the schools and do the swabs.'

'OK, but you expect me just to turn up and argue with them?'

'No, I made preparations beforehand.' He pulled out a letter and waved it. 'I made the arrangements well in advance. I wrote to the Comision Federal Para la Proteccion Contra Riesgos Sanitarios, otherwise known as the Mexican Ministry of Health.'

'To what end?'

'In my guise as an apparently clinical doctor, I asked their permission to collect DNA swabs from schoolchildren. All we need to do is swab their tongues and get the lab to analyse the result. My letter was on University headed notepaper and their response was good. I simply told them I'm researching some medical aspects of DNA and need some international materials. That's not so far from the truth. I got a positive reply and they were keen to help.'

'But I just turn up on the doorstep?' said Wiener.

'Not exactly. I also wrote to individual schools in advance, explaining our purpose, and showing a copy of the Ministry reply. They all gave a positive response—could hardly do anything else— so you,' he said, pointing at Wiener, 'will turn up and turn on the charm.'

'I go by myself?'

'You do.'

'OK, my Spanish will have to do,' said Wiener. 'And we get someone to do the analyses?'

'We do. By the way, you need to favour the institutions farther south, away from the large cities. The local populations are probably more settled. And meanwhile, Carmen and I will be engaged elsewhere.'

'Engaged elsewhere?' said Weiner.

'Yes, we're going to look for lead. But all that will have to come after the obsidian.' Dorkin laughed, aware of how simple he had made it sound. As an afterthought he added: 'No doubt the two are connected. I hope that our swabs will show something in the populations in the far south. And that's also where I expect to see something interesting in the lead samples—that is, if there's anything to see.'

Their hotel was pleasant, but after two days they loaded up, pre-booked their rooms to provide them with a base, and drove south. Again they preferred to drive slowly and watch the scenery. Their route through the Sierra de Los Tuxtlas, a range of mountains running south east through the Veracruz state, was with the coast to their left. On their right the vista seemed to consist of moist rainforest, much of it extending to a high elevation, together with strong sunshine and intermittent cloud cover. Eventually, they approached the San Martin volcano, a peak of about 5500 feet and of a grey-green colour in silhouette against the evening sun. Soon, their path took them away from the main highway onto a rough track. After a short distance their destination, a modest and inconspicuous wooden shack, could be seen in an un-bordered field. Above it, trees replaced grass higher up the slope, but an anarchic rubble of cracked grey stone could be seen near the summit.

Their accommodation, a cheap holiday shack, contained one main room with a wooden floor, and two small bedrooms. A small kitchen was curtained-off in the corner of the living room, but although it had a primus-style cooker, no cylinders of gas could be seen apart from empty ones piled up outside. There was no running water and only a chemical lavatory, but they had known worse. It was undoubtedly the nearest base for their excursion.

They parked nearby, scouted around the property and unloaded enough equipment to make their short stay, intended to be no more than three days, reasonably comfortable. Outside, there was a wooden shed, formerly used for livestock or farm produce, in which they parked their truck out of sight. The two men made camp beds in one bedroom and Carmen in the other. They did not expect to use them more than twice: once before their climb and once on their return. They ate a light lunch and began to view the peak above them. It was shrouded in cloud. Carmen said, 'Well, it's quiet now, but when did you say it last erupted?'

'The last time was in 1794. I don't expect it to erupt again just for our benefit.'

'It's over five thousand feet high, maybe nearer six,' said Simon. 'Do we need to go all the way to the top?'

'No,' replied Dorkin. 'It will be hard work carrying our packs upwards, but we may not need to see the summit at all. We only need to go as far as is necessary.'

'Meaning,' said Carmen, 'that we keep our eyes open for the right kind of rocky slope. It may be covered with vegetation, but we should still recognise it. Then we dig or maybe move on until we find what we're looking for.'

'And don't forget that it's easier to carry rocks downhill,' said Simon, at which they both smiled.

Later they distributed the necessary shovels, picks and rock-hammers and began to climb. Their path, strewn with heavy boulders, was heavy work and they were sweating after the first mile. And they viewed their way with some foreboding; the ominous mass above them, hunched and squat, resembled a broad pair of shoulders. Dark and shadowed, it seemed to lack the majesty of the many higher peaks in the far distance. They were keen to finish, and pressed on with some urgency.

Dorkin kicked idly at a few rocks and said, 'Let's look at some of this stuff, shall we?' Then picking up a handful of fragments, he perused for a while before concluding, 'Volcanic they may be, but they're not what we want.' Not discouraged, they climbed farther, eventually reaching a plateau on which they observed cavities and various other workings that had a certain order about them: clearly it was the first evidence of past human activity. There, Carmen took photographs and recorded their position before moving on. Later, they climbed a slope of ash and lava before finding a convenient place to spend their first night. As Simon observed, 'It's not a place that I would recommend to the boy scouts.'

On the next morning they left camp early, and climbed to 1500 feet. There, they met with a steep hillock, some 200 feet tall, made from cinder, powdered ash and clinker, and which resembled a dead coal fire. It looked prone to a landslide, but they climbed to the summit nevertheless. Looking around, Dorkin said, 'This is a cinder cone: a mini volcano on the main structure. It has its own channel to the core. If we want to see 'our' kind of rock, then it's a good place to start.'

A start, perhaps, but somewhat later they had more success in an old lava flow. There, they unearthed a sample with the requisite olive-green colour, and a hazy luminosity which they were able to polish until it shone. It had a peculiar effect on them, making a profound contrast with the grey desolation all around. Dorkin said, 'And it's like glass, as we found before. It's a good bet for what we came for, so please can you choose some of the better pieces and then we can leave.'

Simon said, 'We can be sure that the Boskop finds came from here?'

'I wouldn't accept it as the only evidence, but there is a very high probability.' said Dorkin. 'All samples from this place should have a similar composition. It's a characteristic of the conditions when they were first made. See this piece with wavy bands in it? It's caused by tiny crystals of quartz or feldspar, or by bubbles of gas. If our sample has them, then all the local obsidian should be like it, and obviously our Boskop sample too.'

They were at last satisfied and started their descent during the early part of the afternoon. Eventually they reached base, where they were pleased to discard their baggage. The next day they were refreshed enough to look at their trophies. Some were as pretty as gemstones, and it was easy to see how they had caught the eye. Yet Dorkin looked thoughtfully at the dark green colour.

'All OK?' said Simon.'

'Not sure. It's just that our Boskop samples were rather different. Sure, we still have to get these samples analysed, but I would swear that this stuff contains a lot of iron. And with these wavy lines too, I reckon that it contains at least some quartz.'

'So now what?' Simon sounded irritated, a fact which Dorkin noted. He was about to propose a repeat performance elsewhere, but let the matter drop for a few minutes. Then he said, 'Well I don't think that these samples are necessarily a very good fit.'

Simon replied, 'But we could collect from ten volcanos and still not get the right one!'

'That may be, but we can still choose wisely. I chose this one because it's near the city of Veracruz, which was already a small port on a main trade route many thousands of years ago.'

'But if we do, the next most likely one would be…?'

'I would like to try El Chichon. It may be just a feeling, but consider this: obsidian was probably a by-product of quarrying for basalt. The local Olmec culture is known to have quarried basalt at El Chichon at least 1500 years ago. And if they did, then I bet their antecedents did, long before.'

Wiener said, 'So we go to El Chichon for obsidian?'

'We could. But El Chichon is notoriously dangerous. When it last erupted, it threw basalt blocks ten miles away. Are you up for that?'

There were good-natured grimaces but they said, 'We can hardly wait!'

'Good,' said Dorkin, 'just in case we miss the next war.'

'Well for my part,' said Carmen, 'I'm keen, but I *would* like a couple of days to clean up.'

'That's alright; already factored in.'

Back at their hotel they made ready once more, and two days later they left late at night in order to reach El Chichon at sunrise. It lay 500 miles to the south-east where they made camp at a lodge near the small town of Francisco Leon. The peak made a grim picture as they left their truck and hiked towards it. On the way they discussed it. 'El Chichon,' asked Carmen, 'is it very dangerous?'

Dorkin replied, 'It isn't quite as high as the last place, only 4000 feet. But it isn't extinct. It erupted less than 40 years ago and when it did, it blew its top off three times in just a few days. Now it's a great dome of cold lava with a huge crater at the top, filled with nasty acidic water. It's not a very pleasant place.'

'And there's a funny smell!'

'When it exploded a lot of poisonous gas came out into the air. It still smells of sulfur dioxide, which can be dangerous if you are an asthmatic like me. And the local soil is full of volcanic ash for miles around, which means that nobody really farms here anymore.'

'So are we safe?' said Simon Wiener.

'I hope so,' replied Dorkin. 'It blows up every 300 years, but it's not due for another 260 so we should be OK.'

They trudged upwards, the ground became warmer and the air carried a smell like a burning match. Their path became more difficult with cold lava flows and rough pumice, all having solidified forty years before. Around them was grey ash and here and there, yellow sulfur. Soon they set to work with pickaxes, first on cold lava streams, then on basalt blocks. It was very hard work, and they revealed only a nondescript mass. Later, Carmen found a different kind of material to work on, among which she soon unearthed pieces that had a familiar lustre about them. They were black rather than green, but they were glass-like and promising. She suppressed a comment about the find having been easy, then brought the others over and suggested they should join in. Dorkin said, 'This is probably what we are looking for.' It was plentiful enough to collect, and having done so they recorded their exact position and took photographs. Yet their job had not been pleasant, and again they were relieved to return to Velacruz City.

Dorkin said, 'That was the easy part. We can get our samples sent off to be analysed straight away. Give them a couple of weeks and they will tell me all I need to know.'

'Which brings us,' said Simon, 'to the next bit. We need to get some samples of lead.'

'Yes, and we shall need to travel about. But Simon, you've got a different kind of travelling to do. It's time for you to get on the trail of the lost genes. You need to brush up your Spanish, and obviously you must telephone the schools beforehand. I'd like you to get on with some swabs while we visit the local lead mines.'

'I was about to say exactly that myself.'

'Good. You can go off in the truck. How does that sound?'

'About right,' said Wiener. 'But you're not proposing to go underground yourself?'

'No. We approach the manager of a mine and get referred to the sales people. They are probably very busy and have to administer a big business. They will explain that galena, the ore, is dug from the ground and sent through a crusher. Later it goes to a smelter and will be cast into sheets or ingots.'

'So we buy some?'

'They will have samples for us to buy. But we want samples smelted in house, not ingots of mixed lead from several mines. I'm sure that they will be able to supply *that*. If not, then they will certainly have samples of galena itself.'

'You still need to get about!'

'Yes. But we can hire a car. The University account will pay, so we can hire something good.' Dorkin laughed and poured more wine.

Four days later, Dorkin and van Brouin drove a hired car down a rough slope of yellow mud. It might have been considered a road to drivers of the trucks, half-tracks and tractors which came there, but to Dorkin and van Brouin it was a slippery path beset with the risk of misfortune, and an immediate danger as far as their tyres were concerned. After a few minutes of sliding around, they arrived at an open area about a quarter of a mile across. It was undulating and unpaved, and the litter of mining was everywhere. There were fallen girders, rusty and mangled pieces of iron, hydraulic gear painted orange or equally often were orange with rust. There were also large holes, apparently bottomless, that were a serious danger. Farther on was an assortment of chalet-like huts made of corrugated iron, other prefabricated buildings and the fallen remains of them. Beyond, and in the distance, tall trees surmounted a ridge that sloped away from the far side of an open-cast mine where from a cavernous hole huge trucks with enormous tyres carried ore to a station for disbursement. There, a bright red stationary engine gave motive power to a moving belt on which the stony ore made a noise like a shingle beach. In accompaniment, the engine belched forth black diesel smoke with a monotonous rhythm. The mechanical clatter continued without cessation, as though the noise of metal on stone was some dreadful punishment levied on nature. And as if this were not enough, the people walked around in hideous orange boiler suits, and wore masks as though forbidden to comment on the cacophony. They had reached their first lead mine, a very unpleasant workplace where presumably, muck was money.

In an office within a corrugated iron hut, Dorkin and van Brouin sat at a table opposite a man who spoke Spanish and Latin American English. 'I am from California, Señor,' he said, introducing himself as Señor Ramon. He seemed not to hear the noise outside. A mask lay on his desk. He pointed to it and said, 'Señor Dorkin, Señorita, you must wear a mask if you go near to the 'ore. The galena dust—not good!'

'Thank you for agreeing to see us at such short notice,' said Dorkin, nodding to Ramon's earlier comment. 'We would like some samples of galena, together with a sample, maybe a few grams is enough, of smelted lead. It could be in pigs or ingots, whatever is convenient for you and you should name your price. We are from the University, here are our credentials'—he withdrew some papers and placed them on the desk—'and we need some lead from your mine in particular. It is for a form of medical research.'

'Señor, if you require samples only, I am authorised to supply a case without question. I also have all the necessary test materials since they are often requested by commercial organisations. Each case contains a sample of our mother ore together with some smelted lead made from it. They are sealed within tubes in the manner required by the metallurgists among our customers, who later may wish to buy larger amounts. Also, Señor, in the interests of good commerce they are complimentary. We ask only that you use the name of our organisation in your report. In the meantime you will have some tequila? It is the best, made only from the agave. You would like salt and lime?'

'Ah, thank you,' said Dorkin, 'just a small one, please.'

Van Brouin smiled doubtfully, but nodded.

Later, they walked back to their car and this time, they did not mind the yellow mud on their shoes. Dorkin said he was indeed able to drive, and their return journey up the yellow slope was less inhibited than before. For the first time Dorkin felt that his behaviour contained a certain Mexican element, and he whistled and made elaborate hand gestures and gesticulations to passers-by, which many returned. On the next day they prepared for appointments at other mines that had been scheduled for the days following.

While Dorkin and van Brouin were enlarging their collection of samples, Simon Wiener, armed with his letters, approached a number of schools in the area. In his reasonable Spanish he asked to take DNA samples from children and assured them there would be no name attached to any sample. His organisation 'remained keen to forge special links in the form of educational sponsorship, and was respectful towards schools that had shown such generous hospitality'. With all agreed, the children trooped into a room to have their swab. They stuck their tongues out with a suitable degree of cheek and departed with their candy bar. Later, there were handshakes, photographs and declarations of friendship, and Wiener was able to proceed to the next most southerly school. Soon, a survey of native populations was complete. Although only a small percentage of the population had taken part, a careful distribution of tests ensured it was representative in terms of geography. Later, Wiener met the others back at Veracruz City. He said, 'So how did the geological surveys go?'

'We have plenty of samples of galena and smelted lead, but I was told there are rumours of disused workings farther south. The galena, they say, is of good quality, but there are problems with working in the rainforest. The Government doesn't want the national park violated by more commercial mining. They've got a point, I must say.'

'And how were the schools?' said Carmen.

'I have representative samples from the indigenous non-Hispanic children from many areas, but it was ridiculous to aim for thousands of samples. We agreed to collect only what we could handle'—the other two nodded—'and don't forget we're comparing them with just a few palaeontological samples, so it's all a bit hit or miss anyway. But some form of commonality might just show up.'

'Well, if it's all done, we can all go home.'

They packed their gear, checked out, and drove towards Sonora and the United States, a distance which they covered in three days. Within a week they were home with their collection and soon settled into their usual routines. These, however, were infused with impatience while they waited for their results. When the reports eventually came, they were greeted by avid hands, but Dorkin exercised his precedence and departed with them all. He knew that when he scheduled the next meeting, nobody would be late.

A few days later, Carmen van Brouin spoke to Walter Stein by telephone. He made polite enquiries regarding their progress and in return, she made encouraging noises and provided him with a short account of their activities which, she said, would be with him shortly. Their conversation ended with no more than a little sense of the impatience which she knew that Stein had suppressed with care.

Dorkin sifted through the envelopes that had arrived. Eventually, he invited the others to a conference a few days later. They were unable to read much from his manner but they remained calm as they took their places and waited. On this occasion his notes were written on paper rather than the whiteboard and he seemed a little more secretive than usual.

He collected himself before speaking. 'We need to remind ourselves that we hoped to find ancient genes in the native population of the southern Chiapas, or at least some degree of special similarity between local native populations and ancient samples from the Cape. I want to pay tribute to Simon for his diligence.' He paused for breath. 'The outcome was strange, but not ambiguous. You will recall the divergence in the Boskop samples when compared to modern man, which of course interested us. They contained several genes that we used as identifiers for the Boskop population, and that were absent from modern humans. Well, the vast majority of our cases showed no ancient genes at all, but there was a similarity in four of them. Four young people from the southernmost part of our range shared three marker genes found in the palaeontological samples from Boskop.' Dorkin showed a great amount of self-control.

'Could it be a mistake?'

'I asked the lab for confirmation. It was as they first said.'

'We could write to the schools, asking for an appraisal of their IQ levels?'

'Hell no! The conditions of our survey demanded that all tests were anonymous. And if the press found that we were trying to link genes and intelligence, there would be trouble. This isn't the 1930s! Believe me, they would take it the wrong way.' Wiener and van Brouin nodded, and stayed silent.

'So we found what we were looking for. But that's not all: the next thing was the obsidian. Our geology department took a good look at the samples we brought home, and I can quote the conclusion of their report.'

"We tested for the presence of hematite and for malachite. We also looked at hardness and translucence together with specific gravity. In our opinion, the samples obtained from San Martin were unlike those from the Cape, above all in their mineral content. The latter samples, however, do resemble those from El Chichon in terms of the parameters described. This similarity is close enough for us to suggest that they came from the same source. Our conclusion therefore, is that the fragments of obsidian from the Cape were originally quarried from the El Chichon area."

Dorkin showed great control, but the other two, despite his outward manner, thought they could hear a measure of elation, or perhaps even well-disguised euphoria in his voice. Calmly, he made a mark on his list and read the next line.

'Now, we need to consider our samples of lead. As you know, we went to several mines, although not the disused workings in the far south that some said are present. We need to remind ourselves of the four isotopes of lead found in nature. None are radioactive, but three are made by the radioactive decay of heavier elements like uranium.'

'So how useful is this?' said Simon.

'We shall see. Anyway, it's the ratio between the isotopes we are interested in, because that can be used to place their source. And at last we have some data.' Carmen's pencil hovered over some blank paper.

'Let me look at my notes.' He picked up a sheaf of papers and looked at the top one. 'Right, lead samples from known South African sources have the following ratios: 1.212 for isotopes 206/207; 2.029 for 208/206; 18.99 for isotopes 206/204; 15.67 for isotopes 207/204; and finally, 38.53 for isotopes 208/204.' He seemed unusually keen to quote the figures in their entirety. Having done so, he waved the papers and let them fall on the desk.

'And the Boskop samples?' said Simon.

'Well, as I said, these ratios tell us about their origin. We could, if necessary, identify Mexican samples and show that they differ from South African.'

'And?' said Carmen. She thought that Dorkin was enjoying his bit of drama.

'The interesting thing is that the Boskop samples were different from both.'

'So the Boskop implement contained no lead from either source?' said Simon.

'That's right.'

Carmen seemed perplexed: 'But if we knew what authentic samples from the Cape and Mexico were like before we went, then why did we visit all those lead mines? Why didn't we simply test the Boskop sample and compare it with information we already had? We went all round Mexico on a wild goose chase!'

'We did, but it wasn't as pointless as you think. Now we know for sure that they are different.'

'But we knew that before!'

'No. We only knew about Mexican samples that had been documented beforehand. We wanted more than that.'

'Alright,' said van Brouin, 'we eliminated a few more possibilities, so what?'

'Well the key thing, which I admit I kept under my hat, is that the Boskop lead implement did actually resemble an unusual Mexican sample which came into my possession a while back. I would point out that you haven't actually asked me what the Boskop sample *did* contain.'

'OK,' said van Brouin, 'tell us...please!'

'Although it was unlike the usual Mexican samples, it had something else rather interesting about it. It seemed to have been manufactured rather than just mined. There was a small chance that we could find more like it, which was really my aim. Shame we didn't.'

Van Brouin sat up straight and said, 'You kept this back?'

'Relax, Carmen, our efforts weren't exactly wasted. The lead was only a part of it. We looked at the rocks and the DNA. Things take time. We had—still have—to build our case. Anyway, I've told you now.'

'Alright,' said Wiener, 'these non-Mexican style Mexican samples. Let's have it!'

'Okay, two small metal statuettes were brought to me, origin certified as Central America. They had a lead content unlike anything else I had ever seen. As you know, lead is used for routine archaeological dating and that's why I tested them. I had never seen the like.'

'So they were Mexican?'

'Yes they were, and ancient. But a story came with them. They were supposed to have come out of the south, near the Guatemalan border. They were small idols, brought in by a native, which ended up with a dealer of antiquities in Mexico. They were sold to a museum here in the States, and I asked to look at them before they went on general display. Do you know anything about native cultures?' Both shook their head.

'Well, the statuettes were of a pre-Mayan god. There are strange legends which surround his cult. All my sources said they were authentic.'

'Joseph,' said Carmen van Brouin, again showing her irritation, 'then why didn't we simply go south and visit a load more potential sources of lead while we were there?'

'It was inadvisable. First, we didn't know whether there was any point. What if the geological samples had shown no similarity? What about the genetics? And we haven't yet seen the place where the statuettes were found. I still need to visit their owner to obtain the appropriate introduction. Without that, we would have had to follow a cold trail back via the dealer to the native who found it. That would have taken us out of our way and wasted our efforts. I had also hoped our existing surveys in lead mines would show something more. They didn't, of course, but if we do things properly then they still might.'

Wiener said, 'So what's the overall significance of the pre-Mayan statuettes?'

'Well that's the mystery we need to solve. Somewhere in the far south of the country there's a source of lead that turned up in two ancient statuettes. The significant thing is that it was similar to the Boskop hammer.'

Wiener said, 'So tell us a bit more about this strange sample.'

'Both the Boskop hammer and the statuettes contained a high percentage of lead-207. Natural samples contain a maximum of 22%, but 'our' samples contained an unheard of 60%. To achieve *that*, they must have been made from depleted Uranium-235.'

Wiener said, 'Which means it came from the decay of fuel used in a nuclear reactor.'

'Ergo,' said van Brouin, 'it must be a modern fake.'

'It can't be. No, Carmen, please don't shake your head! Don't you think I have considered all this: the distance, the age, the metallurgy? Everything else argues against it being a hoax.' They knew that Dorkin had weighed the evidence without prejudice. Yet still she said, 'Couldn't it have been stolen from some government source?'

A STRANGE NEW SPECIES?

'Again, I thought so at first, but let us think about it once more. I can see that it might conceivably have been stolen, but anyone going to such a risk would only do it for commercial reasons: to make depleted uranium bullets, for example. Why would anyone steal it only to make a statuette? And who has even *heard* of pre-Mayan gods, except for one or two academics?' Dorkin shook his head. 'And who would make a hammer from it, take it to Boskop and then hide it in an archaeological site which nobody even knew about? Who would care, apart from *us*? The only motive would be to discredit *me* and I don't have any competitors. And this work is actively supported by the U.S. Government. Why would they discredit someone whose work they support?'

'Alright, so we accept that neither is a fake, now what?'

'Well it's an enigma for sure. The significance is that, if we find a common source, we shall have shown for sure that a trans-continental connection existed thousands of years ago. And if we can do that—we are nearly there anyway—the facts will have shown that a civilisation which existed thousands of years ago was advanced enough to use uranium.'

Simon replied, 'Well, I'm convinced. As Sherlock said, "Once you eliminate the impossible, whatever remains, no matter how improbable, must be the truth". All this must mean that we are the first to have seen the contents of both sites for 65,000 years. And to visit both sites of old, they must have been capable of travel across 8000 miles of heavy seas.'

'Just so,' said Dorkin. 'And would you believe, they may even be akin to the same people who crashed a small craft 75 years ago in the United States.' They fell quiet after these revelations. It had been agreed that, barring the creation of fake lead implements, together with the construction of an elaborate hoax with palaeontological specimens, and with errors of their own making with genetic sampling, this was the only possibility. And they had agreed that such fakes and hoaxes, such ludicrous possibilities, such errors, were less likely than the real thing. In all this, they had shown the correct degree of scepticism, precisely as would be shown by the wider scientific community. Nevertheless they had eventually been obliged to accept it.

Dorkin stood waiting for some comment, anxious not to provoke his colleagues into any course of action. They had a perfect right to back out. In the silence, Wiener reached a conclusion first. 'Obviously, the work must go further,' he said. A few seconds later, Carmen restricted herself to a nod.

'I'm glad you said that,' replied Dorkin. 'I like to think you are both still with me.'

'We are,' said Wiener, 'and there are only two ways forward. Either we shall look fools, which I now doubt, or we shall be three of the most famous palaeontologists ever.'

'Well then, the next steps are clear. We shall have to go back to find the source of the two statuettes. It will mean a bit of detective work beforehand, followed by a trip into deep rainforest.' He paused to write the numbers 1, 2 and 3 on his whiteboard before continuing: 'And while we are there we shall have to find how and where those statuettes were made. It will also mean a visit to a very old lead mine in the far south, although quite clearly it cannot have been the source of depleted uranium.' He paused to write a summary of these points next to numbers 1 and 2.

Carmen said, 'So what's number 3?'

Simon Wiener looked at her and said quite simply: 'We look out for the proverbial lost tribe!'

Dorkin nodded and made his final tick on the whiteboard. Nobody spoke. They had all agreed on a trip into virgin rainforest in search for evidence which might not exist. A certainty, however, was that it would be fraught with great danger.

SEVEN

THE RADIO MESSAGE

It was quite some time since Callum Dood and Freya Sampson had departed for the United States but the remaining protagonists, Peter Pargeter and Adam Shilto, meanwhile had stayed in touch by means of such updates as they could muster. Living farther away, Guy Meredith remained as a telephone contact and was content to go about his work. Pargeter, of course, had his own contacts and was able to elicit from them the occasional comment. In that manner time passed until one day, Pargeter said to Shilto, 'I've heard from Callum. He sent me a package from the US. It contains a computer drive.'

'Oh good, it's nice to hear from him. I take it he's getting on OK?'

'Yes, I think so. He asked me to turn the contents into something we can be beam out.'

'I take it he means a radio message.'

'Yes, and I shall have a go today. By the way, from his note he seems to want more than one person to store a copy. I'm happy to keep one myself. Can I pass the other to you for safekeeping?'

'Certainly, I can keep it with my stock of communion wine.'

Pargeter took a break from his everyday labours and his practised hand took no more than a few minutes to carry out

Dood's wishes. Satisfied, he placed one copy in his desk and passed the other to Adam Shilto who, exactly as promised, stored it among his bottles of Sacro Vino.

—⁓—

David Elliott, Callum Dood and Freya Sampson were at their hotel where they were again in conference. They were discussing Lynch, Mann and Dorkin. Freya said, 'Who is Lynch anyway?'

'He is an ex-materials man. He's runs a small business in town, but before that he worked as a materials scientist for the government. I think he was helping to develop advanced ceramics for the aviation and defence industries. He got out, but the CIA keeps an eye on him anyway. I wouldn't think they would bother with an altogether harmless person. I'm inclined to suspect that he was helping them with reverse-engineered materials. Certainly he let that expression drop on one occasion.'

She replied: 'I expect they think he talks to nutcases about UFOs.'

Elliott said, 'Well, he does speak to people like Mann and Dorkin. But having met them myself, I would say they are as sane as I am. And both are interested in remaining below the parapet as far as the CIA is concerned.'

'We need to think about what to do next,' said Dood. 'Lynch gave you some good leads; Mann gave you a lot of background for your story, but I think Dorkin's work is where the next action will be. The thing is, Dorkin has gone away on some field trip. That leaves our own particular interests to consider.'

'Well,' said Freya, 'I think that we should do something with the data Dorkin gave us. We seem to have done quite well with data, and there's that number from the crop circle.'

'That's if we believe it,' replied Dood.

'We went through all that!' said Freya.

'Alright, we did.'

'So we should be doing something with it. We had some ideas...I spoke to Meredith.'

'You did.'

Elliott said, 'Well, speaking as a journo, we need to chase a story. I think that Freya is right: we need to do something with the leads we already have. And incidentally, I get the feeling that, from what Lynch said, we may have outstayed our welcome.'

'Surely they can't mind *us*, after all, two journalists and a crazy old vicar are hardly a threat!'

'Perhaps we are more important than we might imagine. There would be ferment if the public hears about all that Dorkin has done. I don't think they will trust us to make an uncontroversial story out of it. If that stuff got into the news—and I mean to make it happen—they would have a whole lot of denying to do.'

Dood said, 'I may be crazy, but I'm only seventy!'

'But not crazy enough to hang around.'

Freya said, 'We have been here for two weeks, and David for longer. Perhaps we should go home as quietly as we can.'

With that agreed, they settled their account and Elliott disposed of his car. At the airport they bought tickets home and were able to board an immediate internal flight to New York City. At John F Kennedy, they caught a connecting flight without difficulty and alighted at Gatwick about fifteen hours after leaving their hotel.

—w—

After their two-week excursion, Callum Dood and Freya Sampson were keen to settle into their domestic routines once more. Having done so, their thoughts turned to their recent experiences and they soon proposed a meeting with the others. Of those who had stayed at home, only Meredith had met Elliott, and in return for Elliott having shared his story (Freya Sampson had been worried that, so far, the sharing had been rather one-sided) they were keen to include him in their meeting. Accordingly, Callum Dood made a series of telephone calls and was able to settle on a date ten days later.

When they arrived, Dood described the events of the previous fortnight and his audience were interested or astounded to varying degrees. However it fell to Elliott to describe Dorkin's work, during which Meredith nodded; he had come to similar conclusions regarding the nature of the 'sizeable matter' that had kept the traffic so busy in the Network. When at last Dood and Elliott paused, Meredith was sufficiently encouraged to provide them with a full description of his relationship with Bud Lynch, together with the Lynch's speculations on the subject. In turn, Freya Sampson and the others recounted their own experiences. At last, and with such a large body of evidence before them, any notion of hoaxes, of impossible tabloid tales or of disinformation, finally fell away. They all knew that their small party was working on something considerable; that Dood and Shilto had been sent out by their bosses to find something concrete; and that as for Pargeter and Meredith, their technical skills were to be employed to the full. It was at least an hour before conversation ended with a question on what to do next. During that time, Dood made several pots of tea (which Shilto looked at rather suspiciously but agreed to drink). Questions finally followed:

Meredith promised to monitor the Network, but made the proviso that they ought not to expect too much. He decided not to mention the Firehills projectile without first having discussed the matter with Janice and Charlie. Freya, in recounting her own experiences, said it was useless to wait for more evidence in the form of lights, radioactive materials, power drains or crop circles. At that, Dood nodded and said he expected that any new development would come from Dorkin's activities, which they were aware they would be unable to influence. Then Pargeter said, 'Adam and I still have copies of Dorkin's database. I take it that you brought the other copy home?' Dood nodded.

Pargeter replied, 'So what shall we do with it?' They noted that this was more direct than the possible alternative of 'what shall we do next?' and it was then that the database began to take on more significance as their only possible course of action.

Dood lit a small cigar and said, 'If we agree that our course of action should concern the database, it seems to me that we should try to provoke *them* into doing something.'

'I think that's clear,' said Pargeter. 'But what do we mean by the term 'provoke?'

In her pleasant manner Freya said, 'We need to make our nice alien people aware that we know what they are up to and that they should come to tea with us one day to talk about it!'

Freya's comment might have sounded flippant but it was received as accurate. It took only Pargeter to wheeze a reply that, 'We need to send them the database so they know that we know about Dorkin's efforts in the genetics department.'

Meredith said, 'Yes, but don't expect them to come down and see us! They might prefer to see Professor Dorkin.' Nevertheless talk turned to how they should go about it.

Someone said, 'How about a signal contained in laser light?'

Someone else said, 'That would be no good.'

'Actually I thought a laser might be a good idea.'

'Well think again. We could never lay our hands on one powerful enough. And how do we add a signal to the laser beam? No, we would need use a radio signal.'

Pargeter said, 'But a suitable transmitter would be very expensive for just this one-off use.'

'But if we had the gear?'

Meredith said, 'Then radio wouldn't be as far-fetched as one might think. Scientists already listen to radio frequencies for any evidence of extra-terrestrial life.'

Shilto said, 'Even if we scan interstellar radio waves for strange signals, can we really expect alien intelligences to do the same? I mean, have there been any actual results from all this?'

'Actually, yes,' said Meredith. 'There was the episode of the "wow transmission", for one. That was recorded about thirty years ago by a radio-telescope in the United States.'

'I suppose they happened to be looking in just the right direction, on just the right radio frequency and at just the right time?' said Shilto.

'Well, they had done certain things to cut down the odds. They monitored the skies continuously, so that accounted for the right time. But they were also looking at the best possible frequency, which they already knew beforehand. It was 1420 MHz, the frequency given out by excited hydrogen atoms. It's supposed to be the obvious standard for all intelligent life.'

'So we could send out a signal and expect them to monitor things in the same way?'

'Yes,' said Meredith. 'I'm sure they would be interested. I imagine—I emphasise the word—that they have machines to pick up such signals. And there would be no problem with it getting there, because 1420 Hz is a microwave, which means it can pass through all the general rubbish in space. Visible light and most other radio waves couldn't do that.'

'So about this message, what did it consist of?'

'Nothing,' said Meredith. 'It was a continuous radio signal without any information in it. It was just a flash of energy.'

'Then why did they suppose it came from an alien intelligence?'

'It lasted for about a minute and then stopped altogether. Any interstellar collision, perhaps by excited clouds of hot gas, would have given a continuous signal for days, perhaps months. And then there was the narrow bandwidth; it was just one narrow radio frequency. In fact it was so narrow and so short that the finder wrote 'wow' on it.'

'Where did it come from?' said Freya.

'It probably came from a star in the constellation of Sagittarius,' Meredith said firmly. 'And in case you think it was a hoax, it couldn't have been a reflected signal from here on earth, because that band is a protected radio frequency. It isn't allowed for ordinary transmissions.'

'So we couldn't use it ourselves, just for a once-only message?' said Shilto.

'Not legally, no.' Meredith grinned at that.

Callum Dood called from the window, where he was still smoking: 'So who would stop us?'

'Nobody actually, but in case you're tempted, someone else has beaten us to it. You don't expect a load of UFO nuts to pass up *that* kind of opportunity, do you? Not that *we* are nuts,' he said with irony. 'And that was on the anniversary of the original wow transmission. I think they sent out a whole load of Twitter messages.'

Dood said, 'Well *that* would put any aliens off! But assuming they do listen, how would they recognise a message from us?'

'We would need to attach some kind of starting sequence. It would need to be a set of information, something of a mathematical nature, so they knew it came from an intelligent source.'

'And we could do that?'

'These UFO nuts used a radio transmitter with twenty times the power of a commercial radio station, so it wouldn't be beyond the realms of possibility for us to do something similar. Mind you, there's no guarantee that it would work.'

Dood took a large puff on his cigar, and blew a cloud of smoke out of the window. He said, 'If I have this straight, we send a radio signal into space on a protected frequency, containing DNA data from the Roswell smash and Boskop? That's just *wow*.'

Freya replied, 'If it's *wow*, then we had better get on with it! And I think I may be able to help. Perhaps I could get my radio station in on it? We could give them our data and get them to send it. It would just be part of an everyday commercial transmission.'

Meredith said, 'Well said, Freya! But personally, I wouldn't trouble them. Think about it, we need to send a signal out into space, whereas they are set up to transmit over the Thames valley. And anyway, there's no need. There are organisations that will do it for us.'

'What, for that?'

'Yes. I would call them enthusiasts: a very well-known one is Space Speak. All they ask is for the sender to do it via their website. The size of message is restricted to 500 characters, but they will send a much longer one for a reasonable sum. There are also others who will do the same in return for sponsorship of some kind.'

'And it's that easy?' said Shilto.

'I have to admit I used them once before, just to see how they work. But we need to find the price for a transmission of that size before doing anything.'

Elliott said, 'We spoke about the need to make a listener notice our transmission. So we need some kind of what was it…a starting sequence?' He watched his new friends nod in return. 'Then what do you think about sending that Kepler Conjecture? If they burned it into a hillside in the hope that we would recognise it, then surely we could return it to them!'

Pargeter said, 'David, that's really good. Then we can blast the whole lot into space.'

'I hope you realise,' said Callum Dood, 'that sending the Kepler number will also show that the message came from around here?' He waved away some cigar smoke.

'That's what we want,' said Freya. 'And it would immediately confirm that we are bright enough to have recognised the number for what it is. I seem to remember that that was its original purpose.'

Elliott wondered. He tried to fit this entire conversation into a mental narrative of a story about UFOs, but the contrast between his reasonable newspaper colleagues and his enthusiastic new friends could not have been more profound. He wondered how the story—if ever it came out—would be received. Yet like the very best newspaper 'scoops' it almost had a life of its own. He recognised that he was as hooked as the others. Like them, he waited as Pargeter tinkered with the database, added the Kepler number and loaded it onto Dood's computer. Dood stubbed out his cigar to watch as they entered a website called GalaxyComm. There was room for messages larger than their own, and he guessed that they were not the worst cranks the site had yet encountered. Their payment of $50 was accepted immediately and Dood, the holder of the credit card, pressed the button with his dead cigar. They waited and would not have been surprised had an alien suddenly appeared at the window. Then Meredith said, 'Well, we've done it now, so we can close down our end of the project for a while.'

There was a feeling of anti-climax. Freya said to Elliott, 'Perhaps we can write it up and publish now?'

'No!' he said, 'we still need a reply. It isn't finished without something else happening!'

Pargeter said, 'We mustn't expect too much.' It will take hours for the signal just to get to Pluto, never mind the nearest star, which is probably ten thousand times farther away.'

'Sure,' they agreed. Now we need to wait and see what happens!

EIGHT

THE RENAISSANCE OF CALLUM DOOD

As Peter Pargeter had feared, nothing else happened soon, and it was clear that their radio signal had failed to bump into the requisite antenna somewhere in Sagittarius, or anywhere else for that matter. They were not disappointed because they knew that it would take time, and the ever-present expectation was large enough to dismiss that feeling. Therefore they all went about usual routines with the matter dismissed to the back of their minds.

A full three months went by with the result that Callum Dood felt unusually house-bound. Following his return from Nepal his ankle was healed, yet he remained listless. One day, Shilto, having arrived at Dood's place, observed: 'It's been at least three months since we last saw the others. I think we can take it that our fun has come to an end?'

Dood nodded, and confided: 'If all that is dead, then I shall need another holiday. My trip to Nepal was a disaster, and the other to the US hardly counts—we were too busy. Can you tell the bosses I'm going away?'

'If you do go away I expect you'll miss out on visiting aliens.'

'Well I suppose it was all a bit silly anyway. What I need is some sea air and maybe a quiet guesthouse for a few days. Here's one,' he said, looking at a brochure. 'It's at Herne Bay.'

'What has Herne Bay got that Peckling hasn't?'

'It's the ideal place for a rest.'

'Why?'

'I don't want any bother. You get the most fantastic breakfast and then they turn you out on the seafront. You can wear a handkerchief hat and go paddling or you can collect a few shells from the beach. Then you can stroll for miles, smoke as much as you like or hang around and think. And there's a decent curry at the Rangoon in the evening.'

'Are you driving down?'

'No, that's too stressful. You may remember that I'm the only person ever to write off three cars in one day. I'm going to get the bus.'

At Herne Bay he slept for a full eight hours. Then armed with a copy of the Racing Post, he sat outside in the early morning sunshine. Later in a pub, he spoke to the barmaid, who had an accent. She said, 'I'm from Russia. You'd never pronounce my name properly, so call me Anna Beluga. You look deep in thought.'

'I've been concentrating on sleep and reflection. What do you know of dreams?'

'I know a little about daydreams. Sometimes they are pretty clear.'

'I've made them my recent study. Some say that dreams are, if not *the* reality, then certainly *a* reality. They may be an alternative form of consciousness with a higher state of perception, where distances are minimal and the mind can bend time itself.'

'Wow,' she said. 'That sounds a bit like physics. Where should I start?'

'Try absinthe. It leads one to a state of mind which some call 'crazy' but which is far more complex than its epithet might imply. It is not in itself a real intoxication.'

'That sounds like lucid dreaming? Surely it's more than just absinthe?'

'You have heard of *that*? Good. It is a vivid dream in which events are experienced by the possessor as though actually awake, and widely-regarded as a form of higher existence, a higher perceptiveness. The great Chinese philosopher Chuang Tzu is depicted in a lucid dream as a butterfly; others as the Lotus flower. I have been aiming at this myself through my own researches in the field of herbalism.'

'You won't find much of that in Herne Bay!'

'Oh dear, I think you may be right.'

A week later Adam Shilto said, 'Callum has disappeared. He hasn't come back from holiday and all forms of communication have dried up. He was due back a week ago.'

'Well, I suppose he's his own man and will turn up when he's ready.'

'Exactly, he knows where we are. We shall just have to wait.'

—·—

For Guy Meredith it was a long stretch to visit his new friends farther west, so he restricted himself, during this time, to such visits to Pargeter as were needed for business. From time to time there were others of his new friends there too, but he was still based half a day's drive to the east where Janice and Charlie lived, and it was with them that he most often met.

Charlie asked to use his telescope because it was a full moon that night. Meredith readily agreed, and Janice and Charlie turned up at about 5 pm with a few beers and fish and chips for three. Later, the moon rose in the sky and her pockmarked great face was turned towards them as they viewed the ministrations of the aeons in a night that was almost as bright as day. After a couple of hours they paused, and talk turned naturally to their previous visit when in summer it had been warmer, and when the meteor shower brought forth the Firehills projectile. It seemed the right time to remove it from its hiding place once again.

It lay in a pile of metal objects which, as before, reminded Janice and Charlie of an engineering scrapyard. Some had sharp angles and rivets and a generally rough appearance, and they seemed rather homespun. These Meredith was careful to remove and place outside. A few, however, had something more about them. It was true that they were mostly simple to look at, as though made for some straightforward engineering function. Yet they also had perfect contours and the feel of fine tolerances. Most were smooth and had their edges carefully finished. Such a quality of manufacture made them stand out as something better, and it was from this smaller collection that Meredith removed the Firehills projectile.

Janice and Charlie gathered round to look, and they renewed their acquaintance with the lightness of the object and its perfection of form. Although not an exact sphere, having projections at each pole, it did have a perfect radial symmetry. 'Perhaps,' said Charlie, 'it was designed to spin while descending? Could it be that its shape,' he said, 'like a miniature flying saucer, was intended to be a statement of origin?' The others nodded, although Janice remembered the haphazard and violent way in which it had landed.

Regardless, it was time to look inside, so they propped it up on a bench and took turns to examine its surface. Janice said, 'If we're not going to cut it open, we shall have to find some kind of catch, or perhaps a line to suggest where it comes apart—if it does.' She continued to search the surface, but apart from the marks they called hieroglyphs, the object was smooth, so the only possible means of manipulation remained one or more of them. She used her nails on one and it gave a faint musical note rather like the sound given by the teeth of a metal comb. Charlie suggested: 'Try that on one of the others.' She complied, and the hieroglyph gave a sound of a different pitch.

Janice smiled and said, 'I think we've found something. I bet we just have to do this.' She made another musical note. 'And since they all give out different tones that must be something to do with it.'

Successive hieroglyphs, read from left to right, gave tones that ascended by a regular musical increment, and Janice was able to manipulate them to make a complete musical scale. Then with her long nails she touched several at once so that the object gave out the collective sound of all the marks, a sound like the white noise of radio interference. With that, the object began to resonate, and when Janice repeated her performance, this time brushing the marks more strongly, a gap appeared about two-thirds of the way up. They were reminded of an opened boiled egg. Charlie said, 'Eureka!' and made the lid rock by using his hand. Then Guy and Charlie lifted the lid, laid it on the bench and looked inside as finally, it lay open for the first time.

Guy said, 'It's very like the Silpho object: it's even got copper paper inside!' His words were inspired by a thin copper-coloured sheet held in place by the two arms of a pedestal. Each, running from base and lid, pressed the sheet into position when the object was closed and ensured that it would not touch the inner surface. The sheet, however, was now loose, so Charlie removed it. In the light of a lamp it revealed further hieroglyphic marks, some repeated, and several with spaces between them.

'Janice said, 'What shall we do with it?' She looked at Charlie.

He said, 'I suppose, Guy, we could send a copy to your clever friend? Should we take it that he didn't get very far last time?'

Guy said, 'No, but I only gave him rough drawings. Now we know they have to be touched to do anything.'

Charlie replaced the copper sheet and lid. It settled soundlessly, and straight away no trace of a gap could be seen. He said, 'Let's ask him again, and perhaps he could come down here?'

It was clear that there would be no more progress that night, so with their immediate curiosity satisfied they stowed the sphere back in its hiding place. For a while they looked through the telescope again as yet another collection of shooting stars flashed through the sky. Later, the big bike rumbled outside as Janice and Charlie pulled away. Neither felt in the least proprietorial regarding their discoveries that evening, and Guy was pleased to be able to draw Pargeter's attention to it at long last. Soon Charlie remarked, 'Guy's an interesting bloke—good hobby to have.'

Janice replied 'Yes, he's a nice guy but he needs to fall in love with someone!'

—w—

Elsewhere, Pargeter, Shilto, Elliott and Sampson remained busy, but time passed and like Callum Dood, they had almost given up on any reply to their radio message. Yet their connection with the story was not quite severed because such things as lights in the sky, power failures and crop circles still made the news, and because John Buchanan and his croppies had once again decorated a hillside under the influence of strong cider. News and speculation still ran riot, and the two journalists discussed whether it was time for the scoop which they had so diligently prepared. Pargeter listened but expected little, so it came as a surprise when, on one of his visits to Peckling, Guy Meredith described the Firehills projectile for the first time. He started with an apology: 'I suppose I could have mentioned it before, but I didn't own it, and my friends asked me to keep it quiet.'

'That's fine, Guy, you couldn't have done anything else.'

'But I did give you the marks on its surface. Any more luck there?'

'No, and I suppose it slipped my mind. But I could always come back to Sussex with you?'

On the way back, Meredith described his trip to the Science Museum and said, 'Strange stuff does actually fall to earth quite regularly: large stones, chunks of ice, sea creatures and the like. It's usually the weather which does it. Strong winds can pick objects up and carry them large distances.'

'You don't think this object was such an example?'

'No.'

Later, they managed to open it exactly as Janice had done, and Meredith placed the copper paper flat on the bench. He turned to Pargeter for inspiration. Pargeter said, 'Well there are 10 marks on the outside. Inside there are 12, but one or two look the same as the outside ones. Two are just below the plane of the others, but I don't know what that means. Let's assume that it's deliberately easy to work out.' He walked around and thought for a bit. Meredith, a connoisseur of electrical processors, could almost see Pargeter's brain working.

Pargeter said, 'Alright, perhaps because the outside ones ascend in a regular scale, they are intended to be in that order. And if that's the case, we can number them 1-10.' He wrote numbers down on paper as he worked things out. 'Therefore, if the inside ones also have their own particular number as defined by their place in that scale, then the message must be'—he carried on writing—'17 1150 91 1793. It seems so simple now that your friend—Janice you say?—discovered how to get sounds out of it.'

'Yes, it was Janice, and she's a pretty bright girl. But can it really be that simple?'

'I don't see why not. If it's supposed to be a message, then there's an advantage in making it easy enough to decipher!'

'So, Peter, now what?'

'Well, it's a number, or at least we think it is. Obviously, the next step is to try and find out what it means. Let me put it about to the others and we can see what they say about it. But I'm glad I came down: seeing the object in the flesh has made it worthwhile.'

'Good, let me buy you lunch—I know a nice place—and we can get some fresh air on the promenade.' Pargeter nodded and allowed the tip of his tongue to wet his lips.

—w—

When Meredith was next over at Pargeter's place, the latter made sure that he invited everyone else too. They were all there except for Dood, whose independence was understood and humoured. Lunch was served, a ritual which Pargeter was at last pleased to reciprocate, and they began to discuss the events of the preceding weeks. It was still the case that they hoped for something from their radio message, but they remained philosophical about the lack of action in that department. Message aside, they were encouraged by the Firehills projectile and delighted by Pargeter's deductions therefrom. However it fell to Elliott to pass a first comment: 'We've mentioned some of this before, but it's almost as though we're being set up for some kind of chase. A new toy, the Firehills projectile, falls into our lap. There are marks on it which are ever-so-easy to decipher. Let's stop again and think about it.'

'I had thought the flying ball was aimed for *me*.' Meredith said, 'Perhaps that's because someone, somewhere, knows I listen out for such things.'

'I agree that it's strange,' said Freya Sampson. 'There have been a lot of odd goings-on, all centred around *us*, even though we don't deserve it. We aren't that important. First there were lights in the sky and my car stopped. That seemed a coincidence right enough. Then there was a strange mathematical crop circle on the downs nearby, together with the fact that tremendous heat was given out. We made contact with Guy'—she nodded in Meredith's direction and smiled—'who had experience with clandestine computer practices—sorry, Guy! And through Guy, we obtained real evidence of UFOs and were introduced to a Network of UFO seekers. We went to the United States and met Lynch, who knew a lot. He put us in touch with his own contacts, and they made it clear that a lot of strange research is going on.'

Meredith broke in, 'It does sound too much to believe, I agree. But if we really want to air everything, there's more!'

'Yes, there is!' said Freya, unwilling to stop. 'We met scientists who were using advanced technology to compare ancient DNA samples with materials they said were from the Roswell crash. And as unlikely as *that* was, the two were apparently similar, even though every reason would suggest they couldn't possibly be! Then we beamed all that into space.'

'And here we are,' said Elliott, 'hoping for an acknowledgement! If we put it like that, then we're definitely right in the middle of something strange. Freya is right, we don't deserve it, yet we do, on the other hand, have to accept that we actually chased the story. There were odd coincidences certainly, but we also found things out because they were there for us to uncover.'

Pargeter said, 'I agree, but any other group of people would have been just as unlikely. It was our interest, our sleuthing which turned us into the ten million-to-one lottery winners.'

Freya nodded her head, but it was clear that she wasn't satisfied that all this had arisen by chance. She said, 'Yes, but I still get the feeling that somebody has noticed us. We seem to be following some kind of trail.'

Meredith followed, 'Well if we are, it was laid by one of three sets of people.' He paused to see whether anyone would answer, but since nobody did, he said, 'It's either MI6, the CIA or both, or some green guys from space.'

Adam Shilto had listened intently, and now replied in his thoughtful way, 'I think we agree on these points. But since we are all here for once, it's about time we decided on what to do. I say this with another apology to our journalists here, who may have other ideas. For now, I think we should stay quiet for the same reasons we proposed once before. As I see it, we need to make something out of Peter's numbers, and do it quietly. If not, then we shall have to wait for something else to fall in our laps.'

'So,' said Freya, 'if it comes down to working out what to do with these numbers, perhaps it's an ISBN number from a book!'

'Or a radio frequency,' said Meredith.

Elliott said, 'Perhaps it's a telephone number, but I can't imagine what we'd say to anyone at the other end.'

Meredith replied, 'On the other hand we just might get through to somebody who is actually relevant.' The others nodded.

Pargeter shook his head: 'I doubt whether it's a telephone number, and anyway we can try it now.' He picked up a telephone and dialled. 'There you go, number unobtainable, so it's something else. I would say it's probably an instruction to go somewhere. Perhaps it's a map reference, the size is about right!'

'Well if it's that,' said Elliott, tapping away on his iPad, 'I use a satnav to find my clients. I feed it numbers and it works out the name of the place. And here it isn't,' he said. 'It says "no possible coordinate". Shame, it was a good idea.'

'Hang on,' said Pargeter, 'I wasn't in the boy scouts for nothing!

A couple of hieroglyphs were below the plane of the others. They might be negative numbers. Try minus 91 instead.'

'Alright,' said Elliott, 'so here we go. Yes, it's given me something. But that's odd, it's half way round the world.'

'Where is it?'

Elliott fiddled about with the screen, enlarging the image. 'It's actually in the middle of the Mexican jungle. And if I expand it even more, I can see that it's right near the border with Guatemala.'

'Let me look it up on this machine,' said Pargeter. A few minutes later, he said, 'Ugh! It's virgin rainforest, full of spiders, deadly snakes, howler monkeys and mosquitos!'

'Is that all?' replied Freya.

'Well there's good stuff too, like the architectural remains of an ancient civilisation.'

'Count me out,' said Freya Sampson. 'I've got work to do here.'

Meredith said, 'And me! My clients need me. I've got a full order book anyway!'

But they all looked miserable.

Elliott said, 'Well, I think we've managed to get pretty far. We wanted a huge scoop, so speaking personally I don't want to stop now. Remember how excited we were about the circle on the downs! As far as I can see, it's all or nothing. Either we go or there's no story.'

Pargeter said, 'Well, I suppose if you put it like that...'

Meredith slowly seemed to brighten. He said, 'Well if my most important client is going to be away, then I suppose I can justify it too!'

Pargeter smiled and said, 'And you, Freya?'

'Well if David's going, I suppose I shall have to!'

'Sorry!' said Shilto with some regret, 'I still have to hold the fort here.' That aside, their change of mind had brought about a striking transformation. They were suddenly pleased, as though a trip to the jungle were now inevitable. Much later, Freya Sampson woke in the middle of the night with a sudden revelation which caused her to telephone Pargeter the next morning. She said, 'Peter, that number, it's the same as the one your friend managed to get from the crop circle!'

'Good Heavens, Freya, so it is. Obviously they are trying to get us to go there.'

—∽—

'So, Reverend Dood, you want to do some prospecting in our country, do you?' The speaker was a somewhat sycophantic tour operator called Señor Romeo. Dood had travelled to Cancun in Mexico, there to embark on the kind of holiday that would dispel his own particular dismal skies and winter winds. He had favoured some kind of botanical expedition and in his heart remained a Victorian-style plant collector. There would be rare orchids and fungi and innumerable butterflies! This, after all, was his hobby, and what better place to indulge it than in the jungle? He felt no need to apologise or justify and understood fully that it was a form of escape. Accordingly, he had contacted a small tour operator, and the Señor seemed eager to gain his custom.

'I should like to,' said Dood in a modest and courteous manner. 'I had hoped to see a rainforest and heard a lot about the hospitality of your country. I am an amateur naturalist, but of course prospecting for specimens is probably illegal?'

'Specimens? Do you mean historical artefacts? Yes, it would be serious matter if you were caught trying to leave the country with them. We have a very ancient culture here: archaeological remains, temples, agricultural practices and so on. They have left many valuable traces in the civilisation of our modern country. We, that is to say the tour operators, must warn against collecting even the most modest stone or implement.'

'I quite understand. In fact, I had meant to say only plant specimens, not to remove in their entirety, of course, but to draw them and study their form and habitat. I may need to remove the occasional leaf or piece of root, but that would be the extent of my activities. I believe that the Mayans were renowned for their contribution to…ah, if not botany, then certainly folk remedies and herbalism.'

Señor Romeo looked relieved as he said, 'In that case, Reverend Dood, you have come to the right man. Although the Selva Lacandona has its own tourist trails which, despite it being rainforest are quite popular, there are less-used and very discreet trails which I can show you. Why, only recently I spoke to a small party of Americans. They seemed very serious in pursuit of their own particular interest, that of lost tribes in the jungle. If you prefer similar, well, I can arrange to suit.'

'Do I need any personal protection?'

'Of course, but I can provide all you need. I carry a rifle myself, in case we are attacked... in case we see a jaguar, but other than that our main difficulty will be in avoiding biting insects. But I am experienced and carry all the necessary medical kit. There are a few snakes, of course, vipers, constrictors, but of course, they are not your foremost interest?'

'Well I'm renowned for my interest in butterflies and have many preserved specimens at home. But on this occasion it is mostly the flora of your country that I had hoped to study. Of course I would also like to see relics of the old civilisation, but I would be delighted to accomplish both together.'

'Excellent. Can we agree on a price? I would need $200 US per day. I may not be cheap, but believe me, I can take you to places that the others cannot. Normally the trips are daily excursions, but something tells me that you are the kind of man who might wish to see more: not just the exotic butterflies, but perhaps the things that modern man has not seen at all.'

'That would be excellent. I propose to stay in my hotel for two days, getting things ready. Can we leave on Monday morning?'

'Certainly, but for repeated trips into the jungle may I suggest one of the lodges that are nearer your destination? There are several. They are individual thatched huts with all modern conveniences and a garden in which you are free to walk.'

'Thank you, I shall bear that in mind.'

Two days later, Romeo, wearing modern-looking and robust clothing, checked to make sure his equipment was complete, and slung a rifle over his shoulder. With him were two of his countrymen who, unlike Romeo, were natives of the jungle and non-Hispanic, although bilingual. Their clothing was more traditional than Romeo's own: they wore a hat and a colourful rain-poncho over traditional undergarments of shirt, short pants, and a neck cloth. They chattered in their euphonious Tzotzil tongue as they bade farewell to their women, who also wore traditional dress of a colourful huipil, together with a shawl over their shoulders. The natives were hired to carry rucksacks of essentials such as rations and cooking utensils. Dood was relieved that he would not be asked to carry a very heavy load himself, but besides personal items like clothing, he had included a number of specimen bags in his own rucksack, together with a herbal encyclopaedia and notes on the plants he meant to study.

Señor Romeo indicated that he did not expect to offer an assault course and that if they covered ten miles per day in the first instance, he would be satisfied. If all went well, he would offer a longer excursion using a four-wheel drive vehicle which they could leave in order to traverse the jungle still farther. They walked a good distance on the first day. The jungle floor was a thick carpet of dry leaves, but when Dood kicked away at the surface, the layer below was damp, brown and decaying. He had imagined an intractable barrier of lianas and brush that would require cutting as they passed, but progress was easy at first with lighter shrubs whose branches were displaced readily by the movement of swinging limbs. Walking ahead, the natives chattered happily and to Dood's delight, stopped at ninety-minute intervals for a ten-minute cigarette. He felt more at home in a land in which tobacco was widespread and regularly rolled a construction of it himself.

Eventually they came to a more dense aspect of forest growth which brought about a slightly slower passage. There, the forest floor was damper than before, and with it came an all-pervading smell of decaying vegetable matter. More interestingly the shrubs were especially diverse, and perhaps twenty varieties could be observed growing on the forest floor wherever light could reach them, or higher in the canopy where they were attached to branches from which their roots hung, collecting the dripping water that fell from above. Dood asked to stop and investigate, so they made a temporary camp in a small clearing.

'Reverend Dood,' said Romeo, 'by all means look around, but we are near to a stream over there'—he pointed—'so please watch where you tread. There are often snakes around. They like water and some are green and difficult to see. They can be dangerous.'

Dood nodded. He had seen an interesting shrub nearby and wished to investigate further. He placed his rucksack down and moved towards a nondescript climbing plant that had attained a height of some six feet by wrapping itself around a tree. It bore seed pods and he harvested a number of these, fat with small black seeds. He also picked a few leaves to draw later, brushing off a couple of large spiders with his sleeve. Romeo acknowledged his interest, while the tribesmen nudged each other and said with a respectful and symbolic manner a word that sounded like 'ol-ol-ee-ooh-kee'. They also made a whistled noise rather like a bird call. It was clear that they knew of the shrub and had a profound respect for it. Nodding to them Romeo said, 'We call it 'Gloria de la Mañana'. It is not uncommon here, and is highly-prized for its medicinal properties. You are a religious man, Señor Dood. It is notable that the tribesmen use it in their religious ceremonies. I believe they make an infusion from the seeds.'

Dood inclined his head, bowed and said, 'May I ask for what purpose?'

'Certainly; it is of help to them…they may wish, ah, to commune with their gods. I regret, however, that my Spanish forefathers took the view that, sacred although it is, its use should be suppressed. Nevertheless the tribesmen cling to their traditions still.'

Dood nodded politely and tucked the packet into his rucksack. They had a short break for a cigarillo before eating a light meal and after half an hour, moved deeper into the jungle. As the day wore on, the sun started to decline from its position high above and began to cast shadows from tree trunks. With the light waning, it gave the place a more sinister aspect as though the forest, formerly welcoming, had changed its mind. Yet Romeo seemed unworried and with the tribesmen walking steadily, Dood saw no reason to feel otherwise. Eventually, Romeo suggested that it was time to turn back since their return journey would be of about twelve miles with the evening approaching. Turning, they reached their truck by late afternoon, where, satisfied with his first outing, Dood felt the need to build more fitness before a longer incursion. As Romeo agreed, 'It is better to return tomorrow than to stay the night. Many large animals come out, and things which suck the blood.' Nevertheless there would be progress: Romeo suggested that they should start earlier and go deeper into the forest. Again he offered caution: 'Reverend, we must first be careful to accomplish as much as we can on daily excursions. The jungle can change its appearance at night, and it means carrying heavier gear such as tents, together with more food. Let us work towards such an exploration in due course.'

'Do I take it,' said Dood, 'that some visitors have found deep jungle too much to cope with?'

'Si, Señor Dood. It is not pleasant to see people lose confidence.'

'Were they attacked?'

'No, Señor. The difficulty was the disorienting affect that the jungle can have. They begin to panic when they are lost, even for a short time. But I do not think that you will be the same. There is much jungle near your home?'

'I understand. The concrete jungle—as we say—can be disorienting too, but I am used to it and such a temporary confusion holds no fear for me.'

On the following day the dawn was at 6 am, but the party chose to leave at 4.30 by Land Rover. They ventured farther south than on the first day by using a track, broad at first, although mostly dry, and without the water-filled ruts and churned mud that can arise from regular use by motorised vehicles. Later, they left their truck in a clearing and began to walk. By 10 am, and after three hours, they stopped to rest, boiled water for coffee, and began to examine their surroundings.

They were in a very great wilderness. Their map, such as it was, showed a broad expanse of green together with a few spidery lines of black, suggesting that the jungle was mostly an uncharted domain. It was a huge reserve of vegetation and dripping water, with morning mist rising in the sunlight; a chaos of nature that could not be represented by using a paper chart. They were in virgin rainforest, unspoilt and dangerous to the inexperienced, yet it harboured many relics of past civilisation. Lost villages remained: the fallen walls and moss-covered stones a memory of long-departed peoples who had lived there. But they were long-gone. Their works had turned to tumbled blocks of masonry festooned with lianas, roots and rotting vegetation, among which it became difficult to navigate. Thus, from time to time, Romeo made for higher ground so that he could see the peaks of the Montes Azules, majestic above the tree line. Below, and seen mostly as perturbations in the forest cover, were the major rivers, the Usumacinta and Lacanja. These, favoured by tourists as their main conduit through the country, were avoided by Dood who was in no mood to seek the companionship of other holidaymakers.

The party had entered deeper forest, where rotting vegetation was thick underfoot and mist hung in the air from small rivers nearby. For a while, they followed an undulating river towards a waterfall, where a torrent fell thirty feet to a lake below. There, droplets of water coated undergrowth and clothing alike; while brown vegetation, covered in a white tracery of mildew, decayed at speed in the warmth and dampness. Trees fought for the sun, and their trunks, festooned with vines and aerial roots, rose high to the dark canopy. At his feet, however, Dood could make out a tumble of unusual stones lying in the grey mud. All were heavily weathered, but it was clear that they were made by men and had not been touched for a long time. Some were easy to pull out and wash in water. Romeo and the Mayan tribesmen watched him until Romeo eventually said, 'Señor, we are gratified that you have not attempted to place any in your rucksack. My colleagues are pleased that you have shown due respect and wish only to take photographs of them.'

Dood had actually intended to draw them. He nodded and the others were happy to remove their packs and rest for a while. He began to write a description to accompany his drawing. Each stone was carved into the rough shape of a human figure and was about six inches tall. Below a torso the figure was crude and carved only to stand upright, with no proper abdomen or legs. The torso was fully-detailed, however, and the head, with a deliberately contemplative expression, was surmounted by a broad curved hat. Some had an introspective expression while others were deliberately downcast as though deep in contemplation. All had a small chip taken from the rim.

On looking up, he heard one of the Tzotzil-speakers say 'teonanacatl,' a word accompanied by a gesticulation with his hands to suggest the growth of a plant from the soil. His companion, more bilingual, said, 'piedras de setas' to which Romeo added the translation, 'mushroom stones.' Romeo said further, 'It is so, Reverend Dood. The chip on one side is to represent a bite taken from the mushroom cap. There are many growing nearby. They, the teonanacatl, were highly prized by the Mayans and indeed worshipped.'

'Yes, I see. Hence their reverence towards the piedras de setas,' replied Dood. 'We have similar reverences in my own country.' He wrote a few comments in pencil. 'But if I may, I shall harvest a very few live specimens and will dry them when I return to base. Please would you, Señor Romeo, kindly communicate my respect to our companions? In the meantime, I would like to survey further this very dense part of the jungle. If possible, I would like to find the ingredients for the herbal remedy called ayahuasca.'

'Alas,' said Romeo, 'such herbs are not to be found around here. They are found only in the densest parts of the jungle, a considerable distance away. To find them you would need to journey to the southernmost extremities of the Chiapas. Perhaps we could discuss such an expedition in due course?' He looked regretful. 'It is somewhat difficult to get there.'

'Certainly,' said Dood, and continued to collect the teonanacatl and place them in small bags.

Towards the end of the afternoon, with his rucksack heavier but with the encouragement of his companions, they set off on the return journey with Romeo ahead and the tribesmen following. The latter seemed subdued, and for a mile or two they turned to look over their shoulders rather wistfully. However the party made good progress and regained their transport a little after dark. The tribesmen began to look morose and Romeo said, 'Their natural aspect is one of diligence and perseverance by day, together with reverence by night. Although they are outwardly Catholic and observe the rituals, feasts and ceremonies, they have a superstition borne of their ancestry and culture. They feel that the jungle becomes alive after dark. Certainly it contains life in abundance but as to whether there is a greater spirit, I cannot say. A Catholic myself, I would decline that principle yet observe every respect when there in person.'

The Reverend Dood nodded, smiling at his pragmatism. He said, 'We also have our own reverences towards nature and many still observe the ascent of the sun through stones, or sacrifice to the sickle moon.'

Shortly they arrived, Dood at his lodge and Señor Romeo and the Mayans at their homes. Romeo said, 'I suggest we have a day at home tomorrow? It will enable us to prepare more thoroughly for the following day.'

'Thank you, yes. I think that is best,' said Dood, 'I surprised myself by being able to hike for nearly thirty miles through heavy rainforest, but I shall want to catalogue my specimens, rest and decide on my interests.'

'Si, Señor,' said Romeo, 'and we need to talk about our destination. It is more of an undertaking to get there than I am usually asked for.'

On the next morning, while the tribesmen were elsewhere, Dood and Romeo had a conference in Dood's hut. Dood remarked upon the title of 'hut' not doing his holiday accommodation full justice. He said, 'I am delighted that it contains every convenience.' Then, while Dood made coffee, Romeo considered a map and scribbled on a notepad.

'I do hope your plant specimens will dry,' said Romeo, looking around.

'Thank you,' said Dood from the kitchen. 'As you can see, I have hung the teonanacatl on threads of cotton from the wooden beams overhead. I believe they will dry quickly despite the humid air. And the seeds of gloria de la mañana will be fine as they are. I packed them in an envelope between pieces of blotting paper. Tomorrow, however, you mentioned that I would be wise to carry some pulque or tequila?'

'Yes, you will find that it offers a more potable means of taking herbal remedies if you try them. You also smoke cigars? Then you may find a good supply useful.'

'How long do you think we shall be away?'

'I should bring all conveniences for ten days.' Romeo followed assertively, 'And Reverend, in view of the extra demands you have placed on me and with, some would say, the dangers posed by travelling so far into deep jungle—it is mostly unexplored and even the Mayans look upon it with awe—I must revise my terms to $250 US per day. We shall have to drive as far as we can, and then make...I will make...arrangements to park our truck at an estate I am familiar with. The owner will charge for the privilege, but at least we shall know that our return will be without hazard.' He then said: 'And Reverend, you are sure? You will be heavily laden. If you wish I can hire an extra Mayan tribesman?'

'No thank you, I feel quite confident.'

'It is as I expected,' said Romeo.

The small party embarked early the next day. However although heavily laden it was mostly with extra food and water which, since it would be consumed, would give a declining burden. They had also brought more clothing and on Romeo's advice, medicines such as an antidote to snakebite, together with that for mosquitos, flies and other hostile creatures. They drove inland as far as they could and by mid-day had reached an estate of huts in a clearing. It was in fact a village of about a hundred people, all in traditional clothing and speaking Tzotzil: an agricultural community with one or two merchants trading with the outside world. Nearby were fields of gourds, striped squash and green vegetables. The villagers looked healthy and prosperous, but to Dood's eye, they seemed temperamental and requiring effective leadership. Such leadership soon appeared, however, in the person of an important-looking merchant who waved to Romeo in a familiar fashion and at fellow tribesmen to bring refreshment. They were ushered into a hut and offered a pot of the local coffee, sweetened in the local taste with unrefined cane sugar. Romeo handed the keys of his truck to their host, and they departed with handshakes and courtesies in the Tzotzil and Spanish languages.

'This way, please, Reverend,' said Romeo, 'and may I recommend a particular posture with your rucksack?' A muddy track, wide but visibly narrowing, led south into virgin jungle.

'In this direction, Señor,' said Romeo, taking the lead, 'virgin rainforest lies right to the Guatemalan Reserva de Biosphera Maya, which is on the other side of the Chiapas border. We have very many miles to hike, and we shall enter jungle where few men go.'

They walked in mud and on the compacted vegetation of a thousand summers, spongy and bristling with insect life. The air hummed with mosquitos that danced and dived in the sunlight, rising from wayside puddles, streams and brackish semi-permanent ponds. Drops of water fell all the while from leaves overhead and the temperature increased. By one o' clock the air was hot and humid despite the sun being hidden above the trees. It became difficult to make progress as their boots compressed dead vegetation and made it slide on barely decayed, viscid layers beneath. By two o' clock they had travelled only three miles and were soaking wet, not only with sweat, but also with the heavy rain that had begun to fall. Later, they found higher ground, and on a stony and bare surface finally had a half-hour rest during which they smoked and drank coffee.

The rainforest was thick and wet and less accessible than any they had yet traversed. Dood did not expect to find suitable botanical specimens so early, but had he been a deliberate orchid collector he would have been pleased, for there were many exotic species all around, each with intricate and diverse flowers of rich colour; while around them huge butterflies circled and tiny hummingbirds hovered. It was beautiful, entrancing and without pity. He resisted the instinct to possess, since he knew that few specimens would survive the journey. Finishing his cigar, which he found the mosquitos disliked, he rejoined Romeo and they continued their hike. Later, he asked about the architectural remains farther south.

'It depends upon your fortune, Reverend,' said Romeo. 'We may come across great earthworks and buildings. There are rumours of lost cities, even pyramids. They will be deserted of course, for any working civilisation in these parts would make itself known. Their agriculture would be visible and they would trade their crops such as beans, corn and squash.'

'Were they Aztec in nature?'

'No. The Aztec civilisation arose far away in central Mexico and was prevalent very much later, perhaps by the year 1300. Here, on the Yucatan a far older Mayan civilisation held sway three thousand years ago; possibly very much earlier. The Mayan civilisation has never died; it is here still, and the people live lives and speak as their forefathers did. Yet eventually the Aztec civilisation, more warlike than the Mayan, grew in the plains farther west. They were able to subjugate the other peoples and they gave their name to our country: *Meesheeka* became Mexico. The Aztecs eventually fell to the Spanish, however.'

'What about the Incas?'

'Farther south. They were a Peruvian civilisation.'

Dood mused for a while. They were passing up a mild incline and it was necessary to concentrate. However at the top, he said: 'Would it be correct to say that the Aztec civilisation grew from the Mayan?'

'No. The Aztec language was quite different and the peoples, too, were distinct. But the interesting thing is that just as there were at least some similarities between them, so too the ancient Mayan and Egyptian cultures showed many similarities.'

Intrigued, Dood said, 'But they were many thousands of miles apart!'

'That may be,' said Romeo. 'Nevertheless I find some of their similarities remarkable. It would be foolish to say that ancient civilisations lived in splendid isolation. There was trade, migration, movement, yet even the most committed advocate of such proposals must wonder how the Mayans and Egyptians were able to meet!' There was a pause, and Romeo seemed to reflect before continuing, 'And some say that the remains of another civilisation can still be found near our destination. It may be that a reclusive, perhaps lost people is still present there.'

After considering Romeo's comments Dood returned to the subject of the Mayan and Egyptian cultures: 'Perhaps their main similarity was one of pyramid building?'

'There was much more. Their tongues had many similarities, and I can recall several examples from my studies, *Ahau* is the name for a particular day in Mayan and is also the time of day in ancient Egyptian. Similarly, *hom* is a place for playing ball in Mayan and is also the word for a small ball in old Egyptian.'

'Yes, but surely those few are not conclusive!'

'Certainly not, but I could go on, it seems to me conclusively. The word '*ik*' means air in Maya, while to suspend in air is *ikh* in ancient Egyptian. Similarly *nichim* means flower in Maya, while *nehem* is a flower bud in ancient Egyptian. There are many other examples of similar pairs, which significantly, are also words for which the hieroglyphs are known.'

'So you believe that the Mayan and old Egyptian civilisations were derived from a common origin?'

'Perhaps; it is possible that nations migrated in great antiquity. But there is another possibility that few are willing to discuss since it might seem foolish.'

Dood was encouraging: 'Please speak freely.'

'In this instance I shall go on. Unless we can show how

humans migrated over the great oceans, it can only mean they were sponsored by an outside culture with abilities advanced enough to mitigate the distance. But there are those unwilling to accept such a thing.'

Dood said, 'Scholars have proposed an Atlantean civilisation, consumed in the floods of antiquity and now long gone.'

Romeo nodded, 'And there is evidence for such a thing in the memory of the peoples concerned. Among the Aztecs there were traditions concerning people from the east, so that when the Spanish came, they were welcomed as gods. Similarly, the Mayans deify strange benefactors from the skies. I am drawn to wonder about the origin of such legends and whether they were from experience in the time of the ancients. Or,' he said with particular emphasis, 'more recently.'

They were silent now, and thoughtful as their hike continued. After three more hours the rainforest became particularly dense and the Mayan tribesmen were asked to go first in order to clear a path. They did so with a machete to improve the oft-used animal tracks which, although they gave a recognisable pathway, continually meandered in the wrong direction. Nor could they be followed safely, and it was at this point that Romeo unslung his rifle and removed the safety catch. The danger of confronting a jaguar, together with the heat, humidity and exertion, made Dood and Romeo feel uncomfortable. Only the Mayan tribesmen appeared unworried. Yet after two, then three days more of walking, even they assumed a more morose expression. It was as though the jungle had become as alien to them as to Dood. They did not grumble, yet they seemed relieved to pause at mid-day or make camp at dusk. Romeo said, 'It is as though they feel they are trespassing.' Dood nodded in acknowledgement of the oppressive feel of the jungle, which had gown to an almost tangible hostility. They were under a uniform canopy of vegetation, far from sunshine, and with the imperative of going still deeper into the unknown.

Following an errant compass bearing, conversation turned to the likelihood of missing their goal. Romeo looked confused, and said, 'I carry a compass, Reverend, which I naturally rely on. Yet it is now incorrect when compared with my last observation of the stars.'

'How can you be sure?'

'Mercury can be seen south of east so that our true destination is one day's march to the south. Yet the compass suggests we should walk into the west.'

'I wouldn't worry, Señor Romeo. There may be iron hills nearby.'

'There are none to my knowledge, Señor, none yet discovered.'

'I think it is probably the best explanation. I wouldn't want that to stop our fun.'

'It shall be as you say, Señor Reverend,' said Romeo, who thereafter was silent on the matter.

They continued to march due south where lay the most impenetrable landscape yet. Everywhere, their way seemed to be barred by water. In due course they came to a sluggish river in grey mud banks, where lily pads had collected to provide the perfect hiding place for predatory fish and water-loving snakes. There, the Mayans turned about to avoid wading, and walked east until they found a better crossing-point. That meant a diversion of at least a mile, yet it was the best they could do until, on the far side, they turned to resume their former path. By then all members of the party were thoroughly soaked and they became concerned with finding higher ground, whatever the cost in time. Due south, however, the ground naturally became higher. In the distance they saw new formations of cloud and were certain that they were approaching a significant incline. Most importantly, the jungle began to dry and lose its sour stench.

After a further day during which their morale began to improve, they finally felt direct sunshine and were relieved to stop and make camp. The multitude of flying insects was undiminished, yet it was a reasonable place to make a smoky fire and dry out. Taking stock at last, they were about 200 miles from the estancia of the Mayan merchant and more confident of their position. The Mayans were less morose, Romeo was less concerned with small matters of their hike, and all were pleased to see the Señor Reverend in his element as a latter-day Victorian naturalist.

Soon they encouraged the Reverend Dood to forage around. Inevitably, Romeo spoke about the risks: they had not seen the green anaconda which lived far south in the Amazon basin, yet there were other similar beasts, and he advised Dood to wear long boots at all times. He said, 'Although not all our snakes are poisonous, there are some very nasty ones, particularly the Nauyaca. If you are bitten, try to kill the snake with your machete so that I can see it. Knowing the right antivenom may save your life.' He pointed towards the Mayans who had begun to wear leather boots to the knee. 'You can guard against most bites in that way, but avoid pulling at the undergrowth with your hands and watch the overhanging branches.'

Thus far, he had avoided dealing direct with the Mayans and had reserved a cordial and silent courtesy towards them. It had been Romeo, more correctly, with whom they dealt. After their trials, however, they began to assume a little more familiarity and now showed more reliance on each other. They began to smile at him, and the one called Aapo pointed to part of the jungle as a good place to collect specimens. He muttered the word *ayahuasca* to his companion Atlahua, who nodded and smiled in return. It was clear that they understood his intentions. Noting this, Dood filled his rucksack with a field guide and just enough stores to last the day. Then, slinging a rifle over his shoulder, he followed a trail into the jungle.

Walking about half a mile and looking right and left into the hanging lianas, he eventually found examples of the ayahuasca or 'soul vine' growing innocently alongside the path. Using his machete, he cut several long pieces of stem from the better specimens and placed them in a sack. Then he turned his attention to another plant which Atlahua had seen. This, the chakruna, was growing in profusion, and noting the shiny and corrugated leaves he collected several. Satisfied with his outing and stopping only to harvest some of the 'wild coffee' plant, he retraced his footsteps and arrived back at camp.

By then it was mid-day and they made a small meal. Later, and with the others still at leisure, Dood pushed on towards high ground about three miles to the south, a place notable for having caused the maximum deflection of Romeo's compass. Approaching, it did not look like a hill, more a lengthy cliff running east to west. Above it white clouds gathered in the air, and birds circled aimlessly. Shouldering his rucksack he reached it with the sun still high in the afternoon sky.

It became clear that this slanting elevation, strewn with rubble, would be easy to climb. Accordingly, he ascended using a path made by forest animals such as the coati or the smaller jungle cats, both of which had left their spoor in many places. At the summit, vegetation was limited to smaller shrubs for a few hundred yards, after which the rainforest reappeared. In the farther distance there appeared a derelict township of fallen walls and disused agricultural terraces. Otherwise, the place was silent apart from the wind, and rather eerie. He approached and found walls demolished in a way which suggested that it had been deserted on purpose. Undoubtedly it was a village that had long since fallen into disuse.

Somewhat farther away, and completely incongruous in a position overlooking the summit, he observed a pyramid. Dood noted its incongruity but it would not be correct to say that he was surprised by the existence of such a thing in the jungle. He was, after all, from Wiltshire where far stranger buildings were a general feature of the landscape. Romeo had made a tentative reference to a building if this kind, yet it was not marked on any map and was unknown at large. Perhaps that was because it was enclosed in a curved section of rock and invisible from the forest floor.

The pyramid was small, and bore no comparison with the great examples of Egypt. It was of the stepped variety and like the few examples he had seen elsewhere in Mexico. It had a rectangular base with sides of about one hundred feet long, and it was made of stones so finely shaped that they seemed to need no mortar. It was very old, yet it looked *preserved*. It also seemed particularly clean and barely weathered despite the visible absence of habitation nearby. Sitting in a shallow basin enclosed by a fold of land, it seemed to have been placed there with discretion in mind.

He climbed to the first step and advanced on a parapet four feet wide. Turning the first corner, his way along the second side was blocked by two uprights which continued to the apex above. Leaning around the first to look, he found that between them was an engraving of a wise man on a throne. To one side were impressions of agricultural tools and fields of maize while on the other was a circular calendar. Above were stars, and nearby were spheres with legs. He made a pencil sketch, repacked his rucksack and descended to the jungle. Pleased with his expedition, he reached camp shortly before sunset, noting the growls and warning calls from creatures waking around him. Later, he described his afternoon to Señor Romeo, who translated to the Mayans.

They became animated when shown his sketch and their manner became one of deference. They conversed in Tzotzil and then spoke to Romeo, who assumed a deliberately courteous expression. He said to Dood, 'It seems you have come upon a place, rumoured to exist by tribesmen, but not seen by them in this modern age. They say it is a place associated with a god of the skies deified by the tribe who lived there long ago. They fear the village was destroyed in a war between them and more recent insurgents, and deserted soon after. Yet a few descendants of the first tribe are rumoured to live nearby, and they are said to be of a strange disposition. Our tribesmen regret that they cannot confirm whether the rumours are true.'

'Gracias, Señors,' said Dood, and the tribesmen nodded appreciatively before preparing sweetened coffee and retiring to the campfire.

Romeo and Dood sat at some distance, observing the nocturnal activity of bats and other creatures. Romeo seemed anxious to develop his earlier conversation regarding old civilisations. He said, 'Of course I cannot say for certain that the benefactor in your drawing has any connection with the Mayan Itzamna. Nevertheless I think that it is likely.'

'Why is that?'

'They have a similar appearance. I feel that their gods are of a common tradition.'

'Perhaps he is as alive today as Itzamna?'

'I am drawn to think so. I regret that Itzamna was suppressed by my Spanish forefathers, yet if he is revered today, then I would expect a cousin, however distant, would be the same.'

'What,' said Dood, 'were the spheres to one side?'

'I'm not sure.' Romeo spoke with Atlahua and returned to say, 'A common tradition is that a creator comes from the sky. He is often depicted residing there. From time to time he is willing to visit his children who may offer sacrifices to him. These, which the creator requires in return for gifts, are reputed to be seen to this very day. He asks for young men and women, who are taken away in a shooting star which rides the skies. His arrival is accompanied by lights in the sky and marks on the earth made by great heat.'

Dood nodded. So his experiences were not humbug. He thought for a while of his friends at home, waiting for a reply to their radio message. If only they could hear! He said, 'I suggest we visit the clifftop tomorrow, but in the meantime I am keen to try one or two of the local recreational beverages. I managed to collect some of the wild coffee plant, but would be keen, in the first instance, to make some ayahuasca.'

'Are you sure that's wise?' said Romeo. 'Perhaps we should limit ourselves to coffee?'

'Ayahuasca has been described as a way to the most lucid of perceptions.'

'But there are rumours, which suggest that the effects cannot be guaranteed.'

'Well, I *have* come a long way. And I would regard such an investigation as offering due respect to local culture.'

'I quite understand,' said Romeo, recognising that his employer was becoming obstinate. Turning, he said to Atlahua and Aapo: 'Por favor recolecta suficiente leña para hacer un fuego. Tendrá que durar seis horas[7].'

After about half an hour, Atlahua and Aapo had a fire going in a shallow pit. They allowed it to burn until the embers smouldered very slowly. From time to time they added the occasional piece of wood, and dried further logs next to it.

Over the fire they placed a large pot and in it, the pith of the ayahuasca vine. Then, since the vine would be useless by itself, a layer of chakruna leaves and thereafter, alternate layers of each until the pot was full. Water was added to cover the whole, and it was allowed to simmer very slowly. Atlahua agreed to supervise the boiling pot for the rest of the evening and at about 10.30 pm strained the soggy mass into a bottle. The result was brown and hot, so they agreed to try it the following morning and had a final smoke before going to sleep. In his tent Dood listened to the incessant scratching and scraping of insects as they tried to reach him. Although he was used to the cacophony made by jaguars and howler monkeys, this stopped him from dropping off until late. He was glad to have postponed his experience of ayahuasca until daytime. The following morning, each ate a sizeable breakfast, and then they decided to strike camp and to make a new one nearer the cliff. Suitably fortified, they made ready to leave. Meanwhile, each man was provided with one-quarter of the contents of the ayahuasca bottle to drink at will. Romeo, Atlahua and Aapo drank their shares straight away.

'Ach,' said Romeo. 'It is exceedingly bitter on the tongue.' He grimaced and supplemented his own with tequila. With a knowing wink the Mayans drank their portions down in one gulp and wiped their mouths as though the taste were a necessary evil. Dood decided to defer his experience until he could gauge

---

7   Please collect enough firewood to make a fire. It will have to last six hours.

the reaction of his comrades. Then, setting out, they walked vigorously on a southward path through the jungle. Dood went ahead with Aapo taking up the rear. They expected to reach high ground by about 11 am and to have climbed to the top of the cliff by mid-day. There, they would be under no obligation to leave until it suited them. They could supplement their rations with fresh fruit almost indefinitely and with the rifle could bag something for the pot.

There was no effect on the three who had swallowed ayahuasca until about an hour had passed. Following a stop for coffee and a smoke, Señor Romeo suddenly shouted '¡Puedo ver cuadrados en todas partes!⁸' followed by, '¡Es como las líneas dentadas en una migraña!⁹' and rushed off into the jungle, leaving his pack behind.

Aapo and Atlahua after ten minutes clutched their stomachs and rolled around in anguish as the draught began to take effect. Dood was unable to understand what they said, but it hardly mattered since they rolled their eyes, whistled and made a motion to fly. Then they began to draw strange shapes, particularly squares, in the soil. Shortly, Romeo returned from the jungle and stuck out his tongue at the others. Then after a minute, all three began to dance around the fire, holding hands, before rushing off once more into the jungle.

There was no further sound. By then they were an hour behind schedule and Dood, recognising that the three would soon recover, and then follow his path and join him, decided to move on. He carried his own pack and one more, and in due course returned to retrieve the remaining packs of his colleagues. It was two o'clock by the time he had finally ascended with all the rucksacks. Before climbing for the last time he scrawled a clear message at the foot of the cliff, which read, 'I am at the top.' Then he made camp between three part-fallen walls of stone, and lit a brushwood fire at the narrow entrance.

---

8   I can see squares everywhere!
9   It's like the jagged lines in a migraine!

Dood settled down for the afternoon. He expected to see his comrades emerge from the forest by nightfall, yet nightfall came and went. At dawn the following morning, he collected some basic necessities in a pack, picked up a rifle, and walked to their former campsite. It was deserted. He followed the trail made by Aapo but it petered out in the jungle, as did the trail made by Atlahua, at a wide stream. The bank was of grey mud and there was evidence of a struggle in the form of footprints and deep gouges of the kind made by an alligator or snake. It was likely that Atlahua and Aapo had been overcome and dragged into the water.

He dared not lose his way and returned to look for Romeo. After half a mile he found Romeo's clothes scattered on the ground and his footprints in the soil. A little later, there was evidence of a jaguar kill in the form of pawprints of the beast in the soil, together with bloodstains and a severed human hand. It was the hand of Señor Romeo himself.

Solemnly, Dood shook the hand and then gave it a proper burial, complete with suitable words. As he did so, rigor mortis caused the fingers to contract in the 'thumbs up' gesture and satisfied, he knew that Romeo was at last at peace. He made his way back to the camp with his rifle levelled. There was nothing he could do. Romeo and the Mayans had run off into the jungle under the influence of ayahuasca, there to meet an inglorious end. For a while Dood decided to shelve his own investigations into herbalism and repacked the ayahuasca in his rucksack. Perhaps their dose had been too great?

The Reverend Callum Dood was alone in the rainforest, nearly two hundred miles from civilisation. He sat down by the campfire to consider his future.

NINE

TEQUILA AND CAMPDEN TABLETS

As Simon Wiener and Carmen van Brouin prepared for another field trip they were pleased and ambitious for the discoveries they felt confident were waiting for them. Dorkin, however, had some research to undertake and a friend to enlist beforehand. A week after the meeting at his office in which their future endeavours were agreed, he travelled to see the curator of the Philadelphia Museum of Antiquities, the owner of the pre-Mayan statuettes he had borrowed. It was an up-and coming institution, aspiring to equivalence with the Penn Museum in status and influence. There, he was ushered into a comfortable office and offered cold refreshment which, perspiring in the heat of the afternoon, he gratefully accepted.

His host Dr Steinbeck, a middle-aged man, was well-dressed in the contemporary casual manner, and slim despite a career spent at a desk. He was polite, but had at least some of the assertiveness characteristic of the successful American academic, together with a nervous energy consistent with his responsibilities as curator. They exchanged pleasantries and he rose to turn off his air conditioning, which was running with a pronounced hum. Dr Steinbeck said, 'Welcome, Professor Dorkin. So you are interested our pre-Mayan statuettes. Nice, are they not? We bought them for our display of course, but it can be difficult to obtain suitable artefacts these days, what with certain, ah, licenses that have to be acquired. We were pleased on this occasion to be able to do so, since they did not seem particularly significant to the vendor and from the fact that there were adequate examples on display elsewhere.'

'The other examples were made of lead?'

'No.' Most were of stone. A few were of wood, but they were more recent and of a kind still being fashioned by native people today. There is apparently a continuous tradition.'

'Nevertheless you feel we might need to be careful in case the authorities...have regrets?'

'I wouldn't go that far. Let us say there is no point in antagonising people unnecessarily.'

'But you intend to put them back on show straight away?'

'Not yet. We were concerned that you questioned their origin further, and we thought it best to wait until that's over in case the cultural authorities down there get wind of it.' Dr Steinbeck smiled and looked expectant.

Dorkin said, 'Which brings me to the reason for my visit. We have no intention of working without your organisation being on board. I think it best to collaborate if we are to make the kind of progress we both need...' That was exactly what Steinbeck had hoped to hear. '...so I would like to speak to your broker and see the origin of the hoard.'

Steinbeck said, 'What is your policy on publication?'

'I believe in acknowledging all parties.'

Steinbeck said, 'Excellent. Our broker lives in the south of the Chiapas state. He owns an estate of lodges—holiday villas—that are hired out to holidaymakers and trekkers. People stay there and use it as a base for excursions into the jungle. He facilitates their activities by hiring out canoes and native guides. Most are students, so it might be better to say 'incursions into the jungle' therefore. But among them are serious scholars.' Dorkin nodded and Steinbeck continued, 'But I wouldn't say that trekking is his only business. Since he directly employs native workers he has become a conduit for the many artefacts they uncover. Thus he has become a well-known broker. You would need to speak to him in order to obtain a full description of the site from which the statuettes were removed. He's called Maradona.'

'That's not a particularly common name?'

'I wouldn't think so. And I haven't met him myself. Nevertheless I vouch for him fully. We have a long-standing relationship that we have been careful to foster. We rely on the genuine article, as you know, and he relies on us for the correct form of remuneration.'

'Correct form?'

'He wishes to remain discreet when it comes to the taxman. But there is no reason for anyone to look upon our relationship as being anything other than beneficial to both parties.'

'Thank you for your straightforward appraisal. I shall need to meet him because the statuettes have grown to be of some significance. I hope to see site of the dig in question. I am quite sure that it will be of benefit to us both.'

Steinbeck said 'Excellent.' He went to a filing cabinet and withdrew some papers. 'Here are his credentials. I can furnish you with a letter of introduction.'

—⁂—

Wiener and van Brouin still had a firm recollection of their meeting with Dorkin, yet in keeping a record Simon made assertions in a notebook while Carmen wrote ideas on cards. They were united, however, in their priority of looking for the source of the statuettes since as they agreed, 'We must know whether they are fakes, and all else hangs on that.' Thus it had been agreed, and the small party set off for Maradona's place as a first duty. Their journey was a long way, of over 3000 miles, yet they had one particular advantage:

'We know where we are going,' said Dorkin. 'Central Mexico has a fault-line across it, so it's as prone to earthquakes as California is with its San Andreas Fault. In the south is the Chiapas plateau and still farther is a large area of virgin jungle which is barely populated.

And since Maradona lives near the southern border that is where we are going.'

Dorkin mused on the nature of the task: 'The statuettes were found under some kind of ancient dwelling. It was an unauthorised dig, so we need to be fairly discreet in our dealings. The thing is, it's so remote that we need Maradona on board in order to be able to find it.'

'You expect us to stop after part of the way and walk the rest?' Carmen was driving the truck and she gave a concerned look.

'That is what I was coming to. No, we can cut the time right down if we hire a helicopter at Cancun. That will give us a lot more freedom in the jungle.' He said to Simon, 'I know you can drive one of these things. You did say you are familiar with this model? It can seat six passengers or with three we can carry extra fuel. It even has a drinks cabinet.'

'I can do it, but what happens if we can't find any place to put it down?'

'I don't think that will be a problem. The jungle is usually less than 100% and we should be able to find a clearing without difficulty. If necessary there are roads across the border, but in any case we should be fine at Maradona's place. I'm sure we can land, make camp and move off to do our work. I think we shall need two weeks, but we can stay longer if we need to.'

Wiener and van Brouin looked relieved. There would be no trek through miles of inhospitable countryside. They said, 'We can just about manage that.'

Later, they approached the Mexican border. Their truck was as heavily loaded as before and sat low on its springs. Despite their load they made good time, reaching Cancun via Tabasco where at the tourist area they parked and hired a helicopter. The maximum range of their new craft was 700 km so they flew in two steps, first south to Belize, where they refuelled, and then west towards the Guatemalan border. Over the rainforest, they looked down on a familiar olive green, with the cover broken by open water or occasional elevations in the landscape. They flew west following a prominent rocky spine which made navigation straightforward, then eventually south. Maradona's estancia was easy to find a little to the north of an arterial road bearing trucks and ramshackle cars. There, they set the helicopter down on a patch of bare ground where, after a while, a thin and wiry individual emerged from a portacabin at the side of a wooden house.

The helicopter was unusual enough to attract a dozen or so people, who watched the thin and wiry individual introduce himself as 'Dingo' Maradona. 'It's a name my friends gave me years ago,' he said. Then he spoke Spanish to the surrounding people, who disappeared in the direction of what appeared to be a kitchen, or into a garden of vegetables and colourful flowers nearby. He said to the three Americans, 'Welcome to my estancia, I have a chalet prepared for you: please follow me. Then after you are settled we can discuss business and you will take refreshment as my guests.'

Maradona showed them to a chalet that had two bedrooms. They brought in their belongings, with the two men sharing a room. It was comfortable and pleasant accommodation where, following a brief rest, they were ready for their host's attentions. Dorkin had his letter of introduction from Steinbeck and knew they were assured of premium hospitality.

A map of the jungle hung on the wall of Maradona's office, on which rivers and their tributaries were marked with yellow ink. At intervals were prominent circles which Maradona explained were places of interest for the tourists who went there. 'It is a hazardous journey,' he explained to Dorkin, 'and it will be a relief to reach its conclusion.' With that comment he led them to his dining room where a table was laid for five. The Señora was waiting for them, and she gave orders to a native cook and a waiter. Her husband appeared to reflect as though saying grace and they inclined their heads courteously.

They ate an excellent meal of fish and vegetables. It was hot with chilli and they perspired, as did the Maradonas. It was accompanied by a milky, sticky drink, probably fermented, which reduced the spiciness of the food, as would milk. Carmen drank with enjoyment, but Simon out of courtesy, making polite comments such as: 'Pulque, Señor, is it well-known?'

'It is not as common as it used to be, Señor Wiener,' said Maradona. 'Beer has taken its place in many parts, but we prefer to follow tradition and show respect for older ways.'

They made general conversation, and Maradona produced a bottle of tequila at the end of the meal, which they drank with, admittedly, a more general enjoyment. 'Your visit, Señor Dorkin,' said their host.

'Yes, Steinbeck sends his best regards and was pleased to supply me with the letter of introduction which you have seen. He regards our visit as being of considerable importance. Your agents obtained two statuettes which interested his conservators particularly.'

'Good. Dr Steinbeck has said you would like to see where they came from. Since that is so, I will guide you myself. I know the place, although I was not present at the time.'

Simon said, 'But of course you vouch for the person who brought them to you?'

'They know better than to—how do you say—pull the hair over my eyes. It is simple commerce. The price I pay is good, so they deal with me. Their trustworthiness must also be good or there can be no transaction.'

Carmen said, 'This site, can you please describe it?'

'Well Señorita, there is a large river to the east of us, and many smaller tributaries run into it. The land around was used for a settlement long ago. The people used a form of agriculture based on the clearing of forest by using fire, with the ash fertilising their crops. It did no lasting damage because the population was of a small size.'

'But I suppose this particular place was a more lasting settlement?'

'Yes, there were buildings of stone, Señorita, to make temples and fortifications. They remained when the position of the fields changed. Later, the buildings fell and the civilisation declined so that only tribesmen remained rather than a great nation.'

'And the artefacts?'

'A small party of French students had travelled near there. They stopped to see an old field system on a hill that had been stepped to aid the agriculture of the time. At the top they found unusual remains that had not been seen before. Their guide made light of it and preferred to draw their attention elsewhere. The French were pleased to see jaguars and resumed their journey. Later, the native guide returned to the stony hilltop and found the floor of an ancient dwelling. He dug a little, into a cellar perhaps, and observed a small hoard. He was keen to make sure that the place was not looted and brought the artefacts to me. There may be other things there and I do not think the place was investigated thoroughly.'

'And that was about a year ago?'

'Si, Señorita.'

Dorkin said, 'If it is not too difficult for you, Señor Maradona, we would like to complete the investigation of the site that has remained unfinished until this time.'

'It shall be as you ask. In the meantime, I have a further bottle of tequila, and I would like you to say which you prefer.'

The next day, Dorkin and Wiener transferred much of their additional fuel from jerry cans to the main fuel tanks of the helicopter, leaving a few such containers in storage with Maradona. They then redistributed their stores, making extra space for Maradona and his kit, and flew east to the river tributary which he had indicated on his map. It was a distance of about 100 miles which took them into the deepest rainforest. Near their destination Wiener found it difficult to find any clear ground. Maradona said, however, 'Don't worry, Señor. A little farther please. There will be a clearing.' True to his word, a few small clearings with crops of squash were eventually seen, where they landed and made reparation to the locals for the loss of a few gourds, accepted with nods and handshakes. The helicopter was covered with a camouflage net and they hiked under Maradona's guidance the remaining distance. Just before their destination they crossed a small river by wading through it, an 'ill-advised occupation if any have cuts or abrasions,' said their guide, for their legs would then 'be savaged by piranhas in a place where no injured animal will last long.'

'It looks benign to me!' said Simon Wiener.

'That is the case,' said Maradona, 'yet there are reports that the candiru fish has been found as far north as Guatemala. I would not like to experience its barbs myself, and being required to remove one's manhood to prevent it from being eaten from within.' He looked at the stream rather doubtfully, and at his own clothing.

On the opposite bank they marched on. Soon, they observed a gentle slope rising to 100 feet, while showing the remains of a field system. Climbing to the top the advantages of such a position were clear. Dorkin said, 'Señor Maradona, can we say that crops will grow better here?'

'I believe that the land is better-drained and would receive more sunlight. I also think that a former owner would have wished to pass on an inheritance to children. There may have been primacy of ownership: the field system would be owned by a person of importance, who in a beneficial manner would bestow the tenure of strips upon those of lower status who worked it.'

'I see,' said Dorkin. 'And perhaps such a person, perhaps a king or queen, would have lived at the top?'

'Exactly so,' said Maradona. 'And higher still, their gods were said to bestow all.'

'Let us have some coffee,' said Simon Wiener, lighting a primus stove.

'Be careful to boil the water thoroughly, Señor Wiener,' said Maradona.

Dorkin's supposition about a residence at the top was soon found to be correct. Far from being flat and even, it indicated its former use by the evidence of foundations, which enabled them to choose the best position for a shallow trench. Eventually they located a former dwelling of five rooms, with the position of walls just discernible. Later, Maradona said of the main living area, 'It is here that our pieces were uncovered. Below are foundations and a cavity, although the former are collapsed. And here are signs of the disturbance made a year ago. There is less compaction, and it was opened and covered again in a hasty manner.'

Dorkin nodded. 'Did the guide not wish to uncover more?'

'No, I believe he was happy with the remuneration he would receive from the statues alone. Do you wish to dig nearby?'

'I should like to, but let us finish our more general observations first. If we are the first to study in a scientific manner, then let us act accordingly.'

By the fifth day Maradona seemed restless. Dorkin said, 'I would hope to leave the site in all circumstances by midday tomorrow.'

'Si, Señor Dorkin. It's just that my estancia…'

'I quite understand. A limited inspection will be adequate for us on this occasion.' He considered further: it remained only to extend the cavity that had contained the previous finds. Upon examination, this continued for ten feet under the remnants of a floor, an enclosure in which no organic substance could survive for long. In it, there was little to see apart from mouldering earth and an assortment of black and knobbly objects. He shone a torch, and then covering his face he took the plunge.

Most of the objects were small, but he withdrew two larger pieces: a metal bar and a nondescript earthenware jug. Both were black with dirt, yet they were also covered with white mould, no doubt facilitated to grow there. As it fell away he said, 'It's wise not to breathe in any of that.' Placing them in a bag he said, 'I can see why they weren't removed by the guy who found the statuettes. They don't look much.'

Simon said, 'Let's just get some photographs and go. I'm happy to clean them later. Our guide is restless.'

The return journey was straightforward and they reached Maradona's place without event. On his home ground he was again an excellent host. He served lunch in a flower garden, where every form of insect life throve, and where chair legs protruded from small dishes of water. 'It is to prevent the incursion of ants,

Señorita,' he said to Carmen. Again they noticed that he seemed preoccupied and Dorkin made a suitable comment, 'Thank you for your guidance this past week. We achieved a more than reasonable investigation in a short time.'

Maradona replied, 'To tell you the truth, I'd had notification of a problem concerning some other guests, a party from the United States who wished to visit archaeological ruins farther east. I was told they'd disappeared. I felt responsible, but their journey had passed beyond my own remit.' They nodded, and Maradona seemed resigned. He offered tequila, made further apologies and departed. They thought no more of it.

Simon brought a few pieces of their collection to look at in the light. He said, 'I wouldn't call it a good haul, but I suppose it's difficult to say how it could have been better. Of course, it wasn't us who found the statuettes, and I expect the finder thought different.'

'Perhaps that black junk is better than you think. If it helps us to date the place, then that was our original intention.'

'So what do you think?' Simon passed the rod.

Carmen looked at it more closely. At first sight it bore no more than a few faint marks, none of which seemed interesting. However with polishing she noted that these were on an edge, making the object resemble a ruler. A couple of smaller marks were like everyday implements but they were scattered, and seemed less significant. She passed it around.

With the aid of a magnifying glass Dorkin drew all to scale on paper. The lines resolved into groups of two, three, four, rising to ten, with each group separated by longer lines and spaces. He had a sudden idea and held the rod against his arm, finding that it was exactly as long as the distance from elbow to fingertips. He said, 'This is a cubit measure. I suppose we would call it a yardstick.'

Carmen said, 'We often see those in Egypt. Now I think that's interesting.'

Dorkin disappeared to his room and returned a few minutes later, clutching a small reference book. It contained the writing of civilisations such as the Chinese, Arabic and Egyptian. He said, 'I'm sure I can make something out of this.' After a diligent search in the pages on ancient Egypt, he found several instances in which its contents bore direct comparison with marks on the object. The first was a circle and a cross.

He said, 'To the Egyptians this apparently meant 'perfect', and something very like it is also on the cubit-measure *here*'—he pointed, and his gaze continued to alternate between rod and book. He said, 'And here's another. This time it's simply a rectangle. It meant 'house' in ancient Egypt, and it's on the rod too.'

Simon said, 'I don't like to state the obvious, but I can imagine why they would turn up on a cubit measure. Perhaps they meant 'perfect house.'

Dorkin said, 'The important thing is to decide whether this is just a coincidence. Perhaps they are marks that anyone might draw?' He failed to elicit a response from the other two, who preferred to wait for him to elaborate further. Instead, he passed up the opportunity and picked up the earthenware jug. It rattled, but his attention was drawn first to two characters on the outside:

He said, 'Simon, you rightly said that a second character can change the meaning of the first. The first is 'jug', and since we know the second, the overall meaning becomes perfect jug.'

'Carmen replied, 'Or it might mean perfect contents. Perfect beer.'

'Perhaps its pulque.' He passed it to Simon, who tugged at the stopper, which came away with a crack as though an old and dry seal had finally broken.

Simon said, 'This is a good fit; I guess that cork or wood would have crumbled away long ago.' He turned it upside-down and some pieces of a resinous substance fell out. They were rather like black rubber. He said: 'We need to get this looked at properly; I expect it's the remains of whatever was inside.'

'If that's the case,' said Dorkin, 'we may find them more useful than the jug itself.'

Later, Dorkin asked Maradona if he thought the site had been opened before the visit of his employee the previous year. He took time to answer: 'I believe Señor, that the site was probably the seat of some dignitary. My own guess is that a religious figure once dwelt there. But I do not think it was excavated by professional archaeologists. There would be more order about the place and that would still have been visible when the excavation was uncovered once more. But that does not mean it had escaped from being plundered in the past.'

'My main point is to confirm that the artefacts were not placed there recently, and that the statuettes are not a hoax. Ourselves, we found a few small things, but they were only of passing interest.'

'Of that I am quite sure. The foundations had not been touched for many years. You were obliged to remove the remains of a very old floor and it was in the form of an indiscriminate litter. It would not have been possible to reconstruct its present appearance easily. The cubit rod, the pulque jug, they had not seen the light of day in our lifetime. My own man was completely trustworthy in that regard and was undoubtedly the first to handle the statuettes. He simply left your own artefacts behind.'

'You know of no westerners having visited the place?'

'None. There were the French students of course, but they went elsewhere. There was a party of four Americans, as I have described, but their destination was farther east.'

'Tourists?'

'No, they reminded me of policemen or soldiers. But my guides tell me there is now an English clergyman living wild, now that his native guides have departed. It is not known what he wishes to do but again, he is a considerable distance away.'

'So, Señor Maradona, how do you evaluate these artefacts?'

'They were of significance and must have been important enough to hide when the place fell into disuse. Or perhaps destroyed. The presence of the statuettes would suggest that the place was dedicated to the cult of the ancient god whose image they are. I would expect that the pulque jug was ceremonial. Undoubtedly they are both very old.'

'You spoke of parties of Americans and an Englishman living in the rainforest. They are interested in the same place?'

'I believe so. There is a pronounced ridge that passes east to west. In a prominent part are the remains of structures built by a strange tribe rarely seen today, and about which few even ask. Some have visited the area and never returned. I would be concerned for the prospects for four policemen, let alone a solitary clergyman.'

'This tribe is warlike?'

'It is difficult for native peoples to be warlike in our modern world. Let us say only that they are reclusive.'

'But not so reclusive that Señor Maradona has never heard of them!'

Maradona smiled, but without pleasure. He said only, 'It is not habitual for me to speak of matters about which I know little.'

Later, the three Americans strolled around the estancia and Dorkin said, 'I have absolutely no doubt that Maradona's evaluation of the place was accurate. I think I can type it up and get him to sign it. It will add credence to the description I shall send to Steinbeck.'

'We have enough evidence to date the artefacts?' said Carmen.

'We shall see.'

'And I suppose we go after this reclusive tribe?'

'Offer accepted! In due course, that is. In the first instance we need to find our lead mine. Of course the statuettes were manufactured, so we can't expect to find anything like them underground. I think we're trying to establish a local source of raw material, as much as anything. But before that, we need to see what this trip has done for us. Let's clear up and get back first.'

At Cancun they prepared for their next trip south. Meanwhile, Dorkin spoke to Steinbeck on the telephone. For Dorkin this was a courtesy, since Steinbeck would wish to know how they had got on with Maradona. Understandably, Steinbeck would be keen for the future of his display.

Steinbeck said, 'So, you did well?'

'We had a very successful trip. We found Maradona and stayed for a short while at his place. He was keen to offer us hospitality.'

'I don't doubt that. And you thought him reliable?'

'Yes. I am quite confident about the artefacts you obtained from him. But I found him reluctant. Perfectly helpful, certainly.'

'How reluctant?'

'I might have said, "covering up for something" but it was just a feeling, no more. He disliked giving me information about a tribe living in the south. Of course, that wasn't really his duty anyway.'

'Perhaps he was naturally cautious.'

'Yes, I expect that was it.'

'So about the site, its description was accurate?'

'No, not exactly. I can see why the dwelling was called primitive, because very little remained of it. And even *that* was under a thick blanket of earth and leaf-mould. Yet it had a certain dignity about it, which we felt elevated it from the ordinary. It was probably presided over by some form of dignitary, not just a local landowner. Maradona thought a religious type.'

'That's interesting. You mentioned some further discoveries.'

'Yes. We found a cubit-rod. It was of a standard cubit, about the length of a forearm. But the markings on it were rather like old Egyptian ones. We can only guess why.'

Steinbeck was on the edge of his seat. 'And this could be publishable?'

'Perhaps, but only as part of a larger study. But there's more. As you know, it's rarely possible to date a site without corroborating evidence, but we managed to date one of the artefacts there. It was a ceremonial jug with hieroglyphs, showing that it came from the same culture. And inside was a black solid, the remains of something it contained. It was a probably a beverage, we thought pulque at first.'

'It contained pulque?'

'No. It was nitrogenous, but probably not pulque. It was like ayahuasca, a venerated drink used by the tribesmen in their religious ceremonies.'

'But did you date the jug from its contents?'

'Yes, we did a carbon 14 test. It's a minimum, of course, and it dated the contents, not the jug. Aside from the hieroglyphs, the jug was hardly of interest in the artistic sense. It was quite crude.'

'And the date?'

'It was about of 11,000 years old. And that was no mistake, either.'

'Impossible! But can we get any of this down on paper?'

Dorkin was soothing, 'Soon, soon.'

'So what do you intend to do now?'

'That is something we need to think about. Let's face it, we have a collection of very old artefacts which show a similarity, in the style of their inscriptions, to a very old culture of the middle east. That alone would push back the date for the use of picture-writing. It would also imply a connection between the two sites in prehistory. And there are your statuettes, which can only have come from a more advanced source altogether.'

'You seem to be delving into the realms of fantasy.'

'I'm not. All I did was to recount the physical evidence. Our conclusions, whatever we decide them to be, must stem from *that*, not the other way round. I've tried arguing against it, believe me. But the evidence must stand, and we were first into the market.'

'Ok, ok.'

'So we need to decide what to do. I want to run this past you.'

'Go ahead.'

'I want to find other evidence and I think it may be in the genes of some of the people not so far away. We have already found marker genes in a handful of the general population. Possibly someone had an affair long ago. I want to develop that angle. Let's assume there's a reclusive tribe in the far south. If I can find them, we shall need to show commonality in their DNA. So we investigate right down to the border area.'

'You intend to look for a lost tribe?'

'You're not the first person to say that.'

'OK, but commonality with what?'

'With the Boskop sample and ah, one or two others.'

'If you find it, there'll be a total storm.'

'That's as maybe, but it means a lifetime of public speaking arrangements for you!'

'Well, I've been with you from the start, you know that.'

—⁓—

Somewhat later, Dorkin's party left Cancun for a destination which, following Maradona's help, was no longer the vague 'somewhere south' that it would otherwise have been. They flew west along a ridge until they reached the broad area which had been circumscribed by the wave of their host's hand. Soon, Carmen said, 'It rises to high ground about a mile ahead. Maradona mentioned a kind of cliff face, which I can see. The tree cover is broken there.'

Simon Wiener adjusted their direction and they approached a clearing about fifty yards across. 'This will do,' he said. 'I can get down and we can push the machine a bit nearer to that overhanging ledge. It looks stable and it may give us a bit of protection as well.'

The place was large enough to turn into a base. The ground sloped gently so that water ran out, and it was dry enough to make a fire. Yellow mud remained only a short distance away, however, so that Dorkin mused about the stability of ancient mine workings at such a time. The whole area resembled Ramon's chaotic open-cast mine, except that it seemed to be deserted. There was path from the jungle towards the cliff face, and another along its foot, yet there was no evidence of any use, except by animals.

After a reasonable interval they began to look around. Wiener kicked idly at a pile of rubble. 'I suppose we need to analyse this?' he said.

Dorkin nodded and said, 'Good idea.' Pulling out a test kit he turned his attention to a nearby trickle of water from the cliff face. 'But I think that this will tell us more than the rubble.'

While Dorkin analysed the water, the other two collected samples from heaps of mining waste that lay about. Dorkin applied his test to various samples and said, 'This can give me some idea of… wow!' It was the kind of simple test notable for giving a black colour with lead. He watched it turn very black.

'So?' said Carmen.

'Well it's lead waste, and there's lots of it. This water is full of the stuff, and so must these piles of waste. We can't drink it by the way, not even boiled. We had better look around here, are we all agreed?' There was no better prospect, especially in a period of inexhaustible rain.

Simon said, 'So we need to look for a mine. But why can't we just dig up some of this spoil?'

'I think we need to prove that it was taken from proper workings.'

Behind them the cliff stood, mile on mile of brown rock heaved into a continuous elevated crest. Searching for a supposed shaft, they crept along its face. There was abundant evidence in the form of cavities of water with mosquito larvae and tiny frogs. Yet there was no evidence of an entrance or hypothetical sign over it.

Dorkin said, 'We shall have to climb and look from there.' He pointed to the top of the cliff. 'We might see something if we look down.'

'Well let's do that now, shall we?'

Climbing to the top by a rough path, Carmen picked up a notice written on a piece of sodden card. It was swarming with small snails that had made a meal of some of it, but it was still legible. It said in English, 'I'm at the top.' She said, 'I wonder who?' and propped it away from the snails and left it.

At the top a track led east into the distance. A similar track led southwest towards an encircling arm of rock and a third due west, parallel to the clifftop, where after 300 yards it became a sloping walkway, dipping out of sight towards the entrance to a tunnel. Following the last of these they ventured towards what was obviously an entrance to a mine where finally, they allowed themselves to walk inside for a few yards. There was enough light to see two shafts sloping away, but Dorkin said, 'This is far enough for now. As far as going down is concerned, I might, but not until it's less wet. And even then it will take a lot of careful preparation. I think we need to go back and think about it.' Later, they discussed the idea in some detail. Dorkin said, 'I doubt that mining was very technical when this place was last used. I don't suppose we need to go very deep.'

Carmen said, 'Well I've done a bit of potholing.'

'This is different. We don't want to get asphyxiated by mine gases. And old mine workings are often unstable.' He looked uneasy. 'So any wooden supports would be useless and will probably have crumbled away anyhow. But that doesn't necessarily mean there won't be stone columns. And larger galleries, away from worked faces, are often stable in their own right. A lot of old mines were no more than extensions of natural galleries and we should be able to recognise that. I think we can go in, but we must keep away from water. We can only go as far as appears stable, and we shall need to wear respirators and leave if we don't like it.'

They waited for a period of drier weather and after careful consideration, decided to proceed. Making their first excursion, they chose the right-hand shaft and went slowly forward. All seemed straightforward: their way was stable and the roof supported by columns of stone as Dorkin had predicted. The air was cool and dry and more pleasant than the heat and humidity outside. They were able to walk without stooping on a moderate slope down.

Almost immediately they were obliged to rely on their lamps, and began to experience a feeling claustrophobia. None wanted to walk first, and all wished to be behind the others in case they needed to turn back. Their feelings eased, however, when farther on, the gallery became level and rather wider. Since it appeared stable they pressed forward. However it soon became uncomfortably warm, and when finally they began to cough they decided to test the air. Their protector lamp guttered and went out, and Dorkin said, 'Respirators on, now. I think our oxygen gives out at about knee level. These old workings gradually fill up with carbon dioxide.'

They had been underground for forty minutes and could advance only a little farther. Another short stretch brought them to a worked face characterised by the marks of picks and shovels, and with a floor rutted by wheels. Dorkin proffered, 'No lead ore yet, but I think we need to go back now.' Nevertheless they were encouraged, having done well. Then waiting a few days to confirm the continuing change of weather, they decided on a second descent. 'I think we only need to go a little farther,' said Dorkin. 'Let's get it over with.'

On their next visit they reached the farthest extent of their previous outing and followed another gallery into the hillside. All around was the litter of mining and for the first time that day, they found the dull black and yellow of galena. Dorkin said, 'This is the stuff we want. And it's everywhere, abundant and very probably pure.' He removed several large pieces and packed them away. 'No wonder they made their mine here,' he said. 'But the burning question remains, who were *they*?'

They started their return, but marching past the farthest extent of their previous visit they met disaster. Suddenly a stream of water emerged from the ceiling and a dull 'clump' sounded from a distance. Simon shouted, 'Let's get out of here,' and there was an unfortunate rush as they made for the exit. However a fall of earth followed so that their way was blocked. They were not crushed, nor even damaged, but their prospects had taken a turn for the worse. Carmen screamed, and they felt the full horror of the mineworker caught underground. It was fifteen minutes before they managed to overcome their feeling of panic.

Dorkin checked the air again with his protector lamp. There was oxygen above knee height, but in an effort to save their portable oxygen they stood and breathed through filters alone. He said, 'My lamp only for now.' Privately, he cursed himself for having brought them all down. He tried to clear a path but it seemed hopeless. They were trapped, deep inside an airless mine, far under the Mexican rainforest. They were many hundreds of miles from civilisation and beyond help.

TEN

FIVE IN THE JUNGLE

After some consideration the Reverend Dood decided that not all was bad. It was true that he had lost his guide and native bearers and on returning home would have to carry his luggage himself—that is, if he survived. And he was probably 200 miles from the nearest estancia, a distance that would tax even the most experienced navigator. Yet, try as he might to sympathise with the departed Romeo, and following a decent sleep in the fresh air of the clifftop, he began to regard his predicament more as a freedom.

His mind returned to his former purpose and he decided, bit by bit, to stay put. He had not finished there and his obstinate side considered that, since he was faced with the ordeal of returning whatever might happen, he might as well complete his holiday beforehand. And since he had sought, if not retirement, then certainly a complete change, he began to consider his fortune as a blessing in disguise. Such were the travails of the naturalist; he would carry on. Perhaps the yet-undiscovered butterfly Callumensis doodii was waiting to be described! This period of reflection over, he attended to the practical matter of improving his camp. He sorted through the three rucksacks, burned all items of a personal nature, and kept only useful stores. They would, if eked out, last many weeks. Thus prepared, he ventured inland with a view to making the acquaintance of any people he might find.

There were several paths he could follow but the most promising passed southwest around a spur of rock. Following it, he returned to the stepped pyramid that he had described to Romeo where again, he noted that it was utterly strange there, the only building of large size for miles around. It was still deserted, so he turned south onto brush and scrub using a rough path of his own making. Ahead, the trees began to encroach once more, and walking among them he noted the deserted settlement which earlier, he had seen from a distance.

Still farther, and with his direction unchanged, all evidence of disuse vanished. He observed empty but useable huts, and after 500 yards a couple of larger buildings which, had he seen them at home, he would have guessed were probably tithe barns. Then shortly, he reached a fully working village where thriving activity had produced stores of wood, hay and vegetables, all in piles and waiting to be distributed. All around were modest but obviously inhabited huts, together with smoke and movement, but rather little noise. He had walked farther than he had intended but had been rewarded by a first sight of human habitation. It was a quiet place, but at first he thought little of it.

Thus far, Dood had not been spotted, but he soon forgot his earlier notion of introducing himself because, in the middle of what might be described as a central square, were four men tied to a wooden trellis. Around them a throng appeared to hold them in contempt. The four were westerners with jeans and trainers, and they seemed subdued enough not to care about their treatment. He thought them dazed, or possibly drugged, but it was their captors who interested him more. They were not the usual Mayan natives, he was sure, since their clothes were quite different. Instead of colourful native garments they wore an austere, rough, brown or grey scapular which made them look like monks. Nor did they sound like the expressive Mayans, who spoke their colourful tongue with as much transmitted by a wave or a smile. Their quiet speech was odd: it lacked grace, and sounded like a relentless flow of consonants. They seemed troubled to speak it without effort. And in all cases the villagers were small, so small that at first he thought them adolescents. Whoever they were, they strangely reminded him of those he had seen in the snows of Nepal, many thousands of miles away.

All were highly-developed, but in an unusual way. Their crania were enlarged, and their eyes were unusually large and far apart. However all the lower parts of the face: the jaw, mouth and nose, were much reduced. They had a little hair, but that on the scalp was thin, straight and almost colourless. They looked old, even the children, but it was their manner that was unusual. They seemed to perceive their surroundings rather like a cat, with their vision focussed, concentrated and unblinking. They seemed contemplative but expressionless, and spent much of their time looking into each other's faces. He thought them odd by civilised standards, and doubted whether they could adapt to conventional polite company. And now their behaviour was less than civil. He continued to watch them as they engaged in some kind of ritual. They circled their prisoners and pointed towards them repeatedly. It seemed as though they wished to reproduce the action of pointing with spears: the aggression of pointing. They wanted to intimidate, but without violence itself, and it was as though they were preparing for something.

As a solitary observer so close to an encampment of apparently aggressive people, Dood was ill-prepared for spying. He had a rifle at camp but had not brought it with him. In any case he could not wisely have made such an enemy. He would not be able to help the four prisoners by invading. Crouching low, he backed away and retraced his path. Returning to his camp, he covered his fire and removed his belongings to a small cave in the cliff face. There was nothing wiser than discretion. Later it fell dark, and he made a quick meal. His cave was cosy and warm, yet the fate of those four men could not be ignored. Perhaps they had been left in the dark at the mercy of whatever jungle cat might choose to visit? Could he not sneak in, cut their ties and vanish? He donned darker clothing and brought a knife and rifle for his own safety. Returning by the same path, he made for the settlement. The night was dark, but ahead was a strange glow which, as he advanced, soon became much brighter than would any campfire. He was invisible among the trees but was able to see the village clearly. Before him was the brilliant radiance of pure electrical light arising from a huge pearlescent grey saucer. As he watched, the four men were dragged towards a bench which resembled the medieval 'barter' benches of his own country, upon which goods were exchanged for coins. Yet this barter was different. Tied, perhaps drugged, they were exchanged for tools, salt, bangles and other artefacts, among them small grey metal statuettes. The four were then removed to the pearlescent disc by their new masters, who had emerged for the exchange, and to which they returned after it was done.

In the meantime, Dood had an ample opportunity to observe them. Each wore a one-piece bodysuit of silver, which gave them the appearance of an oversized baby. In other respects they were like their rainforest compatriots with enlarged crania, prominent eyes and reduced facial parts. And their countenance was cat-like, calculating, sentient, and alien. Yet there were differences too; whereas the jungle tribesmen were small, the silver-clothed people were downright degenerate. They had puny shoulders and tiny hands. They struggled to lift even the smallest of goods; yet they had the power from some device to force the four men into their craft. Then with a great effusion of light and the smell of an electrical discharge they were gone. The village returned to darkness, and since there was little that he could achieve by watching further, he returned to base.

In the following days he came and went with more care. He was not so far away from the rainforest people that he could discard all caution and felt that he would be more at risk if he lived in the open. He decided to stay in his cave and do all his cooking with a primus stove, which had the effect of warming his new residence while removing the smoke given by a campfire. Nevertheless, he began to carry out the excursions he had meant to, and on most he began to think. He was interested, and past the point at which he would consider leaving. Who were the four men? From their dress he thought American. Why did the little silver-dressed men want them, and would they also want *him*?

—⁓—

'Here we are,' said Elliott, 'and I'm very glad the flight is over, believe me.' Having agreed to go on this latest wild goose chase, albeit in good humour, he, Sampson, Pargeter and Meredith had finally arrived in Mexico. It had almost been an exercise in making a holiday booking: they had considered Cancun, Tulum, Cozumel, and Playa del Carmen complete with golden sands and palm trees. Yet Tulum was close to their eventual destination and a good base to make excursions farther afield. Not only that, the area was renowned for its architectural ruins so that in the first instance, and having toured the place, they would become more familiar with its people.

Soon, they were settled enough to venture out. Their guide Renata, an attractive woman of about forty, was voluble and demonstrative and waved her hands about while speaking. She directed her party about the port, and to the castle on the cliff. Smiling, she waved towards the sea and said, 'Ladies and gentlemen, you can see how the cliff was a natural defence for the Mayans who used this port to trade minerals overseas. The castle, city walls and towers were important against invaders but it did not help them against smallpox and influenza when the Spanish came...'

In due course, Elliott asked in a temple, 'Please can you tell me about a carving here. It looks like a man, but why is he upside down?'

Renata said, 'He is the deity we called the Diving God. Some say he represents the planet Venus; others the worship of bees. A few scholars feel he is the god of rainfall; sadly we are now unsure, yet the temples here were a centre for his worship.'

'And what is your own opinion?'

'I do not believe in the need for two gods of rain,' Mr Elliott. 'The god of rain was called Chaac, who brought clouds and rainfall. I believe the Diving God was a reverence of the dawn, when Venus could be seen looking down. Our people still revere the sky today. Their legends tell of a people who came from the sky long ago, and who still look down upon us. Sometimes the image of the Diving

God is simplified so that he is represented with a circle and line. Then his image adorns the dwellings of those who revere him, even today.'

Later, the party met in a hotel lounge, where Elliott said, 'The native people cling to their traditions. It is as though they adhere only to the concept of a native nationality.'

In conference, they started to plan their journey. Unlike with Wiener's party, there was no pilot among them and they opted for a truck instead. Soon they set out, using roads above which Wiener had flown to Belize, and in driving they had time to view the countryside. Small shrubby trees grew close together so that progress away from the road would have been impossible. It was a land of distant peaks, jungle, moving water, and of tiny primitive settlements. It was also a land of very large distances between the main conurbations. They crossed the border with Belize and then at Belize City turned west towards the Guatemalan border. Later, they entered the Chiapas rainforest from the south where they observed magnificent mountain peaks in the far distance.

They had no guide, no counterpart to the wisdom of Señor Romeo, but were soon offered advice at the many tourist lodges in those parts. 'Señors and Señorita, you would best go by river,' said Dingo Maradona, a tour guide operating, quite by coincidence, just such a river tour. 'You wish to see the interior? Well, I suggest you go along a small river tributary. By using it one can travel downstream and enter the darkest and most dangerous parts of the rainforest. You wish to see jaguars? The forest is so extensive that it can support many without difficulty. Alas, I cannot take you all of the way; you must travel to the far interior yourselves. Come and see my map. So here is the tributary, Senor, and as you can see, there are small rivers which flow in the direction you wish to take. I can take you as far as here'—he pointed—'using inflatables fitted with oars and small paddles. They cannot sink, but the paddles are necessary when on white water. You will take seven days and I will be your guide for part of the way. You have a similar distance to travel when I leave? I feel sure you are capable. Please, you should confer now…and here is a contract…thank you, I shall need your credit card as well.'

Ten days later, the party embarked in two craft. Their guide had described them as rafts, but they were equipped with a skirt all round, had a definite prow and stern, and were at least boat-shaped. Unfortunately they sat low in the water with their stores, yet Maradona was clear that a lack of buoyancy could not be an issue. It turned out that he would return after seven days, but they could leave their rafts at a staging post and strike out alone.

At first they huffed and puffed with the exertion. But with practice they became adept at steering, and their fitness improved quickly. On occasion they came to minor waterfalls which blocked their way, but they were able to pass either over them or as on one occasion, by beaching their craft and dragging them a short distance through the undergrowth. They made short stops to rest, but less often as they indicated their willingness to press on. Maradona offered tours of various ruins, which they declined, but they did stop to see a freshwater lagoon and the many water plants it contained. Later, they were interested to pass into a canyon made by the erosion of riverbanks over many centuries. In all this, Maradona remained an excellent guide who fully earned his keep. He described and cautioned against the wildlife they saw in wild places. He had infinite patience in dealing with his clients. Yet eventually he hailed another party on their way back. He offered caution on many aspects of the jungle, but they had reached the stage at which they would go towards their goal on foot. The latter, their map reference, loomed large in their minds.

At first the small party followed established trails into the interior but soon found they led towards tourist attractions such as large waterfalls, places where wild animals habitually fed, or to vantage points from which the mountain range could be seen to the north. However on narrow tracks they ventured into wild undergrowth or at times were able to follow a riverbank which meandered in the right direction. After two days, the ground began to rise and they were directed as much by contours in the landscape as by any other method of navigation. By then, they were half the distance to their goal. On the third day their path lost a muddy squelchiness as they ventured over higher ground, but the streams became faster as they coursed from the high peaks.

In this, they felt the natural assurance of a large party and were careful to move at the pace of the slowest member. They learned to tolerate the biting insects and had adopted a manageable and reasonable style of movement with marches and regular rests. On the sixth day they made a final march towards a long ridge in the forest. It rose to a cliff before them, beyond which a plateau could be seen to extend to the south. With this in sight, Pargeter suggested that they should stay in camp for a longer rest. The others agreed and Elliott checked their position. He said, 'We're here in any case. There's no point in going any farther. This is a good clearing and I think we could make it our base.' Like the others, he felt the cumulative effects of their hike through rough territory and knew that Pargeter, as keen as mustard to keep up despite what he knew to be the effects of his previous sedentary ways, was approaching exhaustion.

Pargeter said, 'An excellent idea,' and added, 'of all the rainforest we have seen in the last few days, this is the only place where it strikes me that people could actually live. So let's make it a proper camp, shall we? What about a bit nearer that cliff?'

'Yes, it looks pretty stable and we can go behind those rocks. We'd have a bit of protection on three sides, at least.'

The four companions built up rock walls with wood and stone and made a secure enclosure to the height of a man. It made little difference to the biting insects that pestered them, but even these were less abundant than they had been on their hike, and they seemed to dislike smoke and the resolute use of insect repellents. After a couple of days, Pargeter was fully revived and the others began to imitate boy scouts by whistling jolly tunes in camp.

Freya Sampson had coped particularly well with the trek through the jungle, perhaps because she had the natural vigour of youth. She slapped a mosquito and pulled a wry face. 'As I see it,' she said, 'we may be on a wild goose chase, but it's been quite an experience for me and I would always have wondered if I hadn't come. I wonder what Callum and Adam are up to!'

Guy Meredith had worked hard with hiking and with the equipment, and he had led the march for much of its duration. The others knew he was not given to being demonstrative and often said little. Yet now he seemed at ease, and he had built a close and friendly relationship with them. They might have wished to extend their stay in camp a little longer, but he proffered a certain wisdom, and stressed a 'need to look around.'

They had been exact with their position. Pargeter said, 'I think we should start with this cliff. If I lived here, I would want to do it at the top, not down here.' He added, 'Funny, I could swear I saw smoke from up there. But no, it couldn't be.'

Elliot said, 'You are right. I thought there was a slight smell of smoke, even before we made camp. I didn't like to say anything because I wasn't sure.'

'Perhaps they're cannibals,' said Meredith. 'I wonder whether they use onions in the pot?'

Above them the cliff rose sheer, and higher still a faint haze remained: a thin column of smoke flattened and brought down to them by the wind. They decided to visit while they had it in sight, although Pargeter declined the climb and preferred to look after camp. The others reached the summit with its more open vista to the south and began to look around. Soon, they found a small campfire with the ashes still smouldering. But its owner was nowhere to be seen.

—༄—

Dorkin, van Brouin and Wiener stood, breathing foul air as they considered their fortune. Their path out of the mine was blocked. In a panic, Wiener made another effort with a pick and spade, but there were further noises from above and Carmen shouted for him to stop.

Dorkin made an attempt to impose himself, 'Right you two, calm down, or we're all finished.' He checked the air once more with his protector lamp and said, 'We're OK as long as we don't sit down.' He repeated, 'One lamp only, for now.'

His calmness had a good effect on the other two, who stood and listened. He said: 'We can't shift all this and anyway, some of it may be propping up the roof. We can only try to find another way out. Follow me now and please keep calm. You can leave that heavy gear; if we get out we can get new picks.' He turned and walked calmly towards what he hoped would be safety: it was a small tunnel that ran from the left of their present gallery and from which a faint draught exuded. His choice of escape path veered to the south but it had a moderate elevation, so that at least was right. They had expended much nervous energy and had perspired, and the effect was such that they were now cold and shaking, and wanted to run. It took a considerable presence of mind not to do so, but walking slowly, they were rewarded by the tunnel continuing to rise. Dorkin checked the air once again, and it was good as far down as the floor. Noting that they would not now suffocate, he murmured, 'At last an advance.' Shortly they were able to breathe unfiltered air and soon they saw a pinpoint of light ahead. They stumbled on, and each step brought them nearer the surface. They began to think they were lucky, yet Dorkin realised that Providence had shown him for a fool.

With luck or otherwise they covered the final few yards and emerged in a chamber about the size of a domestic room. It was still daytime and light entered by a substantial opening. A couple of smaller chambers lay on each side, each containing a jumble of black and aged mining ephemera. Ahead was a gulley with high banks, a continuation of the tunnel although open to the air.

Turning back to look before they stepped out, the dark tunnel seemed to grab at their heels as they walked free. But they had won! They danced into the sunlight and then paused, breathing deep. They were dirty, but none minded; and they coughed and retched, and shook away the dust, but were ecstatic.

Considering their predicament, they were about a mile from the cliff, and walking south and into fresh rainforest. In fact they were obliged to do so, since their path was fixed by high banks for about 500 yards, only after which were they able to turn aside. Yet Providence once again, had perhaps dictated their path. Soon, they came across the same collection of disused huts that Callum Dood had seen. And in due course, they found the same evidence of a working village. Unlike with Dood, however, a cacophony of pye-dogs began. The animals raised their noses and ran around, scrapping and investigative.

Dorkin said, 'Stay down.' They backed away, sure that after their travails that day they should leave a confrontation to another time. More careful at last, it remained to be seen whether Providence had finally deserted them.

Later, while descending to camp they observed footprints made by someone climbing up. That fact did not surprise them because they knew that someone, capable of writing a sign on cardboard, had earlier passed that way. However it did make them stop to look at ledges and openings that had seemed, until then, not worthy of investigation. In fact they had arrived at Dood's hiding place, a cave half-way up the cliff, reached by means of a ledge, and invisible until they had passed a promontory. Inside, they found it dry and cosy. A few bats cracked and rustled on a ledge, but the floor was a carpet of dry leaves and there were a few personal effects such as a primus stove and pots and pans. It continued for about fifteen feet: the ideal shelter for a hermit or solitary artist.

And the walls bore an inevitable result. They saw at face-height a collection of colourwashed figures, old and faded certainly, yet still possessed of life. Drawn in black and then filled with black, white and ochre they seemed a window into another world. It was a world of dancing deer and monkeys, but there were also men, aloof, upright and with spears. However they were not quite men, for on broad human shoulders were the heads of snakes, tapirs, crocodiles or birds of prey. And their depiction was exactly that required to show movement. Dancing in the light of a full moon, these animal-headed humans high-stepped and cavorted, and jabbed their weapons. It was a striking picture, and one which had clearly been seen by the current resident of the cave, who had left a candle nearby. He or she was undoubtedly a westerner and as the resident hermit was clearly an individual who had chosen that cave for a reason. Despite their difficulties that day, they still carried their packs and Carmen said one word: 'Photographs!' They decided to remain inconspicuous and left no evidence of their visit.

—⁓—

Very much later it was dark, and they sat around their camp fire while the jungle came alive with hooting, screams, and the incessant noise of insect life. Farther afield, the night sky showed the occasional movement of bats as they fluttered around. Dorkin, regretting that he had taken the others down the mineshaft, said so. Yet it had ended well, and they had achieved their aim of acquiring some ore to test, if not much in the way of anything else. Exactly what it would show they were unsure, but that could come later. Now, they were in a celebratory mood, so Carmen opened a bottle and they began to talk.

Simon was reflective and began to think about the cave paintings. He said, 'I always thought that humans only reached the Americas quite late, perhaps only 12,000 years ago.'

Dorkin replied. 'Yes, but I don't believe all that. And there's evidence too: there are fossilised footprints 23,000 years old, and much more.'

'Enough then, to support our own ideas.'

The two men went on and Carmen began to think about home. The night sky and the silhouette of the escarpment, dark against it, made her feel dislocated from the outside. It gave the jungle a permanent, timeless feel in which modern civilisation seemed not to exist. While the men talked, her eyes were elsewhere. She saw flaming objects in the sky and large white moths among the trees. Her eyes watched the escarpment but her thoughts were elsewhere. She only half-heard when the others spoke about cave figures:

'They are enough to write up on their own,' said Dorkin. 'And if we slot in a comparison with the Boskop art, then I believe we may have something concrete.'

An especially bright star became visible over the top of the escarpment and Carmen tried to guess its distance. Was it fifty light years, or perhaps a thousand? It might be a galaxy in its own right— it seemed to move, a shooting star?

'But do we have enough? And what were they, these men with animal heads? Have we seen anything like them before?'

'They are common enough to have a name,' replied Dorkin. 'We call them therianthropes. They are so common that we can't say they give evidence of a link.'

'That's a shame, what are they?'

'They are man-beasts and they belong to all cultures. In Europe there were werewolves, with supposedly mystical powers. In Africa, man-hyenas were considered common. Here in Mexico, humans were said to be able change into any animal at will.'

'Hmm,' said Wiener. 'I'm sure they found it fun.'

'They were the natural fantasies of imitative people living among animals. I expect it involved the obsessive repetition of rituals and the use of herbal substances. Their leaders were the Shamans and witch doctors: people of power and religious significance.'

It grew late and the whine of mosquitos reached a manic level. Carmen looked at the escarpment and saw that the bright star had vanished. She thought nothing of it. Then it reappeared and seemed to flicker. She noticed it. It moved a little.

'Guys,' she said, 'I don't think we're alone.'

'What?' said Dorkin.

'Up there.'

The light flickered and moved, and then another appeared at a short distance from it. Immediately they drew close and began to whisper. Dorkin said, 'I think there are more than one person. Let's get the fire out. Perhaps there's no danger, but I wouldn't want to draw any more attention to ourselves than we already have.'

They put earth on the fire and carried their odds and ends to the helicopter, still under the overhang where they had left it. Hastily, they covered it with netting. Inside, it was dark and they were quiet, their nerves on edge. They continued to speak in whispers as the minutes passed. It became a colder outside, so that dew fell on the windows, but they heard no sound and there was no further disturbance that night.

The day brought a change in the noise of the jungle. The shrieks and howls of the night were replaced by the hooting of birds. The sun began to warm the tree-tops and the green foliage began to steam. Behind the camouflage netting their windows cleared and they looked to see whether their hasty efforts at hiding the fire had been enough. Were any visitors present or had they remained unseen? They doubted it: their campfire must have been as visible from the clifftop as the burning brand was to them. In the light, much of the fear of an enemy was removed, and of course there might have been no enemy at all. Until that became clear they could probably still leave, and Dorkin, remembering their escape, felt that he had a duty to ask whether his companions wished to fly out. Yet Simon and Carmen measured their prospects in an instant. Their reply was clear: they had come far and would stay. Dorkin smiled in gratitude.

Before long they saw movement outside and heard a low murmur of conversation in a guttural tongue. Then followed a knock on the cabin, and after a few minutes the conversation moved farther away, where it remained a muted undercurrent, waiting. A meeting was inevitable. Wiener grabbed a rifle, but was dissuaded by Dorkin. He carried no weapon himself, recalling that their visitors were simply fulfilling his own wishes. He had wished to meet them and they had obliged by turning up. Their visitors, about twenty men and women, could now be seen waiting patiently. Their low murmur became louder as Dorkin and his companions stepped outside, the object of considerable critical attention.

They stood in line and tried to seem unmoved by the strange faces and clothes before them. The tribespeople wore the local version of a monk's habit, a rather austere garment, beneath which they had taken considerable care to ornament their arms and neck with artistic and colourful squares and stripes. Their faces seemed alternately like the work of headshrinkers, then of humans. They were undoubtedly residents of the village they had seen earlier, and none showed any aggressive intent. All however stood with enough of an attitude to make it clear that they expected their curiosity to be satisfied.

Dorkin had emerged first, and with as much dignity as possible. His appearance, that of a very tall man, caused their onlookers to back away and close ranks. His helicopter, although not a pearlescent spacecraft by any means, was at least the right colour for a flying craft and knowing this, he reached towards the sky with both hands and made a gesture as though drawing down benefaction towards them. They relaxed visibly and seemed to understand. Then calmly, he waved to Simon and Carmen and said, 'Here's our lost tribe. Our dream has come true. Collect some things to use as gifts: knives maybe, or rock-picks, anything useful. And bring some small specimen bags. For each gift ask for a hair in return and by the way, make sure you wear gloves. Now's our chance to collect the DNA samples we need. I bet they'll be useful, and I am pretty certain what they will tell us.'

They carried these gifts outside, sat on chairs and their admirers formed a line and willingly accepted them when offered. Then Carmen showed them how to pluck a few hairs and place each in the proffered specimen bag. After a short hesitation this apparently harmless gesture was carried out with goodwill, and finally they departed, apparently pleased with their gifts. Yet as they did so, two of the older men turned round, gesticulated towards Carmen and looked at them all in a considered way. Dorkin was not sure quite what that meant, but felt they might have known the three scientists were going through an act, and that perhaps they had behaved similarly themselves. Their manner made him uneasy, but he said nothing. Later, Wiener said, 'What now?' His manner suggested that he was very tired after the trials of the previous 24 hours.

Dorkin said, 'We take it easy. Then tomorrow I shall send both of you back to dispatch our samples while I stay here.' He hoped that a break was some kind of recompense for them and smiled inwardly at the thought of them on the beach.

—◊—

Two weeks later Dorkin heard that their results were ready and so asked Simon to take them all to Belize, where he received the expected electronic package. Then he locked himself away in his hotel room. Only later was he disposed to present to his colleagues and in the meantime seemed happy just to think and contemplate. Eventually he donned a ceremonial air:

He said, 'Lady and Gentleman, we are vindicated. But first, the galena was of no particular interest. I'm glad to get that out of the way first. Let's face it, we hardly expected it to show much.'

'So how are we vindicated?'

'It's exactly as we expected: there is a close correlation between the DNA of our tribe and the Boskop samples.' He paused, expert at creating suspense. They knew that this was not particularly for their benefit; he was simply exercising an obligate skill that could be flourished in a larger auditorium. He continued: 'Their appearance—we could hardly talk about it at the time—the enlarged cranium and strange eyes: all this was reflected in their DNA. They are half-way towards being a separate species.'

'I think we guessed that,' said Carmen. 'But you seem a bit cagey about a certain unspeakable word.'

'Roswell?' said Dorkin, promptly saying it.

'Yes.'

'Well our 'tribe' was more like the Boskop evidence. There was none of the loss, none of the degeneracy of the Roswell sample. But apart from that, all three were more like each other than any single example was to us.'

'And can you tell us anything else?' said Wiener.

'I think I can. We found that the Boskop population became separated from modern man 450,000 years ago, and from the Roswell men 600,000 years ago. I find, however, that the Boskop folk were only separated from our jungle tribe just 65,000 years ago. This then, is the proof of what happened. We anticipated it, but now we know. Our aliens, the Roswell people, left earth 600,000 years ago and they revisit from time to time. They kept an interest in the Mexican jungle—perhaps some of them had stayed there. And a few survived for a short while at a settlement in South Africa. They didn't prosper.'

'And perhaps,' said Simon, 'there are still other pockets of that very old population in remote places.' Dorkin shrugged his shoulders.

Carmen said, 'So our spacemen return from time to time and revisit their jungle relatives. They bring gifts, which are probably paternalistic goodwill. Perhaps they feel some kind of kinship with their relatives.'

'No,' said Dorkin, 'I think they *need* to visit.' Why would they travel all these light years just to give their relatives a few ploughs and mallets? It doesn't make sense. No, there has to be another reason.' It was clear he had been turning just that over in his mind.

Carmen said, 'Well if they need to visit, then it must be for something our tribe has which they need.' She added: 'It can't be material wealth or technology. I think it must be something to do with their DNA.'

'Carmen, I think you must be right!'

—⁓—

When they were in Belize, Carmen van Brouin had received what was unusual for her, a text message from Walter Stein. In fact Stein rarely used such a low-security means of communication, and it was clear that he wished to speak to her urgently. She had telephoned him straight back and could tell by his manner that he was downright angry: 'Four of my men have disappeared in that damn jungle. What can you tell me?'

'They were nothing to do with me. I never even knew they were there.'

'Well they were.'

'Do you want me to keep my eyes open for them?'

'Yes, do that. And if you see them tell them to clean up their act or I'll cancel their ass. Now tell me what Dorkin has found out!'

For some reason, Carmen felt inclined to give Stein only the barest of details. She supplied him with what she felt he would probably already know, namely the results of the DNA tests, but she left out Dorkin's conclusions and all their experience with the mine and their encounters with local people. It was strange, but she felt a shift in loyalty. Perhaps it was Stein's manner? Or perhaps it was Dorkin and Wiener's continued friendship and care.

—⁓—

Gradually Callum Dood became less concerned with caution and began to make regular journeys into the rainforest. He was never without an adequate means of defence. He used fire, but chose to prepare meals at some distance from base so that if anyone came there, he would be long gone. Over time, he became used to jungle living and became self-sufficient. However these everyday affairs did not satisfy his curiosity. On many occasions his thoughts turned to the strange people who lived above the escarpment and to the south. Even more so, he became fixated on their relationship with those who visited from a silver craft. Who were they, and where did they come from? He speculated often, but had few facts.

On several occasions, he went into the rainforest and observed the forest tribe about their business. They were a pastoral folk who worked a kind of collective, with all the fruits of agriculture and hunting stored centrally and shared equally. Their lives were simple, yet not quite as simple as they might have been. They were not a large community, yet they had an apparently powerful ally. From time to time they received these visitors, and on such occasions Dood watched while lights flashed in the sky and various ceremonies were enacted at suitable places in the forest. He came to possess a circumspect opinion about these times, which he decided were occasions for transaction rather than friendship. And they were conducted among the architectural remains of a great city that had once propagated to the south, rather than the sorry and fallen relics he had at first seen. In his discrete, cautious and careful observations, Dood passed into large buildings, avenues, and stairways. Farther afield were miniature pagodas and temples, together with terraced pyramids like the one near the cliff-face. And there was a special place where exchanges took place. He had previously observed the four westerners exchanged in a clearing, but at other times the occasional unfortunate was treated thus in the small stepped pyramid enclosed by an arm of rock, near the cliff itself. Then, the individual concerned would be dragged forward, drugged but still able to walk, and taken away by the people Dood had called the silver men. Each ceremony was completed by the receipt of gifts, apparently valued by the forest people but considered trivial by their counterparts.

Dood did not know what this was for, but he continued to observe, and became adept at surreptitious movement. By then he had adopted a rather extreme appearance with a beard and long hair, and with the minimum of clothing. Taken together, his outlook and demeanour made him seem like a wild man, fully adopted by the jungle and at ease with it. He had, by that time, none of the clumsy awkwardness of the westerner therein, but seemed able to live at one with his surroundings. Mosquitos were no longer any concern; he had established that they were repelled by the essence of wild garlic. And the nights were interesting with a sweet smell of flowers, and when moths were on the wing. It came as a surprise, therefore, when in the midst of this, and on an occasion in which he sat at his fire roasting yams, that he was surrounded by small men with spears.

They jabbed their spears toward him. He was careful: he knew that they were tipped with deadly alkaloids, the essences of poisonous plants nearby. He did not move, but continued to roast some yams. Bravely, he offered these to his visitors and his manner: amiable, equal, conciliatory, seemed to impress them. They sat down and he was careful to share hot yams all around. Later, he smoked a cigar and proffered further examples to them, a habit they were clearly familiar with. Finally, and in a spirit of great generosity, he gave each a slice of teonanacatl, which they swallowed without hesitation.

After an hour of social discourse, Dood rose to his full height and bowed low, an act which caused the forest people to nod and accept all as a courtesy. Then, armed with the few things he had brought with him, he slipped off into the jungle. As he left, he could hear them laughing and weeping as the teonanacatl took effect. He believed he had made allies rather than enemies that day, and that they now regarded him as akin to themselves. Such a conclusion was later reinforced when baskets of fruit and vegetables were left for him near his cave. It was quite clear that they had known of his presence but now accepted him as just another forest dweller with no aspirations of a predatory nature. In due course there were several other occasions when this relationship developed, and Dood began to learn one or two words of their strange tongue.

ELEVEN

A DESIRE FOR WOMEN

Dorkin and company prepared for what they knew would be the summit of their endeavours. All the strange reasons they had applied to inexplicable evidence depended on finding a final proof of a relationship between the so-called lost tribe and its mentors. Who were these strange people who visited on an unknown mission? And what was it?

As they approached this final conclusion they were purposeful, relaxed, prepared. Carmen and Simon, by then, had developed a warmer friendship and began to make decisions as a pair. For Dorkin, this was the ultimate substance of his career and he intended to savour it. He became hard to reach, an aesthete, devoted to this higher task. Yet with so much to find out, there remained so few means of doing so. It seemed that there was rather little to investigate, and they could think of no more than watching and waiting and putting themselves about.

Carmen said, 'We need to think of a name. "Lost tribe" hardly does them justice. We can't call them Mayans either.'

'No,' said Dorkin, 'in fact they don't sound like Mayans or even look like them.'

'Well let's give them a name anyway. What about the "Ixchel," after the Mayan moon goddess? They are as quiet as the moon and just as mysterious! It's the best I can do, anyway.' The other two agreed it would do, at least until the clicks and tut-tut sounds of the Ixchel language could be translated into something better.

The Ixchel had a habit of appearing unannounced but the small party wanted to be the ones to do the surveillance. First, they decided to find where the Ixchel lived so that, sooner or later, they would meet their silver-clothed friends. 'We know roughly where they hang out,' said Dorkin. 'We need to sneak up behind them in the rainforest just south of the cliff.'

Simon said, 'We need to be careful. They knew enough to find our camp, remember?'

'Alright. I suppose we don't want to blunder into them and make their dogs bark again. First of all we need to find out what else is up there, so I think we need to look around. We could make two parties. One—that's you and Carmen—can go west. I can look east. We can leave early and take enough to last us a day and keep in touch by radio.'

'Okay,' said Carmen, 'we can turn back at about midday and go inland a bit as well.'

The next day they left camp early and climbed to the top of the cliff face. They parted after having walked inland for a mile, whereupon Dorkin turned towards the rising sun, leaving as few footprints as possible and seeing none. He saw, however, a rough path of a kind, but it was as much the domain of wild animals as humans. To his right the landscape sloped away towards the jungle; to his left the ground was covered by lumpy turf and corrugations. Nowhere was there any sign of the Ixchel. As he walked east, his long shadow followed behind.

The other two walked west with their backs to Dorkin, passing a natural fold in the landscape. Their attention remained with their present path as it veered southwest, upon which some booted footprints lay. Their owner seemed to have had some strange purpose, because his path meandered to various bushes where he had picked leaves and small branches, some of which lay scattered around. All this smacked of the presence of another westerner, and

Carmen suggested that they should speak to Dorkin. He could not yet have marched more than four miles and she reached him with ease. Dorkin said, 'Well, I'm glad there's someone else to talk to. Are you OK to carry on or would you like me to join you?'

'How long would that take?'

'I could be with you in a little over an hour.'

'We would have to wait for you. These prints are fresh and we think we can discover who made them. He may be the owner of that cave.'

'OK, I'll press on as planned. Who knows, there may be something equally important this way.' He doubted it, but was determined to keep his share of the bargain. Later, his return, with the jungle to his left, was easy.

Carmen and Simon followed the footprints but they continued to meander, at one point towards a clump of bushes covered in butterflies, before eventually leaving the path altogether. The trail then changed direction, returning east along a parallel route north of their own. Carmen said, 'Perhaps these tracks are a day old, otherwise we would have seen him.'

Walking on, their way led to a natural amphitheatre with a sloping bank around. They saw a suggestion of flattened grass on the perimeter, suggesting that people had reposed to watch whatever had taken place there. For a while, they were concerned with it to the extent that they forgot their own safety. Instead of their former cautious style, they stood fully upright and spoke in loud voices, concerned only with what they saw before them. They did not see the Ixchel approach quietly, nor the fact that they closed and surrounded them. When they finally turned to see that escape was futile, they stood close with an instinctive loyalty to each other.

At first Simon and Carmen felt unable to gauge their intentions. Instead of showing aggressive behaviour the Ixchel circled, closing slowly. They were a small people, but they began to mill around, giving a press like that of many children in a playground. Then both felt a pinprick on their ankles and immediately, the Ixchel withdrew to a distance. They watched while, standing together for support,

Simon and Carmen's legs began to feel numb; and they closed again as the two finally collapsed into paralysis.

They were paralysed below the knees, and lay helpless as the Ixchel bound their ankles, and their hands behind them; but the two were fully conscious. Yet the painful end they expected was not forthcoming. And it became apparent that they were only really interested in Carmen. Strangely, they left her ankles free, while her wrists were bound tightly. With Simon, his wrists were bound in a kind of loose halter, while his ankles were tight enough to hurt them.

Shortly the numbness began to fade and the Ixchel dragged Carmen away. Meanwhile Simon managed only to sit upright. It took time to free his hands, but once achieved he was then able to untie his ankles. The Ixchel had meant only to immobilise him while they escaped, and it was clear that they had meant to discard him. They were interested only in Carmen, but why?

Perhaps there was still time to catch her, and so he ran as fast as his ankles would allow. They had gone east, but he could see no sign of them. However, Dorkin hove into view, having completed the return leg of his foray. Simon quickly explained what had happened. Dorkin realised that no good could come from recriminations. In fact, he doubted whether any other man could have done more. He said to Simon, who was visibly upset, 'Let's face it, these guys know this place better than we do.' They continued searching for a while, but Carmen had vanished without trace.

Simon said, 'Why Carmen and not me?'

Dorkin replied, 'Well if she's not for the cooking pot, which she can't be otherwise they would have taken you, then she's for some other purpose. And that can only be because she's a woman.'

—m—

Guy Meredith had seemed to lose some of his awkwardness. His obsessive ability with practical matters and his acerbity, the characteristics that gave him an obsessive cast at home, were displayed to an advantage under the forest canopy. His friends came to rely on him for help and in getting things done. It was Guy who found the best firewood and the most effective medicinal plants; Guy who was the least affected by insects and could best dress a wound. They began to look up to him. And with the others: Freya, young and energetic; Pargeter, huffing and puffing but so astute with all matters; Elliott, quiet, calm and as devoted to his work as any newshound, the camp resolved into a generally competent group of people: some quiet, others less so, but all respectful of each other's abilities. It was this group that now stood at the clifftop, looked back over the way they had come, and marvelled at the fact of having reached there at all.

Yet their objective remained vague. They constantly reminded each other of the fact that it was only a map reference, and *that* sent to them by means which at best were unusual and at worst absurd. Even now, they could not confirm absolutely that their set of numbers was anything more than an idea. It took repeated words from Peter Pargeter, who had a particular ability with weighing evidence, to renew their confidence. Yet despite all this, they knew that unless something happened quickly, their present undertaking would peter out in disappointment.

As the high ground sloped away to the south they saw that it was curiously featureless as though the summit of the climb, the clifftop itself, was the only fact of aspiration. They saw only low scrub, with the rainforest recovering after about a mile. However rising about half a mile to the west, a thin column of blue smoke did catch their eye. After a short walk they found a camp, smaller than their own, and with many suggestions of recent use. Beside the smouldering embers was a small pile of wood, a collection of assorted plants, an old can of water, and a seat cut from the surrounding turf. It was probably used by a single individual.

Elliott said, 'There's not much here in the way of personal belongings, so I wouldn't be surprised if the person who comes here only regards it as a temporary place to hang out. It's a bit too exposed to sleep here, anyway.'

'That,' said Freya, 'is just what I was thinking. It's the sort of camp where a person would sit and contemplate.'

They waited, but the camp remained deserted and the embers eventually burned out. Later, they made for folds of ground nearby, where they were surprised by the amount of land enclosed from view. Even more so, it contained a small stepped pyramid, which Pargeter said was like a statement of ownership of the place. They stared, and Meredith said, 'Well since it's at our map reference then it must be something to do with us.' But none could see how.

They walked farther and found a few remains of other buildings, and that encouraged them. Then they decided that their next expeditions would be to the pyramid once more, followed by the rainforest to the south. More immediately, they settled to spend that evening in camp. The mosquitos whined and the night-time cacophony started. They arranged mosquito nets and wood-smoke rose from the fire. Pargeter felt it necessary to sum up in his soothing voice: 'At least we're at our destination and there's an interesting stepped pyramid and other ruins.' On that positive note they drank coffee and Irish whiskey and watched the stars come out. At ten o'clock a cloud passed over the stars and they decided to turn in for the night. Then a violent squall of rain came, which extinguished their campfire. It soon passed, but the sky stayed dark as they made for their tents. Suddenly and without warning, a blinding white light issued from the top of the escarpment. It lit their surroundings to the extent that they could see each other as silhouettes inside their tents, then it flickered and died and all was still and quiet. They called to each other and said they were fine. Early next morning Freya told them that their experience was like the effusion of light she had seen from her car. Later, they found that their compasses had failed, and thereafter they knew they had come to the right place. Pargeter no longer felt the need to bolster their confidence.

The rest of the day passed without disturbance and in their foray to the pyramid and beyond, they saw no sign of strangers. The pyramid was interesting, but they were unable to get inside. Farther south, they saw evidence of the presence of people in terms of paths and fallen buildings, but had no sight of them. They had not, as yet, entered the jungle farther on. That night they shared another evening in camp, where talk turned once again to their expedition. Elliott said, 'There's something special about that pyramid. It seems very much more than just a building up there on the clifftop.'

Freya agreed: 'No, it's not just a pyramid, is it! That big electrical discharge last night must have been near it. It was almost like a lightning conductor.'

Later, the jungle seemed particularly noisy. The howler monkeys were vociferous, their screeching loud and anguished. There was also much rain, which beat down on their tents and made them unwilling to venture outside. At dawn, all ceased and the rainforest began its particular ritual in which nocturnal animals fell silent as the sun lifted, and the smell of Turkish bath and dank vegetation rose once again. And Peter Pargeter was up early to put the kettle on. Soon, Meredith and Elliott appeared and they sat drinking coffee, sleepy after their disturbed night. It was unlike Freya to stay abed and eventually they called her. Yet she did not rise or shine and Pargeter went to her tent.

Her tent was riven, a neat cut down one side, and she was gone. Her day-wear was left, although she must still have had her shoes. Pargeter shouted to the others: 'Quick, come and see!' They stood aghast and quickly made a few presumptions. Meredith said, 'Look at that cut in the canvas, it's neat. This is the work of men.'

Elliott replied, 'I thought it was noisy last night, and now we know why. And it's not westerners who have taken her either.'

A trail of footprints made its way towards the cliff face. Pargeter said, 'Please don't panic, that's the worst thing for Freya right now.'

Quickly, they doused their fire and equipped for speed, set off in pursuit. It was a straightforward task since four sets of footprints led away from their camp, Freya's with them. Meredith was angry, and the others wondered what the outcome would be if faced with her captors. They climbed quickly to the summit, at which point the trail veered south towards the forest before being lost. There,

Pargeter stopped. He said, 'I expect they had an advantage of about four hours over us. Perhaps they covered her mouth so she couldn't call out, or maybe they even slipped her something to make her feel drowsy. But the point is we can't go blundering on. We have to approach slowly.'

Their anger had been dissipated by the strenuous climb: Meredith in particular was now cold and calculating as he nodded to Pargeter. After a short pause to catch their breath they followed a direct line towards the trees where further marks of her passage reappeared. They had no plan of what they would do if they found her. Pargeter cautioned Meredith not to barge in, and they began to crouch low.

Just as several others had seen before them, the outskirts of a native village eventually changed to become a place which appeared still to be inhabited, with various cooking pots, piles of firewood, everyday utensils and a still-warm bakery. Yet the people were absent: either busy or in hiding. The three stopped crouching, began speak in normal tones and widened their search. Yet there was no sign of Freya or her captors and the whole place was completely silent. After a while they were obliged to make their way back. Pargeter said, 'They've all disappeared because they expected us to barge in. Right now, Freya's best hope is that we should work 'wise'. I don't think we can expect to find her in any laborious pursuit.'

Meredith replied, 'I think that's obvious. Perhaps we should try to meet the owner of that camp on the clifftop. He's probably the only person around here with any experience of the place.'

—⁂—

In Washington DC, Walter Stein sat down at his desk and interviewed a member of his staff who, responsible for liaison with Carmen van Brouin, had information of significance. 'Sir,' the colleague said rather formally: 'Van Brouin. We usually get a message about once per month and if things are urgent, more often. We haven't heard a thing for ages.'

Stein valued her call, particularly under the present circumstances in which he was required to provide regular assurances to those in positions above him. He said, 'If we hear nothing in another two weeks, make sure you divert some personnel to see what the hell is going on.'

'That's just it, Sir, there's nothing from the others either.'

'Well try to get in touch if you can.' Stein dismissed his colleague and turned his attention to a manuscript on his desk. It was long and entitled The Seneca Guns are Active. He read:

> 'Today, repeated sounds of an undersea explosion shook houses in the area and made furniture vibrate. The local populace were alarmed and made representations to police forces and politicians. Seismologists scanned their data for the area and said there was little or no unusual seismic activity that could have caused it. The military say they had no planes in flight that could have made a sonic boom. Meteorologists examined atmospheric conditions prevailing at the time and found nothing to explain them. Scientists proposed that the sounds were derived from inversions of water temperatures, but we understand such conditions did not prevail on the day. Similar sounds were also reported inland, well away from deep water, and they are also unexplained.'

To Stein, that was old-hat; he had seen their like before. He then read a following paragraph:

> 'Bright lights were seen off the Carolina coast, and they were accompanied by loud detonations in the sea. These strange lights flickered on for a few seconds and illuminated considerable areas so that fishing boats as far apart as twenty miles reported the same phenomena. Such vast releases of light must require the expenditure of great energy, yet there is no explanation for it apart from the fact that fishing boats reported flying discs in the area and described them as pearlescent silver with a halo of

light emitted from the edge. They appeared at the same time as
the disturbances reported elsewhere.'

He wrote at the foot of the memorandum: 'Advise local press and radio of US military activity in those places. Reports of flying craft are to correspond with training flights of stealth bombers in the area.' Then he appended his signature.

Stein paused to look out of the window. He was not a reflective man and had become used to this continual output of disinformation. It hardly worried him. Yet he had come to feel that it was all for nothing. His department had managed to keep a lid on all matters extra-terrestrial, but recently the lid of the pressure cooker had blown off. Now his career was on the line.

—⁂—

Callum Dood sat at his campfire with four elders of the forest dwellers. It was an evening visit, and a social one. They had brought several green snakes which they nailed to the ground by the head and tail. Then, first eviscerating each snake, they selected the gall bladder and emptied it into the cups of brandy that Dood had passed round. Thus fortified, they sliced each snake into short pieces and steamed it with yams and corn. With gestures of their hands, arms and torso they explained to Dood that the flexibility of the snake would improve his own suppleness and that the gall, while astringent, would improve his digestion. The yam contained an elixir to improve fertility and he could be sure of many children, which was what interested the Pragya, the gods of the silver machine. The corn, too, resembled the male appendage, so that his masculinity would improve in the course of his efforts at siring them. And further, he should come to their city where they would repay his considerable hospitality and perhaps, if all was well, he might see the Pragya himself. With due solemnity they ate this excellent meal and Dood was generous with the brandy he had brought with him. The elders had heard they were called 'Ixchel' and found it acceptable. They taught him how to say 'Pragya' and his vocabulary was further enhanced by the words for woman, child and snake. Under the stars, which they described to him with an expanse of gestures, he could see a small white disc hovering. It was close, but would not descend that night. They would know when to expect it because the light of the sun would appear briefly during the time of the stars.

Dood felt invigorated; his years fell away. Like the Ixchel, whose lives were prolonged by the use of natural remedies from the jungle and like the Pragya from the skies, his existence would be prolonged too. At one with nature, he would soon meet the Pragya and help them in the struggle for their very survival.

On the following day he became aware that some other people had visited his camp and were trying to find its owner. He did not, at that time, wish to be found, so he let his campfire smoke and watched to see who the visitors were. In fact he was surprised to find no fewer than two distinct groups, both searching for something and becoming increasingly frantic. He thought their behaviour directly connected with the Ixchel and therefore indirectly with the Pragya whose requirements the Ixchel accommodated. At once he felt that his present equilibrium might be upset by bad feeling between the various factions. He wished to avoid the trouble that he knew would follow if more westerners were taken away. He hoped to continue there for some time yet and found it a comfortable life. His hair might be long, but he was not inconvenienced by sleeping rough. He felt a greater cognisance of time, and solitary reflection had made him feel almost in a continuing *déjà vu*. At no other time had he such a constant and shifting appreciation of the future, and later he could write much. His was the counterpart of Indian tepee living, or that of the one-man yachtsman on a round the world cruise. He did not wish it to be disturbed. In this clear comprehension he knew that the Ixchel had taken women from both visiting parties. And it was *that* which would shortly cause trouble. After considerable reflection Callum Dood extinguished his campfire altogether and walked towards the jungle. Now was the time take up the Ixchel's offer of hospitality.

—⚹—

David Elliott kicked once again at the embers of Dood's campfire and looked around. The fire had been alight for 24 hours and was now only a pile of embers. The camp was again as deserted as it had been the previous morning. They had tried visiting in the evening, but to no avail: its owner remained as elusive and secretive as always.

'Perhaps this is a decoy?' said Peter Pargeter, but the others shook their head. 'Nobody,' said Elliott, 'would light a fire just to draw attention to their absence from it!'

'And in any case,' said Guy Meredith, 'I believe we need to look elsewhere. He or she must gather food and firewood from time to time.'

That this was clear and logical was self-evident. They had, at other times, seen smoke issue from the rainforest below the cliff, although a little to the north. That, too, was the area of the densest rainforest and farthest from the Ixchel. 'If we wait at a strategic position watching the foot of the cliff,' said Meredith, 'we could expect to see this stranger sooner or later.'

Accordingly, the three men waited and watched. They became adept at avoiding the ants that held station within the trees, one hundred yards from the cliff face. They made a hide of a kind, the better to remain inconspicuous. They learned to avoid soap, aftershave and the odours of cooking, each of which seemed to entice the most vicious of mosquitos. And on the third day a grizzled and grim-looking person, outwardly a native, and yet bearing a rucksack, descended to the forest floor at dawn and strode towards them, a hand-axe in his right hand. This strange native whistled a tune from the book 'Hymns Ancient and Modern' as he approached and had a gait that was strangely familiar, although they could not place it. He stopped to light a cigar, and then swung his axe a couple of times as he entered the forest. In an attempt to avoid the axe, Guy Meredith waited before saying, 'Hey you!'

The strange native turned round and his features became clear. They realised that his beard made it unlikely he was a member of the Ixchel. In a moment there was recognition on both sides. Peter Pargeter said, 'Dr Dood I presume!'

The Reverend Dood said, 'What the hell are you doing here?'

Pargeter replied, 'Hey, you can't say that!'

In short measure they shook hands and decided to invite Dood to their camp, where they prepared breakfast and drank some of the best coffee he had ever tasted. Afterwards, Dood gave a brief account of events. 'I suppose you must think me strange,' he said. 'Nothing much happened after we sent our radio message and so I went on holiday.'

'You disappeared from the seaside!' said Pargeter.

'I suppose I did. But I did leave a message with my landlady. I went off travelling. I'm actually on a botanical excursion and ended up here because this is the best place for interesting plants. Unfortunately, my guide was eaten by an alligator. By the way, where's Adam Shilto. Is he here?'

'No,' said Pargeter. 'He had to stay behind to manage things at home. But have you any idea what's been going on here recently?'

'A little,' said Dood. 'And how did you get here yourselves?'

Elliott recounted the fact of their having solved the marks in the Firehills projectile, then finding that it agreed with the information in the crop circle. He explained that it was a map reference that had brought them so far. He said, 'We still don't really know why they sent it to us.'

Guy Meredith described more about their recent adventures and explained how Freya went missing, believed in the hands of the Ixchel. He added, 'We have not been able to find her,' and glanced at a rifle. Dood caught his look.

He said, 'If you attack them then you can say goodbye to Freya. You—or rather we—can only barter with them. I had planned to visit them again myself because I guessed they had taken more women. I expected an upset and wanted to talk them out of whatever they intended to do. I shall have to bring that forward.'

'So,' said Guy, 'where is she?'

'I think she will be OK. She's probably asleep. Up there.' He pointed towards the clifftop.

Elliott, who had been listening carefully, said, 'You said women?'

'I did. You may not believe it, but there have been two other parties around here recently, one a party of three American academics, and the other a party of four Americans watching them. One of the academics is a young woman and the Ixchel have taken her away as well. I expect she's with Freya now.'

'They were following them?'

'Yes. Strange as it may seem, these academics are on a quest rather like your own. It's all about this odd place. The other lot, well, didn't we discuss the CIA once before? It seems like ages ago.'

Elliott replied, 'You are saying that there are CIA people here?'

'I am. But the leading man of the three is that guy Dorkin. David, you met him in the US I believe.'

'So we are just as likely to be picked up by the CIA?'

'No.' Dood's reply was straightforward: 'These four CIA types, they were collared by the people you call the Ixchel—nice name, by the way—and I won't exactly say sacrificed, but disposed of might be better.'

'What!' said Pargeter.

'Yes, we won't see them here again. And I think they mean to do something similar to the girls.'

There was a pause, after which Elliott said, 'What about the academics. Have they found anything out?'

'I'm surprised you haven't met them. I suppose they have been hiding, though. As to what they've found out about the Ixchel, you would have to speak to them.'

'Callum,' said Pargeter, 'you seem remarkably cool about Freya and this other girl being sacrificed!'

Callum Dood lit a cigar while he collected his thoughts. He said, 'From their point of view it might seem a sacrifice, but don't worry, the Ixchel don't intend to cut their hearts out with a knife, if that's what you mean.'

'Alright, so what do we do now?'

'Well I intend to vanish now and go about my business. I don't want to be seen colluding with you, because I have been developing tenuous links with the Ixchel recently. I've also been watching things from a distance. But chiefly, I've been concerned with promulgating a feeling of harmony. The forest people have decided they can tolerate your presence only because of my efforts. I drank tea with them only yesterday, and said I intended to visit them.'

'Visit?' said Elliott, rather frustrated by his absence of contact with prospective journalistic sources.

'Indeed. And there's another understanding between these people, the Ixchel and the wanderers from the stars, the Pragya.'

'So what's this understanding?' said Meredith, reflecting his long-standing interests.

'I think it's somewhat paternal. The Pragya regard the Ixchel as their nearest relatives here, but they are no less inclined to be friendly towards the rest of us, and indeed, I hear they admire some of our achievements, especially in the areas of music and literature. They cannot understand how we produce so many venerated philosophers and yet fail to live by their philosophies. Our science, of course, is puny by comparison with theirs, yet they still have great regard for our vitality and ebullience. It is something they have lost and they cannot seem to acquire it from the Ixchel, despite having tried.'

'I suppose that explains why they visit on a regular basis?' said Meredith.

'They have visited, for sure. Despite their advanced science I don't think they have been successful with what they desire. That may change soon, however.'

'And what are they doing with Freya and this other girl?' said Elliott.

'That's next. I need to find out exactly what they intend to do. I shall go tonight. Meanwhile, I think you need to try to get in touch with Dorkin and the other young guy he's with. You're all stronger as a group, and perhaps wiser. But I would suggest that, although you may meet and talk, you should maintain two smaller camps. That way the Ixchel may not notice a change. I can come and see you when I'm ready, perhaps…give me another day.'

'Alright,' said Meredith, 'but one more question, please. What has this got to do with spacecraft?'

'Everything,' said Callum Dood, and walked off.

—◊—

A mile to the west Dorkin and Wiener continued to search for Carmen and their searches led them to examine in detail the many local features of the landscape. They made a visit to the place enclosed by folds of higher ground behind the cliff. Later, they spent a day looking again at the outskirts of the part-fallen Ixchel township to the south. Towards dusk they ventured farther, approaching the inhabited parts while staying far enough to stop the dogs from barking. Although they found no secretive way to visit Carmen, they conducted all in calm and quiet, which belied the fact that they were frantic with worry.

It was a welcome divergence therefore, when, descending to the forest floor, they observed three men climbing up. One was slim and athletic, another gaunt and wiry, and the last rotund and perspiring. Dorkin and Elliott recognised each other immediately. Pargeter said, 'Well if you guys are going down, perhaps we should lead the way?' He was in fact pleased not to have to climb higher.

They shook hands, and Pargeter invited the smaller party back to camp. Both parties felt relieved, since although the two girls were not yet back, their meeting seemed to be at least a step towards it. Pargeter said, 'We knew you were here and expected to bump into you before long. I suppose we were half-looking for you anyway.'

Elliott eventually said, 'Thank you for your computer disc, by the way, we beamed the contents into space.'

'Is that how you got here?'

'We don't know for sure. We think that our 'interplanetary friends' sent their map reference to entice us here.' He went over the story about the Firehills projectile and the data in the crop circle. Neither Dorkin or Wiener had heard about these. Wiener said, 'I guess there's a whole other side to this matter. It's about time we all told each other everything.'

There followed a cathartic, hour-long discussion by all of the events which had led them to that strange place. In this, they were relieved at the lack of secretiveness and the fact that the need for furtive behaviour was abolished. They continued to listen and reflect, each group adding small details to the overall story.

Finally Dorkin said, 'It strikes me as unrealistic that your radio message made them send the map reference down. From what you say, the Firehills projectile came quite some time before.'

'In that case,' said Elliott, 'they must have sent the map reference as a way of enticing any people here: anyone with the wit to work it out.'

'Then, they must think that all interested people are of use to them,' said Pargeter. 'And by the way,' he added, addressing Dorkin: 'I love your work on DNA and those ancient palaeontological sites.'

Dorkin nodded. 'Thanks, but the question remains, what do they want with Carmen and Freya? I do have some ideas, of course.'

'Go on, tell us!'

'It has to be something to do with DNA. I said earlier that the DNA of those guys was like the Ixchel, but it had loads of bits missing. I think they are on a quest here to do something about it. No, I don't think that the girls are likely to get sacrificed any more than this guy Callum Dood did. But I reckon they want what girls can provide.'

'Not sex?' Wiener sounded worried.

'No, more like useful body parts: ova. I wouldn't be surprised to find that our visitors are trying to restore the deleted sections of their genes. They probably use the Ixchel to get a supply of people.'

'My God,' said Pargeter, 'even our tour guide spoke about such legends. She mentioned strange visitors from the skies.'

'So what do we do now?'

Pargeter said, 'Dood said we can't rush in. Even if we have rifles we can't defeat them, and don't forget they also have their clever friends to help. Callum said he's going to find out what's going on. I hope to hear back in 48 hours. Can we last out until then?'

'I guess so,' said Meredith and Wiener together.

—�⁓—

Callum Dood collected a selection of his best cigars and a fresh bottle of brandy and walked towards the rainforest. It was a clear afternoon without rain, but the sun beat down from behind light cloud cover and there was very little wind, so it was particularly hot and sticky. Ahead stood the olive-green canopy and upon reaching it he was pleased to be removed from direct sunlight and make for the Ixchel's city. He wondered why the city had fallen into disuse at its edges but not in the middle. Perhaps they had defended it against the incursion of another tribe? Or perhaps it was better to display an outward dereliction to all newcomers? Nevertheless it had once been a larger place but had now shrunk, so that only the middle one-third remained in use. Undoubtedly the Ixchel were now fewer in number; he doubted whether they could be more than three thousand people. From all that Pargeter had told him, he could not see how they would remain a viable community for long: they were different, and he would expect them to be absorbed or fade away in this modern world. That must be it: their isolation, the surrounding dereliction, it was an intentional posture the better to remain undisturbed. Yet that posture was immeasurably more complicated by their relationship with the Pragya. The latter were the key to all the events that had taken place. He wondered at the seeming coincidences that had brought his friends all this way. And he wondered at the Pragya themselves: were they a predatorial species, or were they no more than pragmatic about their own fortune?

Turning these questions over, Dood ambled over damp ground, soon reaching the jungle settlement where he was surprised to see a deputation of the Ixchel waiting for him. They must have had lookouts. They were as courteous towards him as they had been before, and to emphasise the fact that he was similarly inclined, he bowed low.

In the middle of a grassy square was a fire, and around it many small people sat, their scapulars replaced by a simple loincloth. Men and women were similarly clad, giving an ample opportunity to observe the strange contrast between narrow shoulders and feeble limbs, and their enlarged crania. What evolutionary process had produced them? Callum Dood could only think that their best specimens had been taken as slaves and that the brightest had managed to avoid that fate. Nevertheless they were now happy. There was dancing and a kind of rhythmic music made from many people humming the same tune, while clapping their hands together. He stood and joined in, his young female counterpart in a dance smiling and charming. Behind her, and in the centre of the square, a cooking pot steamed in an ominous manner. The dance over, all sat down on coarse grass and proffered their bowl towards an old man who circulated with a ladle, dispensing the contents of the pot. Dood was reluctant to take it, fearing a concoction of bones, but was relieved that it was only yams and corn, supplemented with something like *pan de elote*, the cake of maize bread eaten in parts of Africa. An adequate amount was eaten by all, and then bowls were refreshed with a strong, sweet tequila-like spirit which all drank with a brisk and cheerful readiness.

Once again the ladle was brought round, and to Dood it was clear that he had joined more than just a village feast. It was to be an evening of celebration. The ladle was dipped into an altogether different pot, and a smaller measure of a dark brown infusion was provided for all. Yet he noticed that the village elders, those that had visited him at his camp, all avoided this infusion which he suspected, from its appearance, was ayahuasca. It would probably be a long evening. He accepted his share but made a motion to drink it without swallowing and was careful to make his bowl capsize on the grass. The ayahuasca would have taken a while to work and in the first instance he was careful to moderate his movements without the stamping of feet and egregious expressions that would have been inappropriate at those stages. Later, with the sun falling and the mosquitos beginning their work, he rubbed garlic onto his exposed limbs and settled to watch whatever festivities would follow.

There was more dancing, and music made by woodwind instruments and drums. Yet in all this the elders, those he knew from earlier meetings, were silent, watchful and careful to act as stewards rather than participate themselves. Dood now rose to join them and as if by unspoken agreement two elders walked away and invited him to follow. By walking due south they entered deeper jungle, where after ten minutes they reached a building of stone that had the appearance of being a communal place of storage. Inside were bales of dried grass, yams, maize and the like. More particularly there were the drying leaves of tobacco supported from the roof by string. The elders of the Ixchel noted his interest, smiled, and offered some, which Dood gratefully accepted. They entered an anteroom and waved for him to follow.

The anteroom was a place some fifteen feet square, a quiet room with mats on the floor and a latrine behind a screen. On mats lay Freya and another girl whom he had not met before, but knew to be Carmen. They seemed to be asleep, yet it was deep and immotile without the involuntary movement of muscles. It was a drugged sleep and featured laboured breathing.

Dood knew enough from guttural words and gesticulations to understand what the Ixchel intended. He pointed to his own manhood, shook his head and made a wry face. Perhaps at a more propitious time? The Ixchel shrugged their shoulders. Instead, he made an attempt to sponge the girls' faces and turn them on their sides so that their laboured breathing would ease. Aware of the purpose of the Ixchel at last, he rose, showed more interest in the tobacco, and gesticulated for a return to the festivities.

There, under the watchful eyes of the elders, he assumed his most inscrutable manner and was careful to show respect to all as he danced what could only be described as a jig. By the next morning, having eaten, drunk and smoked his fill, he acknowledged the elders with thanks and returned to his camp. Then after a day of thought, at the end of which his view of events was exactly as it had been that morning, he made for Pargeter's camp. There, with all parties assembled, he recounted his observations and conclusions to the five conspirators.

'Okay,' said Dorkin, 'how are Carmen and Freya?'

'They are alright.'

'You saw them?'

'Yes.'

'Can we get them away?'

'I doubt it. If you try that, you would face a load of nasty little poison darts, and the girls would be just as badly-off afterwards.'

'So what do you advise?'

'First of all we maintain contact with them, or rather, I do. I shall act as though I'm complicit in their intentions in case they er—want me back again. Somehow I or we will manage to grab the girls and bring them back here. But there's just one more thing.'

'And what's that?'

'I hope you do realise that if we are successful, it may put an end to your investigation here? I say this because I assume you want to learn about the Pragya?'

Wiener and Dorkin nodded; Meredith opened his mouth but decided not to say anything.

Dood added: 'But fear not, the Ixchel don't intend to slit Freya and Carmen's throats.'

Pargeter followed, 'Well if not, can you finally tell us what they *do* want with them!'

Dood said, 'I can do, but Professor Dorkin, can you first give us your description again, of what exactly your DNA investigations led to. Don't worry, it is relevant.'

'Alright, we eventually managed to build quite an interesting picture. We originally compared ancient DNA from a palaeontological site in South Africa with frozen samples supplied by the US government from the Roswell smash. Other evidence suggested that we should also test samples from people around here. Believe it or not they were all similar, and quite different from modern human DNA. And looking back— and this is something that has only just struck me—I also tested a sample of hair that was collected from a remote place in Nepal by some guy and that, too, was unlike modern human stuff. So in summary, we are not the only masters of our planet that we thought. There are other ancient peoples here who still share with us, although how they have managed to survive all this time I don't know. We collected all kinds of evidence to prove it.'

Dorkin paused as though deciding what, from all the mass of evidence, they might wish to listen to. He went on, 'You asked me about these samples of DNA. They showed that we became separated from these strange people long ago. But even more strange, the Roswell DNA had diverged long before that, as though those guys left earth, leaving some of their kin behind. And the DNA of the people they left behind, well, that was more complete. The Roswell sample was simpler: it'd had parts excised, cut out, the non-coding bits that perhaps they thought served no useful function. Only they probably do. That's about it.'

'Very concisely put,' said Dood. 'And that helps me to explain. As far as I understand matters, the Pragya, so called, are the end result of some kind of genetic experiment. So they return here for two reasons: yes, they have a genuine interest in their earthly relatives and want to help them, but their prime motive is to fix their own mistakes. The Ixchel provide them with the raw material, and by that I mean ordinary people. They particularly want women. I can't say why, but I do have a suspicion that they are interested in the scientific aspects of procreation.'

'Aha,' said Dorkin, 'I had guessed that! I thought they would eventually start playing around with hybrid embryos…or worse.'

'Then maybe,' said Dood, 'that would explain why the Ixchel thought I might be interested in the girls. I managed to make them think I'm not up to the job, at least not right now.' He added with a smile, 'You should see me in the broom cupboard with the campanologists!'

He went on: 'But they collared four guys a while back. I expect they want them for something similar.'

Dorkin replied, 'If those guys were CIA, there will soon be more of them when they don't report back.'

Elliott said, 'I suppose we can expect some kind of exchange with the Pragya soon?'

'Yes,' said Dood. 'We shall probably know when it's about to take place because that damn great silver bird will come down, along with lights in the sky.'

'Then what?' said Simon Wiener. He had shown such disquiet throughout their discussion that Pargeter had placed an arm round his shoulders.

'I can see that I shall have to do a lot of talking to them. We need to meet here again, when the lights appear. Please prepare for a trip to their city at short notice. No guns, it won't help.'

—m—

In the meantime Callum Dood began to think about maintaining social discourse with the Ixchel. On a few occasions he visited them in a hail-fellow-well-met manner, openly smoking tobacco and taking part in minor routines. He acquired a scapular, the local form of monastic dress which he found dry and airy, yet cool in the direct sun. Eventually he felt that his presence hardly merited a second look, which was his precise intention.

In due course he was able to visit the girls, whose plight had continued, to ensure that they remained comfortable. He noted that their drugged sleep had become shallow, with tossing and turning, and that they were now guarded. Throughout, he was careful to ensure that all common courtesies were shown to their guards by offering cigars and by smoking with them in a companionable manner. While not quite obtaining free access he had been able to confirm their whereabouts and ensure their continued wellbeing. By then he had acquired a working vocabulary of their strange tongue and they smiled at his mistakes and offered their corrections. But the elders, while accepting him, appeared preoccupied as though their minds were on greater things.

It was in this atmosphere that Dood, having built workable bridges, returned to his own campfire one evening. Immediately, the pigeons ascended into the sky and began to fly round in purposeless circles. Soon after, a minor storm brewed overhead, complete with fast-appearing dark cloud, a squall of heavy rain and a seemingly early nightfall. Rain then fell, a shattering downpour which beat the trees flat and that left him without the troublesome flying insects for a while. Then thunder followed, and white light which had the brilliance of a small local sun; while around him the air was filled with static electrical activity and a strange magnetic effect such that all metal objects were pulled together. Most of these effects were observed by his friends a mile distant. Shortly, he walked the distance to their camp and spoke to Dorkin alone. He asked that he should accompany him in a proposed visit to the Ixchel and added, 'But I don't want any impetuous activity when things are in the balance.'

Dorkin said, 'Impetuous?'

'Yes, can you get the others to guard the camp? Tell them they need to be here if the girls arrive. That should do the trick.'

Dorkin saw the wisdom in Dood's proposal: the younger men had been rather *gung ho* in their attitude recently and he doubted whether they would refrain from the kind of aggressive behaviour that would cause an upset. He said, 'Anything I can do myself?'

'Yes, wear your scruffiest clothes and bring some tequila and these cigars.' He handed some over. 'They can be gifts. Do you have something like a cycling cape?' Dorkin emerged with a blanket. 'Good, make a hole in it.' Dorkin spoke to the others and to Pargeter privately. The latter understood his role in keeping the others out of trouble.

Dorkin and Dood entered the rainforest after its particularly heavy drenching. The forest floor was squelchy and the trees dripping so that they were pleased to walk on whatever broken pavements they could find, stumbling in the dark and worried by the few growls and slithering noises around them. Yet eventually there was firelight ahead and the sound of a gathering. The pye-dogs were quiet or at least distracted elsewhere, and soon they joined the throng where Dorkin, in his blanket-poncho drew only the occasional glance. Yet despite the milling crowd it was not wholly a time for celebration: there was an underlying urgency in the behaviour of the people which suggested some other, more important purpose.

The elders had begun to marshal the tribe, who were shortly arranged so that the women were placed towards the front, and men and younger individuals to the rear. They sat, and were fed from a rich and satisfying stew as before. There was no beer or tequila, nor even pulque, and the throng, satisfied but expectant, was arranged with a large space in the middle.

The thin hair of the Ixchel began to rise with static electricity and in the case of Dood the effect was magnified by his luxuriant grey locks to the extent that he assumed the appearance of a wild man, which brought considerable deference from those around him. Nodding, he dispensed a few cigars and an equitable manner was assumed by all. Then after a minute the proverbial silver bird descended and the Ixchel were hushed. The elders, four of them, approached solemnly and stood waiting for it to open. It soon did so, revealing light behind an open aperture from which one individual walked out and faced them all.

Dood and Dorkin, who had managed to avoid any undue interest through having adopted clothing like that of the Ixchel, were about fifty feet from the open aperture. The proceedings were not designed as a religious ritual, yet the Ixchel behaved as though they regarded the Pragya with awe or at least an excess of respect. Dood thought that the spokesman for the Pragya acted with arrogance in the way he held his puny body erect. Both men felt a measure of assault as his cynical and knowing eyes passed over them. Perhaps he had more mental power than might simply be expressed in a glance?

The Pragya now showed that they regarded the gathering as a form of nursery. Several young women were ushered forward, but rather than showing fear or injustice they seemed to regard it as a privilege and honour to be offered in this market. The throng pressed forward with the women to the fore so that Dood and Dorkin, just behind, were brought forward to within twenty feet of the representative of the Pragya who presided. At last, they were close enough to see that his clothing, while silvered, was only partly opaque, and that they were able to examine him in detail.

He was a short and puny individual, who held his short arms out in a gesture of welcome, revealing a hollow, barely muscled chest and narrow shoulders. His pale flesh was enclosed by androgyne clothing in which his genitals were either reduced in size or internal, or absent altogether. His legs were short and his body long in comparison, while his overall height was little more than five feet. By comparison the Ixchel were a paragon of athleticism. Dorkin wondered what circumstances could have produced such a body: was it a lack of evolutionary challenge? And in that there was no doubt that the individual before him was deficient.

Not wholly deficient, however. He held up his head with hairless eyebrows and the enlarged forehead prominent, and watched them all, knowing, through lidless black eyes. He was not quite human, nor yet wholly alien. He was similar to men, yet distinct from them. His eyes held them with a sentient understanding, yet it contained an alien viewpoint. He brought forward metal tokens such as statues of gods, together with various useful materials of which bags of salt excited the most interest. But their weight was such that the Ixchel were obliged to collect and carry them. In return he waved his arm towards the young women at the front, and for a second he reminded Dood of Pargeter's cat as he cocked his head to view them, perhaps entranced by their beauty. Certainly, he was choosing from them, and having done so waved his hand so that three walked forward, a choice which again they seemed to regard as a privilege. There, in front of all, each removed her scapular and completely naked, was dressed again in the same semi-opaque silvered clothing worn by the Pragya. Turning to face their audience they bowed low and entered the silver machine. They showed no fear and the Ixchel no sense of loss. As far as Dood could see, the exchange had been grossly unequal.

Shortly, the edge of the machine began to shimmer as it rose in the air, and the nacreous quality of the object was once more manifest. Then iron or steel objects: knives, kettles, flew towards it as it sped aloft, while a metal object in Dorkin's pocket was tugged with considerable force. The celebration had ended and all now departed, Dood and Dorkin through the undergrowth with particular caution, for the pye-dogs were out again.

The next morning Dood walked to Dorkin's camp with more urgency than before, where he found that the others had been briefed concerning the events of the previous night. Dorkin had already made it clear that Freya and Carmen had not been the object of interest, and some of the anxiety of the previous day had gone. As they spoke about what to do next, their talk was open and palliative, revisited a few coincidences, and was then enquiring of the future.

Joseph Dorkin said to Pargeter: 'I thought all this was my own affair. I'm sorry that Freya and you guys seem to have been drawn into it. And all that stuff about the crop circles and the Silpho and Firehills projectiles, it showed a good bit of detective work.'

'Thank you, but we were the amateurs in all this. I would never have believed that your side of things was possible.'

Simon Wiener directed a question to Dood: 'Callum, we all wondered who had the campfires and kept his own company all the time. We still wonder how you managed to arrive here at the same time as we did. It seems the most remarkable coincidence.'

'Well, if you consider that there are only 195 countries, most of which would have been useless for jungle exotica, then it's not as much of a coincidence as you might have thought. Once I was here, it was my guide who brought me to where the action was.'

Elliott said, 'All this sounds so understated! There's actually enough of a story here to fill a year's worth of glossy magazines. But how will it end? And what exactly do we do next?'

'What next?' repeated Joseph Dorkin. 'Perhaps we need to think about what the Pragya are going to do; and the Ixchel for that matter. Callum, that's where you come in, you've spent a lot of time watching them.'

'Perhaps, but I can only tell you a little about both groups. The Ixchel are reclusive, formerly a city-dwelling tribe, but now they choose to live in a small remnant of their city. I believe they know that publicity would mean the end of them. I think they also know that their sponsors, the Pragya, are hugely powerful and valuable friends to have. That, I think, is why they allow the occasional woman to be carried away—and the occasional man, especially if not one of themselves. But instead of making that into a punishment, the Ixchel seem to have instilled a feeling of reward into the proceedings. They do receive gifts in return, but their elders are not as simple as one might suppose. They are probably interested in being a longer-term protectorate.'

'Are they almost alien?' said Guy Meredith.

Dood paused to consider the question. He seemed to find it difficult. 'I do wonder—some of you have seen them. They are human, but not quite. They are a little removed. I would say that the men are only about as powerful as a fourteen year old boy. But they are clever. They live in perfect equilibrium with their surroundings, never fight and they don't need to. They may have fought *us* in the past, and it is that which they remember.'

'But I believe they live in a world that is more spiritual and cerebral than our own. I think they can communicate by telepathy. We know that some of *us* can do that, but only sometimes. If that is so, it may explain why their language is a bit of a mouthful: perhaps it's because they don't use it as we do. When they converse, I think they use a bit of each.'

'Do you think they actually read minds?'

'No, but I believe they would know if you carried a gun. So in the bigger things, for example if you went to see them with the intention of physical violence, I believe they would know. I also believe they have the ability to 'project their minds at will' and see things at a distance—but only if they are inclined, which may not always be the case. Certainly they seem to have anticipated my own movements from time to time.'

A long silence followed, but eventually Guy Meredith said, 'So that means we cannot plan to take the girls back?'

'I didn't say that. I did say 'if they are inclined.' They are not necessarily inclined because they regard me, and therefore you, as reasonably benign: just curious people. That's why I said don't carry a gun.'

Meredith replied, 'But they must know we want them back?'

'They did suggest that I should actually have my way with them. Perhaps they thought that going off with the Pragya, after my having done so, would be as much an honour for them as it is for their own women.'

'I see, so they weren't ready to be dispatched then?'

'No. But if you want me to answer questions about the Pragya, I shall have to pass you over to Joseph, I am afraid.' Dood waved towards Dorkin and sat back.

Dorkin's mid-west tones were cultured and precise. He made no attempt to go over old ground by talking about the background to his work, or the interest of the CIA. He limited himself to saying, 'A lot of people began to think I might be of use to them. My route here came from agreeing to look at strange tissue samples. Then someone let it slip that the issue itself was connected with what the US government knows about alien spacecraft. And I was more clued-up than most because I know Bud Lynch. But I let them lead me on, because I was grateful for things like the licence to dig at Boskop.'

Meredith interjected: 'It did get around though—even to me!'

'That was inevitable. But it all led here, and there's a bigger story'—he nodded towards Elliott—'so the question remains, who, or what are the Pragya, and what do they want?'

Dorkin let those words sink in before going on, 'So what the Pragya actually want must be connected intimately with what they now are. And that, at least, is clear. I was astounded when we ran the DNA comparisons. Of course I'm making the assumption that the Pragya are identical to the people who smashed at Roswell in 1947—we cannot complicate matters by supposing that there are two sets of aliens.'

'So it turned out that the Roswell samples were similar to the Boskop material, and more recently to the Ixchel. We even managed to date when they became separated. And in the case of the Pragya, depart they did, about 600,000 years ago.'

'Now more about the Pragya: I felt—still feel—that they are the product of some kind of genetic engineering that went wrong. As Callum has intimated, the reason they return here is very much more than just altruism. The Ixchel have something the Pragya want and it's nothing to do with material wealth.'

'So the fact that they take people suggests to me that they are interested in correcting their mistakes. I think they want to tinker with their own genetic makeup. At the very least it could be to develop a larger gene pool. But I think it's more than that. There must be some kind of genetic experiments going on.'

'Why would they need expectant mothers?' said Elliott, bluntly.

'I can immediately think of embryonic stem cells,' said Dorkin, 'even though such experiments are widely regarded as unethical. But my instinct makes me think more about hybrid embryos.'

'So why,' said Peter Pargeter, 'do they not simply cart off the whole damn lot of the Ixchel and bring them up as their own?'

'Would you agree to be carted off?'

'No. I think I would start to be difficult.'

'Well perhaps the Pragya want to invade then!'

'That did occur to me. If they supplanted or absorbed the Ixchel down here, they might then have the numbers and the reason to take over. That might make them our own enemy. But of course we know nothing much about them.'

Guy Meredith said, 'They have been visiting for thousands of years. Why now?'

'Why indeed. There may be some new imperative. They may be dying out. Or they may want to finally stop *us* before we trash the planet.'

There was a pause, then Dorkin said, 'But if it were me, I would say it's a little of all these reasons. I think they are opportunists, cynical to a degree, users certainly, and ethical only as far as it suits their purpose.'

Dood, who had been sitting quietly, said, 'And here we are in the middle. The Ixchel want to exchange our women and the Pragya want them for their genes. The CIA wants to eliminate us and the big cats and mosquitos want to eat us alive. The question now is what *we* want. As I see it, there are two things. We want the girls back, undamaged. And we want to put a stop to the Pragya and send them on their way. Oh, and we want to get home!'

The others nodded and poured more coffee. Thus all was agreed, if not the practical means of going about it.

—◠◠—

Callum Dood decided to spend some time at his own camp, not for reasons of dissimilitude, but because he found it easier to think when he was by himself. There, he pottered round building a new fire and collected interesting botanical specimens from far and wide. In so doing, he turned their current predicament over in his mind and came to a quite simple conclusion. It was clear that the relationship between the Pragya and the Great and Good could not be their concern; and that they must simply infiltrate and release the girls. Then, and having done so, it would be possible to take them home. However, in this he suspected that the younger men would be impulsive and therefore a nuisance. But while it was important that he and Dorkin should do the infiltrating, they would need to keep the others onside. That, in turn, meant that he and Dorkin would need to exert influence. Soon he returned to speak to Dorkin and Pargeter, which he was able to do when the others were busy with *grands projets* outside camp. 'It's like this,' said Dood, and recounted his thoughts while the others nodded sagely. Pargeter, in particular, recognised that his abilities remained with the respect he was able to engender in the others, rather than in climbing cliff faces and secreting himself among the Ixchel. Thus he was more than happy to remain in camp with Elliott, Meredith and Wiener.

That evening the lights in the sky returned, together with a squall of rain and a dark cloud, and at once they were sure that the Pragya had arrived. Yet it was very soon after their last visit, so that in the absence of new captives it could only mean that Freya and Carmen were finally to be passed on. In a desperate effort to avoid whatever this might mean, Dorkin and Dood enacted their plans without delay. In the meantime Pargeter tried to instil realistic purpose in the others: they were to pack all their goods and chattels, await the arrival of the girls, and make preparations for a fast departure. Later, Dorkin and Dood made their way through the outskirts of the Ixchel city, making use of whatever rocks and walkways gave the best path. Soon they were absorbed into the throng, and they waited among the other scapular-clothed people for whatever festivities were to be offered. Unlike the others, however, they felt no pleasure in the prospect at all.

The proceedings had reached the stage of the communal meal, whereupon the familiar vegetable stew was passed around by the local chef. As before, it was eaten without much delicacy, and all were happy to pull out pieces of food to cool in the air beforehand. In turn, this was followed by tequila which Dood and Dorkin happily tasted but declined to drink, preferring to keep a clear head. The throng behaved otherwise, swigging with gusto and spluttering with the strength of the brew. All this added to the revelry, which was welcome as far as the intruders were concerned by making it easier to move around unnoticed. Soon, there was singing and dancing. Dorkin and Dood joined in, allowing themselves to be drawn slowly towards the place where the girls were kept. It remained dark away from the fire, and they hoped they wouldn't be noticed as they drifted towards the shadows by the hut, which shortly they entered.

Even as the door was closed their surroundings were lit by a blinding light, and Dood's hair stood on end with the static electricity. It was clear that the Pragya had arrived, and the noise outside fell to a low murmur. Inside the hut it was bright enough to see that the girls were no longer drugged. They wore the usual Ixchel clothes, but their only constraint was that their wrists and ankles were bound, and their mouths gagged. There were no guards, all presumably being busy elsewhere. Dorkin and Dood were just in time and they made a gesture to emphasise the importance of silence. Dorkin cut their cords and the girls stood, rubbing their wrists and shaking away the last vestiges of whatever knockout drops had been used to pacify them. There was no time to lose, and Dood estimated that they would have only a ten-minute advantage in a chase, and that if they could avoid being seen.

Carmen said, 'What kept you?'

Dorkin replied, 'Talk later. Let's get out while nobody's looking.'

Freya's only response was a grunt as she removed her gag and cleared her throat.

Outside, with Freya's garment covering her untidy blonde hair, and with all stooping to blend in with the Ixchel, they walked slowly away. In front, Dood tried to give the impression of being under the influence of tequila by a form of wayward dancing, which the rest soon imitated. A casual observer might have thought the girls were following two rather intoxicated men into the undergrowth, a perception which they were happy to endorse. Thereafter they hurried away, making as straight a path to the north as they could find. Behind them the pye-dogs were quiet, but the dark forest remained as sinister as it had always been. Eventually their ten minute start was up, and although shouting was not in the style of the Ixchel, the sound of hurried movement could be heard behind them. It was getting nearer, and the four were obliged to accelerate. Shortly the night sky could be seen once again, and they were at last able to run properly. Yet soon, Freya and Carmen's unfortunate period of captivity made itself felt in a dramatic way, with their barely-used legs becoming cramped. They knew they faced being drugged again and carried back; while Dood and Dorkin probably faced worse: the fate of those the Ixchel had accepted as friends while bringing about the girls' release.

Freya was forced to stop and catch her breath, whereupon Dorkin said, 'Leave me behind, I can carry straight on and draw them away. Don't mind me. Carmen, let me leave you in charge. Here's my bag, it has a few things in it. Take them away down the lead mine. I'll let the others know. You can get out through one of the other exits and they may not follow you there. Veer left now, over there. Now run!' He turned and ran off towards the north east, while Carmen was too surprised to exercise any reluctance and immediately carried out his wishes.

It was a relief for the three escapees when, having followed instructions, the approach to the mine was visible in the form of a long embankment stretching before them. They could now see by moonlight and ran along it as quietly as possible. To their right they heard their pursuers turn after Dorkin, who had made himself noticeable by speaking into a radio. Continuing to run, the three entered the shaft of the mine, passed the storage rooms on either side, and strode down the musty mineshaft. They then slowed as the shaft narrowed and sloped away. The air remained fresh, but they noted the increasing temperature and felt, for Carmen, the half-forgotten feeling of claustrophobia. Behind her neither was familiar with potholing, let alone a mine, and required regular reassurance. Yet they kept up with Carmen, still anxious to avoid being followed and imprisoned again. Farther down, the cool draught failed altogether, but now the strange garb of the Ixchel came into its own. In the absence of breathing apparatus the dust was stopped by the hood of the scapular, which could conveniently be arranged over the face and nose. Underneath they were hot and perspired freely, but she said, 'At least it cleans the pores out!'

Carmen knew that the air would soon become foul from the heavy gases that can collect and fill any mine, and regretted the absence of respirators. She knew that Dorkin had sent them on a hazardous journey in which experience was all, but she remembered the places that Dorkin had tested on their last visit and prepared to repeat his advice on how to avoid that danger. 'I've been this way before,' she said, 'and the thing is not to panic or lose concentration.

Don't try to think. We're better here, even if we have to go back up again. This is a good hiding place at very least, and we can leave at the top when those guys go home.'

'Is there another way out?' said Dood.

'Sure, but I hope we don't need to go there. In any case, it's blocked, or was, by a fall. I think it would take a day of digging to get out that way.'

'Thank you,' said Dood. The thought of a dig in darkness sent shivers down his spine.

Some twenty minutes later they paused at a place that was wide enough for three people to stand together. The air was dry and hot, but the faintest cold draught from the top was just discernible. Holding their breath, they were able to listen for the sound of pursuit. There was none, and the mineshaft was eerie and quiet. They waited in silence for ten minutes and gradually their breathing became slower. Soon, Freya said, 'I think I've had enough of this standing still. I need fresh air. Can we go back now, please?'

Dood, who had long ago lost his wristwatch said, 'What's the time?'

Carmen said, 'No wristwatch either, I'm afraid, but it must be getting on for about one o'clock. We've been free for about ninety minutes. I wonder whether they've given up on us yet? Let's give it another fifteen minutes. Are you OK with that, Freya?'

'I suppose so. It's just that this place smells like an old garbage tip. It's almost as bad as Callum's cigars!' In response Dood made a face in the dark. Funnily enough, he would have given a lot for a smoke just then.

With the fifteen minutes up they began the rather more laborious ascent, but were drawn toward the faint draught of fresh air from above. They were obliged to pause a couple of times, but eventually reached the exit where, as with Carmen's earlier escape, they hurried towards the prospect of freedom. Yet there was no light ahead. As they approached the exit they were unworried: it was night, after all, and at last they were able to stand comfortably. Yet eventually they found that their way was blocked by a large rock that had been rolled into the gap. They were imprisoned in the mine, far from their friends and farther from home. Carmen burst into tears and was obliged to be comforted. Then they sat in one of the smaller chambers to the side and tried to rest among the collection of dusty relics, each with his or her private thoughts.

—∭—

Peter Pargeter received a radio message from Dorkin. It seemed hurried, and Dorkin was short of breath: 'Hi Peter, we've got the girls out but they are after us. I've sent them off with Callum through the lead mine. It's dangerous for them but less so than staying around. Speak to Simon. He's been there and he knows how to get in and out. I think that's safer than having the Ixchel chase us straight back to camp.' Dorkin's manner was imperative and hurried.

'Do you reckon it's time to break out the rifles?'

'No, Peter. Hide the chopper as best you can. And all our gear as well.'

'Should we come and get you too?'

'No, don't do that. I'll try and draw them off. I'm running east now, along the top of the cliff. It's an easy path. And to be honest, this is my mess anyway. Perhaps I shouldn't have brought them into this kind of danger!'

'OK, Joseph, but remember one thing, you didn't really bring them, did you? We all came under our own steam.' The radio went dead as he finished.

Dorkin had jogged slowly while using his radio, but as soon as he finished he accelerated. Luckily he was reasonably trim and his lifestyle enabled him to run either far or quite fast. He felt he should choose fast and then hide, so breathing deep, he swung his arms as he ran along the path east. Under the moonlight he could sense rather than see the Ixchel following him. Perhaps they could see him? Or more likely they could *sense* him as he almost could them. He decided to stop thinking and felt more secure immediately. He ran on.

After about a mile he entered rainforest again, and it was not an area that he had visited before. It was pointless going very much farther since by then he had drawn the Ixchel away and the others surely should have escaped. Or if they had not done so, then no more running would make any difference. He stopped and listened, but heard nothing. Changing direction he walked north towards the clifftop and reached it after about ten minutes of clambering through heavy undergrowth, where it was completely dark. There, the slope was shallow and despite the absence of a path, he was able to climb down past boulders and the occasional crumbling ledge. He descended about twenty feet before finding a suitable place to hide under a slight overhang. There, he stretched out in silence on his narrow ledge, with the rock face to his left and a sheer drop to his right. Around him the air was cold, and he found the slight breeze refreshing after his exertions. The moon shed light over the surrounding landscape and he could see that he was about a mile east of Pargeter's camp. Shortly, his attention was diverted by a large brown snake which, coiling near, luxuriated in the warmth of his body. With his scapular close around him and the snake in mind, he lay still until dawn, when the animal vanished. Coming to his senses, he climbed towards the clifftop. However at the top twenty small men emerged from the trees and surrounded him. They were the Ixchel, and although they showed no anger, they waved for him to join them. Some carried blowpipes and the dart with its sharp tip showed brown and sticky. He nodded and walked back with them.

—⁓—

Freya and Carmen had only recently emerged from a protracted period of imprisonment during which they spent many days bound and drugged. The events of the previous night had therefore left them exhausted, so that Dood suggested they should rest upon reaching the mine exit. Both had done so after sprawling on soft earth in one of the side rooms near the mine entrance, and by dawn, each had had about six hours of sleep as evidenced by the trace of light visible from outside. In his own way, Dood had found enough privacy to indulge in a smoke as an alternative to sleep. By about 7 am the girls were finally called, when with the vitality of youth neither had any remaining aches or pains. Similarly, Dood was refreshed by his cigar and all hunger fell away. Ready at last, they sat together to consider their fortune.

'They must think they can pick us up at this entrance,' said Dood. 'Since they blocked it last night, they either want to dispatch us all together or keep us trapped until they can hand you over to the Pragya again.' He wondered whether the Ixchel meant the same fate for him too.

'I think that's about it,' said Carmen. 'I can't imagine they would suppose that we can come out the other side.'

Neither responded directly, but Freya said, 'Then I think we had better get it over with.' Her face was smeared with dust and she looked like a chimney sweep in the faint light, a fact that Dood found rather enchanting.

Standing and stretching, they gave a mighty push to the rock blocking the exit, and then tried to lever it away by using a long piece of old wood, which promptly broke. Faced with the unyielding rock, Carmen grizzled a bit, but bit her lip and said, rather bravely, 'Well we can't just wait. We shall have to dig our way out the other side. I'm sure I can find it, it's quite easy to get there, but the difficulties will start once we do. Let's get there first and then I can explain.' The others made ready, and followed her once more; down and down, they marched slowly but surely on a route made more difficult by the declination. Dood's ankles ached; it had been easier to ascend. Perhaps his were not fully healed after his misfortune in Nepal? All thought of similar matters as a way of diverting their minds from darker thoughts. The air became still, warm and stuffy and it held dust, so that Carmen advised them to arrange the hood over their faces.

Dorkin's bag proved useful. It contained torches and bottled water, and they made use of the first of these in the dim light. Down farther, where the oppressive feel was almost unbearable. Would the Ixchel return them to captivity? If so, why had they not done it that morning? Perhaps they still meant to do it! Dorkin should surely have spoken to Pargeter by now, who must know of their predicament and would surely meet them. At least all this was better than being drugged again. As long as they didn't panic!

Eventually they reached the place that Dorkin had described as a mine-face. To Carmen it was familiar as the gallery in which he had found no oxygen below knee height. Nearby were the picks they had discarded on their last visit. Freya, looking even more like a chimneysweep said, 'We can always climb back up again if we want fresh air!' Dood thought that such was the origin of the expression 'black humour'.

Carmen said, 'This pile of earth is our way out. It's all we can do now, short of going back up to wait.'

They set to work in a space enough for two people, with the third holding a torch. Formerly it had been wet, and it was that which had caused the subsidence. Now that it was dry Carmen felt more confident. All felt, however, the dreadful feeling of weight above them, and the claustrophobia was enough to make them cry out.

Progress was slow, but a small cavity eventually grew in front of them. For a while, they chose to dig in darkness in order to save the first torch, which by then was becoming feeble. In the absence of light altogether, they indicated that they would rather return to the surface to wait. Later, they began to use a second torch very sparingly. At intervals they stopped for a rest and drank water, and at all times were careful to avoid sitting down. They were perpetually hot, breathless and terrified.

Eventually Carmen said, 'I think we must be half-way through.' But that was after three hours of digging, and now the second torch was low. 'We need to save it,' she followed, 'let's keep on without it for a while.' Working singly now, they swapped places so that Freya dug while Carmen and Dood rested, then after fifteen minutes they made a rotation. Eventually Carmen flashed the torch only for seconds. It revealed still more earth before them: deep, brown and never-ending. The pile behind was large, their arms and backs ached, and they coughed continually. Their appetite for more was fading. They were trapped, and faced a choice between still more endeavour or a slow asphyxiating end.

—⁓—

Peter Pargeter had taken Dorkin's radio message at a time when he and the others were hopeful of good news concerning Freya and Carmen's escape, and it was with some concern that he passed Dorkin's news to them. Nevertheless, although the very best news would have amounted to all having escaped, and the very worst that they were captured and about to be sent to the Pragya, the actual turn of events was somewhere between the two. They were free but in danger of entrapment. Dorkin was free but in danger of being captured. It was with urgency, but not panic, that they gathered to decide what to do.

'I think we need to do just what Joseph said,' said Elliott. 'He was quite clear that our priority should be the girls, and we know where they probably are.'

'Just the girls?' said Wiener. He was of course exercising a certain wit, although it was not the best time to do so.

Meredith's reply suggested that he had taken Wiener seriously. 'I guess not. The Reverend Dood might be a bit crazy, but I put that down to the stuff he swallows. He's a pretty decent guy really.'

'All this assumes that the Ixchel will chase them down the mine,' said Elliott.

'It does,' said Pargeter. 'And we shall have to assume they want to get out the other side. Of course if they double back and manage to get out that way, then there's no harm done.'

'Joseph inferred that they would get out our side,' said Wiener. 'If so, then we shall have to dig them out. There was a blockage when we were there. A load of earth came down; I would think it made a pile about eight feet thick. It's drier now, so that should be OK, but we still need to dig our way through. It was pretty soft stuff, so we shall need shovels. And oxygen.'

'And how long will it take to get there?'

'For them or us?'

'Well, both.'

Wiener said, 'The fall was about half way through, so I would say we are in for a tramp of about two hours. There's a bit of a descent, of course. That will also apply to them, but obviously I can't say what they will do exactly.'

'In that case,' said Pargeter, 'let's get the stuff and get going. And bring three extra masks.'

The four, who quite liked to call themselves rescuers, collected enough to fill a pack each and then struck out for the clifftop. This was an occasion on which Pargeter demanded to accompany them, although with the climb itself he suggested that one of the others should lead. By the time they reached the top he was breathless, and the others gently ribbed him with the comment that it would be easier going down the mineshaft, a comment he accepted with good grace. Then, walking west he recommended, and the others accepted the general notion of silence. He also suggested that they should crouch against the night sky. They reached the entrance without incident and with no suggestion that anyone had seen them. 'All parties,' suggested Meredith, 'are now at whatever place events have decreed.' This seemed rather a melodramatic thing to say, and he probably became aware of it because he immediately added, 'and I feel very optimistic for all concerned.'

In fact all four were optimistic. The approach to the mine was large so that moonlight entered easily. Paradoxically they were able to see more clearly than in the day, when the bright light outside made the contrast inside greater. Their eyes now found it easy to adjust to shadows and the faintest of silhouettes. Led by Simon they began their descent, while some distance farther north Callum, Freya and Carmen were sleeping. Had they known it, the trapped party were about two hours from starting their own descent, and both would start digging on their respective sides within an hour of each other.

As had been the case before, the old mineshaft became warmer, and with the very little fresh air that could reach them it soon became unpleasant to breathe. And as with the others, by now no more than half a mile distant, they felt the oppressing claustrophobia and wondered that anyone could ever have agreed to work there. Elliott was in a cold sweat and thought of possible excuses for turning back. There were none, but soon their descent gave out into larger horizontal galleries and he was able to stifle such thoughts and follow where Simon indicated. Later, they reached the obstruction where the earth had subsided. Their progress had been as good as could reasonably be expected. Elliott energetically wielded a shovel and worked off his panic. In turn, each man dug for thirty minutes before handing over. A pile of earth grew behind them, as indeed one grew on the other side; but neither party could hear the other and both worked mostly in silence.

—⁓—

Carmen also dug with some fury, then Freya, followed by Dood. But they began to fail with the oppressive heat, the knowledge of foul air below waist height, and the acrid black dust which coated them from head to foot and made them cough. Carmen said, 'This is no time for modesty,' and shed her clothes to provide a last comfort. The others followed, and upon Dood's turn he said, 'Lucky it's dark,' and carried on digging. Their humour managed to prolong their endeavours by a few more minutes, but eventually, they came to a slow and brutal stop, exhausted if not past care.

Then Dood said, 'We could go back up top, at least there's fresh air there.' But they knew it would be a case of waiting in the cold and dark. Waiting for what? Then Carmen, who had worked so hard, collapsed. Quickly, the other two raised her to a standing position and by clutching an arm each, walked her up the tunnel so that there at least, she would be able to sit for a short while. They rested for twenty minutes, after which Dood exercised whatever authority he still possessed. He said, 'You two stay here. I'm going back.' The girls nodded, happy to rest for a while longer.

The Reverend Dood's time in the mountains of Nepal, then back home at the seaside, and more recently in the tropical rainforest, had not been some foolish whim. It had been a period of many months during which he had shed much of the social, material and intellectual baggage that he had collected over the years. He had needed a significant change, and after three attempts had found it. He was genuinely rested, truly better, and his mind was sharp with the rigours of solitude and the life of a hermit. Aided by his experience with herbal remedies he was able to last for a week without food, while his stamina was now that of a younger man. At once he realised that only this new training could help them now. He placed a wad of dream root in his cheek and the bitter, astringent taste drew spittle into his dry mouth. His mind grew sharp and focussed and his aching arms were relegated to the facility of a painless automaton. Quietly and calmly, he tied a band of cloth about his face and returned to digging. He dug with a silent purpose, his mind distinct and separate from his endeavour so that he never tired. The continuing element of dream root in his bloodstream gave him strength. His mind floated free and he saw the white mountains of Nepal once more. He dug on: one, three, five feet through heavy soil. Behind him he heard coughing as the girls slowly recovered. One last push…

Suddenly he had a vision and thought he was dying. A voice said, 'I say old chap, are you alright?' Then an arm grabbed him through an opening, and a beaming face which reminded him of Peter Pargeter looked at him. The voice said, 'Doctor Dood I presume,' whereupon he croaked, 'Mine's a pint—the girls,' and jerked his thumb back up the mineshaft. Then he collapsed, and felt the cold and metallic smell from an oxygen mask as he succumbed into unconsciousness.

The Reverend Callum Dood awoke in a tent and there was light all around. There was also a quiet humming as a few mosquitoes patrolled and alighted on him. He watched fascinated as in slow motion they bit him and drew blood. He felt in his pocket and then rubbed some wild garlic on his bare arms.

They had let him sleep. He had reached exhaustion and was very dehydrated, but slowly he felt strength return to his limbs as the sun rose in the sky. Suddenly he received the full glare and realised that he must be at Pargeter's camp. Strictly speaking it was Dorkin's camp of course, but Dorkin had gone away. Had he returned? Callum Dood sat up.

Shortly, he opened the flap of his tent and he poked his head out. 'Coffee?' he said.

The others had been quiet, the better to let him sleep. However they became more animated when he emerged invigorated, just like a butterfly from its chrysalis. The young women had taken a surprisingly short time to shake off their experience and pottered about happily, while Wiener and Elliott looked upon him with a new wonder. He pulled his scapular, a surprisingly practical garment, close around him and joined them for a reinvigorating meal. Yet Professor Joseph Dorkin was not among them.

'I suppose,' said Pargeter, 'that you couldn't get out by means of the forest entrance? I'm not quite sure, but perhaps Joseph only wanted you to hide in the mine?'

'Everything happened quickly,' said Dood. 'We were being chased, and those guys meant business. I'm not sure if they really meant to harm us, but the threat was certainly there, and I don't think that Freya and Carmen fancied being hauled back.'

'And anyway,' said Carmen with a shudder, 'they rolled a great stone in front of the entrance, so the only way out was through the mine.'

Elliott listened with avidity, and his mind couldn't help composing headlines: 'Long lost tribe with poison-tipped darts threaten jungle explorers.' However he restricted himself to saying only, 'So they meant to trap you there and kill you after all?'

Carmen said, 'No, I think they had several reasons. Certainly they knew we were there. They probably wanted to stop us escaping, so they blocked the way as soon as we were inside. Or if they thought they were too late, which is equally likely, I would suppose they doubted whether anyone could get through the mine workings in the dark. In that case they were waiting for us to sit plaintively by the exit and emerge into their arms at their leisure.'

'So why didn't they follow us here?' said Guy Meredith, drinking his third coffee.

'Well I don't think they would have done that in case it led to a direct confrontation, and let's face it, we are only two women. It's not as if we are a declining species. They may want us back, sure, but the Pragya can always wait for some other poor captives.'

'Well, I think they are more interested in keeping out of sight,' said the Reverend Dood. 'I think I know them quite well. My feeling is that they won't want whatever outsiders we could bring down on them if we wanted. So anything they do around here is surreptitious: a quiet kidnapping or a drugged dart in the leg. No wars, you see. I really don't think you will hear from them again; not unless you walk into their city, that is.'

'Talking of walking into their city,' said Pargeter, 'we need to decide what to do about Joseph. He wasn't that far away, and he ought to have been back by now.'

Callum Dood said, 'I think the Ixchel hold him responsible for the girls' escape, but even that isn't really a hanging offence. Possibly they will give him to the Pragya as they did with those CIA people.'

'So our next job is to extricate him!' said Wiener.

'No, not you,' said Dood. 'They would just quietly imprison you too, so the whole thing would start over again. No, I had better go and get him.'

'You!' said Meredith, 'but surely they will just do the same with you too?'

'Not necessarily. Think about it. They know me, and there's probably nothing to connect me with the girls.'

'But you helped them escape!'

'I did, but they may not know that. They are more likely to think that Joseph did it. They caught him, remember, and they may not have seen me go with them. And there are a whole host of other things they might think too.'

'Such as?' said Elliott.

'Well, I'm not sure I should say this in present company.'

'Oh go on!' said Freya.

'Well, they wanted me to have my way with them. Then they could be given to the Pragya.'

'Oh!' said Freya. Her eyes were huge.

'So they will probably take a relaxed view about my turning up in camp again, if not Joseph.'

Elliott considered another mental headline: 'Lost tribe imprison young women for romp in the jungle'.

Peter Pargeter summed up. 'We need to get this right at last. We want all our people extricated, and we want our research preserved. And there's still one thing we need to do before we can consider leaving.'

Elliott finally said, 'We still need to get something on the Pragya.'

'Exactly. We need to support whatever Callum suggests. Callum, I want you to relax today—you and the girls, and in fact everybody. I want you to think, get it right. Later tonight we can set things in motion.'

That day, they ate and drank well, cleaned whatever clothing they preferred (in Dood's case, his scapular), and they also washed themselves to remove the ingrained grime from the mine (it was no exaggeration to say that the water ran black). Later that evening, they were all in a suitable frame of mind to confirm their next move.

Callum Dood said, 'I had better be off now. I aim to look completely innocent. I'm just going to turn up and look expectant— hey, are you alright, Freya? Here, have some more coffee—and then I shall just have to play it by ear. There's just one thing I need: I can keep you informed with a radio. No, not that big thing, a small handset please. Oh, and I want some best brandy and a handful of cigars. Is that OK?' The others nodded and David Elliott fetched them. Thus armed, Dood walked off and the others sat back to relax, at least for a while.

Later, Dood, suitably dressed and looking as indistinguishable from the natives as he could muster, walked into the Ixchel's camp where the evening congregation was about to take place. The Ixchel ate and drank communally and instead of singing a melodious song or dancing they sat and in their particular manner gave forth a rhythmic humming noise, full of the clicks, pops and the staccato snaps he had come to associate with their so-called speech. But of course, he reflected, they were looking into each other's eyes...'

Nobody turned a hair as he approached. He dispensed a few cigars to the elders and smoked one himself. Then he tried a glass of brandy and was pleased to receive a drop of gall from a green snake, which he placed in the glass and drank with gusto. It was all alright, he thought—then he wondered whether the snake gall was as bitter as it had been last time. He thought no more that day.

—⁂—

Dood awoke in the same hut that had held Freya and Carmen. He was tied by the wrists and ankles and next to him lay Joseph Dorkin, similarly tied. He tried speaking, but his tongue seemed twisted and dry. However he managed to salivate enough to speak, and soon he wriggled and twisted so that he could sit up. Shortly, he addressed a few words to Dorkin, who was awake. 'Hello Joseph, so they've got you as well. I came back to effect a rescue!'

'Too bad. Now someone else will have to effect a rescue and get caught themselves.'

'Ah.' There was a pause for a short while. 'If we sit back to back, then I can probably undo these bonds.'

Dorkin said, 'Look, Callum, I know you mean to help, but to be honest, I have gotten this far and I'm pretty sure they don't mean to eat me. I think we can expect them to give us to the Pragya.'

Callum Dood reflected on this for a while. Then he said, 'You mean like those last four guys? So what happened to them?'

'I don't know for sure. If they were going to get bonked on the head it would probably have happened straight away. Perhaps they were sent off to some kind of stud farm—ha ha. Seriously, I want to meet the Pragya now that I've come this far.'

The more Dood considered this, the more he realised that such a course—meeting the Pragya—had been his own private wish. He said, 'OK, Joseph, I'm with you. But I'm damned uncomfortable tied up like this. If you can only untie my hands then at least I can sit up. I promise I won't run!'

Soon, Dood and Dorkin were sitting up, their hands and legs free. And as they then said, freedom without having run was as powerful a reason for their future endorsement by the Ixchel as they could provide. Dorkin declined a cigar, but Dood soon had a particularly fine specimen alight and as he puffed away, the fragrant blue smoke wafted out of a window and brought the Ixchel in. Dood then dispensed a couple of cigars to the pair of elders who had joined them and he 'strongly advised' Dorkin to do the same them on grounds of civility. This Dorkin did, rather amateurishly, puffing away and coughing. The Ixchel noted their unbound hands and feet, the fact that they hadn't run, and accepted their obvious courtesies with what seemed to be a gracious nod. Then Dood began to speak. He used their primitive tongue and made sure that he looked into their faces while he did so, the better to emphasise the finer aspects that his incomplete mastery of the former was unable to provide. The Ixchel looked thoughtful and nodded from time to time. He said, 'Dorkin and I helped our women to flee because they told me of a fear of being tied. Both had experienced poor treatment at the hands of people in the past.' The Ixchel nodded.

'And to show my good faith I have returned, as Dorkin would have done, had he been able to do so himself. It was not necessary to add the sleeping draught to my brandy last night.' The Ixchel nodded again and looked at each other. 'So finally, we wish to adopt your purpose in their stead, and we agree to go with the Pragya.'

The Ixchel looked doubtful and one said, 'You cannot be an adequate replacement for the women, but it is true that men are useful to the Pragya on some occasions. We agree to your offer, but do not consider running if you are of honour, since we would find that distressing.'

'How long will we need to wait?'

'Perhaps two nights.' The Ixchel held up a single finger of each hand. In the meantime we shall feed and entertain you.'

Potted entertainment was just what Dood had in mind. He and Dorkin left their hut and took part in the communal meal outside, with its characteristic shared stewpot containing a very nourishing and pleasant broth of vegetables, supplemented with corn bread. Alcoholic drink was once more a feature of their hospitality, and upon trying this generous concoction Dood immediately identified it as a form of pulque, which he had in fact observed the Ixchel make from the maguey plant. Later there was tequila, but although he preferred brandy, he was careful to accept it when offered. He also shared several smaller cigars, the better to preserve the larger for special occasions. Dorkin also looked as though he had thrown off some of his austere habits and ate and drank his fill, following which he could be seen dancing with one of the portly women of the tribe. Meanwhile, Dood preferred to sit and contemplate while listening to the strange rhythmic tone of speaking voices, and the peculiar music that reminded him so much of their tongue itself.

On the second night, however, and true to the word of the Ixchel, a minor weather perturbation struck the community. Dark clouds and a rainstorm were manifest, followed by the release of white light and the sense of static electricity all around. It passed quickly, but Dorkin and Dood had seen the signs before and they knew that a craft of enormous power was close.

Callum Dood switched on his radio and very quickly obtained an answering signal from Pargeter. He said, 'Peter, we have struck up a kind of truce with the Ixchel. We are free, so long as we don't escape. But neither of us wishes to escape, not now.'

'So what are you going to do?'

'We have taken the place of the girls. I doubt whether we are as good, and I hope they don't try—well anyway, we intend to walk the plank and go off with the Pragya. Lord knows where it will end. As far as I'm concerned, it was probably inevitable. I managed to expand my mind in Nepal and here in the rainforest, but now it's time for outer space.'

'That's alright, Callum, you always were a bit spaced out.'

'Exactly, and these particular measures can make us all grow as people. I still have the radio, and I will use it if I'm able. Can you hang around for a month?'

'I expect we can. After that time we shall want to get back to civilisation.'

'That's fine. Best regards to all.' He turned the transmitter off.

—※—

Pargeter explained to the others that he had given a broad commitment to staying for about a month, and that this should be considered as support for Dorkin and Dood, who might turn up again or might not, depending on circumstances (normally, he would have used the word 'might' only once, but that seemed an overly-optimistic weighting of possibilities). None of the others seemed to begrudge that time even though they sensed his doubt: they had, after all, been devoted to their present cause for so many months that one more could mean no great hardship. The girls said they had no wish to miss the endgame, if that was what their present position was; neither Freya nor David wished to write their article without a proper conclusion; while Guy, conscious of his links with the 'Network,' said he preferred to be able to explain to Bailey T. Mann and Bud Lynch exactly what a flying saucer was really like. Yet together with their doubts about Dorkin and Dood's return, none liked the thought of poison darts or abduction, and the girls wished to avoid being captured again or a repeat of their ordeal in the mine.

'They may not mean to kill us,' said Pargeter, 'but we need to make sure that we stay out of their way.'

Wiener replied, 'And if this is leading onto what we can do for a whole month, I think we need to do a bit more careful looking around, without antagonising them. Certainly, we can't sit and do nothing.' Carmen, sitting next to Simon, seemed pleased to have his familiar face around. She nodded, seemed happy with this, and followed, 'We could look at some of those old buildings again—as long as we make sure we can get out.'

Guy Meredith said, 'We never really looked at that pyramid properly.'

David Elliott said: 'I think the pyramid is a good idea. It's not too near the Ixchel and we should be able to get up the cliff without being seen. We always said that it made some kind of statement as the most considerable structure in these parts. Let's put it like this: what's it for, perched on that clifftop, but hidden behind those folds in the landscape?'

'What indeed,' said Peter Pargeter, 'and I agree that it would be a good way to spend our time. But just one thing: if we're going to do that, then I'm going to disagree with Callum and say we should take our rifles.' He felt that it would add to their confidence, if nothing else.

The others looked relieved, and Pargeter added, 'Let's call it a defensive measure.' There was a renewed purpose, and by mid-day they were all standing outside the pyramid. There, the question of getting inside was quickly resolved when Guy spotted a large block that was more loosely-fitting than the others and which had the appearance of having been handled before. There were scuff-marks on the ground before it, as though it had been pulled forward, and it contained small holes into which levers could be inserted. After making attempts with various strong implements they were able to pull it out, as had apparently been done before.

It was not dark inside since a reasonable amount of light entered by various apertures, particularly a large one overhead and by the front door, which they propped open. They could see that at certain times of the day the amount of light that entered would become greater, when rays from the sun fell straight on shafts in the ceiling. As they looked on, one such ray made a large oval shape on the floor, and small particles of dust could be seen in the air above it. However, there was none of the foul air that Freya and Carmen had encountered in the mine and all felt confident enough to wander around, look for clues, measure things up, and tap at various surfaces.

These features aside, the pyramid was essentially a hollow place with few internal walls, but with a number of stone blocks to act as seats or tables. Each was plain, without adornment or comforts of any kind, and placed in a semicircle about a central area covered by a mat of woven grass. Raising an edge, Guy Meredith revealed a design engraved on the floor. Calling for the others to join him, they removed the mat altogether and saw an engraving of interlocking maps of the world and heavens, the whole highly-detailed.

David said, 'Can we assume that this has something to do with the purpose of the place?'

'Inevitably,' replied Simon. 'Let's face it nobody would carve that on the floor for fun. By the way, the mat, I doubt whether it can last very long. I think the place is still in use.'

'Quite right: it's still in use,' replied Peter. His style was not one of proclaiming his wisdom to all, but he said, 'Once upon a time I actually saw the pyramids in Egypt. The main difference is that hardly anything of the inside was actually space. This one is the other way round: it's mostly space inside, and with a thin outer wall. It was built to let light in. I think it's some kind of meeting place, not a tomb.'

'Then as far as we are concerned,' said Simon, 'the interesting thing is the maps.' They walked round, looking from various angles.

Peter said, 'Yes, it's the maps: and all those boyhood hours in the reading room are coming back to haunt me! But this is fascinating. Ancient maps go back to the 5th or 6th century BC, but as one would expect, they show the 'known world' of the time and therefore only one or two continents; and those usually misshapen and to the wrong scale. Invariably the 'home' continent was placed in the middle, and any farther continent towards the outside. We still do this today: for example, modern American maps always show the United States at the centre.'

The others nodded; Pargeter mopped his forehead and continued: 'So the interesting thing is the sight of all seven continents despite the fact that not all were known even a thousand years ago. Also,' he emphasised, 'they are correctly-shaped and of the right size. But there's another thing: the southern continents lie in the middle as though they were important to the people who made it.'

Carmen crouched low so that she could look at smaller details. She said, 'And there are all kinds of small pictures here, there and everywhere. There are little boats, rivers with fish, frozen wastes, flooding, and wall-building. I'd expect them to describe the present activities and events of the time.'

Simon, looking as directed, said, 'And there's even something in the Middle East. Dare I say that that's of particular interest to me?' The others smiled. He crouched beside Carmen and said, 'This wall-building, Carmen, where would you say it is, exactly?'

'Oh, in modern-day Israel.'

'OK, but where exactly?'

'It's a long time since I went there!'

'All right, I can tell you. It's roughly where Jericho is today, and I happen to know that the first evidence of building there is from 11,000 years ago. At least, that's what the archaeologists say.'

'I see!' Pargeter smiled. 'So you think we can date the map from the inscriptions?'

'I hadn't assumed exactly that, but what if we assume, as Carmen suggested, that they made pictures of ongoing events?'

David said, 'No, I'm sorry, but it's just stretching the imagination too far. The seven continents alone would tell us that it was made recently.'

Guy Meredith said, 'Then, what about the map of the heavens? Back home I keep a telescope. And I don't recognise these stars. If the maps are recent then the stars should be!' He pulled out a flask of cold coffee and took a draught. 'And a whole lot of them are in strange positions.'

'Such as?'

'Well, there's no Dog Star, for one. I can't see any point in a star map that doesn't have the brightest star in the sky. That is, unless it was missing at the time!'

'How could it be missing?' said David.

'Well, it wasn't visible above the horizon until 10,000 years ago,' said Guy firmly.

'So,' said Simon, 'if, as I was saying, we accept that the maps show ongoing events, then with Jericho being built and the Dog Star missing, it would date the map as…'

'Come on,' said David, 'anyone with a knowledge of old star maps could make this: all they would need is a computer!'

'Well if it is a fake,' said Meredith, 'that must make it no more than 30 years old.'

'But this place was mentioned by Callum's guide as being part of long-standing tradition!'

'As did Maradona.'

Carmen said, 'Alright, if it's more than 30 years old, then the place is probably thousands of years old. And if it's the latter, then they had some advanced means of transport. Advanced enough to—well, that doesn't need to be repeated.'

Peter Pargeter had directed an ear towards her as she spoke, but turned towards her when she finished. He said, 'I suppose that's what we all think. But there is one point which does bear repetition: If this place is owned by the Ixchel and if they made it, then they relied on their unusual friends to help. We think that we know who their friends are. It seems to me that we are getting close enough for Freya and David to write their pieces!'

'And for us to blaze our way through the journals!' said Carmen, nodding to Simon as she did so.

'I agree,' said Freya. 'It's only the Pragya who are the mystery now. I wonder how Joseph and Callum are getting on!' Neither had returned, and their absence was felt enough for all to wonder how the Pragya were treating them. Later, the small party returned to base and they were pleased to have completed an interesting excursion on their own terms.

TWELVE

THE PRAGYA

The township of the Ixchel seemed to have a particular attraction for its many citizens who, having apparently been busy elsewhere, now began to congregate so that the place resembled a convention of monks, each wearing the same peculiar dress. Meanwhile, all observed the odd purposeless flight of pigeons which continued until they were exhausted, after which they fluttered down to roost on a ledge or nearby bush. It was clear that a visit of the Pragya was nigh.

Callum Dood happened to be looking into the dark sky when a bright light appeared and he was as dazzled as if he had looked directly into the sun. Then his vision was beset by zig-zag shapes and squares, as though as a sufferer from migraine headaches he had looked directly at a flashing television screen. Around them the air crackled, while metallic objects were displaced. All turned to face the oncoming pearlescent saucer-shaped craft, which slowed suddenly and finally stopped before them, where it remained hovering, two feet off the ground. It had a remarkable presence, reflecting whatever light fell on it while seeming to sparkle at the edges. The Ixchel were hushed, and there was a pause of five minutes before an opening appeared in a side.

With a mind to remaining domestic courtesies Dorkin pulled out a mobile phone, and despite being unsure of a signal, tapped out a message to Simon Wiener. On re-reading it, it sounded ridiculous—

Hi Simon,

A flying saucer has just arrived and I think I'm going to be asked to enter it. I don't know why, but in case I return as damaged goods or not at all, please keep up the good work and above all, listen to the advice of Peter. I have taken a collection of personal ephemera with me.

Joseph Dorkin.

—nevertheless it was accurate. Picking up his rucksack, which contained some rations, water, a camera, pencils and paper and a radio, he stood with Callum Dood in expectation.

The Ixchel seemed to fawn somewhat, preparing to greet their visitors with a mix of obsequiousness and servility. By comparison Dood and Dorkin had no reason to ask for gifts or exchanges. They preferred good terms with equals or otherwise and were happy simply to be civil and welcoming. Therefore they stood their ground and waited as the minutes passed. In fact, they all waited and no visitor emerged, and with the crowd becoming restless, it became clear that Dood and Dorkin were expected to step forward and enter. This they did, turning to wave at the Ixchel, a duty acknowledged as such by the elders who waved in return, honour satisfied on both sides. Inside, they were greeted by five small men who stood in a row before them. They resembled the Ixchel in size and appearance, each with a head large in relation to his body and with the forehead particularly so. In each case the torso was degenerate, with narrow shoulders, a hollow chest and puny arms. They were no more than five feet tall.

Yet each face was very much alive, and while mouth, nose and the various wrinkles seemed expressionless, a multitude of expression remained in the eyes. These were black and enlarged, and beheld the world as the Ixchel did. Their gaze was contemplative and lucid, but it differed in that it contained an extra element. Dood had thought that he saw cynicism, but was finally able to dismiss it. It was grief. It was the expression of a people who had suffered and would not now do so. He bowed low and held his palms outward in a gesture of courtesy that the Ixchel had accepted. Dorkin followed, but neither made an attempt to move forward.

One member of the five spoke: 'Welcome Professor Dorkin and Reverend Dood. I am called Coalascan. We have arranged to visit in the assurance that you will help us.' His accent was impeccable: mid-Atlantic or perhaps Boston, but it had a trace of the staccato born of speaking a language of many consonants, as was that of the Ixchel.

'You speak English!'

'Certainly, it would be impossible to have studied this world for many thousands of years without having learned to do so. Would you prefer another form of speech: perhaps that of a thousand years ago, or alternatively the ancient language of the Caucasians?' He followed: 'Mé lícaþ éow tó métanne.'

'No thank you. But please tell me, how do you propose that we should help you?'

The spokesman directed his words to Dorkin: 'Your scientific work has been of interest to us. We are engaged on a quest. As you may have suspected our forebears made errors of judgement.'

'I'm sorry to hear that. May I invite you to enlighten me?'

'Our principles directed us towards significant foolishness. We became egalitarian to the point that a difference even of sex became unacceptable. It became possible for this absurd culture to exist through an unwillingness to tolerate free discussion in public. Our leaders became an illiberal elite.'

Professor Dorkin nodded expectantly.

'You see, we expunged the X and Y chromosomes from our genes.'

'So what did you do instead?'

'We made a replacement chromosome using the most important parts of both X and Y. Sadly, although we achieved our stated aim of homogeneity, we ignored the most fundamental requirement for living things: that of heterogeneity. Our entire prospects, at a stroke, were diminished. Our viability fell. We became androgynous, so that as hermaphrodites each of us had an ambiguous sexual identity.'

'And you were unable to correct it?'

'We resisted all notion of it being incorrect until a major symposium that we called the Great Acknowledgement, following which it was too late. We had purposely expunged all details of our former composition so that our repairs were always faulty.'

'And I suppose that made you as you now are?'

'It did. We took an interest in the Ixchel, our nearest kind on earth. They had a more elementary wisdom; they were in some ways an object lesson for us. They remained here, avoiding any notion of self-effacement and became unlike us.'

'You carried out the occasional restorative experiment?'

Coalascan made an affirmative gesture with his hand. 'We did, yet they were not satisfactory.'

'I sense that you have some greater sadness.'

'You are perceptive, Professor. The fact that we became androgynous became, in turn, a discouragement from the normal processes of evolution. We disregarded that aspect of our existence. Our bodies, if not our lives, became degenerate. We are the result. After the depredations of our experiments we came to consider that our own bodies were barely adequate. Our forebears became degenerate when compared even to those you call the Ixchel.'

'And so you are here to put that right?'

'Yes, but the realisation of our problems took a long time. And even that was long ago. We became concerned with a high prevalence of muscle wasting and with progressive brain disorders. We knew that they are the result of unstable repeated DNA sequences which accumulate in successive generations: these became common in our small population—you may be familiar with muscular dystrophy and Huntingdon's disease yourself.'

'A very little.'

'And at least some of this arose from a decision we made, aeons ago, to delete what were considered to be unnecessary parts of our genome, the parts for which, as you know, there is no obvious function.'

Dorkin was silent; he sensed that Coalascan's words were cathartic, a release for him.

'So we sought redress and repair. Our scientists were able to recreate a working body from first principles, yet it lacked an essential spirit and was aimless. Some called it a living robot. It lived but its purpose was corrupt, decayed.'

'But perhaps we had better invite you to a more comfortable sitting area.' Dorkin nodded. Thus far the Pragya had made no attempt to imprison them, and there was no apparent hostility.

Another of the five men said, 'Please come this way.' They followed the Pragya but the porthole remained open behind. Conversation continued, and became more of a negotiation.

Dorkin said, 'You wish me to help you make an improvement to your physical bodies. Are you aware that humans have reached the stage at which all selection is equated with evil, with Nazism?'

'We are aware that the purposeful selection of humans was attempted several times throughout your history. It was practised in the plantations of the southern American states and also in Europe in the early 20th century. It was obligate: the individuals concerned did not necessarily wish to participate. They were enslaved. Yet selection occurs in another sense: during evolution. It is clear that it is not necessarily the best option for those less fit for survival. The slowest may not choose to be caught and eaten. Thus evolution is cruel, but not immoral. We are aware that you choose to protect such people, as we should do. We have simply turned against the quest for homogeneity. We would choose only to repair those mistakes we made long ago.'

'I think your distinction between the two is clear.'

The two men had followed the Pragya into a comfortable room with chairs and couches. They were offered, and accepted, water. The minutes ticked by, and the Ixchel remained outside waiting, the porthole still open while discussion continued over these small comforts.

'So we were concerned to improve and change. Our rainforest friends helped us by offering gifts of people who could provide us with eggs or sperm cells. The Ixchel saw these people as gifts, but we did not receive them as such. Those who wished to leave were released unharmed, their memory of our meeting gone. As far as the work was concerned, there has been a little progress, but we came to the conclusion that we should seek a full fusion: a human or an Ixchel fusion with one of us.'

'There are ethical considerations in that also.'

'That may be true, but there are similar considerations in ignoring our need for help.'

'Am I to help you under duress?'

'No, we will release you without obligation.'

Dorkin thought intensively, and the room was quiet. Dood said little, but continued to study the faces of these strange people. He thought he had seen their like once before.

Dorkin said, 'Can you not approach a national government?'

'There are none suitable. We think they would seek advantage— try to obtain technology which they cannot properly handle— and then try to destroy us. It would be too dangerous for all parties.'

'Well, please give me a few minutes to consider further.'

Dorkin stood and considered for a while, but in truth he had already made up his mind to help. He had, however, one remaining test. Raising his head, he said, 'I am sorry, but I cannot become involved. I don't consider that I could be useful.' He walked towards the porthole and onto solid earth, and Dood followed behind.

Coalascan stepped forward and said, 'We regret your decision but must respect it,' and moved to close the door.

Dorkin said, 'You pass the test. I shall be happy to offer my full help.' In an uncanny way he felt their euphoria, as near to telepathy as he had ever experienced. He stepped back into the craft and Dood followed him again.

—ᵐ—

Joseph Dorkin was a rational man, composed and assured, and at ease. Yet he had never been placed at such a disadvantage with other people in his life. The inside of the silver ship was completely quiet: there was not even a hum. It was anodyne and white, neither warm nor cold, and a perfect calm. The five people there were peaceful but they were not complacent. They were purposeful. But Dorkin had never been inside an alien spaceship before and was unsure of how to behave. There were no courtesies that he could fall back on, such as avoiding the use of someone else's chair or holding a door open. He did not feel free to touch anything, make any move that could be misconstrued, or take advantage of any material object. He made a heart-hearted remark: 'Which one of you is flying this thing?'

One of his hosts replied, 'It does not require a constant manipulation of controls. We had small devices implanted in our brains—I think you would describe them as microchips. If we wish the craft to undergo flight it will do so. Your kind has learned to use a similar method to work the limbs of those damaged by accident or illness.' He added as an afterthought 'Or by genetic factors.'

Dorkin sat down on a chair. He found it interesting. It was comfortable, ergonomic and it pleased the eye. It could not be said that his companions designed only functional objects. That was also true of the inside of the craft, which although functional, gave a sense of lofty ceilings and space. It was as though the placement of furniture and the design throughout had been made with the knowledge of Feng shui. However the universal white colour was strange. One of his new companions noted his expression and said, 'If you find the colour unusual, you will find it will change during the course of the day. Soon it will become warmer as the day passes and it may, according to our wishes, become green in the afternoon. Green is a restful colour as is that time of day, but by evening it will become dark and may even change to give the appearance of a study with panelled walls.' Dorkin nodded.

There was so much he wished to ask. He said, 'How is this craft powered?'

'We can control vast magnetic fields and enormous masses. They distort space-time in our favour. There are other factors of course, but we can reliably reach considerable proportions of light speed and make great distances seem less significant. Our travel requires much energy, which we can release. It would not be helpful to display the equations at this stage.'

'There only five of you?'

'There are many more, but they are not here. This craft can accommodate enough for our purposes but for far interstellar travel we use another. I believe you would call it a cigar. It contains the motive factors that I have described.'

'What may I call you?'

'We have names of course. In fact, they are chosen from a list of forebears we wish to venerate, and these are used for everyday discourse. However there are also up to four further names, each with 50 choices that we use less often, to avoid any one person sharing names wholly with another. You can easily work out that no name would be duplicated unless there are more than 312,500,000 people.'

'I suppose you should call me Dorkin. I hope that it carries enough meaning to be commensurate with my seniority and experience.'

'That is fine, Dorkin. My name is Handel and these are Kakatak, Botticelli and Poppatak.'

'They are interesting choices. May I ask about them?'

'Certainly, Kakatak is revered as having provided us with the means of overcoming the cold during an ancient ice-age. Poppatak was a leader of the people you call the Ixchel; he lived many generations ago. He preserved their independence and culture for eighty years under difficult circumstances. It was at a time of the advance of other peoples into their territory; yet he was not warlike. By comparison Coalascan was a significant statesman of our people; he lived two hundred thousand years ago during the Great Acknowledgement.'

'The symposium?'

'Yes, you are not familiar with our history, but at that time many doubts had coalesced into a general understanding that our future would be bleak despite our great technical and artistic prowess. For aeons we ignored the fact that a lack of evolutionary selection had made our bodies weak. As Coalascan has described, we valued only humanity and the equality of all. Differences of gender were regarded, foolishly, as being either weak or strong and therefore eliminated. Once we had begun to tinker, the process was self-perpetuating: we tried to eliminate the ostensibly unnecessary parts of our DNA, those for which the function was obscure, but our designs were at fault. We could not understand why. We, the brilliant, the creative, the humanistic cousins of the Ixchel were degraded and faulty. There remained only a purposeless existence and we could not survive in a world in which all were artists, poets and musicians. We desired risk. Eventually it was accepted that it was inhuman to continue in this manner.'

'And that was The Great Acknowledgement?'

'Yes, a protracted symposium where our troubles would supposedly be settled.'

'So you, the cousins of the Ixchel, revisit earth regularly?'

'We do. Over the years we helped them, and in turn, we were able to enhance our project with their help or in a few cases, help volunteered by your kind.'

'Volunteered? You were going to abduct Carmen and Freya!' Dorkin's voice contain a hint of anger.

'Not abduct; we intended to offer them a fair exchange in return for gifts of stem cells.' Handel's face was expressionless, but his eyes gave a new indication of concern, as though he realised that such a trade might have been less than welcome. He said, 'The worst that happened was no more than the Ixchel's way of being tied until we arrived.'

Dorkin replied, 'OK, but if you wish to enlist my help, why cannot your own scientists do all that I could?'

'That is not necessarily the case. Our creations, as I have tried to explain, lacked a spirit. They were living as an electrical cell is alive, yet they did not have a life as you or I do.'

'As far as I can see, you have made clear the difference between mankind and God.'

Handel might have nodded, but it was clear that his catalogue of gesticulations did not contain such a gesture. Instead he looked straight at Dorkin and their eyes met in an exchange of complete frankness. He said, 'That is the kind of conclusion which the first Coalascan recognised during the time of the Great Acknowledgement.' But Dorkin recognised humility in the exchange.

For the time being the conversation came to an end and both parties, now wiser, began to meditate. Dorkin and Dood returned to their seats and watched while the five busied themselves with technical matters. Later they rose and offered refreshment in the form of warm water and a plate of assorted vegetables. They ate and found it surprisingly appetising. Hunger was appeased and the water, tasting and smelling mildly of an essence like mint, was attractive to the palate and gave a suggestion of freshness. There was little conversation, although Kakatak, Botticelli, and Poppatak introduced themselves and suggested their own specialisms. 'But,' Poppatak assured him, 'our preferences for artistic matters or for statecraft or science are not strictly relevant to our mission today.'

While he spoke, Dorkin watched their puny hands grasp the food and take it to their mouths where, after much mastication, they swallowed with the help of water. Meanwhile, Callum Dood refreshed himself with a small cigar and the vapours, appreciated by some, were circulated by currents of air nearby but eventually removed, although not before Coalascan had made a comment about it: 'Reverend Dood, I am intrigued by that herbal substance which you burn, I imagine for the beneficial quality of the smoke?'

'Yes certainly. We call it a cigar, which contains an herb we call tobacco. It can induce a feeling of reflection in its own right, but from time to time I add other substances for various effects. For example, I could suggest another which enhanced my ability to play chess; I assume that it improved my spatial cognisance. I suspect that a further example may have enabled my thoughts to transcend the dimension of time.'

'In due course you must demonstrate that to me. Of course, we have machines that can do similar, but I am keen to learn...'

Later the Pragya repaired to chairs. It was a time for social affiliation, when the bright white light of morning activity changed to green. They seemed to welcome conversation and Dorkin asked the questions that had been foremost in his mind:

'Where is your world,' he said, 'and where are we going?'

'For me to answer that question,' said, Poppatak, 'I would first need to describe why we left the earth all those aeons ago. It was a time of the ascent of mankind. Our lives prospered on the rich and sunny, open grassland in southern Africa. All around were wild animals, competing with us and dependent upon each other too. Yet all around us other forms of mankind arose. We continued to prosper but realised we should eventually compete with them, the more primitive, the more warlike, and yes, the more competitive.'

'How long ago are you referring to?' said Dood, anxious to confirm that particular point.

'All humankind became distinct from chimpanzees about five million years ago, while Neanderthals became a separate line a mere 500,000 years ago. A little earlier a particular group of humankind developed, that had advanced social and mental abilities. They became our own forebears and progressed quickly, making an ascent to a technical civilisation in 50,000 years. Meanwhile mainstream humans progressed more slowly—there were long ice ages and much disease yet they—you—are now strong.'

'Is that why you left these shores?'

'Yes: I understand the colloquialism. Several hundred thousand years ago we began to look for a place to live in which we stood no fear of assimilation. Our knowledge enabled us to establish colonies around the world, and some were successful, at least for a time. Others, in remote places were less successful, and only small relics of our civilisation remain today.' Poppatak looked regretful, but apart from his eyes, which were full of emotion, the rest of his face was unmoved. Dood wondered: how could this be an advanced social ability?

Poppatak continued to speak of matters long past, 'Yet all the time, mankind was spreading north and into other continents where northern forms of mankind, the Neanderthals in particular, would face our own fate. It was clear that to live in a manner which our principles dictated, we should have to depart.'

'But surely,' said Dorkin, 'your abilities would have enabled you to have mastered these insurgents?'

'We could simply have pressed a button and annihilated them all, but that was not our way. And sooner or later it would have had to be repeated. To what end?'

'So your leaders decided to leave?'

'The decision was consensual rather than imposed by any leader. Those that wished to remain were encouraged to do so. By then our kind was diminishing, and the main body of our people decided, as you have said, to find a new world.'

'Those that remained were settled in middle America and at the Cape?'

'Yes,' said Poppatak.'And of course we visited them. But despite our help with tools and more advanced agriculture, the emerging competition on the open veldt of the Cape was not conducive to long-term survival. We became smaller and dwindled. Finally, we could only prosper in the hostile rainforest where the Ixchel survive through their reclusiveness.'

Dorkin did not wish to be unkind; he had heard quite enough to agree their basic proposition. He said, 'I don't wish to seem cynical, but perhaps it was in those times that you began to appreciate the essential wisdom that to survive in this world, you must be able to compete?'

'Not exactly.' Poppatak showed no sense of pique. 'We knew these principles long before, yet we imagined that our wisdom would enable us to live as we chose. It was later that the inevitable outcome became clear. We did not wish to kill in a world of kill or be killed.'

'Yet you still prospered away from earth?'

'Prosperity can perhaps be measured in numbers. Handel'—
he turned courteously in his direction—'mentioned that we have
five names and that all could be employed without duplication
by 312,500,000 citizens. In practice our first name, the name by
which we wish to be known, is chosen later, but only after a period
in which the honoured earlier citizen is first studied. Therefore in
the first instance we use only four names. You can judge for yourself
whether we prosper.'

Dorkin made a metal calculation. He said, 'That is the
population of one city in America.'

'So therein lies your conclusion.' Poppatak showed little sadness;
there was no bitterness or anger in his words. He had shown only
a desire to make good and to repair and advance his own kind.
Dorkin held them in his gaze for a minute. He thought, 'They hold
the highest principles and deserve no pity. Perhaps it's my own kind
with our relentless greed and need for expansion which qualifies for
that.'

Dorkin had watched them, but so had Dood. He wondered that
the Pragya, unanimated, unmoved, could be considered advanced.
He thought they might fare poorly in France or Italy where, in the
absence of demonstrative behaviour they would be handicapped.
At very least they were bound by eye contact, but there was much
more. He was sure they were advanced telepaths. He was drawn
back to Dorkin's question: 'So you settled far away?' and added, 'I
am pleased that we have been able to discuss some of your history.
It has certainly helped me to understand how I came to be here.' He
thought, 'Courtesies! What a roundabout way of speaking!' But he
felt no sense that the Pragya had discourteously tried to read his
mind.

Poppatak paused to think. He turned to the other four and
spent a minute looking into their eyes. There appeared to be a
consensus, so he turned to Dorkin and said, 'We made our home
on a planet in the system of Luyten's star. It was found to be only
a little larger than earth, although with greater gravity. It was also

colder, but these things were soon overcome. We were able to travel there, twelve light-years distant, for our purposes. In a small way we have prospered, but our eyes have long been on this beautiful and dangerous blue planet.'

'So we are returning there today, a distance of twelve light years?'

'No. In our vessel now we are waiting, not travelling. We have remained above the earth and will return to a suitable place for your researches shortly. You will be supplied with all you need.'

—⁓—

Peter Pargeter and his five friends weighed the advantages of leaving for home or staying in camp. There were several on each side and at first they had equal measure. Yet eventually the consensus came down to a question of loyalty. As Carmen said with her pleasant voice, 'We owe it to Professor Dorkin not to desert him.' Once that was said, it completely tipped the balance of the argument in favour of remaining. And their stay had already given them new evidence: had they gone their separate ways they could not have found the floor map and all it suggested. Only one week of their proposed month had passed. Perhaps there might still be other things they could find out. With these points aired, they reached a renewed consensus and resolved to stay for a while longer.

A couple of days passed. They spent their time foraging or sitting in camp with their notes, sketchpads and diaries. Carmen had long dissociated herself from the demands of Walter Stein and had heard nothing more from him. The evening was their favourite time, with a campfire and a glass of tequila. Then the dusk fell as quickly as it can at that latitude, bringing forth the night-time cacophony once again; paradoxically a time for reflection.

Suddenly, all steel objects around them, the knives and tools, were compelled to fly in the direction of the cliff where after a second they became scattered over the ground in the intervening distance. At the same time, the night sky flashed, and it became as light as day as an arc of lightning connected ground with the sky above. The jungle cacophony ceased all around them and in the flash of light they could see bats fluttering, confused. The light then flickered and vanished, leaving the night as black as before. They stood at once, listening to a jungle that seemed to have been stunned into silence. Presently they returned to their campfire, where Pargeter said, 'We need a sentry tonight. I am happy to do two hours if you lot will follow me. And again I mean to keep the rifle handy. Simon, can you follow me, then Guy and David, please? That will take us through to breakfast.' Any notion of abandoning their camp had vanished completely.

—⁓—

'We are waiting, not travelling,' Poppatak had said. From Dorkin's point of view it was not clear that he could tell the two apart. There was no sense of movement or the turbulence that one can sometimes feel in an aeroplane. Nor was there any sound of an engine. The silver disc seemed to have a mind of its own: a mind to watch, wait and listen just as the Pragya did.

Soon, Dorkin enquired of the nearest of the Pragya, Coalascan, where they were and how long they would wait. As had been his habit, he tried to make his enquiry as courteous as possible. Coalascan replied in a like manner, 'We remain in whatever cloud is nearest to our beacon. You may have seen the beacon yourself in the guise of a rectangular pyramid. We are a little to the east. Shortly there will be an exchange in which we collect the energy that has accumulated there. Later we shall dispose ourselves to your instructions.'

'I see, thank you. By the way, just as we try to compliment the native tribesmen with the name Ixchel, may I ask whether you have a preference for something similar?'

'You may ask, certainly. I think the best name for us is 'Pragya,' which you already know. It is from the Sanskrit and refers to a higher state of wisdom.'

Soon, Dorkin and Dood were encouraged to observe the Lacandon jungle below them, which had become visible in a gradual descent from cloud cover. It was dark in the moonlight, an olive green that had changed through slow stages to black. That colour was soon changed to a universal white in a sudden exorbitant flash when in an instant a picture of lightning emanating from the top of the pyramid was firmly etched onto their retinas. Their companions seemed pleased with the result.

Dorkin said, 'Where on earth does all that energy come from?'

Coalascan replied, 'It is indeed on earth, and that is its value. We use it to harvest the great energy from the earth's core. We have many such beacons: Reverend Dood, you may have experienced one of these on the Downs near your own home. There are similar places elsewhere and at times, sound may emanate from them which we regret. Perhaps we are best-known for our activities under the sea, which occasionally sound like cannon-fire.'

'Is that its only purpose?'

'No, we also welcome our friends the Ixchel there in the kind of ceremony they prefer.'

Dorkin was summoned to a conference with the five, while Dood listened in accompaniment. They sat on chairs as before and he was encouraged to make use of his pencil and notebook as he thought about the work he might do. He said, 'The best place for our project is my own laboratory. And I may have some examples already of the end result you desire.' Dorkin was thinking of embryos he had created. 'You will be specific in your requests, however?' As he considered these ideas, he dwelled on the word 'created' and wondered whether he had usurped the position of creator.

Their spokesman on such matters was Botticelli: 'We offer you complete freedom, because if we specify an outcome we will only direct you toward the mistakes we made in our own efforts. We also accept your choice of venue and feel your responsibility is to use your freedom in the best way you can. Perhaps you will need assistants? If so we can collect Carmen and Simon, who are still here with their friends.'

Dorkin followed, 'By all means I could do with Simon and Carmen's help, although I doubt whether I would be much slower by myself. But these friends, do you know much of this second party?' He nodded towards Dood.

'We do. We intercepted their radio message within a few seconds of it being dispatched. It was in response to earlier cues we sent out. We always seek enthusiasts to help us, as you found yourself. They were intelligent enough, and interested enough to be drawn this far from their homes. We knew that you had been experimenting with hybrids because of their message, and we may yet find a way of rewarding them.'

'Right, well I need to get a message to Simon and Carmen. I'll write if you will deliver it. I'll ask them to join me shortly. It will take time to make their farewells.'

Like his colleagues, Botticelli's face was immobile but his eyes were very much alive. They positively glowed with excitement when Dorkin finished by saying, 'We need to get back to my laboratory. But if I'm going there, then the expectation will be that our foray here—and I mean the work with my friends—will end. No don't worry, you don't need to give them a lift in this machine: it doesn't seem particularly dramatic inside anyway. And they can go home via Belize very easily.'

—m—

It was early in the morning and Guy Meredith was awake before anyone else in camp. He kicked at the campfire, placed a couple of logs near it to dry, and then raised a blackened camp kettle over it to boil water. The fire began to smoke heavily so he sat down to watch, whereupon the scrubby bushes parted ahead of him and two native men approached. They were the Ixchel once more, and their manner was conciliatory and friendly. Meredith was not drawn to any defensive behaviour and they left a package at his feet before retiring into the distance. He opened the package, which consisted of a hastily-made envelope with a single piece of paper inside, and read the following:

'Hi Simon, Carmen and everyone else,

I hope you are not worried about my safety. I am with friends nearby, and will be with them until further notice. I think it better that you should return home now, because the focus of my activities will shortly be at home, in my laboratory. Simon and Carmen you will need to see me there in about two weeks' time. The Reverend Dood has decided to stay with the Ixchel for a while longer, until, as he says, he is fit to return.

In the meantime, Guy will wish to speak to his US contacts before returning to England. And David and Freya, now is the time to prepare that big scoop: I'm sure you have enough news at last! Peter, the Pragya have promised to send you a solution to a mathematical problem that will make you famous if you publish it.

My friends, of course, are the Pragya, and they are concerned with the contents of the radio message which Peter, Guy and Freya sent out. As you might imagine, I shall be helping with work in that direction, which will mean returning to my laboratory for a while.

In due course we can take up our normal routines again, and when we do—

The best,
Joseph Dorkin.'

Meredith thought about it and then roused the others who, by then, were appearing at intervals anyway. When they were all present he passed the letter around, described the men who had brought it, and explained that it would have been fruitless to follow them in the hope they would lead back to Dood and Dorkin. They agreed to act on the suggestions it contained and were reassured that if he had been in any danger, Dorkin would not have written the letter in such a manner. Within ten days, all had taken up station as had been suggested by Professor Dorkin, and there was a general sense of euphoria as they began to adopt their former routines again.

—⚹—

Back in Washington DC, Walter Stein made a telephone call to Carmen van Brouin, whose arrival home had been confirmed to him. He said, 'Hello, this is Stein.'

'Hi Sir,' she said. His call had not been unexpected, but her ordeals abroad had made her feel more loyal to her companions there than to Stein. His sinister voice made her bite her lip. 'Sorry that I haven't been in touch recently. I have to make sure I'm clean.'

'That's OK. How's it going?'

'We have returned. Professor Dorkin has decided to return to his laboratory'—she knew that Stein would be aware of that anyway, and could guess what he would do there—'and he's gonna make more hybrid embryos.'

'Why?'

'It's for his new friends: the extra-terrestrials—I kid you not. He managed to bring them down with him.'

'And where will they be?'

'That I can't say.'

'Good. I need to get my hands on one of those sons of bitches.'

—⚹—

Dorkin was pleased to be back in town and celebrated with a couple of hot dogs with mustard and a rare treat for him: a pitcher of Rolling Rock. The next morning he rose early and despite his solitude was able to hold an imaginary conversation with his colleagues, still so far away. He often did this because it enabled him to develop a mental narrative, a rational argument for the steps he intended to take.

'We have,' said the imaginary Carmen van Brouin, 'collected DNA from our lost tribe: the Ixchel, and we struck lucky. It was similar to that of Boskop man and was also like the 'crash' DNA, except that it retained all the 'unknown purpose' sections which the crash samples lacked.'

'Yes,' said Dorkin, 'and remember we thought the crash material was the result of a massive genetic experiment? Well, we were right about that! They tried to simplify things to make them work better. They played God, and sadly, that's where they went wrong. Now they want me to play God too.'

'Quite clearly,' said the just as imaginary Simon Wiener, 'now that we know what happened, we can help to put things right. We have the 'Ixchel' result as an example.'

'In that case, why don't we just give them an Ixchel embryo? Why don't they raise a lot of Ixchel children as their own?' Carmen was genuinely perplexed.

'Because,' said Dorkin, 'I think that over the centuries the Pragya developed positive things too, which the Ixchel might presently lack. They are even more cerebral; I saw them communicate by means of thought transference and the Ixchel, despite their abilities, are perhaps less developed in that. Humans can sometimes achieve psychic communication also but *they* were much more advanced. They might lose some of this if they turn wholly to the Ixchel. And there may be other reasons too. I doubt they would tell me everything.' He thought of ethics, but remembered how they had been able to define ethics in their present interest.

Dorkin finished shaving and came down to metaphorical earth. He was clear in his mind, and mentally thanked his younger colleagues for their inspiration. In the laboratory, he set about his objective: first to make an Ixchel-monkey embryo and then, armed with the requisite experience, an embryonic Ixchel-extra-terrestrial. He doubted that the first would live long. The question was, however, what genes would he need to edit in order to improve the result?

—⁓—

Walter Stein sat in conference with the Deputy Director of the National Clandestine Service, together with a representative from the presidential office in Washington. Also present was a tame geneticist called Girault, brought in to translate science into plain English.

The Deputy Director was called James Davis, a respected and moderate individual and an ideal 'chair' for a discussion like the present one. However Arnold Schickel, answering to the President himself, had no time for anything other than the most direct interrogation. By comparison Stein's own particular brand of assertiveness was different: it was sinister, more concerned with the unspoken and less with overpowering a subordinate by talking over him, or by appearing on the verge of anger. Under the circumstances, Stein felt at a disadvantage as he was questioned about Professor Dorkin.

'So tell us,' said Davis, 'what is Dorkin currently doing?'

'He is making hybrid embryos,' said Stein. 'He snips out useful bits of DNA from cells and then…look, perhaps Dr Girault, you had better answer these technical questions.'

'Yes, thank you. Well I have looked at the reports handed to me—'

Schickel interrupted: 'Sent by whom?'

'My main contact,' said Stein, 'recently returned from southern Mexico, where she was watching a party of individuals there. I had recent doubts about her loyalty, but she informed me of Dorkin's current activities in his laboratory, where I have two or three other useful operatives installed in various positions.'

'Good. So you were saying, Dr Girault?'

'Yes, their reports were handed to me, and it seems that Professor Dorkin started working on an ET-Ixchel chimaera. He cut out certain stretches of DNA, certain genes from an Ixchel embryo. He repopulated the embryo with stem cells for things he wanted to implant: such as brain cells from the ET. The resulting hybrid embryo is usually only allowed to live for a short time, especially if the fusion is considered unethical—an example would be between a human and a rat. However in this case, the hybrid was allowed to develop.'

Schickel said, 'So what's the method actually used for?'

Girault replied, 'It could be used to grow human organs inside pigs, for example. But many scientists consider that unethical too.'

'And what traits did Dorkin aim to get into the Ixchel embryo?'

'Well, Dorkin had the advantage that there was apparently nothing unethical about it: both species are closely-related, apparently. He was aiming to introduce genes for intelligence. Effectively, he made Ixchel embryos with an ET brain. The cells were so happy growing together that the embryo looked altogether normal.'

Davis said, 'And is there a name given to this kind of practice?'

'There certainly is,' replied Girault. 'He made a chimaera, an animal made of cells from two different species—but not too different in this case.'

'It sounds completely unethical to me!'

'Perhaps, but the idea has been around for a long time. It was understood by the ancient Greeks, whose mythical vision had the body of a lion, the head of a goat and the tail of a snake. It's the stuff of everyone's bad dreams—except for the scientists, that is.'

Shickel did not appreciate Girault's attempt at humour. He said, rather dryly, 'Well I happen to know that human-animal chimaeras are not eligible for public funding.'

'We all know that,' said Girault. 'But in this case they apparently do qualify since Ixchel and ET cells are each human-like, or perhaps even totally human.'

'You say that the hybrid should be more intelligent?'

'If the ET source were more so, then theoretically yes.'

'It sounds like eugenics, but without the selective breeding.'

'That's arguable: if the Ixchel brain were defective, then a perfectly valid description would be gene therapy. It's all a question of attitude; various 'religious' chimaeras were thought of as bringing only good: some have said that angels are the chimaeras of men and birds.'

Like Dorkin, Girault was an accomplished public orator. However he found it difficult to deal with Schickel's persistence and assertiveness. Schickel, without showing any degree of anger but with the dogged need of the official interrogator, said: 'I have no idea whether the Ixchel brain cells require gene therapy, but I do want to find out about the significance of this hybrid. We may go on funding him, but if we do, then I hope it doesn't turn out to be a monster. So tell me, what do you expect Professor Dorkin to do next?'

'I can't see him making an Ixchel-human embryo, but I wouldn't be surprised if I heard about a full human-ET hybrid. That is, if he uses brain cells as before. If he goes off the rails, then Lord knows what hybrid he might make.'

Schickel said, 'God help us all.'

Walter Stein noted the tension and closed the meeting before anything could be said that was harmful to the project or less directly, to his own Department which depended on clandestine operations like these. He disliked these meetings and preferred his own offices where he had complete hegemony. A recording was passed to a secretary, who prepared a typescript for very limited circulation.

Time passed, and back in his Pennsylvania laboratory, Dorkin reached a crux in his investigations. His hybrid embryos had reached the stage of continued cell division and he needed to decide—they needed to—whether the embryo would be taken to term. For that, it would need to be implanted, but with whom? Was that where the Pragya had gone wrong?

It was straightforward to arrange a meeting with the five, requiring only a brief conversation using a radio. Later that day, Dorkin drove out of town to meet them. They had descended to earth in sparsely-populated countryside far from evidence of present use. The vista was flat and unpromising, with many fallen pine trees and a discarded industrial operation leaving a place protected from view. There, he supplied Poppatak with details of his latest work and explained why he had come.

'You will need to decide whether you wish the embryos to

develop,' said Professor Dorkin. 'And for that, well you are already aware of the demands of the next step.'

'We were undecided how far to take this,' said Handel. 'You have made embryos with the body of an Ixchel, and we can see that this will resolve several errors we made long ago. You may have understood that we are men, but that is not so. We are uniformly a combination of masculine and feminine character, and gender was discarded long ago. Our form is therefore ambiguous, which for us was a poor outcome. We can see that this would be resolved by the embryos of different sexes that you have made.'

Professor Dorkin nodded, 'That is correct.'

'And with our neural cells, the hybrid embryos should retain our particular mental abilities. It is quite remarkable that our own scientists tried to build a complete genome without seeing an easier way in which this could be achieved. In one, you have also managed to restore the deleted sections which they removed to our great regret.'

'I am pleased to have been of help.'

'So,' said Handel, 'I must converse.' He spent a minute looking into the eyes of each of his companions. Finally, he turned to Dorkin and said, 'We are as one. Having come this far it would be inconceivable to turn back. We will take the embryos and make arrangements for their continued growth although we cannot disclose what form that will take. Please can you arrange a suitable time for us to visit your premises; we shall need to come when you are alone. There will probably be two of us and it will be no sooner than fourteen days from this time.'

'No fewer than fourteen days? Certainly.'

Dorkin made ready for the Pragya and worked into the small hours, a solitary and single-minded individual. He was clear that this was his great work, a contribution to human history that would eclipse his oft-repeated archaeological digs and his grubbing through scholarly histories of the Middle East. He became a hermit, unapproachable even to his staff, and stimulated only by thought of his project. He became thin and increasingly gaunt, a middle-aged version of Meredith, and like the latter was quite happy in his lonely endeavours. Unlike Meredith, however, who had grown into more of a social creature through his recent experiences, Dorkin was growing less of one by keeping only strange company.

Eventually, he sent a message to the five who responded that they would accept his suggested time for their visit. Two of them, they confirmed, could be expected the following night. However unbeknown to him, that information also reached Walter Stein, the recipient of a dozen recorded telephone calls, bug emissions, confidences and surreptitiously opened letters.

In preparation, Dorkin spent yet another day in his laboratory where he prepared a portable incubator and waited for his guests to arrive. They would have attracted attention in anything other than a disguise: their strange expressionless faces, all-knowing eyes and enlarged crania standing out in any crowded place. However he knew they were intelligent enough to avoid confrontation and had chosen a quiet time in which to pass the short distance up the granite steps outside. There, he met Poppatak and Handel as planned and they were quickly ushered indoors. In silence and secrecy they walked the corridors to his laboratory, pressed the code on the door that had been renewed by Dorkin to admit only himself, and entered.

Dorkin's companions were immediately surrounded by half a dozen burly men in combat gear, their helmets and visors, bulletproof vests and huge boots making them large and impregnable. They avoided Dorkin but grabbing Poppatak and Handel, wrenched their tiny hands behind their backs, which caused them to howl in pain. Dorkin shouted: 'For God's sake don't do that. Pinion them at the front if you must!' The six 'security guards' changed their minds and did so.

Dorkin and Handel held each other's gaze and one said, 'It's alright, we understand that this isn't your doing. Please see what you can do for us.' Then they were whisked away, leaving Dorkin with his incubator, in darkness and in a state of confusion. He could do little except, as an interim measure, replace the embryos in storage. Then he hastened home where, shocked and awed by the speed, violence and purpose of the assailants, he lay down to sleep in an armchair.

The next morning, Dorkin arose late, the shock of the last evening making him sleep long: a weary and disconsolate individual. Soon, dressed at last and keen to make amends with his friends, he sat down at a window and resolved to think for that morning before doing anything. Perhaps it was that which had let them all down: had he, naively, thought only of work and nothing of those, the unseen and unseemly, he had been warned about? If he could make amends then he would not be so foolish again. At last he saw his own fatigue.

First, he knew his assailant: Walter Stein, the man who was 'gonna squeeze.' Since that was so, he knew that Stein had no immediate interest in him, only in what he could deliver. And he had delivered his friends to him, lock, stock and barrels. Further, Stein might be interested in the embryos but was more likely concerned with Poppatak and Handel for reasons of harder technology. That gave him an opportunity. Quickly, he grabbed a coat and made for the door. Outside he drove to work, entered his laboratory and replaced the embryos in his portable incubator. Realising the origin of Stein's all-seeing creativity, he ignored the telephones and made no noise as he padded carefully about. Upon leaving, he took the incubator with him, returned to his car and made a call from a new mobile phone. Obtaining an acknowledgement he refuelled his car and at sunset, drove to the meeting place out of town. A silver craft awaited him, where he explained the events of the last twenty-four hours and passed the incubator to Kakatak, Botticelli and Coalascan.

Professor Dorkin was apologetic: 'After all this,' he said, 'I am so sorry you have lost your friends. I should have been more careful.' He explained who Walter Stein was.

'So,' said Coalascan. 'What can we expect Walter Stein will want from them?'

'Stein's department is concerned with security. He is interested in suppressing all public knowledge of so-called UFOs and he does it by disinformation, fake news, anything else that will ridicule it or create Twitter conversations which oppose it. But there's more: he wants your technology. And by that I mean smart materials, ray guns, explosive devices, methods of harvesting and controlling energy, information technology and above all, methods of propulsion. I expect he will make Poppatak and Handel work for him in fear of their lives.'

'And at the end?'

'I'm sorry, but Stein's department cannot let them live. He could return them to you, but otherwise could never take the risk of having them paraded through Washington DC on a limousine.'

'So he would kill them?'

'Even he would only do that as a last resort.'

Coalascan held Dorkin's gaze. 'So the answer is yes, then?'

'It is.'

There was silence and the three gathered together and looked into each other's eyes. Their faces were as expressionless as usual, but their eyes, usually serene and sentient, were troubled. Dorkin thought he saw a trace of anger, but then he thought, surely not? After a full five minutes during which the contact between them continued, they broke away and stood before him in a line.

'It is our fault also,' said Kakatak. 'We judged you all according to our own wishes and it is clear that not all are as beneficent, altruistic or humane as you. We cannot let our friends be killed at the end of their usefulness, but neither can we bring about the death of their captors.'

Botticelli continued to talk, a task that was shared between them, 'In the first instance we need to find where our friends are being held. We must get a message to them explaining our goals. We agree to transfer our technology to Walter Stein, yet it cannot be our greatest secrets. Not at present anyway, since your society is primitive to the point that we cannot tolerate its dispersal and plenitude throughout the universe.'

Dorkin felt anger, 'You wished to restore evolution and competition to your own kind. You will not be able to preserve the weak as though they have an equal share of providence; nor will you be able to seek equality, that absurd notion in this world of chance and unequal outcomes. Will you not, once again, be as primitive, as unethical as us?'

Coalascan replied, 'That may be so; our view of the universe has been directly challenged by the facts of survival. We shall need to consider, perhaps in a renewed great symposium, to what extent such matters infringe on our views.'

Botticelli followed, 'But we do not feel that our cautious advancement can compare with the effect of humankind acquiring technological secrets they cannot control. We will help Walter Stein in order to preserve our people, but only as an interim measure. We shall need to remove them as soon as we can.'

Professor Dorkin shook his head. He did not understand why a great symposium was needed to discuss these matters. However he said only, 'You must do what you will with the embryos. They cannot stay for long in that portable incubator and will need a more sophisticated machine. You have seen my design for something suitable.'

'And you?' said Coalascan.

'I shall work in such a way that you can conceive it as an apology from my fellow man. I will try to find out where your brothers are imprisoned, and how they can be released. In the meantime, I need to arrange a gift of technology for Stein. It should be in the form of individual steps so that I can show him an incremental increase in results. Stein must be led on to accept that in return for further freedoms for his prisoners. Then, when I am able, I shall call you down and try to release them.'

'I was about to propose something similar,' said Coalascan. 'Please first get in touch with Stein and make a suitable proposition. We shall need a few days to make something suitable. Come and see us here when we are ready.'

Dorkin was able to contact Stein by telephone. He seemed very pleased to hear from him and said, 'Professor Dorkin, I was about to call you. It seems you know more about our 'foreign' friends than meets the eye. I do hope that we didn't use excessive force yesterday.'

'Well you did.'

'Well, we got what we wanted.'

Dorkin stifled an oath. 'There is that,' he said, 'and there is also another reason for my call. I expect that you want to put them to work?'

'I had been thinking that.'

'In that case, you need to let me supply them with their special requirements. Put it this way, if you were on Uranus, you would want a bottle of Scotch just to keep going. They need to see me.'

'Why can't you just pass it to me?'

'Because you need me, too. You won't get anything from them unless they speak to me first. They need to agree it with their friends, and I'm the one who can make that happen.'

'And what do you get from all this, Dorkin?'

Dorkin resisted saying, 'It's a question of what I've already had.' He knew that Stein would be suspicious of an idealist. Instead, he said, 'If you want me to be frank, then I prefer a situation in which the agency needs me.'

'That's wise. Ok, I'll set that up and get back to you.'

Pleased, Stein saw the prospect of his captives, satisfied with their comfort, working busily in order to supply the technological wizardry that could be passed on above. By contrast, Dorkin saw the prospect of providing comfort and useful information to the pair, together with instructions about their release. But how far would their comrades go if they needed to use force?

Dorkin busied himself, and Stein eventually returned his call a week later. Stein said, 'Things are ready. Those guys are set up someplace.'

'Can I meet you there?'

'No. I'll collect you by car and then take you there. Don't worry; you'll also get a trip back.'

'That's fine. Say in about another week? I'm busy here with my own work—it's going quite well.' Dorkin wondered whether the three would be ready to see him beforehand. Later, he left his laboratory and used his mobile telephone to make a suitable call, switching it off afterwards. A day later, he met the three after driving out for that purpose.

Coalascan was the first to volunteer an instruction, 'We think that we can give you something on an interesting carbon-based fibre. It has no resistance to the transfer of an electric current and will keep them all busy in being shown how to use it. They will be able to build a very fast computer, under instruction of course. We cannot see that this would be particularly harmful, and in fact it may do some good.'

'Very good, I will present it to Handel and Poppatak. But I shall need to take them something more personal also, to satisfy Stein's understanding of the need for individual gain.'

'Yes,' said Coalascan, 'here is a package of food. They will have refused to eat much and will be in need of it. You are the only person who will know how to prepare it.'

Dorkin accepted these and drove home. Later, he set up a meeting by telephoning Stein who, when Dorkin explained about the packages, offered to take him the next day. With that arranged, Dorkin sat down to think. He knew that he would be blindfolded on the way there and would have his pockets checked and his mobile telephone confiscated, at least until they returned to his own doorstep. He decided to let them, since they would have at least the knowledge of that success. But the question remained of how to trace their movements. Then Dorkin had an idea. His neighbour kept a pet cat as a companion, one notorious for long walks in the neighbourhood. It wore a location tracker on its collar so that it could be found when necessary. He would borrow the tracker himself, while Stein could not possibly complain about a keyring in his pocket. Later, he would download the data, faithfully recorded. Suitably relieved, he would make sure the cat's pleasures were accommodated as a trade-off for staying indoors.

The next day, an important-looking black car arrived for Dorkin, who joined it with his packages. They were examined by Stein and accepted, as was the technical data and samples he also brought. His pockets, as he had expected, were checked and his phone confiscated, but it was not the same device he had used to make his calls to the three. Finally, he was blindfolded. The car went a considerable distance, calculated by Dorkin as approximately 90 minutes at 60mph. Since it was mostly freeway driving it meant their destination was about 90 miles distant—unless Stein had arranged to double back. Eventually, it drew to a silent halt, disgorged its people and security precautions were relaxed.

They were at a military-grade institution with a camp enclosed by barbed wire, but with two disused, unpaved runways and a single large hangar at the southernmost end. Clearly, it was a disused airfield that had been taken over by the US military. There were a few concrete buildings near, together with evidence of continued use in the form of strip lighting visible through windows. Outside a security fence the landscape was varied, with agricultural fields in the foreground and trees farther distant. Dorkin thought it a rural area, without the hum of a freeway or the overhead cables needed by heavy industry. There, it was approaching mid-day when they were taken into a building where Dorkin was interrogated more thoroughly by Stein. Dorkin said, 'First, can you tell me whether Handel and Poppatak have eaten anything?'

'Only a bit of spinach and some distilled water. I presume they eat more than that?'

'I think they need a fortified substance too. It's based on some kind of plant. It looks like green jelly. And they drink a kind of mint-flavoured water, but that's supposed to contain a supplement as well. When I see them can you please make sure I have access to hot distilled water and some basic utensils to mix it with?'

'Yeah, I'll do that. How long will they take to chow down?'

'Give me an hour, will you, and can you get me a something too?'

Poppatak and Handel looked as puny as their kind always did, but were neither too cold nor hot in their silvered, yet colourless suits. Their morale, however, was low because they knew their freedom was taken away, and they were concerned about the nature of their work. It was with pleasure that they welcomed Professor Dorkin, although only he knew it. Watching them, Stein saw only expressionless faces and thought them dull and forlorn.

Dorkin moved to provide them with food, passing them the package of pleasures he had brought. It was with a trace of pity that he watched them mix up their green pap and add hot water. Yet their mood seemed to improve after they had eaten it, and calmly they enquired after Dorkin's wellbeing and listened to his instructions from Coalascan. They seemed to accept them, and Stein noted only passive complicity. The latter was strange to him, yet welcome, and he began to see the fruits of his endeavours.

Dorkin said, 'Coalascan has suggested that a conducting fibre would be acceptable as an item of technology to pass on. The specifications are here: it has no electrical resistance and if used in a computer would make it supremely fast, and run without the need for cooling.' Significantly he added, 'We are to believe it will give this country a great lead in all aspects of technology that require fine electronic control. They understand that it is in fact a widespread goal in all competitor countries.'

Stein nodded and seemed grateful, yet Dorkin held the eyes of the other two and was complicit in the understanding which passed between them. Stein did not notice, but Poppatak and Handel understood quite clearly: they were to make conducting fibres from a chemical kit; they were to make a very fast computer but somewhat slowly, and then demonstrate its prowess in a conspicuous manner. In the meantime they were to remain passive, seek privileges, await rescue. Above all, they must avoid the transfer of what might become military technology; and similarly, they should avoid the use of great masses and gravitational waves to distort spacetime. It was strange, for that was an exact list of the knowledge which Stein's political masters sought to obtain. Later, Stein reported to Arnold Schickel in Washington. Schickel, for once, seemed pleased and his manner less interrogative. He said, 'So Dorkin delivered the two aliens.' He sounded as though he relished the word, for once used without irony.

'Yes, and they are hard at work.'

'Good, you know what we want.'

'I do. They are applying themselves to something chemical at the moment. I have never smelled such a stink; it's almost as bad as their food.'

'Something chemical?'

'Sure, a special fibre for use in computers. You want a control system to beat the Russians or Chinese? Well this is part of it.'

'Okay, but make sure they finish that pretty quick. Our team thinks they can help us control the movement of immense masses.'

'Eh?'

'Let me look at this brief. Ok, yes. I'm told that gravitational waves are disturbances in the curvature of spacetime; they are made by an immense accelerated mass. They deliver waves outwards at the speed of light and they transport energy, so that if we could make them, we could propel an object in a particular direction. We would be able to make a starship.'

'And you would be the next President, no doubt!'

'Maybe, and if I am, you get rich and famous, too.' From his tone, Stein knew he was serious.

'So how long do I get for this work?'

'I want it finished in a month. Then, you get as long as it takes. Just don't fuck up.'

Stein said, 'Over and out,' with some relief.

—m—

Professor Dorkin said to the three sometime later, 'I know where they are.' He had arranged a meeting with them and they had chosen another place out of town to descend in their machine. 'They are used to me by now and they have stopped searching me when I visit. I wore a gps tracker and downloaded my own movements when I got home. So I can say for sure that they are being held at a disused airbase.' He passed them a piece of paper with the position. 'Unfortunately, they said that any rescue attempt would make it worse for Poppatak and Handel. I think they mean it, so my suggestion is that we don't try; not there, anyway.'

'I don't think they appreciate what we could do,' said Coalascan.

'Our abilities far exceed those of Mr Stein and his compatriots and in a direct confrontation, there could only be one winner.'

'Perhaps, but you would risk the loss of your friends. I think that even Stein would be reluctant to dispose of them, but he is under such pressure from his masters that I couldn't predict the outcome.'

'We take your point. There can be no question of placing them in any more danger.'

Kakatak said, 'Have you seen the results of their work, and if so, is it finished?'

'Yes,' said Dorkin. 'I brought some food to them and they stopped work to take advantage of it. I think it's interesting that Stein made no attempt to follow me here. I'm sure he could try, but he would have placed the 'order of things' in doubt. Had he made an attempt on your craft, he would have lost his source of supplies to Poppatak and Handel.'

'It would have made no difference,' said Kakatak. 'We could easily drain every bit of energy away from them so that they would be incapacitated. Nevertheless I accept your point: they want a complicit source of technology, secured with veiled threats which we are obliged to agree to.'

Professor Dorkin sometimes felt a little impatient with their equanimity, but he restricted his following words to: 'But to answer your question, they made a superconducting fibre and assembled a computer which stays as cold as its surroundings, and is much faster than anything which Stein's people can compare it with. They tried it against a large machine which took up enough space to fill three basketball courts. It was so-called state of the art, but Poppatak and Handel made something much faster, much to their delight.'

'And what did they barter in return?'

'They obtained more personal freedoms: more leisure time, more time to rest, and the opportunity to walk out in a garden.'

'Good.'

Dorkin said, 'Do I take it that your own devices are still better?'

'Of course. Control by using electronic communication is in

itself primitive. In our own case, we use control systems based on the movement of light, which is instant. We are surprised that you remain committed to metallic wires. And there are many other improvements also.'

Dorkin said, 'Which brings me to our next difficulty. Poppatak and Handel are under pressure to begin work on atomic particles.'

Coalascan looked concerned. Although his face was as impassive as ever, his eyes held a complex mixture of emotions which, without difficulty, he managed to pass to Dorkin. He said, 'Please describe this work.'

'They—Stein's people—have built a giant centrifuge and they want advice on making it work as a sphere instead of spinning in a circle. It is immensely strong and of a very large radius. They intend to place a very heavy object on the circumference and spin it.'

Coalascan and his friends looked, if possible, graver than before. Their eyes, as black as always, were dark with doubt and worry. Coalascan said, 'And can you tell me what it is that they intend to spin? For example, did they mention a source of this heavy material?'

'Yes, but that's not all. They spoke of a further quest, which involves accelerating the atoms of a heavy element to great speeds. They mentioned that when these collide they are destroyed and release radiation. They are also seeking to make the tiny black holes which arise in the resulting confusion of particles. They want these home-made black holes to use in a following step.'

'And what is this next step?'

'They spoke of accelerating them to high speeds in their own right, and looking for evidence of a distortion of space time.'

Coalascan said simply, 'They are fools to do these things here on earth, but I doubt they will be successful anyway.'

'Remember, they have Poppatak and Handel.'

'Yes, they do, so I think we should stop them if we can.'

'They may be more successful than you think,' said Dorkin. 'For a start, their scientists were accelerating gold atoms, which gave interesting results but were not particularly useful for their purposes. Instead, they want to use a very heavy element which they believe exists in the earth's core, and they are working on those principles.'

'And what is this element, please?'

'I was told it is called a superheavy element. It has no name.'

Coalascan sighed and looked down: 'Perhaps we are the ones who have been arrogant and foolish. We might have guessed it would come to this one day.'

Botticelli tried to console his compatriot: 'Our contacts with Earth have led to many good things. We have helped our people here in many ways. And for ourselves, we must thank Professor Dorkin, who has helped us also.'

Coalascan replied, 'Yes, that's true. His efforts with genetic manipulation have ensured that our new offspring are better than their forebears. It may be that after all, our kind has a prosperous future to look forward to.'

THIRTEEN

BLACK AND WHITE HOLES

Inside the airbase Poppatak and Handel, together with Professor Dorkin, were set to work. Stein, who was with them, had by that time a certain measure of disbelief: how could two members of the Pragya, by themselves and in an old and empty hangar, set about the seemingly impossible task of testing a large centrifuge, together with a particle accelerator? Such things required great engineering works, large premises and estates of land; together with much manpower. And what source of heavy elements did they intend to use? It should of course be impossible, yet Dorkin came to understand that Stein had arranged all of these with his large airbase and not least, a plentiful supply of conscripted labour.

Over the weeks therefore, the large hangar filled with what could only be described as a giant fairground ride with moving arms and a complicated means of driving them in variable radii. Similarly, the fairground analogy held true with the construction of what Dorkin felt able to describe as a ghost train, the long tunnel of which swept around the base, hidden by folds in the land and various forms of camouflage. He didn't quite dare to call these things a centrifuge or particle accelerator, yet built with the knowledge provided by his two captives, that is precisely what they were.

Professor Dorkin, however, was disbelieving. He understood that they needed to obtain a super-heavy element, not in great amounts, but by drilling some 1800 miles into the liquid core of the earth where the desired material lay. By comparison, the deepest human accomplishment of 7.5 miles had taken 20 years to dig! How could two Pragya, supported by a few power-hungry people, do any better? His doubts were eventually passed to Stein, who had a considerable sensitivity in the matter. In fact Stein was sensitive enough to seek reassurance from Arnold Schickel, who replied, 'Stein, you've got the two aliens. That's enough as far as I'm concerned.'

'How do you suppose I'll know if they are raising obstacles?'

'If nothing gets done inside a couple of months. Then you withhold that green mess from them or whatever it is they eat. Or use thumbscrews, I don't care.' Stein pulled a face and put the phone down.

Dorkin and Poppatak conversed: 'We don't think we can withhold the raw material without retribution. We shall have to deliver it. But we think we can stop them later. In the meantime, can you speak to the others?'

'Certainly, I'll let them know of your plans.'

Over the next few days, Poppatak and Handel seemed, if not amused, then certainly bemused by Stein's offer of a drill rig of the kind used by oil explorers. Stein's 'engineer' brought with him a diagram of a drill string and bit, together with descriptions of how used. It was the first time that Dorkin had seen the rather dour Pragya show what he guessed was a sense of fun. He felt that this improved them, but it also suggested they were more in control of events than they had indicated.

The airbase came to contain a giant machine; that was clear. It dealt with power and energy, and was controlled by the Pragya who were able to make it perform by an effort of will, just as they instructed and controlled their spacecraft. There were no flashing lights; no levers, only small hieroglyphs which from time to time became visible on a wall near them. At night, the place seemed alive enough to receive great arcs of electrical energy from the clouds above, where some knew their silver machine waited, unseen.

This machine seemed to be a great store of energy, yet no batteries or capacitors could be seen. On one occasion, Dorkin spoke to Poppatak: 'How?' he said simply. It was then that they used new gestures to show the covert, and also elation or zeal. Was zeal part of an elaborate hoax to mollify Stein? Possibly, yet Dorkin had felt their satisfaction with the power and process of their design; they had shown what it meant to be the Pragya. Their machine worked silently; the Pragya worked efficiently; Dorkin was reduced to housekeeper; Stein reduced to lackey. But eventually all was ready.

On a fine morning about six months after they had begun, the Pragya asked Stein, Dorkin and the guards to leave. They said, 'You must not be within two hundred yards.' Later, when all were at a distance and the security guards looked hungrily on, a white aura of electricity arose and the air crackled with static for half a mile around. Still farther, those at a distance felt their hair rise in the air and small fragments of leaves began to hop all around them and fragments stick to clothing. This static electricity was enough to bring a spark to metal objects or to make a discharge fly from finger to finger, so that it became impossible to shake hands. Then, on a nearby open runway an arc of electricity began to make a deep wound as the substance of the tarmac, and then of the earth itself, was vaporised. The arc diminished to a consummate point and the heat became blue and infinite. It began to focus lower—still lower, and the depth of the shaft increased. Within a couple of seconds the point of vaporisation had passed down to the depth of a standing man and Dorkin, watching, made an automatic calculation: if a shaft of 6 feet could be made in two seconds, so 1800 miles could be excavated in 36 days! How could it be? Well, now he knew.

The Pragya continued, neither sleeping nor resting. But with their attention firmly held, Dorkin eventually decided to return to their company. There remained the static electricity, for sure, yet he held the suspicion that the Pragya had meant only to be undisturbed and had not feared for his safety. He brought his usual offerings and

Poppatak and Handel were grateful enough to turn to more modest pleasures for a short while. Quizzically, he said, 'Now I know how you can fly so far across space?'

Handel replied, 'All the energy you have seen would not take us anywhere near the speed of our craft. That is a trick which you may someday learn, but not from this.'

The days passed and static electricity remained. Birds could no longer be seen overhead and metal objects were soon avoided by the guards and by Stein, who felt insignificant in this display of awesome ability. The security guards outside seemed helpless without their weapons but stood around looking gung-ho anyway. Meanwhile, the shaft continued to emit a cloud of vapour and continued its descent as the burning arc was focussed lower still, and as it approached the core of the earth. It was then that Stein realised he could no more control the Pragya than the wind or tides.

Dorkin asked, 'Why doesn't the cloud of vapour cool and condense to block the shaft as it rises?'

Poppatak replied, 'The particles are highly-charged and so they repel each other and bring about a high pressure in the shaft. The clouds we see emitted are the result.' Dorkin smiled and nodded as though that had been obvious to him, too.

Eventually, the Pragya suggested that they were approaching the liquid core of the earth, where vast amounts of molten metal could be obtained quite easily. It would naturally flow upwards, they said, being under great pressure, and so could be collected and refined. Yet that pressure could be controlled and the shaft sealed; indeed it would naturally seal itself as soon as they withdrew their interest. The temperature was about 5000°C, but would be cool enough to manage by the time it reached the surface. They were not to confuse the liquid metal core with molten lava, and they would be able to extract their desired metal quite easily, since the hot substance of the earth contained a notable amount of the raw material: the heavy element they required.

One morning, Dorkin remembered a part of an earlier conversation and said, 'Are you going to extract gold and make an accelerator for atoms of that?' He was probably only making conversation, not knowing much about the science involved. However he added, 'But of course, physics is not really my realm!'

Handel, however, looked at him with respect. He said, 'No, we don't intend to accelerate gold atoms. There's nothing in that for us. A few super-heavy atoms would be made, for sure, and we know they would fall apart and give interesting subatomic particles. But our aim is different. We want to obtain significant amounts of a super-heavy element that we can accelerate to high speeds in our particle accelerator. We think, in fact we know that it can lead to tiny black holes, immense gravity waves. Stein will want to see it and he may wish he hadn't.'

'So it's a white elephant contrived for Stein's purposes?'

'We agreed we need to deliver. He's not stupid and must see a result.'

Soon, Poppatak and Handel, working at their most dedicated speed, advised Dorkin and Stein that they had broken through to the core below. A channel would remain for as long as they prevented its seal; and the liquid contents of the core would pass up under pressure. The Pragya had seemed reluctant to discuss any science, but after persuasion, Handel said, 'We intend to vaporise the molten core and place it in a gas centrifuge: a big one. We have used that method many times to obtain useful materials for our purposes. Come this way.'

He entered an entirely new hangar. There, a huge transparent cylindrical casing could be seen, inside of which was a rotor that could spin at enormous speeds. Handel said, 'I acknowledge that this is similar to centrifuges which your people use to purify uranium, but ours is very much larger and faster. The centripetal force will cause very heavy elements to pass to the outside, where they can more easily be collected.'

'So,' said Walter Stein, 'If not gold, then what exactly are you after?'

'Had we been after gold we could have simply dug some up. That also applies to uranium and thorium. No, we are after a super-heavy element, one which humans have described, but of which they have never managed to obtain more than a few atoms. But the essential principle is that in the core of the earth, where heat is released by diverse forms of radioactive decay, atomic nuclei undergo many impacts that you have not yet begun to describe.'

'And can I take it that one of these impacts is the origin of this super-heavy element?'

'Yes it is, exactly so. We know that this element can be purified from vaporised core material. And our centrifuge is so large, fast and efficient that we can purify a considerable amount.' Handel seemed to show some pride in these accomplishments.

Stein said, 'You had all this equipment ready?'

'We did. As you may have surmised from the sonic booms and various noises which emanate from under the sea and other places, we obtain many useful materials in large quantities and refine them in this manner. There are, of course, many other sites beside this one.'

'You seem to think you own the place!' Stein replied.

'No more or less than you,' said Handel. 'In fact we behave with more respect and less of a proprietorial attitude than any part of the human species. Look at what your activities have done to the seas, for example; they are almost dead.' Dorkin had not yet seen any of the Pragya show what appeared to be a feeling of irritation. This appeared to be a first, which Stein noted too, because he closed his mouth and stayed silent.

'And this super-heavy element will be?'

'Do you wish me to name it or perhaps describe its properties?'

'Ah, both please!' said Dorkin.'

'Well, your people have already made element 118 in a particle accelerator, but it was unstable and didn't last even for a second before falling apart. But that little foray illustrates how keen you are to make progress with experiments of this kind. In truth, though, you seem to have ignored a much better prospect. Element 122 already exists in recognisable amounts in the Earth's core, and in fact it is stable. We call it by an unpronounceable name, but I would like to suggest that 'Fundamentum' might be suitable for our purposes today. It is fundamental to many physical processes that we shall seek to carry out very soon. We can purify a lot of it in our machine and use it in our experiments. But more of that later; this is enough for one day.'

After a short rest the Pragya returned to their work. Their machine worked soundlessly and the crackle of electrical energy continued; a stream of red-hot liquid metal began to emanate from the shaft and was collected in a container made of a ceramic-like substance and from which it gave out great amounts of heat. Further electrical energy was expended in vaporising it and in rotating the huge centrifuge; regular discharges of lightning were seen to travel from clouds to ground; the many people watched and waited in the knowledge that a momentous experiment was being undertaken in their presence.

—⁓—

Inside the hangar the centrifuge spun and spun and Poppatak and Handel conferred. Time had passed and their measurements indicated that a large supply of their preferred element had been extracted from the molten metal of the planet's core. Their machine stopped spinning and the electric arc was switched off. The place fell into a kind of torpid silence as though nature were exhausted. It took a day or so for birds to return, but the Pragya were quite obviously still busy. Dorkin fed them, Stein observed them, the security guards paced around. Eventually, however, they let it be known that it was time for their main experiment to begin.

'We have,' asserted Poppatak, 'obtained much of the element Fundamentum. It is the largest quantity that has been collected within a distance of twelve light years. We believe that we have more than enough for our experiments.' There was a pause: Poppatak clearly wished to emphasise that the experiments were ongoing. He was behaving as though he were an active and keen member of Stein's workforce. Stein was aware of this, as was

Dorkin. Perhaps it was the easiest path to take: it would have been foolish and counterproductive to have been obstructive. Yet Dorkin was worried: how would the Pragya stop their experiments from becoming too useful to Stein's people? What then would Stein do? That time was coming closer still.

One morning, Stein asked of the Pragya, 'What experiments do you intend to do? We want to see Fundamentum spinning in our giant centrifuge.'

'We thought that would come,' replied Poppatak, 'but we actually have more interesting work to do. It is true that interesting effects can be observed when heavy objects are spun, but we think that that would only be of use to you as a means for developing your centrifuge machine. We want to do something else. Perhaps you could leave us to it?'

'No,' said Stein, asserting himself. 'Not unless you let me in on it.'

Poppatak and Handel conferred for a short time as Dorkin and Stein watched. 'Then you had better come with me.'

The Pragya, accompanied by Stein and Dorkin, entered a subsidiary chamber in the building. There, before them, stood a device which resembled the inner workings of a giant barometer, and which continued outside into a tunnel like a ghost train. It consisted of the tight turns of a capillary tube wound, coil on coil, in circles of increasing diameter so that by resembling coils of the intestines it had the effect of placing a very long tube into a space of moderate size. It seemed polished and it shone, but it was unclear what material it had been made from; while on the largest coil was a sphere with small symbols on the outside. 'They are light-sensitive areas,' said Poppatak, 'which we use to control the device.' Sundry other controls were close to the machine and a transparent barrier lay between it and the operator. The Pragya took turns to describe the purpose of the place.

'This is a particle accelerator,' said Poppatak, smiling at Stein's disbelief. 'We can accelerate atomic particles of our choice to immensely high speeds and smash them into each other.'

'But you need a giant tube for that: like the accelerator at CERN, which is over 16 miles long!' replied Stein.

'Ha!' said Poppatak. 'Our accelerator is miniaturised so it doesn't need to be that big. But it is also of a surprisingly long size: we have miniaturised the whole thing so it's at least as long as the largest machine on Earth today. We can accelerate particles to immense speeds and watch them smash into chaos. And that can happen right here!'

Handel added, 'And it is in this chaos that we have successfully made—and preserved—the black holes that Mr Stein, you seek. Our atoms of Fundamentum are heavy and very interesting as a raw material, but it is our experience that you are—I believe the colloquial term is—buying into.'

'Buying into;' it was clear that there would be a price. Whatever the outcome of the forthcoming experiments, Stein knew that because they had cooperated to the full, the two members of the Pragya would expect their freedom. What could he do when they found out that that was the one thing his own superiors would refuse? They were too valuable; Schickel would want more. He would ask for weapons, and as he had already said, perhaps also a starship! He foresaw problems for all, and didn't think that even the patient and diplomatic care provided by Joseph Dorkin could gloss over the disagreements that would arise. But that lay in the future. Stein's position depended on the successful outcome of these latest projects and so far, they had been a success.

Stein did not really understand the science. It was a little clearer to Dorkin, although he could not claim to be anything like a physicist. Dorkin could see a simple picture: Handel and Poppatak, aided by the machines they had built, had obtained a superheavy element from the earth's crust where it was naturally found in the great heat and radioactivity there. That alone was an astounding accomplishment, yet their main work still lay ahead. Their intention remained to accelerate some of the element Fundamentum using their miniaturised particle accelerator, the manufacture of which was an outstanding achievement in its own right. The gravitational field of the tiny black holes they hoped to make, in what they called the 'resulting chaos', would be so strong that it could bend space-time. Dorkin's vision of a future arising from these events was from the point of view of a space-ship visiting stars far afield: he would see from close the points of light they had all seen in the sky at night. Theirs could be a distant journey made feasible by the science of these two modest, pathetic figures, degenerate in all except their minds and principles. Yet sadly, it was only this scientific ability that Stein's masters coveted.

Yet why had the Pragya cooperated? They had revealed their enterprise and determination and it was strange that they should have applied it to a cause favoured by Stein. Given their abilities, it should surely have been possible to disable Stein and escape. And Stein would probably have been happy with much less than the wonders they had already shown him. One morning he made an attempt to ask but they remained inscrutable, their thoughts hidden.

On that day came the first trial in which their accelerator received a test substance, the heavy atoms of mercury which they decided to bombard with fast neutrons. In this first test the device worked perfectly and chrysopoeia, the alchemist's dream of a transmutation of a base metal into gold, was finally achieved. This was communicated immediately to Schickel, who seemed pleased. He said, weighing in his mind the comparative qualities of riches and power, 'Keep this going for a bit longer, but don't let it deflect us from our main purpose.'

A week later, the Pragya finally indicated that they were ready to try Fundamentum, and were Stein, Dorkin and the others ready? Had they thought of the consequences of matters going awry?

'Professor Dorkin said, 'How can matters go wrong with you guys in charge?'

'Quite easily,' said Poppatak. 'If we create a black hole here on earth, and if we cannot contain it, then it will fall to the centre of the earth where under the force of immense gravity it will suck the whole planet into itself. You will vanish forever; the black hole will increase in size and gravity bear down on all the contents of the present solar system and engulf them. Eventually a growing black hole will engulf perhaps even the sun itself so that no light can escape, and this place will be a dark, cold and dismal reminder of the beauty that was here.'

'And yet,' said Stein, 'if it is a success?'

'Then you may hold, if you can understand it, the secret of bending space-time so that vast distances can be travelled, or apparently travelled, in the twinkling of an eye. Your kind will visit new places, both rich and poor, yet one in the experience they will offer. But beware; you will either become like the Pragya, of the highest and purest form of wisdom and understanding; or it may remove your wisdom altogether in a lust for riches and possessions. If, Mr Stein, you are responsible for light or dark, will you be the one to unleash it?'

Stein said, 'Let me press the button!'

Poppatak sighed, 'Something told me you would opt for the latter. If it must be, then so be it.'

With difficulty, for it was heavy, Handel picked up a transparent phial with a lid of steel and with tiny pipes issuing from it. He held it to the light where little of the contents could be seen, except for a slight discolouration, which he alleged was the vapour of Fundamentum. He connected it to the coils of their machine and as promised, suggested that Stein should touch a mark on a surface. There was an immediate demand from the machine for power and, uncharacteristically for a device made by the Pragya, a hum emanated from it, rising to a crescendo as it began to accelerate particles within its long, winding tube. This phase continued for five minutes, during which Poppatak and Handel watched a wall nearby that had pictures and symbols, moving and flashing, displayed on it. Eventually the symbols gave way to one picture only. It was of a sphere, white inside and bordered by a thin black line, pulsing as though alive, so that the sphere alternately grew in size and then contracted. Around it, many numbers appeared, but they continually decreased in value until they reached nought. Shortly the white sphere turned black and the border around it became a line of white. All numerals became negative values and then became vast; and with it the demand for electrical energy became immense. Poppatak said, 'It will draw any amount of power that it needs.'

Handel said, 'We must decide whether to let it grow to the next phase or stop it now.'

They looked at each other, seemed to agree, and they brought their thoughts to bear on the control system so that the demand for electricity fell slowly, and the mathematical figures on the wall began to increase and then turn positive. The moving and dancing illustration began to reverse through its various stages until it finally disappeared. The Pragya seemed pleased with their work and said to their audience, 'Another success. We accelerated atoms of Fundamentum and they smashed into fragments. In the riot of particles and forces we observed a black hole and managed to contain it.'

'Was that dancing sphere an actual black hole?' said Walter Stein.

'No. It was a representation of it: a picture made by presenting innumerable mathematical values. It came about when the sphere appeared to change colour and from that time onwards the demand for energy was devoted wholly to containing it. We exercised our will in bringing the incident to a close before it could grow further. It was a calculation that you could not conceive. Without us the black hole would be growing now, sucking all matter into it and leading to destruction. You could, Mr Stein, bring such a creation into being, but you could not end it as we have done.'

'Perhaps you have made the ultimate weapon,' said Stein.

'If we have, then it would be a Doomsday weapon in the wrong hands; a weapon with the potential to destroy all.'

Poppatak began to look uneasy as though he was aware that the conversation was drifting towards the acquisition of power. He said, 'We feel that this demonstration is enough for a while. We need to reflect on our experiments and decide what best to show you.'

'You're in no real position to argue,' said Walter Stein.

'Sure,' replied Handel with resignation. 'You have control over many small matters.'

———∞———

Later, the Pragya began to speak about their next project, volunteering their services willingly, and in fact acting as the instigators of this next step, which in itself confirmed what Dorkin instinctively knew about their intentions. He was again called on to help them with their creature-comforts while they plotted, manufactured and assembled. Neither he nor Stein had seen them as animated, or indeed as secretive. They dismissed questions, made endless calculations and moved apparatus about and about again, until quite satisfied. Never before had either seen them struggle so, their hands failing to grasp objects that should appear trivial. Yet finally they were ready, and it was then that they agreed to speak about their intentions. Poppatak invited the first question.

Stein said, 'We have kept you supplied with all you need, but I am keen to understand this latest step please.'

Poppatak replied, 'As you know, we successfully made tiny black holes. We checked our calculations and it was so. We were able to contain them, and they did not bring about our destruction.' He waited in expectation of a further question, but they preferred him to continue: 'This however, is our aim. We will now make an antimatter black hole as well.'

'You will?' said Dorkin, in amazement.

'We shall. And if the two should fuse?' Stein stayed silent; Dorkin's eyes were averted.

'Then all the matter of each will be changed to energy. As you know, vast amounts of energy are required by any space-craft in order to approach light speeds. That is the secret of interstellar travel. In essence, all the matter of the universe will be our fuel. We require only a source of antimatter. You, Mr Stein, would like these secrets for your masters?'

Stein nodded and looked at his shoes. 'Then you may watch.'

Later, Stein spent a day with the Pragya, watching these strange people, human and yet unlike any others he had known. He finally knew they were playing with him, but also that he was fair game, caught in a trap between the assertive and dangerous Schickel and the all-pervading competence of the Pragya, whose abilities could cause him to be crushed at any time. Thus all along, their only purpose had been to demonstrate their superiority, together with the fact that neither Schickel nor any army of his supposed scientists could ever be expected to approach this unassailable quality. 'We suggest you watch from outside,' they said. 'We shall be ready at 9 pm tomorrow night.'

Stein and Dorkin spent a fitful night in anticipation. Stein had spoken to Arnold Schickel again, explaining their intention. This time, he felt the menace in Schickel's voice as he said, 'This is the culmination of all our efforts. Make sure we can do this too.'

Dorkin and Stein stood outside in the dark. It was a cold night, with the moon illuminating the forlorn acres of airstrip. Around them there came the hum of vast amounts of electrical energy and soon, a connection via a flash of lightning with an object above the clouds. The electrical hum rose to a crackling crescendo. Immediately rocks, shrubs, stones and other objects were pulled forward in a violent manner which exceeded all they had seen before. In the near distance, objects were elongated and came to resemble spaghetti: crushed at the sides and pulled out into long strings. From the farther distance light seemed to struggle to reach them and the moonlight itself dwindled to a pinprick. Around them, the very space seemed to be squeezed and diminished. Ahead, a boundary emerged, totally dark, while attracting all outside to become a part of itself. Then Stein and Dorkin were dragged towards this miniature horizon by an almighty pull and they felt small and trivial as they experienced it, a force greater than any they had known. Yet they were just far enough to avoid their end. This dark, destructive, spherical blackness ceased as suddenly as it had been made, to be replaced by a vastly brilliant white light which flashed and flickered so that the airstrip became as bright as daylight, and in which onlookers experienced an immediate snowblindness that took minutes to fade. Then they were released and fell violently, with no regard for any safe landing. They struggled to stand upright, rubbing hurt limbs, and observed broken and spaghettified objects before them, long and thin, crushed, destroyed and in some cases bloody. They alone of all nearby creatures had survived, and that only due to their distance from it.

Stein tried to pick himself up and found he was half-blind and in severe in pain. Professor Dorkin (he felt how ironic it was to be called Professor after that demonstration!) was worse, with his shoes pulled bodily from him and after a severe fall in which he struck his head. They rolled over on their backs and looked upward, only to see the vague impression in their part-sighted eyes of silver overhead. It hovered, it seemed, contemptuously. Stein wept and said, 'Schickel doesn't know what it is that he wants. I can't see how he can use this!'

It grew quiet and the Pragya emerged from their building: two strange people of consummate wisdom and unimpeachable principles. Any notion that Dorkin may have had, regarding his own help in removing them from Stein's clutches, seemed hopelessly absurd. It was the Pragya that were completely in control of events, not he, nor Stein. Yet with humility they walked over and with their weak bodies tried to raise Dorkin and Stein from the ground.

Later, Dorkin felt rather foolish as he offered the Pragya some of their mint-smelling edible pap, which they accepted with equanimity. A few minutes later, Dorkin said, 'Will you describe what we saw, please?' The Pragya held each other's gaze and Poppatak said, 'We made a miniature black hole, so very small that its effect was small also. You observed the event horizon nearby, the darkness, around which time seemed to drag out to nothingness. Nearby, objects were stretched or destroyed by the enormous gravitational field. Instantly we fused it with another of antimatter, so that all was converted to energy. That was the source of the great light you observed, and of the great energy which our vessel has collected overhead. Yet these things were small and local. You can image those of immense size.'

Handel then followed, 'Throughout, we were aware of your intentions. You wished to acquire these skills for your own purposes.' Stein nodded as he realised that the Pragya had known of all his intentions throughout. He could think of nothing worthwhile to say, but that void was filled by Handel, 'We wished to show you what is possible, yet also to give you an idea of the forces that would be released. It should be clear that you cannot control them, nor even understand them. They are a step far greater than splitting the atom in a nuclear reactor or the construction of an atomic bomb.'

Stein mumbled, 'It would lead to our end, for sure,' and added, 'so what next?'

'First,' said Poppatak, 'you must realise that this particular excursion into the acquisition of power must finish. You must contact your masters and tell them. We are prepared to help you in more modest ways, as we have done with the Ixchel.'

'You will help us?'

'Certainly, but we can discuss that later. For now, please notify your masters that their little game is over.'

'And if they disagree, as I know they will?'

'Then explain to them that we will deactivate their entire defensive networks so that they lack the power to defend themselves.'

—w—

Arnold Schickel was in conference with the President. 'Sir,' he said. 'We have been very successful in finding the source of the many scientific phenomena experienced recently. We made contact with a science-based culture of high technical ability.'

'And what became of our relationship with them?'

'As for that, Sir, we observed many advanced experiments which had been demonstrated for our benefit. Yet we do not think they can help us with our immediate goals. They did not respond well to persuasion. For now, they have given us some interesting engineering materials that could be useful in advanced robotics.'

'Is that all?'

'Professor Dorkin helped them by carrying out some kind of genetic enhancement. Their 'improved' offspring are being raised in a normal way. They are pretty keen on him.'

'He can still help them?'

'Perhaps, and they hold him up as an example. I think that—Dr Girault, perhaps you could take this one?'

'Thank you, Mr Schickel.' Girault's oily manner irritated Schickel: 'It seems that long ago, the Pragya tried to eliminate all differences of gender. They blamed some of their misfortunes on that foolish step. Dorkin helped them put it right.'

'Well, let Dorkin help them some more. Perhaps that could lead to more?'

'We think so,' said Schickel, 'but the fact is that their help will depend on us being helpful back, and not in threatening them.'

'So what of Stein?' said the President.

'He's had some kind of conversion. I think he needs a new job.'

'OK, bring him back and give him something else to do.'

—◊—

Carmen van Brouin and Joseph Dorkin were talking. Carmen had struck up a deeper friendship with Simon Wiener and remembered the care with which Simon had considered her troubles. It came as no surprise when, one sunny morning, she announced their new relationship. However she first said, 'I'm afraid I fell under the influence of Walter Stein, and that affected my judgement. I can't say that I was wholly honourable in my loyalties. But now he's a fallen man, I feel free.'

Dorkin replied, 'Well you're not the only one, Carmen, but I'm pleased that you finally told me. There's still a place for both of you here, of course.'

'Thank you, but Simon's reached the writing-up stage, and we have both decided to go out west and live together. Or at least try.'

'OK, but do me a favour and wait about a month?'

FOURTEEN

BEVERLEY HILLS TO OUTER SPACE

Coalascan said to Dorkin: 'Professor, we have completed our appraisal of the embryos which you so kindly created for us. They are carried to term. We believe they are an advance for us and will introduce *vitality* into our kind—oh, how suitable is that word!' While his face was expressionless, pleasure was evident in his eyes.

'Good,' replied Professor Dorkin.

'Now we think the whole surreptitious aspect of our relationship with humans can end. We have finally decided to announce our existence to the wider world.'

'Good idea. How do you mean to go about it?'

'We thought of suspending our ship over a prominent place so that it can be seen and evidenced by thousands. There could be no doubt about our presence, at long last.'

'So you want to hover over New York City? Well if you do, I have one or two requests.'

'I am sure we can accommodate them. What are they? You wish to take part in chat shows and conferences?'

'No, that's not my style. I'd rather be working in my laboratory. But I do know someone who would like to take my place. He's a guy called Steinbeck. He's the curator of the Philadelphia Museum of Antiquities. That would be right up his street.'

'You wish me to invite him onto this ship?'

'Yes, and a few others. I would ask that you make a place for Pargeter, Meredith, Sampson and Elliott. The last two are journalists and they would like the 'mother of all scoops.''

'Yes, I think I understand the colloquialism.'

'And Simon Wiener and Carmen van Brouin: I expect they will get married in California. Can they arrive at church in this spaceship? It would make a change from a coach and six!'

'I will see what I can do. And what about your friend Callum Dood?'

'He's with the Ixchel still, but he still has one of our portable radios.'

—◊—

One month later, all the protagonists were on board, including Dood, who had made a special representation to include Adam Shilto, so busy these last few months. They flew west into the setting sun and shortly, approached Beverley Hills. Dood said, looking out of a porthole, 'Down there, isn't that Glendale?'

'Yes,' said Carmen.

'And that yellow building with the brick-red tower: that's Dreamworks isn't it?'

'Oh yes.'

'And that slim, handsome man with the spectacles?'

'He looks like a film director. Perhaps it's Steven Spielberg!'

'Let's hover overhead so he can see us!'

'Yes, then we can hover over LA for a while before we arrive at church!'

—◊—

A few weeks later, Freya Sampson and David Elliott published jointly the many photographs and other evidence they had obtained, giving direct evidence of the existence of UFOs and the Pragya.

They avoided all mention of the Ixchel, rightly assuming they would prefer isolation to the presence of a multitude of tourists. In addition they were given statements by Bud Lynch and Walter Stein, now a transformed person. Sampson and Elliott became major celebrities and appeared in chat shows on television. Their careers flourished with city broadsheets, where they easily held the most fierce of editors in abeyance.

Guy Meredith expounded a new method of powering supremely fast computers and became a multi-millionaire by generating Bitcoin. Thus he attracted the interest of many young women and was a married man within six months.

Pargeter published a novel conclusion to a maths problem and won a $1 million prize, whereupon he gave all to charity and won a further prize for his philanthropic action.

Dr Steinbeck, the curator of the Philadelphia Museum of Antiquities, spoke at length on television and wrote ten scientific papers in half as many months. Becoming famous for his contribution to knowledge, Steinbeck expounded at length during his many parties, and his organisation became as famous as the other well-known museum across town.

Bud Lynch, too, became famous for appearing on television cooking shows; while Bailey T. Mann benefitted from help with powered flight and achieved a world-wide record for the least power consumed in the flight of an aeroplane around the world.

That, however, left Callum Dood, who asked to be the first to step onto the streets of Beverley Hills, where he was accosted by a policeman, followed by a reporter from the Los Angeles Times.

'—Callum Dood here, itinerant vicar, naturalist and naturist, at your service.'

'Ah, Reverend,' said the reporter, 'I hear you've come from outer space—'

Later, Callum Dood, by then alone with the Pragya on board their craft said, 'That's an interesting-looking drink you take. And it smells pleasant, not unlike mint.'

'We find it very nutritious.'

'Would you like to try this essence that I prepared? The Ixchel also drink it, so I expect that it's suitable for you as well. I must apologise for the bitter taste, however.'

'By all means.'

'And I find that this dried fungus has a sweeter taste. Again, the Ixchel eat small amounts as a luxury on festive occasions, so once again—'

'We would be keen to enter into the spirit of any festive occasion.'

Later, in LA a policeman said, 'Look at that spaceship. It's ascending—no, rocking now, it's just on the limit of gyroscopic stability—now it has a strange falling-leaf motion. I hope those guys know what they're doing!'

On board, Coalascan said, 'How do you fancy a further step towards understanding the Cosmos? The Pragya need a lively, youngish individual as a companion, at least for a time. And we have noted how you value a form of consciousness in which through exciting herbal essences you have apparently acquired an elementary ability to bend time and space. We feel this has added a further dimension to our celestial navigation.'

He said, 'I'm up for that.' And in a twinkling of an eye Callum Dood was twelve light years away, a journey that took no time at all.